GAY.

PEOPLE WILL ALWAYS BE KIND

Also by Wilfrid Sheed:

A Middle-Class Education
The Hack
Square's Progress
Office Politics
The Blacking Factory and *Pennsylvania Gothic*
Max Jamison
The Morning After

WILFRID SHEED

People Will Always Be Kind

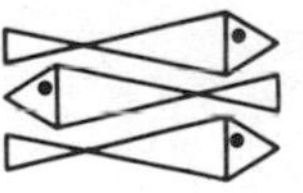

FARRAR, STRAUS AND GIROUX *New York*

Second printing, 1973
Library of Congress catalog card number: 72–97000
ISBN 0-374-23071-4
Printed in the United States of America
Published simultaneously in Canada by Doubleday Canada Ltd., Toronto
Designed by Paula Wiener

For my parents: a very different proposition

Contents

Does it matter?—losing your legs? . . .
For people will always be kind,
And you need not show that you mind
When the others come in after hunting
To gobble their muffins and eggs.

Siegfried Sassoon

If God doesn't exist, that's His problem.

Brian Casey

PART ONE

Backgrounder

1

The wall is straight at that point, although later he would always think of it as curved. He sat on it for some three hours, embarrassed to tears. The clock on Riverside Church kept him abreast of the hours, halves, quarters, who could tell? Night couples wandered past, glowing fiercely. A professor and his dog, nobody he knew. Fifty yards behind him cars hummed sweetly along the river edge, smiling to themselves. Their lights were blinding and the buildings in front of him blazed like an iron foundry. A sudden late-summer carnival was in the works. The professor's straw hat gleamed and his dog shot a golden arc under the street lamp. The number 5 bus rocked past like a holiday camper.

Brian didn't want to approach the blazing building just

yet, the fiery elevator; his mother's face would be blackened with heat. It was cooler out here on the wall. Still, he couldn't stay all night. He lowered his feet to the sidewalk, and immediately his knees buckled. He was barely able to clamber back without being caught. In his bones he'd felt it coming. Two stumbles yesterday, followed by little reassuring gusts of strength. This evening the same, throwing some sweet forward passes, delicate as a jeweler, and sitting down with his back bursting and his throat too sore to speak. He'd felt lousy for three days and nights, and Dr. Devlin had said flu, as usual, but he'd told his mother he felt O.K. and had gone out and played football like a maniac. He knew all right.

A thin ribbon of thought slanted across his mind: he could make it from the tree to the railing, from the railing to the parked cars—but then what? How to cross the street? He would simply have to get down on his knees and paddle. In a few minutes, when the professor was out of sight, he might give it a shot.

The professor left, at last, a happy man on two good legs; but as Brian was about to make his move, a couple came and sat on a nearby bench and began laboriously to neck. The girl's dress was a sizzling white, the man's sailor suit, white white white. That particular year, people used to neck for distance. Even if they weren't going overseas the next day. It gave Brian a bitter taste tonight. He ached from his throat to his feet, and the wall was a gravelly slab gnawing at his rump. He couldn't wait for them to finish.

"Mister," he said to the man. Much too softly. "Mister"

louder, and then no doubt some kind of scream. Brian had never asked for help in his life, and he made a hysterical mess of it. They carried him across the street, big firm hands in his armpits, all his problems solved. The apartment was cool as crystal. He was put to bed, and the fever had a chance to settle, and the next day he was off to the hospital, the twenty third recorded polio case that August.

It was difficult to be solemn about a wise guy like Brian. "He was a great guy," Hennessy said. "He was neat," said Bernie Levine. Hennessy had heard somewhere that only the best physical specimens got it. "That lets you out," said Phil Marconi, who was usually best ignored. Levine suddenly remembered an act of kindness and Fatstuff came up with another. ("He wasn't that good," said Phil. "I mean he was just a guy." They stared at him in frozen horror.)

"I guess he was my best friend," said Fatstuff Hennessy.

"Mine too." "Definitely."

"He could understand what you were thinking before you thought it."

"How'd he do that?" said Marconi.

"Ah, shut up," said Fatstuff. "How would you like to get it, Marconi?"

Marconi was too tough to hit, so the thing to do was sort of whine at him.

"Hey listen—is that why you're being so nice about Casey?" said Phil. "Because you think you might get it yourself? It won't help, baby, believe me."

"Go fuck yourself," said Levine. "If you get it, I'm going to celebrate for three whole days."

"Sure, why not?" said skeptic Marconi. "Crying wouldn't help me."

The feeling was that arguing with Phil cheapened you. Phil was the kind of fellow who said that Germans were better soldiers than Americans. The Italian campaign in Africa and the jokes that ensued had made him bitter about things.

"I really got to know him in the last year," said Sam Hertz doggedly.

"Yeah, we all did," said Phil. "Never knew a guy with so many dear, dear friends."

"I'm really sorry for you, you know that, Marconi?" said Hennessy. "You're really twisted."

"Everyone crowd round Casey for luck, now. Touch the hunchback," said Marconi. "Anybody want to play some football? While we still got a leg to stand on?" Philadelphia matrons could not have looked more shocked. "Suit yourselves, sickies," said Marconi and wandered out, with his football under his arm.

There was fear in the air now. "Jesus," said somebody. "Football!"

"That guy ought to grow up."

"He makes me puke."

It was steaming forenoon in the Casey apartment, a fan carried soggy air around on its wings. The boys had come over to get the poop on Brian and give awkward comfort to his parents. But there was no one there except a slow-motion cleaning lady.

"It was funny that night," said Levine, trying to recapture the mood after Marconi's ravages, "how he wouldn't stop playing. You remember how it got dark, and we wanted to go to Loew's, and he'd say, 'Hey catch, Fatman,' or, 'Big Bernie, let's see the ball.' "

Hennessy could feel his own legs drain of strength as he listened. He moved them slightly to make sure. So did Hertz. Marconi would have pissed himself from laughing. So would Brian.

"How'd he get home finally?"

"I don't know," said Hennessy. "I couldn't see the ball no more. So he waved me to go on home. He was just standing there the last time I looked back." Brian's thin, mocking, Irish face looked in retrospect saintly: Christ in his garden. Hennessy had hung around simply because Brian had asked him to—which now made him the closest thing to a good disciple. The others had trickled off to Loew's long since. "Hey Fatstuff, don't jump through too many flaming hoops now" was Marconi's parting word that night. But Hennessy's subservience now seemed prophetic insight.

Kevin Casey, Brian's father, came home from the hospital, looking grave. In sorrow, his thin, black-Irish face seemed younger than usual. The boys sat crushed and small as Mr. Casey talked. Brian's legs were their legs now. No man is an island, when there's an epidemic around. "It's too soon to tell," said Mr. Casey. "He's still delirious. We'll know the extent of the damage in a few days."

Hennessy stuttered. "Does he, *you* know, know?"

"I honestly can't say," said Mr. Casey.

Delirium was a golden garden where Brian wandered, with his football under his arm, while the dice were rolled for a piece of left leg, possibly a hand. Lungs? We'll see. That's a tough point to make. Mr. Casey explained what he had just learned himself, about how polio worked. Think of a switchboard in the spine, he said, think of nerves blowing out like fuses. This was certainly something new to worry about. Hennessy's chronic appendicitis moved around to the back. The virus was still mincing through town, swishing her purse. Maybe *you,* Hennessy. No, I won't go. Take Marconi. He deserves it, not me.

"When can we see him, Mr. Casey?"

"I can't say. I'll let you know."

The gang went off, sorrowing. Phil Marconi was still lounging on the stoop. "You're all scared shitless," he said. "That's why you're so worried about Brian." He had stayed around just to say that. He spat it out hard, no joking this time. They heaved off in their different directions, not answering, not wanting to hear another blasphemous word.

Beatrice Casey had stayed longer at the hospital, straining her eyes in the bad light of her son's room. When she closed them, she could see nothing but running. Hadn't Brian ever walked anywhere? She couldn't remember it. Not in all his years. Legs of all ages pounding solemnly. Now his legs were swathed to the hip in hot soggy flannel. The room smelled like a laundry, it was hard to believe that anything healthy could come out of such a place.

She had been too foggy to notice much the night they brought their son here. She remembered entering the emergency hospital through a dim liver-tinted foyer. Why had he lied about his flu? Why had she believed him? And would it have helped to know sooner? She wanted to discuss all this with someone.

Brian was taken upstairs for processing. They were told to wait down here, and were swiftly forgotten about. They mingled with some old people who had been sitting here forever, as if waiting for Immigration to decide their cases. Bare pipes lined the off-yellow walls. "This is the kind of place Dickens got the English to abolish," said Kevin.

A pretty place might have been worse, was all she thought. A polite receptionist, a bowl of flowers would have made her cry. An old man with a bright black mustache daubed at her feet with a mop made of seaweed. Kevin had to walk over to the desk every few minutes and ask if it was time to go up yet. Otherwise, they would be squatting there yet, like the old people.

"Downtown Moscow," muttered Kevin. Why was he going on about the hospital? What difference did it make? As an architect he had a right to his interests, but there was a time for everything. She herself wanted a place that reminded her that life was short and foul.

Now, two days later, she saw Kevin's point. Brian needed sunlight at least, he would never get well in the dark. Think of the plants in city apartments. The fever was almost played out, and he looked as if nothing too serious had happened. She smiled at him with all the tenderness she could muster, and he smiled back politely. He obviously didn't know what a fix he was in yet.

The tenderness dried in her throat and stuck like paint. She could not for the moment look at her son naturally. It would take time and practice. She studied the nurse, for composure. Miss Withers moved in a brisk monotone, pumping up the bed, putting a napkin over the urine bottle as if it were vintage champagne—regulating the room's mood at a steady 70. No laughter please in the hospital zone, laughter is paid for later at night and you know who has to clean up. Tears? Just don't get them on the patient. As soon as Beatrice looked at her son again, tenderness came back like a blush. She got up to go. "Will he be all right?" she asked Nurse Withers. "I think he'll live," said the nurse, winking grotesquely. "Won't you, sonny?"

Living would hardly be enough, for a perpetual-motion machine like Brian. She could see him now, the size of her thumbnail, playing ball down in Riverside Park, making the trained-monkey moves of baseball: holding glove to mouth to jabber something, swinging three bats, and crouching down with the handles in his lap—none of it made any sense to her, so she watched with special attention, between swipes of the duster. Bend and straighten and jiggle and spit. Strange things to be doing, but he seemed to enjoy them.

She cried automatically when she got home. As soon as she saw the living-room furniture. (Yesterday, the hall closet brought it on.) And Kevin calmed her, an old practice of theirs, but not as satisfactory as usual. "Don't *you* ever cry?" she said.

"I just express myself differently," he said. Kevin was the worst man in the world to criticize. He took an awkward lurch on the arm of her chair. "I wouldn't think I'd have to prove how much I feel."

"I'm sorry," she said quickly, "I didn't mean anything like that." God's truth. It was just a point of manners. She had hoped vaguely that his response to grief would be perfect.

Kevin put his arm around her. They probably should love each other a little more consciously than they were accustomed to. Which meant that an agreed-upon dullness of bodies must be waived, and the hedgehog defenses of the spirit. He thought that perhaps lovemaking would help. She thought not. Not after just seeing Brian. Their cross-purposes made for an awkward seating arrangement. Kevin stood up and went looking for a cigarette or anything else he could find.

"There's a good sunset," he said. She could tell from the violet in the room that this must be so. A rich flush suffused the sofa cushions, the color of Christmas.

"Do you suppose he knows yet?" Kevin asked casually.

"Knows what? That he's got polio? I guess so. He must, don't you think?"

"I don't know. It's hard to think straight when you're in fever. Do you think he knows much *about* polio?"

"Oh, he must. All those pictures of little boys in leg irons." My God, was he one of *those* now? A March of

Dimes poster? "You can't miss those pictures." Don't think. Just keep talking.

"I guess not. And our gallant President." He rocked with his hands in his pockets, and the sky flared in front of him. His shoulders looked skinny with the waistcoat hunched up on them. Beatrice thought, What is he doing, talking about sunsets and gallant Presidents? Has he no feelings? And thought, I must not get hysterical. Kevin was a dry, cheery man and you couldn't ask him to drop everything overnight. His style of mourning would be different from hers, equally acceptable in its own way. It seemed, in fact, to consist of an endless keeping up of morale, like the British in 1940—even when you wanted morale to sag a little. It didn't mean he didn't feel things, though.

Father O'Monahan, expert in grief, turned up that afternoon. She was pleased: he might lay down some guidelines, about sunsets and jokes and things. She walked him along the corridor and into the living room. Kevin didn't fancy O'Monahan in a general way, but surely they would both be above personalities today. Kevin managed a greeting of sorts and winced over the priest's soft handshake, in a way that might have passed for sorrow, she hoped.

"This is a sad thing," said O'Monahan, sinking down in his favorite sofa . . .

"We think so," said Kevin, starting in on him right away.

"You'll need a lot of faith. And hope, too. They tell me cures are being found every day."

"Not for polio. You must be thinking of something else," said Kevin. "Will you be having a drink, Father?" Oh dear, an Irish accent.

"Er, the usual. A little Scotch and soda."

Kevin went out to the kitchen, wooden-faced and prickly. Beatrice was appalled. His sarcasm was usually as light as pastry . . . in fact, he used to be quite funny about O'Monahan, claiming that he couldn't believe in spiritual leaders over 250 pounds. But today he seemed vicious, as if O'Monahan were to blame for the whole thing; or as if, anyway, *some*one should be punished for it. She hoped he stayed in the kitchen until he came to his senses.

O'Monahan seemed ill at ease, for all his experience. She felt like telling him not to worry.

"How is the boy?"

"He's much better. He—smiled at me today." A flash flood of grief. Freeze it at once. Practice not crying every day, until your tears harden like cement. Women with strong faces. Beauty hint.

"That's wonderful. He'll be his old self in no time."

"Not quite," said Kevin, back at the door already. "He'll be missing a thing or two."

"But his wonderful spirit will still be there."

Kevin's face was ugly with mischief. The charm turned into poison.

"How do you know his spirit is wonderful?" said Kevin. "That's what we're about to find out, isn't it, Father?" He handed over the drink with elaborate disdain, which O'Monahan strove to ignore. Kevin was a *funny* man.

Was this what happened to funny men under pressure?

"Give us your advice, Father," she said. "What should we tell Brian about his condition?"

"Yes, Father," said Kevin, "tell us about that."

O'Monahan writhed a fat man's writhe, and the sunset flashed across his chest. "Am I the only one that's drinking?" he asked.

"That's right," said Kevin.

"I don't care for one right now," Beatrice added more politely.

"Well, then," said the priest, looking at his glass wildly, as if wondering whom he could plant it on.

"Oh, go ahead and drink it," said Kevin.

O'Monahan took a temporizing sip and said, "I don't set up as an expert, Kevin." Then what the hell are we paying your salary for? said Kevin's face. "I've never had a son of my own, it goes without saying." All right then, don't say it, said the face. You've probably never even been sick, have you? Ah, but you read about it once, in the seminary, in Latin.

"But I think I would emphasize the miracles of modern science, the marvels that take place hourly in our labs." So that's it. Bow your knee to the man in the white coat, ye sinners. "And don't forget the power of prayer. It can move mountains, you know." Oh yes? Name one.

Beatrice's head was splitting. She had heard Kevin giving the works to Monsignor Sheen on the radio, settling scores with some old nun who had once slapped his face for talking back. She bet he was doing it now. She guessed she had hoped that the warm heart inside every comedian would be coaxed to Kevin's surface by tragedy; but perhaps it was cold hearts comedians had. Anyway, she hated to see O'Monahan all guileless, feeding her husband straight lines.

"Thank you, Father," said Kevin stiffly. "I'm sure that's very helpful."

O'Monahan got up. He knew the score, knew that he couldn't win. His cloth stood on end in the presence of an Irish anticleric. Kevin was usually politer than this, but the hatred was always there, for the connoisseur. Kevin was a good enough Catholic, outside of that. His confessions were dry and scrupulously correct. It didn't seem to mean any more to him than brushing his teeth, and O'Monahan sometimes thought he would be a mellower man if he just gave it up altogether: not that mellowness counts for much in the courts of the Lord.

Beatrice saw the priest out. "Kevin is upset today. I'm sorry if he was sharp with you."

"That's all right," he whispered back. "It may be one way I can help."

She stalled by the door. She would not go back in a temper. A fight would be just awful. "Who the hell is he to be giving us advice? This is a real problem, not one of those spiritual ones." Kevin purple and shaking with clown's rage. She went straight to her bedroom. Brian would sense it if they had been fighting. She credited her son now with supernatural powers. She tried briefly to feel sorry for Kevin and his ancient wounds, but she just couldn't. She felt quite isolated. A sarcastic man was no company at a time like this.

Later in the evening, Kevin told her that he hadn't meant to be critical of O'Monahan at all. Maybe a little tasteless joke at first, but what the hell, they were old friends. He was really most anxious to hear what O'Monahan had to say. And she really hoped that this was the truth.

2

"Good night, kid," said Nurse Withers. She seemed to be all right. He listened with half an ear while she told him about some fellow she was dating. He sounded like a real creep, but maybe it was the way she told it.

He would miss the opening of school, which was no great loss. It would probably take several months to fix this thing up. The doctor was vaguely optimistic about it. His mother's sad smile had puzzled him. He didn't know of anything that called for that. He lay in the dark now, feeling the wet ooze around his legs. The fact that the legs couldn't move was neither here nor there. He was used to it already. They would move again in their good time. But the hot packs were a nuisance. He felt as if he'd been out in the rain all day and was now drying out in front of a stove. But as soon as he got anywhere, the night nurse would dip some more flannel, and he would be back to go.

"Too bad you don't talk," he said to the nurse, a placid Russian lady.

"I talk a little," she said, nudging the pack under his knee.

"This priest, Father O'Monahan, one of God's holy fools, Dad calls him, he was in today, and he said, 'My son, you're being very plucky about this, hmmm, hmmm.' So I said, 'What's with pluck, Father? Lying in bed and being looked after by beautiful nurses is plucky?' And he shook his head, and told me I had a grand spirit. I don't know what gets into these people."

Night nurses should be able to talk. He felt lonely with nothing but his wet flannel. There was this to be said for the nurses, though; they didn't take it all so darn seriously. Madame Kutchakokov here could have been moving furniture, for all the concern she showed.

He shut his eyes and imagined the scene as he sauntered into a touch-football game on the block. "Hey, it's Casey." "Yeah, it's Casey. Fellas, it's Casey. You got out of the hospital, I see," etc. He hoped they would think of something more interesting to say when the time came, but right now, it was the best he could do for them. Admiring glances, soundless pats on the butt. Casey is back. "Shut up and just gimme the ball, will you?" Fatso came running and handed him the ball like a chalice. Marconi threw him a grudging smile. Not bad, not bad at all . . . Cut it out now, Casey. Nobody thinks you're that hot. But it was a pretty vision to sleep on.

The next few days were busy as a diplomat's. Visitors were whisked in and out, bearing flowers, magazines, and from his old man, detective stories. He began to distinguish between the "very plucky's" and the "how's the boy's," the tender smilers and the hearty laughers. It was quite a game adjusting to all of them. Even his friends, Bernie Levine and Fatstuff, had to be reconsidered. They started out very solemn, dressed up as if for a job interview, and wound up chasing each other around the bed and knocking over his water jug. Fatstuff asked if Brian could feel anything in his legs, and he said, Go ahead and touch. I can see you're dying to. And Fatstuff touched, as if expecting the mummy's curse to strike him.

Bernie said, "How're the nurses? Are they any good?"

"Not bad, not bad." He had been too weak to think about it in that sense. "They're probably kind of cold, though."

Bernie giggled. "Do they, you know, wash you?"

"Oh for godsake," said Brian. "Yeah, sure, they wash you until you can't stand it." Fatstuff was looking at him as tenderly as a woman. Good grief, he thinks my balls have got it. "Of course, the nurses are frightened at first by my amazing proportions," he said, smothering his own panic. He really didn't know. The area was numb for the moment with the packs jammed against it.

"What happens when you have to take a crap?" asked Bernie, from his list of topical questions.

"They got pots and pans for that. You lose the taste for

it after a while." Fact. He was brimming with constipation. But did they really want to hear about that? He sensed it was up to him to keep the conversation going. Stranded between jollity and reverence, his friends hardly knew where to turn.

"How's Phil?" he asked.

They glanced at each other. "Don't mention that guy," said Bernie. "Please."

"What's the matter? Burning candles to Mussolini again?"

"Nothing. He's just a rat, that's all."

"Go on, he must have done *something*."

"Well." They hesitated again.

"Come on fellas, you don't have to look at each other every time you talk. What'd the wop do?"

"Well," said Bernie, "we were talking about, you know, you, and what a lousy break you got, and he was kidding around, and he wouldn't take it seriously."

"Is that so?" How dare he not take it seriously? It was strange, being talked about at all. Brian didn't realize he was an issue. "It was nice of you guys to stick up for me. You *did* stick up for me, didn't you?"

"Definitely."

"What'd you say about me?"

"Well, you know, that you were a good guy and all. That you had a lot of guts." They obviously resented being made to say it, and would think twice about sticking up for him next time. Saints don't reach for compliments. He had certainly botched that one.

"Yeah sure, I'm a prince. What I really want to know is, what did Macaroni say that was so terrible?"

"He said that, *you* know, you were just a guy."

"Why, that's a *ter*rible thing to say."

"Well, it was the way he said it, right Bernie? All sneery and *blech*."

"And he said we were just being nice to you because we were afraid of catching it ourselves."

Brian smiled. "That's interesting. Is there any truth in it?"

The silence was horrible. They had come to worship at the shrine, and the old saint had pointed a bony finger at them and told them they stank on ice. No more pilgrimages for them, boy. He would have to look for new clients, new friends; but right now he didn't care.

After that, things degenerated, and out of sheer social inadequacy, Bernie landed a punch on Fatstuff's biceps and the chase was on. Brian lay there, aware of his dead legs, thinking, Those guys are afraid of this, and I've already been there. A grotesque sense of power creamed through his veins, right down to his toes. Yes, his crotch was alive all right. He saw their horseplay as fear and weakness, the high thin farting of virgins, to use Marconi's favorite expression. They didn't know the secret of his power—that polio wasn't really that bad.

Nurse Withers threw them out, and they said a worried but fervent goodbye. The young diplomat figured it this way. They were on record as thinking he was a great guy, magically improved by polio; and they would stand on the record and try to forget what had happened in here today.

The next encounter was a surprise. Phil Marconi himself; a triumph. "What are you doing in here without a present, Phil? Don't you know that everyone brings me presents?"

"Yeah, I figured that. So I thought you wouldn't miss the one I didn't bring."

"You don't understand, you fascist pig. It isn't the present, it's the respect it shows."

You couldn't accuse Phil of sneering, because his lips were shaped that way and he didn't have to move them. "How come all the presents go to you, anyway? You sick or something? I think you should give some presents to your friends, to keep things even."

"You came here just to tell me that?"

"Yeah, I thought this place might be ruining your character. Which was shaky to begin with."

Phil would be a great guy if he could ever stop saying the same one thing, over and over. Fifty-seven variations of "you're not so hot."

"I hear you upset my friends, Phil. You told them I was just a guy."

"Nicest thing I ever said about you. Those little shits were sucking up to you for luck. Getting polio doesn't change anything in my books."

Yeah, maybe not. Phil was so desperate to get everything straight, after the wartime propaganda, he never knew when to stop. Brian was getting sick of the subject of polio, however cunningly served up.

"Have I missed any triumphs of the Italian forces?" he said.

"Boy, you guys are boring. If the enemy fights good, you call him a fanatical killer. If he fights bad, you call him a clown. Italians don't want this war and you should be grateful."

"Is it true they fought a draw with a flock of sheep?"

"You make me sick, Casey. When did you last hear from the Irish Army? Fifteen-oh-two, in the Battle of the Bog, was it? Unfortunately, the limeys routed them utterly."

It was good to shoot the crap like this. Marconi's Irish accent had to be heard.

"Den dere was de Battle of McGonnigle's britches in 1603, where alas de Irish was forced to flee, but [switch to solemn Edward R. Murrow voice] they got a great song out of it, which is still heard wherever free men gather." Marconi laughed rackingly at his own invention. "Yessir, the strains of 'McGonnigle's Britches' were heard above the battle at O'Donegal's Downfall and again the following year at O'Donovan's Disaster."

"You're full of shit," said Brian. His stomach felt drastically weak and any more laughter would blow it apart. Miss Withers came in to check on the racket. Marconi's laugh was a wheezing bark that could alarm anyone. He might be trying to kill someone in there.

"See you, Brian," he said abruptly and left, stumbling past Miss Withers.

Marconi was defiantly clumsy. He was the kind of guy who sneered at baseball and hit the ball a mile with a grudging, what's-it-to-you swing. In the movies he and Brian lived at, he would be the hero's best friend, the one who chewed him out about his values the night of the championship. It was no accident—they studied those parts closely. Brian saw himself as a natural John Garfield.

They rested him and fattened him up for the next round of visitors—his aunts, Brigid and Portia. There was no escape around here, except to get so sick *nobody* could see you. He felt more than ever like a mummy in a glass case, as the aunts looked him over. Brigid looked at his legs as if she expected them to tell her something. Portia stared above his head as if nothing had happened. People were really a scream, in this situation.

Aunt Portia had a leather shopping bag, Aunt Brigid's was made of wool. Brigid hauled out a missal stuffed with holy cards. "This one is St. Jude, patron of lost causes—not that your cause is lost, by any means. And here is St. Dismas, the good thief. He's always handy. I'd like you to keep these, Brian. They've done wonders in their time."

"And if you should want something a little more substantial, I've brought you some medical magazines." Aunt Portia sprayed her selection over Brian's knees. They looked like the kind of two-bit sun-and-health nudist magazines that Brian and his friends occasionally browsed for cheesecake.

"Do they say anything about polio?" he asked.

"Well, there's one about a Dr. Steinmetz who does nerve

grafts. Here he is." She flipped to a marked page. There was a fuzzy picture of a small man in a two-piece bathing suit, standing next to a smiling brunette, twice his size. He had a chin beard, which looked hastily glued, and rimless glasses. The caption said the doctor was honeymooning in Atlantic City with his third wife, a former patient. Miss Olivia Schenk, if anyone wanted to know.

"Dr. Steinmetz has had a terribly hard time from the medical world," said Portia. "They hate new ideas, you know."

"Nerve grafts? What's that got to do with polio?"

Portia didn't blink. "I'm not sure. The article is mostly about amputations, I believe. But don't you think the same principles might apply?"

Maybe, maybe. His options were many at this point.

Brigid surged back into the picture. "The nuns at St. Cecilia's are praying their hearts out for you, Brian. And Father McShea mentions you in all his masses." He imagined a votive light burning through the night in a dark chapel. Just for him. Hot spit.

"You won't be needing medical help in that case," said Aunt Portia, who was something of a needler.

Brigid laughed. She was a big woman, not easily rattled. She had fifteen or twenty children. Brian couldn't remember which. Altar boys with sniffles, flower girls: you only saw them in church. "God prefers to work in natural ways if he can," she said. On another day, Portia would have given battle. "It's the only way he ever works, have you noticed?" Leaving the Church had been a convulsion for her, her moment of highest intensity, and she never missed a chance to rekindle it.

"There's no conflict between religion and science," said Brigid, and Portia gave a hopeless snort. "We'll both be working for Brian in our own ways," said Brigid.

Religion and science made sleepy, after-lunch peace in Brian's mind. They were both just ways of getting cured. He pictured nuns praying in shifts around the clock, scorching their wimples, trying to shake a miracle loose; while at the same time brilliant scientists worked feverishly in mile-long labs, holding test tubes to the light and squinting. "Come here a minute, Watson. I think I'm on to something." Also quacks in bathing suits, mad enough to try anything, grafting the legs of a goat, the heart of a chicken. Something had to come of it all.

Meanwhile Brigid and Portia fought with their eyes. Don't destroy the boy's faith. Well, don't you fill him with superstition then. Or rather, "My life good, your life bad." Brian had heard them at it, at family get-togethers, and didn't care. They were both right. Brigid had special powers. She breathed in time with the tides and had a baby every spring. She knew something. But Portia, his father's older sister, was pretty smart in her own way.

They left in uneasy truce, and Miss Withers scooped up their cards and magazines and stuffed them in his bedside drawer. "Open the cage and let my crazy relatives out," said Brian. "I've seen worse," said Miss Withers.

She seemed annoyed at having to fix his flowers and tidy his presents. He could understand that. Her petulance was comradely, us against them. "Those magazines are putting my aunt through college," he said. Miss Withers held up his urine bottle and he nodded—a sordid exchange in most instances, but Miss Withers made a fine thing of it. "How'd you make out last night?" he asked her.

"I don't know. They're all after the same thing, aren't they?" She said it provocatively, a little gift for Brian. He thought about that thing they were after for a moment, golden and glowing. Then felt tired and dizzy. The packs sagged cold on his legs and Miss Withers began to cook up a new batch. Dr. Samson looked in on him at that point, peeped under the packs, and nodded. What did he see? He asked Brian to flex his right knee. Brian couldn't, but the doctor nodded again anyway.

"How does it look, Doc?" he asked.

"Very good. No sign of atrophy," said Dr. Samson.

"Yeah, but is there any sign of life?"

The doctor smiled. "Don't be in such a hurry. These things take time."

You see, you see? He said I'm going to get better. Brian wasn't sure whether to press the inquiry and shoot for more specific assurance. O.K.—shoot. "What would you say the chances are, Doc?"

Samson looked at Nurse Withers, as if this were a routine they'd done together before. "These kids," he said. "Always trying to pin you down." Miss Withers looked back without expression, bless her. The doc straightened up and swung into a man-to-man match-up.

"Brian, I can't give you odds. People are working night

and day on this thing. And your own spirit could make a big difference."

Ten years in medical school to learn that? Brian expected a better brand of cheese from this man.

"What about Nurse Kenny?" he said.

"Yes, well, she's done some very useful work. Mostly in cutting down atrophy. That's about all she's proved so far."

"What about Dr. Steinmetz then?"

"Dr. Who?"

Brian was embarrassed already. "Dr. Steinmetz. He does nerve grafts."

"*Nerve* grafts? For polio?"

It did sound pretty silly. His aunt had led him into this. Samson didn't laugh, because he didn't have to. "I'd rely on real scientists if I were you, Brian."

"I heard the medical profession was down on him."

"Is that so? Well, I'm not surprised. He probably should have his license revoked." Samson was an official in the American Medical Association, and he couldn't let it pass. "Men like that fatten on silly old ladies and make it that much harder for the rest of us. Don't you think that if he had a cure for polio, we'd know about it by now? Don't you think we'd *welcome* it?" The thought of Portia as a silly old lady was crushing. His own family didn't belong in those categories. Silly spinster, fat fool.

Samson's anger was so darn *distinguished*. "I'm sorry, Brian, but those people give me a swift pain. Nurse Kenny, too, if it comes to that. Just another exhibitionist, raising false hopes in sick people. Put your faith in real doctors, Brian. And in your own fighting spirit."

The doctor left, still smoothly raging. His neck was too thick for a doctor's. Brian's fighting spirit felt as hollow as Nurse Kenny. In defense of his stupid profession, Dr. Samson had just about admitted that there was no hope. Fighting spirit, indeed. If they were relying on that, the game was up.

He gathered from Miss Withers's expression that he must be showing some distress. "Don't worry about him, he's an old fud," she said. But the rows of scientists were waxworks figures now, and the nuns at prayer were just silly old ladies, baying at the moon. "What about Dr. Steinmetz?" he said ironically.

She frowned and said, "Well, maybe he's on to something. Dr. Samson would be the last to know."

Brian shut his eyes, too tired to feel seriously scared. There were some good things among Samson's ravings, weren't there? That you never could tell. That scientists were working. That these things take time. When he woke, he found he had regrouped and added Samson to the good tidings.

3

"I say we tell him."

"Tell him what, dear?"

"The score," said Kevin. "About his chances. You can't feed a boy of sixteen fairy tales. It's bad for him in the long run."

"Oh dear, not that again. We're *not* telling him fairy tales," said Beatrice. "There *are* such things as miracles. You believe that, don't you?"

They were in front of the window again. The back rooms were all as dark as underwater dungeons. So the Caseys met at the front window every evening. The trees in Riverside Park were beginning to shed, and the coming of winter had to be borne in mind.

"Yes, I guess so. Occasionally. Not too many miracles in New York, though," he muttered.

"There's not too much faith in New York, either. Do you suppose that might account for it?"

They looked at each other fearfully, as if they had both felt the first drop of the monsoon. "Look, let's not fight about it," said Kevin. "It's just one small point."

"I'm not fighting and personally I don't care *what* you think about miracles," said Beatrice, "though it seems a pity to have that emptiness in your life."

Kevin mumbled, more to himself than her, "I didn't say that they couldn't happen. Just that they don't."

"But I'm afraid you'll say something to Brian when he gets home," continued Beatrice.

He turned his head. Sick of memorizing the Jersey shore. Palisades Park was shut for the winter. The Crisco sign was out like a light. Everything dead or dying over there. Each time you have the same discussion, it gets a little bit worse. "I won't say anything at all to him until we've talked it over together. Meanwhile, I plan to do everything I know to make him happy. O.K.?" Kevin always liked to cut domestic quarrels short, before they got sloppy. But it was sometimes hard to do that and still make his point. Brian was due home tomorrow and would spend his days in the bright living room. From now on, they would have to do their arguing in whispers, and in the bedroom. So, if they wanted a last noisy one, this was the time for it.

"I'm sorry," said Beatrice. "I know you want what's best for him."

"I do," said Kevin, reaching an arm for her shoulder. They stood for a moment side by side, as if there were an altar in front of them and a beaming priest. They had weathered some standard-issue storms in eighteen years: miscarriages, hysterectomy, no more children. Nothing terrible recently. Not much more money of course, ambition flogged slowly to death like most people's. They could surely survive this one.

"Look, I just want to ask this one thing," he said. "We agree that Brian has got a fine spirit, right? So—why don't you think he can face the facts?"

"Oh, can't you leave it alone? Why is it so important to you?" She disengaged herself, and he began to prowl, to the sofa, back, anywhere.

"I don't know." There was some other quarrel between them, but they couldn't find it and had to keep settling for this one. "I don't want my son living in an unreal world, that's all."

"You don't mean the Catholic Church, do you?"

"No, of course I don't. The Catholic Church is realistic." Kevin groped. The Church taught a little of everything, didn't they? What was the teaching for this? "They teach you to accept suffering, not to run away from it, and they teach, I think they teach, that it's presumptuous to expect miracles. But besides all that— Don't you see that accepting the facts could make a real man of him? If we lie to him, if we offer him a Hollywood cure, we leave him a kid forever, like everyone else in this damned country."

"It just so happens his own faith is a very important factor."

There was a sense of scandal and shock between them. They had never really argued religion before. Kevin's anticlericalism was just a mannerism. They agreed about the essentials, because the essentials never came up. And Kevin's good humor always suggested that he would be right about them if they did.

"You and Father O'Monahan seem to think a healthy body is everything," he said. "Damnit, if the spirit is so important, why don't you concentrate on that for a while?"

"I don't understand you, Kevin. Don't you want your boy to be well?" Oh God, the power of a non sequitur. "Of course I do. But what if he isn't?"

"He will be. I know he will be." What monster of cold rationality could doubt it? "If it's God's will that he isn't, there'll be time enough to face it then. But how can you give up on him so soon?"

Lack of faith was a terrible accusation. It was better to be wrong than to be a doubter, a life-denier. He tried to rephrase it. "All right. I believe it. I believe that he very probably will get well. I don't see what we've ever done to rate a miracle, but maybe we'll land one anyway. More likely it will be science that does it."

"That's perfectly fine with me."

"But, anyway, *I* don't know—" silk cords of custom kept them from fighting properly and ending it. He wasn't allowed to say, You can't face it yourself, can you? You're more Hollywood than you thought, aren't you? And she wasn't allowed to say back, what she must be thinking, You're being very brave on your son's behalf, I must say. Could you have taken a blow like that yourself? Could you take it now? It was as if the sick boy were in the next room already and they must talk in flurried whispers.

At their last anniversary, Kevin had toasted the happiest couple he knew and the man who made it possible. Now, one badly phrased word could release old poisons they hadn't known about. They groped for that word and pulled away from it. To stall, Kevin gave her a good-old-boy squeeze and she responded slightly like a faithful chum.

The next day, Kevin Casey dropped by the hospital to assist at Brian's removal. It was a cold, raw day, a cold-blooded killer to all that grew, but Brian thought the fresh air was simply great as they slammed open the iron door and hoisted him down the ramp and into the ambulance. "I don't know when I've felt so great," he said. "Just feel that air, will you." Kevin's bones had long since turned to stone, but he did as he was told. And for a moment he shared his son's elation.

What could he do for this wonderful boy? Brian was talking thirteen to the dozen in the ambulance. His face must be the only one in town to have escaped the first frost. Outside people with grey faces peered in whenever the driver stopped for a red light (the ambulance was in no hurry) and it seemed as if their skin would fall off with the next wind and have to be raked away. Or line the gutters like rind. Legs or no legs, his son was at least alive.

Brian talked of the wonders of home, what he would do first, second, who he would like to see (not see), and the

Grade A spookiness of hospital life. Miss Withers, he said, had broken with her creep and taken up with another equally creepy. She was plagued by sex fiends. The night nurse was hoping to get back to Russia and rejoin her "people" as soon as the war ended, and had actually managed to convey it in English. Brian had been patient with her, and she could now say words like "drop dead" and "so's your old man," with that sad, faraway smile of hers.

"It sounds as if you had a pretty good time after all," said Kevin.

"Yeah, except for things like the early-morning washing. I told you about that, didn't I? The night nurse likes to give you a last lick before she checks out. And then the morning nurse wakes you again for a quick scrub—mind you, you're still wet from the night nurse." He was more talkative than he used to be, almost like an actor. "And then there's temperature-taking practice. You know, after the first week, you don't really have a temperature to take any more, but boy, try telling that to the nurses. The trainees come sneaking in with their thermometers and whammo, in the mouth, under the arm, anyplace they feel like. Wow."

Any change was worrying. This was definitely a new boy. There was a smoothness about him, and the rattling charm of a salesman. Had he been listening to too many daytime radio shows? Or was this the tinny echo of somebody's bedside manner? Kevin hated blather; Brian sensed this, and slowed down a little. "It's funny about the temperature part," he said. "You know, polio only lasts about a week. What you have after that is the *remains* of polio."

Perhaps it was possible to become both glibber and more thoughtful. Anyway, the synthetic thing, the prattle, would become worse if the boy was lied to about his condition. (Why is this such a mania of yours, Kevin? Because I cannot bear to deceive him. Because he'll find out and say "You deceived me." Because I cannot bear it that *I* know and he not. Because. A good confession is never done.)

That morning, before picking Brian up, Kevin had talked with Dr. Samson, to make absolutely sure. Samson had been his usual evasive self, squirting smoke screens of "wait and see's" and "early to tell's," but when he saw that Kevin would settle only for the worst, he said, "Unless science comes up with something, I guess his chances are only fair."

God, he hated people like Samson. There was a sense of no Irish need apply about him. And of "Fordham? (pause) I see." "Less than fifty-fifty?" Kevin badgered. "*Much* less than fifty-fifty?" Let's have a little mental discipline, Yale.

The doctor nodded. "There should be *some* sign of life by now, Mr. Casey. The arms seem to be all right, especially the right one. He nearly broke my hand testing his grip. The neck and stomach are weak but hopeful." And then he launched into a stream of Latin names, *glibius flatulus, ponderus maximus,* not Latin a Catholic would use, indicating that Brian's legs were a wasteland where no life would stir again.

Was that what he wanted to hear? Pain was ambiguous, some people laughed from it. Kevin was delirious, flayed alive, laughing to death, but glad to *know*. Nothing could now get worse, that was the important thing. Jerk the adhesive off smartly. Brian could still live a wonderful life, but they must get started on it right away. No more prayers to St. Philomena.

"I wouldn't tell your wife about this," said Dr. Samson.

"What about my son?"

"Why tell him? He'll get used to his condition in a year or two, and he won't mind knowing then."

If Samson had his way, no one would ever be told anything. Everyone would pass through life knowing nothing at all, caressed by lies. His only medicine was anesthesia.

"You don't trust my son, is that it?" Kevin said as pleasantly as possible. "You don't think he's strong enough for the truth?"

"Few people are. Remember, Brian is only a boy of what? Sixteen? Precocious in some ways. But don't be misled by that. It will take all the courage he has, to face it when he has to."

Please, Doctor, spare us your wisdom, O.K.? You have utterly failed to help us professionally. In fact, you have done nothing at all, so far as I can see. So do not lecture us on how to live . . . Kevin felt for a mad moment that the doctor was to blame for the whole thing: his sly evasions, his passivity had held Brian in check for precious weeks.

Samson looked as if he was used to this. He came around the desk and stood by Kevin, ready to shake hands or whatever Kevin preferred. "I'm sorry, Mr. Casey. It's hard for you too, *I* realize that. It's your decision, of course. But I think Brian will figure it out at his own speed. The facts are there." Translated: everybody really knows that polio is incurable, don't they? I, Dr. Samson, have not deceived the public.

A weaselly compromise. Dr. Samson was paid by the minute, and his handshake was metered. Kevin was uncomfortable with professional men. Of course he was one himself, but he didn't feel like one. He left the doctor's office and had a couple of drinks for lunch to steady himself. It was indeed his decision to make. The truth hurt like hell, he could hardly bear to keep his own eye on it for more than a second. But two years of ghastly charade and dwindling hope were unthinkable. You wouldn't string out, say, an amputee for two years, would you? All right then. Whether Beatrice liked it or not, he would share the truth with his son and join him in battle. The truth could make Brian a hero: how many people ever get close to the truth? With only one son, you wanted to go all the way. It wasn't enough just to make him happy.

Kevin still had blood in his eye, with a little Scotch, as he joggled in the ambulance. But now Brian had lengthened his view from the first days at home and was burbling about the months ahead.

"Basketball, yah, who cares about basketball? I'm not tall enough anyway. The doctor says I'll never make seven feet. I expect to be out and around by then, of course, but it'll take awhile to get my legs back in shape. You can definitely put me down for the opening of the baseball season."

My God, he was talking like a child. The baseball season! Kevin jerked his head, but there was no place else to look in the narrow ambulance. Brian must have thought his old man was nuts, like all the others: trying to hide his fixed grin and his streaming eyes.

4

So Kevin gave up, for now, the idea of telling Brian his chances. He still thought he should, but he hadn't the heart to. As the only one in the neighborhood to face it, Kevin began to feel that he carried an unfair burden. He watched with heavy eyes the pantomime of cheerfulness and unreality forming around Brian: the holy-card vendors setting up their stands, Portia and her crazy magazines, the quacks with their optimism, ten dollars an ounce. He ached to scourge them away, and have everything very pure and simple, but he couldn't bring himself to do it. And every day he felt weaker and more out of it.

Brian didn't spot much of this. His father seemed his old brisk self—altogether too brisk in some ways. For instance, he brought up the question of schoolwork on Brian's second day home. "Can't that wait a little?" said Beatrice. Exactly Brian's feeling about it. "It's possible to get lazy in bed," said Kevin. No, no. Polio victims are a compendium of all the virtues. Brian knew his old man had a point, but felt nettled with him for bringing it up at this particular time.

It would be unspeakably dreary to have this thing and to have to study as well. What Brian wanted now was magazine subscriptions. He proposed to his mother that they put out for *Look, Collier's, Time,* and *The Sporting News,* a nicely balanced lineup. Kevin said, "You won't have time for anything else." "Nobody in the world has more time than I have," said Brian. They compromised on *Time* and *Look*.

The days were pleasant enough, except for the grunt and groan with the physiotherapist. Mrs. Schmidt demanded an hour's work and a pound of flesh, and a ten o'clock scholar. "You're not pushing," she'd say. "How can you tell? I don't have any strength there yet." "I can tell." She pumped his legs, as if she were training him for the Rockettes. When he didn't push, she noticed it, and when he did push, she accused him of doing it with his hip, a low form of cheating. There was no easy winning with Mrs. Schmidt.

"When am I going to get better?" he asked from time to time.

"Never, if you don't push."

"Yeah, but if I push?"

"Just keep pushing."

That was all the sense he could get out of her. But she was a good kid. She lit on a flickering muscle as if it were a gold strike. "Do that again." He usually couldn't. "I thought I saw something. All right, let's get back to work." She would never give up on any leg that came her way. But after a month or so, she began to allow herself a five-minute cigarette break. And it turned out she was quite different at rest. Her face smoothed out and she looked beautiful, for forty-two. She talked about music a lot, although Brian told her he had a tin ear. Never mind, he should hear about music anyway. It was part of being a civilized man. Did he speak German, no? 'Fraid not. He spoke French then, yes? Sorry. *Ach*, you Americans. One thing she wouldn't talk about under any circumstances was the war. It seemed she was some kind of refugee with a husband still over there. But whether this husband was in a concentration camp or the German High Command, there was no way of telling. Brian couldn't tell a Jew from anyone else, even though he'd lived in New York all his life. He didn't think he'd met any, although Levine might be one.

They had him in a cranked-up bed, and he sat by the window watching the grim last of the touch-football games and the appearance of mittens and sleds. There was no place for real sleighing down there, but they paddled along hopefully until they came to a rise. They were smaller than they used to be.

Enthroned in clean pajamas in the middle of the living room, he came in for a good deal of random attention. All the Caseys' visitors paid their frantic respects, the "how is everything" brigade, and the "you're looking wonderful" division. After which, they would forget him and talk business and politics, so that he went from being petted to being bored. The way it goes. He read a lot, mostly junk, but some good stuff. Damon Runyon, Chesterton, Plato's *Republic*. Decided Socratic questions were a crock: "Oh yes, Socrates, truly, Socrates; how do you want your ass kissed today, Socrates?" Still, he liked the book. Father O'Monahan came around and gave him the sacraments at Christmas. Very embarrassing to confess masturbation to a man who could actually see you, but there was no way round it. O'Monahan took it like a sport. A man came over to cut his hair, and a fine mess that was, trying to tilt his head around on the pillow. His neck was still weak as water and they talked about putting it in a brace—scare talk that came to nothing.

It was like living in a luxury hotel, where everything was brought to you on trays. Even the men's room was brought to you. He was embarrassed the first time his father took out the steaming bedpan. It was things like that which made him ache to get back on his feet. Otherwise, it was a pretty good life, at least in the daytime. People seemed to think he was going through something, and if he said he wasn't, their eyes glowed double with admiration.

The nights were kind of crumby. He prayed a lot (1) to get better and (2) to avoid the roaring temptations of the flesh. He didn't sleep well, for want of exercise, and he usually succumbed to number 2 around three in the morning, in agonies of remorse. Please don't hold this against me, Lord. I still want to get cured and will make this up to you eventually. No one in good health should ever have occasion to masturbate. Linking the problems like that gave him an exhilarating sense of purpose, and he slept serenely in his wet pajamas.

In February a little man came around with a roll of brown paper and began tracing his legs. It hadn't been explained to Brian, or he hadn't been listening, that he was about to be measured for leg braces. A disgusting idea. "What do I want those things for?" he bellowed at Mrs. Schmidt. "I'm going to walk on my own legs."

"*Ja,* but in the meantime . . . You don't want to spend all your life in this room, do you?"

It felt like a betrayal. His muscles would never come back in those iron grilles. He had seen people heaving along Broadway, dragging them like chains. In fact he even remembered throwing a pitying smile to one such—old fellow with a beard and a shiny black suit. God, what a horrible thing to do.

"You didn't even ask if I wanted them," he raged. "How can you make decisions like that for people?"

"I'm sorry, Brian. It's routine."

"Do my parents know about this? Get my mother."

Mrs. Schmidt was not someone you ordered about, but this time she went meekly enough and came back with Beatrice.

"What is it, Brian?"

He wanted his anger to hit her, level and hard. "Did you know about this, Mother? Did you know that Mrs. Schmidt was planning to put me in braces?" The little man shoved a second piece of paper under Brian's other leg and began sketching. He either was deaf or had heard it all before. "My God, not my right leg too. Mrs. *Schmidt!* You said my right leg was improving. Mother, *did* you know about this?"

Brian had not yelled at his mother since he was five, and he half-expected her to slap him sober, especially for saying "my God." But to his surprise, he got away with it. She bowed her head and said, "I'm sorry, Brian, Mrs. Schmidt said it was a normal part of your treatment."

"Oh, she did, eh? You thought that putting my legs in iron braces was going to bring them back to life, is that what you thought?" His mother was crying, and he felt a queasy mixture of contempt and confusion. "My God, Mother, why didn't you *tell* me about it? That's all I ask. I don't want things *done* to me . . ."

"I'm sorry," said Beatrice. She shook her head and then half-ran from the room. Did I do that? thought Brian. The cause and effect were of different sizes. It was weird the way the cheerfulness around him would spring these sudden cracks: his mother crying, his father making faces in the ambulance.

"This has nothing to do with whether you get cured or not," said Mrs. Schmidt coolly. "Your physiotherapy will continue as before. It is a healthy sign of progress that we've brought you this far."

When Mrs. Schmidt bursts into tears, *that* will be the day. The little man rolled up his papers and left. Brian tried to stay angry over the deception. He still thought he was going to get it in the neck from *some*one for shouting at his mother, and he wanted to maintain some righteous indignation for his defense. But when he next saw his mother, she was still very gentle and repentant. And when his father got home, Brian heard them murmuring in the hall, and then his father was very gentle, too.

The braces arrived, gaunt steel scaffoldings smothered in straps, and he was jimmied into them and strapped tight and hoisted aloft, like a knight helpless in his armor. It was a giddy feeling, lurching about at this altitude, with his feet trailing off in the distance. He jerked a leg in a memory of walking, and only Mrs. Schmidt, a former circus strong man, it turned out, kept him from crashing to the floor. His knees hurled themselves against the leather caps, they would certainly flop out in a moment. He was scared spitless that he would just fall apart if he tried to move again. Straw would fly out of his chest. But Mrs. Schmidt was everywhere, under his armpits, around his chest, doing it all.

She urged him forward in a stately waddle in strides of no more than six inches, all the way to the window. He felt giddy with achievement. It was a clear, sharp day, you would know it was New York blindfold. But looking at it *standing up*—now there was something. He rested his head lightly against the glass, savoring his sheer tallness. He had no idea how high five foot ten was. If somebody comes in now and talks about my gallant struggle, I can at least grab him and fall on top of him. Bite his leg, if necessary. Oh boy. He felt drunk up here and half-mad with power.

"Are you ready to walk back now?" asked Mrs. Schmidt. "Try not to do it all with the hip. And not so much drag, please. Keep the toes pointed." She was at it already, before he had even had his measure of gloating. What difference did it make which way his toes pointed? He'd be out of these things in a twinkling. However, something warned him not to raise the question right now. She would only say, "You'll never get better if you don't point the toes."

As she commenced her endless unstrapping, he thought, She's right, this isn't much of a triumph. He thought again of the old men heaving along Broadway, some of them not really old at all but solemn little boys in glasses: they had probably had their moments of glory like this, the first day up. It was no time to get complacent. The braces looked malignant when they were off: like something in an Amsterdam Avenue store window, between the pink trusses and the corrective corset. Dwarfs humping in to be measured for dwarf equipment. He didn't belong to that world, and never would.

"I hope you didn't pay too much for them," he told his parents over supper. "Because I don't intend to stick around in them for long."

He knew that this proclamation came under the heading of gallant struggle and fighting spirit, but for once it couldn't be helped. He had to put his intentions on the record. His mother said, "Of course you won't." And his father said, rather blankly, "We didn't pay too much." And then recovered himself to say, "Not that that makes any difference."

5

Fatstuff and Levine looked in occasionally, but they seemed more at a loss than ever with their bedside manner, now that Brian was only half-sick. They clunked in and out of the kitchen for something to do, polishing off his Pepsi ration. Otherwise they sat around and picked at their socks. Brian brought up his plans for the coming baseball season and the guys seemed slightly incredulous. "You really think you'll be back in time, huh?" said Levine. "Definitely." "That's great, Brian."

No use talking to them about it. He didn't give a shit what they expected. He would just have to show them, just as he would have to show his old man. He had asked the latter for a baseball glove for his birthday in February, and his father had agreed with that worried look of his and had given him something else. All right. We'll just see.

Also, some new friends wouldn't be a bad idea. He sensed that the old ones were coming around now out of remembered kindness, and he sure as hell didn't need that. Polio had lost its terrors for them, he would have to get cancer to see that again. "You remind me of a couple of old ladies from the parish going door to door with a bag of fruit," he told them one day. They grinned sickly and didn't answer. Hey—he might still get a rise out of Hennessy if he waved a skinny leg at them and sang, "It could happen to you." Phil Marconi was still O.K., if you liked that kind of thing. He came by himself and talked about socialism, his new kick. Solitude was driving Marconi insane.

"What do you do for girls up here?" Bernie Levine asked one time.

"I have them flown in. From Paris."

"No, but really."

Really, what he did over them was writhe, twist, and sweat, holding his penis to keep it from exploding. Outside of that, nothing.

"What happened to Marie Snyder?" said Bernie.

"She sent me a get-well card. It made me cry."

"You want to meet something good?"

"Now tell me, Levine. In your frank opinion, what the hell would I do with something good up here?"

"You could talk."

"Yeah. Thanks mucho, buddy." In fact, all he had ever

done with a girl was talk and attempt such necking as could even now be easily performed in a wheelchair. But he understood that Bernie at least had moved on from that, which elevated the rhetoric for all of them.

He temporized. "I'll be getting around pretty soon. I'll wait." Outside of the feeling that he was now an enormous cock with a six-inch man attached to it, he was in no special rush.

Three days a week now, a man called Mezzerow came around and coached him in various subjects—algebra, English, and whatever came up. Mezzerow was some kind of a nut, if you like. He had shiny, thin black hair and a red beard, and Brian never did place his accent. "It doesn't matter," said Mr. Mezzerow. ("Probably Armenian in that case," said Kevin.) He taught at Fordham, which Brian had always taken to be a jockstrap institution. But Mezzerow went to a different, exotic Fordham. "There are many strange birds of passage up there," he said.

He didn't teach Brian a damn thing he was supposed to. Although he described a huge, rich syllabus to Kevin, he never got close to it with Brian. Before his corduroys had crunched down, he was off on a discussion of, oh, medieval monasteries, or whether men were inherently different from women. One day it was genes, the next it was the social contract. His little eyes would dart like a bird's and he would light on a fresh subject. Pick, pick at it, until he'd got hold of a thread. Then up and away.

Brian loved the sessions and hoped that nobody else would discover that his teacher was crazy. He got especially hooked on Roman history—his own temperament seemed suited to the years 133–44 B.C. He thought Sulla was kind of like Roosevelt. "No, no—he's like your General MacArthur." Mr. Mezzerow would leave with his green algebra book under his arm, convinced that he had been teaching from that all along. Kevin would ask, "How's the algebra coming?" and Brian would say, "Fine, fine." He even tried to learn a little on his own, to cover for Mr. Mezzerow.

The one thing Brian did learn was how to argue with a bird in flight. The opening would be pedantic, a discussion of ground rules. "What do you make of theocracy, Casey? Don't you think that priests make more disinterested rulers than lay politicians?" Brian could have been anybody at that point. Besides wearing the same shirt for a whole week, Mezzerow took no interest in individuals as such.

"That's ridiculous. I mean, isn't it?"

And they'd be off, Brian pouncing and the little man skimming away over the grass, into the trees. "Do *you* believe in theocracy?" Brian would say, winded and exhausted. "I don't know." Mezzerow's eyes would suddenly look troubled. "Sometimes I think it's better than what we've seen in our lifetimes, don't you?"

He never knew what Mezzerow had seen in his lifetime because the little fellow was unmasked all too soon. Brian had to be shown a real algebra exam, to see how he would do in the Regents, and he couldn't make head or tail of it.

Mezzerow had a confrontation with Kevin. "Do you know any algebra yourself, Mr. Mezzerow?" Kevin shook with rage. Brian hoped to God that Mezzerow knew a little.

Mezzerow walked over to Brian and said, "You know how to do this, don't you?" He took the paper and wrote the answers on an envelope without pausing and handed them to Kevin. He had taught Brian how to do this, he knew he had. Kevin thanked him speechlessly, and he left and never came back. Later Brian heard that he was released by Fordham (which Brian now pictured as a refugee camp, with gypsies boiling kettles and singing) and had disappeared into the Midwest. Along with Mrs. Schmidt, he conveyed the sense of some dark outer world which would catch up with you someday in a cheap hotel room or in back of the "Y."

He was replaced by a poopy regular teacher named Walton and the old dullness settled in. Brian was used by now to reading what he liked when he liked and this man's assignments simply bored him out of his bedpan. For a while he did them in a rush at the last minute, and then he stopped doing them altogether. How do you like those apples, Mr. Whatzit? Mr. Walton, who, mind you, was so dull that Brian couldn't remember what he looked like between visits, shrugged. How do you punish a boy who already *has* polio? Brian had been raised thus far in the Catholic school system and was used to working under the whip. This guy was a pussycat. Walton was replaced—tutors were nomads, always moving to a new mining town—by a Miss Crowther, who was just ridiculous. She looked as if she was going to cry as she snuffled out her sixth-grade arithmetic. Kevin gave up trying to look for competent tutors in New York after that. It didn't matter, Brian had been top of his class at Conception (God knows, a humble achievement), and he could spot the guys a year.

In April, Mrs. Schmidt thought she sighted something in the left anterior tibia or someplace. Push, you buggers. Sorry. False alarm. Next they installed a galvanic battery to smoke out any live nerves that might be lurking in there, but it only burned his skin and left it sore as a boil. Mrs. Schmidt said she was pleased with his right leg, which was O.K. as far as it went but not the big cigar.

"You should concentrate on that one for a while, Brian," she said.

"Yeah, well, you see. I know that one's going to be all right. It's lefty I'm interested in right now."

"Pardon me. You *don't* know that the right one's going to be all right. You don't know anything for sure. If you stop working, progress will stop instantly."

Ja, ja. Vurk is der answer to der problems. "Look, Mrs. Schmidt, lefty is the ballgame, as far as I'm concerned."

Orders came straight back from the Reichstag. "It is imperative that you have one good leg as soon as possible." Done and done.

"You mean you're not sure the other one's coming back at all?" he said playfully, not meaning any harm. It was just an average day.

"You can do wonders with one good leg. It's like night and day, the difference."

Ho hum. What was that she said? *One* good leg? What the hell use was one good leg? "You're kidding, Mrs. Schmidt. You think I'd settle for that?" he said, smiling.

"What you settle for is your business," said Mrs. Schmidt. "I'm just telling you—" She stopped. Physiotherapy conversation was mostly prattle, the kind of thing you might say while doing a jigsaw puzzle, and you sometimes launched into a sentence without planning its future.

"*What* are you just telling me?"

"I don't *know* what I'm telling you. I'm telling you you have to work on your right leg, that's all." She began ferociously pumping his left leg, as if to appease it. He watched her with panicky disdain. Unfortunately, he could not afford to let this pass.

"You've lost faith in me, haven't you, Mrs. Schmidt? You don't think I can do it?"

"I didn't say that," she muttered.

"Come on, I'm not that stupid. One good leg, you said. Admit it." She worked away fiendishly as if she would cure it all by herself this very afternoon. Her silence was maddening; he must make the next words land a bit harder; he must force her to say that everything was going to be all right.

"I don't believe I can make it with someone who doesn't have faith in me. Are you listening, Mrs. Schmidt?"

She looked up from her hopeless task. She looked as beautiful as she did off duty. "What do you want me to do, Brian?"

"I want you to say you believe in a complete cure. And if

you don't, I want to get someone who does." He hadn't meant to force her hand. In a way, it was only words anyhow. Like the Pledge of Allegiance. Go on now, just *say* it.

"Do you really mean that, Brian?"

"Yes, I do." You can keep your fingers crossed if you like, he almost added.

She took a deep breath. Oh God, you don't have to take a deep breath for this. "In that case, maybe somebody else would be better for you. I'll talk to your mother." And she picked up her stuff, just like that, and was gone. She was almost psychotically incapable of crapping around.

He heard her voice out in the hall and was tempted to shout something. He was losing everybody. He must keep Mrs. Schmidt at all costs. But then he thought about the one good leg, and how Mrs. Schmidt had probably given up on life *as such* for some personal reason, a dead child or something, a murdered husband, and he thought, I can't have people like that around me. It would deaden his willpower. She was some kind of Jewish refugee, he bet, beaten way down. This was one of those turning points (he hadn't expected one today) where you decided to become a cripple or not. He must toughen his mind starting now, and have no truck with losers.

Final snapshots of Mrs. Schmidt: walking the streets in her belted raincoat, boiling a rationed egg in her lonely apartment, finally being gunned down in an empty swimming pool by the S.S. Brian told his parents that he liked her very much, and always would, but he couldn't afford to be around defeatists. His father looked depressed and didn't say anything. "Don't you agree, Father?" Kevin murmured something. "I said, don't you agree?" "Of course we do," said Beatrice.

Mrs. Schmidt's replacement was no defeatist, but a serene old lady with iron fingers, name of Miss Seton. Miss Seton did not know much of the mechanics of polio, but she did believe you could do anything if you tried. She herself had recovered from some disease which Brian had never even heard of, while she was still a small girl. She had also met Owen Wister, the author of *The Virginian*. A delightful man. Brian knew he would feel those fingers drumming on his legs as long as he lived.

"Miss Seton thinks there's life in your left leg," said Kevin.

"Yeah, well you see that comes mostly from the hip."

Kevin looked inexplicably proud—another of those out-of-synch expressions. "I'm glad you admit that," he said. "A lot of people would kid themselves."

"Listen, I'm not that far gone, that I need to kid myself."

Miss Seton didn't know many exercises. She had never actually handled a polio case before, though she had some acquaintance with arthritis, and her only notion was to knead him with baby oil and pound him until the blood roared. Any sign of life anywhere fooled her, and on lazy days, Brian liked to thrill her with fake heaves from the torso. The old lady was beside herself every time. He was beginning to lose his faith in orthodox physiotherapy anyway, it seemed like an awfully plodding way to get there. What this thing called for was a blitzkrieg, with General

Patton streaking through the Ardennes, General Bradley reaming in from the South—those slashing arrows in the paper every day should be applied to his spine.

So, re-enter the swamis. Aunt Portia was still peddling Dr. Steinmetz, who had turned up again in Arizona. His new clinic had been doing famously until the government impounded his white mice. A very transparent move in the A.M.A. plot to discredit him. Portia was trying to get in touch with Steinmetz, and if he ever came East, she would make sure he got a look at Brian.

Aunt Brigid, for her part, was high on one Blessed Herbert Weatherby, who needed one more miracle to move up to saint. "Of course it would have to be authenticated, but you wouldn't have any trouble with that, would you? You could get a doctor to sign something, couldn't you?" "Yeah, if anyone could read the doctor's writing. I'd certainly hate for Blessed Whatzit to waste a miracle."

Steinmetz countered with a daring new plan involving leeches. These, if applied to the jugular vein, would suck off all the poisons in the system, and then some. Unfortunately, Steinmetz was having trouble taking his beasts across state lines, and had been arrested in Kansas when one of them escaped from a shoe box. Blessed Herbert Weatherby was having his problems too, serious doubts having been raised as to his very existence. His name had originally been scratched in the Tower of London, and his initials had become an inspiration to Catholic fugitives everywhere. But whether he had actually existed was not known for sure.

In a final raising of stakes, Portia began talking of taking Brian out to Kansas to see Steinmetz, while Brigid spoke of Lourdes, now that the war was ending. Kansas was dismissed for now on the grounds that Steinmetz would probably be somewhere else when they got there, but Lourdes seeped into the regular family consultations.

"I think it's a wonderful idea," said Beatrice. "Don't you, dear?"

His father's new mumble was the answer to that. His mother agreed to accept it, though Brian was nettled by it.

"Maybe by next spring it'll be possible to get over there," she continued.

"Next spring? I'll surely be better before next spring." Brian's litany. "You'll have to get me there fast if I'm not going to beat them to it."

"Isn't there a shrine in Canada or someplace?" asked Kevin, joking thinly. "Lourdes is an awfully long way away."

"You know there's only one Lourdes, dear. Even pagan scientists are stumped by it."

"I guess so."

"If we can just get Brian there, our worries are practically over."

It was only true, if everybody said it together. "Don't you agree, Father? Our troubles are practically over?"

Kevin looked strangulated. "Yes, I guess so."

"You don't seem very happy about it. Does he, Mother?" They both smiled at Kevin, a spontaneous ganging-up by the Faithful.

"I don't think you should take miracles for granted," Kevin said in a low voice.

"Don't worry, I won't." His father looked so small and weak, Brian felt he could say anything to him now. "But it's better than going in there hopeless. Don't you think so, Mother?"

Kevin looked at his wife. She was still smiling. She was on Brian's side. Faith was vitality, doubt was death. Cornered like a rat, Kevin said, "Beatrice, I think you're spoiling him," and left the table.

They dropped it, of course. The Caseys in quorum never discussed personal matters for more than a minute. But Brian heard them at it again later, like distant thunder, in their room. They must have calibrated the house, to see exactly how loud they could speak without quite being understood. It was maddening, straining from his bed, to catch it—another three feet would have done it for sure. But with the sixth sense of the bed-bound, the one that picks up doctors' evil whispers, he imagined his mother was saying, "How can you talk about spoiled, after all he's been through?" And he thought, I haven't been through anything yet, have I? Still—if enough people thought he had, maybe he had, at that.

6 By March, they had him up and out in a wheelchair.

The second time, Bernie Levine almost cracked up the chair, racing it down the hill on Claremont. Brian was shaken by the four-miles-per-hour, the giddy rush of air on his indoor face, and screamed for him to stop. After that, they took him on a sedate grand tour and he thought, Oh gee, you don't have to be *that* careful. They plodded gently past Riverside Church. "Could you go a little faster, Fatman? Good grief, but you're in terrible shape." Hennessy plugged along gamely, not yet realizing that you can say "fuck off" to a polio victim. On Brian's side, it was difficult making jokes with a guy who treated you like a piece of glass. "O.K., Fatstuff, take five, I was only kidding." Gee, but his friends were second-rate.

Important lesson about human nature: they didn't say "fuck off," they just stopped coming round. Fatstuff was involved in the Glee Club, anyhow, and spent long afternoons practicing "Stout-hearted Men" for Commencement Day. Levine was rushing some girl in Westchester. Fuck spring, thought Brian, who swore liberally in his head these days. He missed his ration of raunchy conversation and didn't want his thoughts to get *too* soft and girlish. Faithful Phil Marconi pushed him around the block once and quit for good. "It's too much like work," he said. Brian's picture of Phil as loyal, cynical friend had to be adjusted downward. "I can get you a guy from Chinatown for six yen an hour and no questions," said Phil.

So it usually ended up with his parents pushing. It seemed a bit of a chore after that, like walking the dog, and he wished they'd change the buildings around here. He went at a crawl, with a blanket over his knees, and got annoyed with people who looked at him and asked how he was doing. "How are *you* doing?" he asked an old lady, who seemed startled.

Half an hour a day, he lunged around the apartment on his braces. Miss Seton let his toes point where they would, and he found he could work up a good, ungainly speed, slurring his feet across the living-room carpet. In due time, he took the elevator, to the cheers of the doormen, and held a small parade in front of the house. Neighbors and well-wishers gathered to cheer him on, with cries of "take it easy" and "that's the boy" and lots of vague gurgle and buzz. He felt like the Second Coming.

Flushed from the attention, Brian said, "That's only the

beginning, folks." And damned if someone didn't praise his fine spirit. Ah well, tolerance, tolerance. His arms were limp as rags from pushing the crutches, and he felt like a marathon winner as he slumped back into the house. He had a picture of those admiring faces, felt their love on his skin like velvet. He would see them again in dreams, in Roman togas, or bobby sox, his basic crowd face from now on. That very night, he played basketball in a jammed arena, floating around the court like thistledown, making miraculous lay-ups between motionless opponents, and the crowd was there.

When he woke, he could not believe it had been a dream. He made the first moves of getting up as usual, slipping his legs over the side of the bed. He had felt them move just a few minutes ago, their strength had returned during the night. All was well.

Ah goddamnit. You can't sneak up on it like that. His feet touched the floor, and he knew that they were the same old feet. He hoisted them up again sulkily. The dream was a dirty trick. He ran the dregs of it around his mouth. Dreams had taste, all right. The funny thing was, he'd been floating with a slight limp. Ah fuck it.

That evening Brian tackled his father again. Kevin said he'd had a bad day and he certainly looked it. His face was still steaming from the heat and he couldn't seem to get his collar loose enough. Had he always looked like this? Anyway, it was imperative that Brian take some of the management of his own case away from this very tired man.

"I dreamed I was playing basketball last night. All right,

it's nothing to get excited about." God, he hated sentimentality. "But it made me want to get things moving. I mean, are we just going to sit here and wait for something to happen or what?"

"Miss Seton is very satisfied with your progress." Kevin had poured himself a huge drink, and seemed overwhelmed by it.

"Yeah, Miss Seton. I've taught her all I could about polio, but she doesn't seem to catch on."

"Do you want another physiotherapist?"

"No, I really don't think it makes that much difference. If a muscle's dead, you can't help it with exercise, right?"

"Right, I guess." His father looked as if he just wanted to go to sleep. He finally said, "What do you suggest then?"

"I don't know. How about that place I keep reading about, in the South. That must be pretty good, I bet."

"It must be pretty expensive."

"What's that got to do with it?"

"I don't know," his father continued. "I may not have enough money for it."

"Couldn't you do some extra work or something?"

Kevin began to speak and then changed his mind. God, he's drunk. That's what it is. He must have gotten stoned on the way home. Brian was disgusted. His father suddenly seemed terribly drunk, awash, rheumy-eyed, with booze rubbed right into his suit. He was falling apart under their eyes, just when they needed him.

"Would you just look into it?" said Brian.

"It's been an expensive year," mumbled Kevin. Beatrice,

who had been darning socks at the window, glared up at this. "Polio's an expensive business," he said. Beatrice *would not* argue in front of Brian, but she left the room pointedly, and Brian assumed that they would argue later.

"I'm sorry I'm a burden on you," he said sarcastically.

"Oh God, I didn't mean that." The old fool was on the verge of tears. "It's just been a very tough year."

Well, his sickness had clarified a few things around here. Brian had always felt the neutral, equal love for both parents that Catholic boys were taught to feel. "Felt" was even putting it too strongly. Now he saw that if he was to make the Big Push, he could not afford to love his father equally. Not until he got back on the team– Go on, challenge that, give me a reason to love you equally. But his father seemed paralyzed now, in the soul. Counting his pennies, with a cure in sight.

"I'll write to them myself," Brian said. "Maybe they have scholarships or something."

"That's all right, I'll write to them."

"Don't you know somebody influential who might help?"

"I'll have to think about it," said Kevin.

Think about it. Oh God, that was too much. Too priceless. Brian turned away and rolled his own chair silently out of the room, leaving his father staring into his glass.

Kevin did raise the money somehow, and he even came up with an influential person, sort of: a school friend who knew the head of the Polio Foundation. And they found a place for Brian in the overflowing hospital at Salt Rock. Brian practiced turns and fast stops in the living room to prepare himself for train travel, landing hard on the carpet a few times, memorizing its harsh flavor.

His father saw him off at Penn Station, drunk not drunk, who could tell any more. He was off the team now.

Brian took all the credit for being here. For three weeks he more or less hadn't talked to his father, and Kevin had submitted to the silence. That was all: Brian had willed this thing into happening. "Goodbye, then," a worried face at the window, and gone. His father was only one of a hundred small anxious people disappearing up the platform. Most lives were terribly insignificant, from a moving train. A fight to the death with polio gave your life some point. Those people on the platform hit him like a vision. He hadn't moved fast for so long he'd forgotten how people shrink as you travel away from them, how they melted into each other, cloth and flesh all in one, and became the public, humanity, and then nothing at all.

A harassed porter checked on Brian every hour or so to see if he needed to go to the bathroom. By evening, things were pretty frantic. Sailors went heaving past with their duffel bags or hunkered down on them, to jam the aisles. An enlisted man plopped next to Brian and fell instantly asleep. The conductor tried to wake him to see if he had a Pullman ticket. The soldier said, "Wha' wha'," and rolled his head away. It was pretty neat, to Brian's eye, after seven months of nothing much. The conductor asked a sailor to help with his ticket problem, and the sailor professionally raised the sleeper's eyelid and pronounced him next door to dead. "Probably on drugs," he said. "You didn't know that, did you, conductor? A lot of civilians don't. Yeah, all combat soldiers are doped to the gills, the poor bastards." The conductor edged off to find an MP. The sleeping man waved a finger at him.

Everyone was very nice to Brian. Some of them called him "sonny" and some of them called him "sir." The sleeping man asked if he'd been in the army. "Watch out," said Brian suddenly. The MP had snuck up on them. The man's eyes shut and his head lolled expertly. The MP gave him a shake and then tried to lift him by the armpit. The sleeper collapsed in the MP's arms, causing him to stagger like someone in a dance marathon. Then realizing that the jig was up, the sleeper gave a woozy salute and they moved off together. "Did you see that guy's combat ribbons?" said the sailor. "Shit, he should be allowed to sit anywhere he likes."

When Brian had to go to the john, they passed him from hand to hand like a fire bucket: scary at first, on the rolling train, then exhilarating, being touched by so many friendly people. Swaying over the toilet bowl, fumbling at his buttons, he felt like giving a war whoop. It was like coming back from the dead.

The porter made up his bed, but he couldn't sleep. It was raw excitement, no cause, no nice thing he had to tell himself, but the rush of a train through black country, the feeling he was moving again. He jerked up the shade and smiled out at the moonlit fields. Gr–eat!

The train was a wartime special, seven hours late, which was fine with him. The juice that had accumulated in bed like hog fat was jogged to life by the motion, and he wanted it to last. The stillness when they stopped was like the first moment after death. He was met at the station by a big Negro in a white coat. "You fer th' foundation?" asked the Negro. Brian guessed that must mean Salt Rock and he started cautiously shuffling forward. But the Negro stepped up smartly and scooped Brian into his arms like a kitten. "This quicker," he said. God knows how, he snapped Brian's braces open so his legs bent and proceeded to trot him along the platform. It was damn humiliating, in front of all these people. Another Negro, smaller, already had his crutches. There was no way of getting down. "Put you arm roun' my neck," said the big one. The neck was huge and slick with sweat, and although Brian was a liberal of course, it made him feel slightly sick. "Go ahead, drop you on you ass if you don't." So Brian clung there like a doll, feeling a nuance of helplessness that he had missed up to now. Goddamn, I'll get well, he thought, to get even. Fuck it, I'll get well. Cocksucking right, I'll get well. He could say no more than that. Last night they were saying, "Sir, have you been in the army?" And now this.

The man dumped him in the back of a station wagon, where he bounced like a laundry bag. The car started up with a retching grind, and Brian bounced some more. It was a scalding, airless day and the countryside looked like a dirty old bum. Brian saw a man dead in a field, with a white handkerchief over his face, or maybe he was just sleeping. And houses with collapsed lungs, split bellies, caved-in roofs. Everything very, very sick around here. Brian had his theories about the South, of course. He tried talking to the two Negroes, but found he literally couldn't understand their answers. (Not sure they understood his questions, either.) Well, cockfuck it, he'd get well, suck-damnit, he'd get well, godgoose it—cursing was pretty funny, when you came down to it. The dead surroundings charged him with crazy energy. He'd shake this place until its teeth rattled.

It was a long drive, and the two Negroes never once spoke to each other. They drove him eventually into a compound that looked like a deserted army base. "They all at the movies," said the driver. Then he said a lot of other stuff, which Brian couldn't follow—would just have to wait and see what it meant. Brian was already thinking in a new dialect. The driver carried him into a prefab, the big neck no problem by now, and flipped him onto an operating-table-type thing and whipped off his pants with surprising delicacy and threw them in a corner. That was a clue. The big dinge wants to examine me. Everybody wants to examine me.

"What are you doing with those?" Brian piped. The guy had whipped the braces off, too.

"Won't be needn'm no more," he said and flung them after the pants hard enough to shatter them. What the hell? Brian was lost without his braces. He doesn't mean I'll get well that soon, does he? Who is this nut anyway? The man finished undressing him and scooped him up again and hustled him into the next room, which contained a bathtub on stilts and a big slow-witted fan. The Negro was quite gentle once you got used to him. He lowered Brian with a plunk into the lukewarm water, which had just been sitting there, and left, and that was the last Brian saw of him.

Now bathing had been a big deal at home. A bathing suit, for decency. A bath thermometer. His old man lifting him with trembling back. You got to know what your parents *felt* like in this racket. How small they were. Who had dandruff. What suit should be thrown out.

He had not bathed unattended since the old days. His mother would leave the room while he soaped around inside his trunks. Otherwise, there was always someone watching. Bathing seemed highly dangerous. You could drown in the course of a blink.

But here, they let you soak like a pickle. Very nice. He assumed the Negro had told him what to expect next and not to worry. Everything was so slow, there could be no danger. The sun splintered down through a dusty skylight, putting a smoky shine on the bath water. They certainly saved on overhead around here. Everything must go into research. A bug the size of a horse began climbing the far wall. Brian eyed him lazily. That couldn't be your household roach, could it? They must be breeding them big down here, to play football and eventually take over the world. The bug changed its plans and disappeared from sight: only to surface again a minute later on the wall next to Brian's head, just a few inches away. God he was ugly; Brian imagined the black metal skin crunching under a human foot and the small idiot brain rolling out. Brian wasn't scared of insects, but this was no insect. It was a lousy panzer division. No trick at all for it to drop in beside him and wrestle him to death. What the hell would Brian do with it? He couldn't get out of the tub. The son of a bitch would eat him alive.

He flapped the water hysterically with his weak left arm. A drop landed on the bug just like that and it slid skittering down the wall. Hah. Score one for the Western mind. A minute later, though, the bug was back. Maybe he just wants to play. Like a St. Bernard. Brian nervously splashed the water again, but the bug shook it off this time. He'd learned from his last encounter with the white man. God, this could go on forever. Brian was pumping water on the wall when the door opened.

A sandy-haired man in a white apron looked in, and began to shut the door again. "Hey, wait, wait," said Brian. "Could you get me somebody? Are *you* somebody?"

The man said, "You through with your bath?"

"I guess so, yes."

"I'll get somebody."

Ten minutes later, Brian was out of there, and in another twenty he was dressed and in a wheelchair. People came and went and sent for other people, no one seemed to have any special plan for him. If there was any way of speeding up these zombies, they would make wonderful pets. They told him he could check in tomorrow, everybody at the movies right now. He was wheeled to a cabin and left there. The freedom still tingled. Both the beds were smothered in comic books of the Jungle Queen type, and the walls were brilliant with Petty girls. Already a roach was crawling up a pinup's shining flank, bent on rape. The metal body shook with desire.

"Go get her, baby. Screwgie-doos." Brian was so busy with lust and death that he hadn't noticed his roommate come in. "Hi. I'm Joe Santini. I'll move my stuff. Christ, what a bomb. Fucking Andrews Sisters."

He was a little dark guy with lightning-quick moves. He took a couple of jog steps over to one of the beds. Belched like a gong and struck his chest. This guy was *sick?* He bundled up his funnies and stuffed them under the bed.

"You an Italian kid?" said Santini. "You look like an Italian kid."

"No. Irish."

"Yeah, well, you could be Irish, too."

"*You* haven't got polio, have you?"

"Sure. A little trouble with my stomach." He patted what looked like a perfectly good stomach. "I doubt I'll fight again. Well shit, I wasn't that good anyway. What branch were you in?"

"I wasn't in any branch. I'm still in school."

"Oh yeah? Hhh." He grunted. "Hey, it really winged you, didn't it, kid? Bad, bad. Well, got to be running along." He jogged back to the door. "Ping-pong calls," he said.

Brian decided to get out of here himself, before the combination of pinups and roaches drove him crazy. His groin was filling like a balloon in the heat. There were two screen doors, and he banged open the one that led to the patio. It dragged against his wheelchair and slammed shut behind. Nothing much back here, a burned-out patch of grass and a concrete path, leading to yet another prefab. They must be putting *everything* into research.

He wheeled around the corner: more concrete, more prefabs. People moving softly, as in dreams. Happy? Unhappy? We do not know these words here in Shangri-la. As he got to what he took to be the outskirts, he thought, Ol' Porgy gon' roll all de way to *New* York. He finally came upon some solid-looking crew-cuts standing by the gates, chatting and leaning on golf bags. "Excuse me." He wheeled up. "*You* fellows aren't patients, are you?"

"Damn right we are," said one of them.

"You'll be getting out of here soon, I guess."

"Not if I have anything to say," said a big fat one. "My anterior tibia may never come back," he said, doing a little shuffle step.

Well, that was a rotten shame. Taking up space that was needed. Still, he was in now himself, and it was good to see how they cured people around here. He wheeled back through the pale heat. His left wrist was sore as rust from pushing.

He had his supper in a dining room that seemed like a Quaker restaurant with another bunch of outstandingly healthy GI's. Two of them said they had gotten polio in the South Pacific, another lucky bastard got his at Fort

Dix. Better than having your balls shot off, no? There was a rumor that one of the nurses put out. They would look into it, especially if it rained tomorrow. At other tables, elderly civilians sat hunched, a few of them drinking their dinners through glass straws, others with drastically short legs or hands as small as a child's. They had gotten here too late, or too long ago, for the miracle cures the GI's picked up as a matter of course. It was a tough world, and Brian felt, for the incorrigibles, some of the tenderness a healthy guy would feel.

After supper, he expected a whistle to blow for bingo or something, but nothing happened. The big recreation hall filled up randomly; wheelchairs were drawn up around the bridge tables; old men wrote letters. Brian continued to cruise like a ghost trying to pick up the principles of bridge over people's shoulders. He watched the big boys in the army fatigues booming ping-pong balls at each other, and then he went to bed and read Santini's copy of *Forever Amber*. He was still waiting for Amber to actually *do* something, when his roommate came roaring in, frisky with booze.

"Hey Irish kid, you want a drink?"

"No thanks." It didn't seem like a great time for his first one. "Are you allowed to drink here?"

"It isn't easy. Hey, you little bastards!" He had spotted the night's roaches. "I'll teach you to eat shit around here." He picked up a checkerboard and began flailing at them. "You've eaten your last shit on *my* time," he shouted, as a huge one splashed to his death.

"You play checkers?" asked Brian.

"Checkers? Oh, you mean the board. That's just for the roaches. Take that, you Japanese cocksucker. Ah, Son of Rising Sun. Here's a message from the good old U.S. of A."

The room was already black with corpses. Santini looked around satisfied. "Let me know if you have any more trouble, ma'am." He took his three jog steps to the door. "See you, kid. I hear there's a nurse on corridor 3 that puts out."

Brian turned out the light, and slept in his sweat and his bower of roaches.

7

The next day, they gave him a brief examination at the main building, which was an actual stone building in the middle of this polio boom town. The doctor kept adjusting Brian's legs to make sure they were the same length: first pulling one and then the other, till Brian couldn't tell himself. The doctor gave a final tap with the gavel, to see if any reflexes were at home, and started to pack up.

"Is that all you're going to do?"

"They seem to be all right, although maybe the left one's a *teeny* bit shorter," the doctor said to the girl in white. "We'll just have to keep an eye on it."

"I said, is that all you're going to do?"

"That's it for now, son. Miss Prendergast will fix up an

exercise schedule for you. Welcome to Salt Rock. I hope you're happy here."

He was gone in a flash of white hair and glasses. Were all specialists required to have white hair? Were doctors' hands pinker than other people's? From all that scrubbing. Also, Miss Prendergast seemed awfully young for a physiotherapist.

"When do I get my braces back?" he asked her.

"We'll make you some new ones while you're with us. You probably had horrible old heavy ones, didn't you? Salt Rock makes the finest braces in the world."

She was a pretty girl, and Brian was passionately attracted to her, even though she spoke like a Chamber of Commerce. It seemed that the pool schedule was very crowded, with all those servicemen, and that he could only work out every second day. She wheeled him over for a quickie that morning. He lay on an underwater bed, and she worked his legs gently, side to side, up and down. "Is that *all?*" he said again. On both sides, he could see malingering servicemen, grunting over their small problems, hanging on to what was left of their polio, so they wouldn't have to go back to war.

"That's all we have time for," she said.

"But how do you cure people?"

She smiled and said nothing. She wouldn't say cure anyway, she would say remarkable improvement. Goddamn, they'd handed him a lemon. "What do I do now?"

"Whatever you like. Have you tried ping-pong?"

They didn't like the patients to walk, she explained, even on their own fancy braces, because it led to bad habits.

Well, that was good. In his bones, he still felt that braces were the enemy. They were on the side of death.

He wheeled back to the rumpus room, where his friend Santini asked if he would mind buying some cigarettes to share. Santini had used up his own ration, but Brian was a new face at the counter. Santini gave him a buck and told him to keep the change.

The line was abuzz with fresh rumors of the nurse who put out. She was the sports page and the financial section, all the news there was around here. Reports had come in this very morning, there was no doubt about it. She was a tiger.

"Which one is she?" Brian asked the man in front.

"That one, over there."

"You're kidding." A mousy little blond girl, standing by herself with a manila folder, looking for someone to give it to: a nice enough body but surely no tiger.

"You'd be am*aze*d," said the man. "From what I hear."

Brian quickly wished he hadn't been told about it. He could already see her biting and moaning under the hot blankets, as one huge GI piled on after another. "More, more, give it to me, give it to me." Once, when he was thirteen, he had stumbled over a couple humping in the bushes of Riverside Park, and the girl's moans had to be believed. Until she said, "Get lost, you nosy little bastard." So he associated women in sex with spitting rage.

"Give it to me, Brian, give it to me." The night transformation of the mouse into a raging whore was too much for his fragile glands.

Impure thoughts were bad enough, when the girls had

no faces. But when you had a specific target, that was a real sin. In the gospel it said that once you had lusted after a woman in your heart, you'd as good as frugeled her. In which case, of course . . .

"Next," said the girl at the counter. "Er, Chesterfields, I guess. And a big Hershey bar." Would the same man order both? And was there any way in which he was eligible for a crack at the tiger? Or was it just servicemen? And if he got there, how did he manage the mechanics? Heaving and fumbling for his gold. Would she help him, or would she curse impatiently and tell him to make way for a real man?

All afternoon long, he imagined her pounding his back with her fists, cursing, face alternately scarlet with desire and white with disgust; ah, forget it, Casey. It's a sin, and besides it's impossible. He did try a little ping-pong, his right arm was plenty strong enough, and he enjoyed playing from a wheelchair, taking the ball near eye level and swatting it back with an overhand shot. But it didn't help materially with the nurse problem.

The heat roasted his crotch till it was a purple inferno. Any moment it would combust and bury the place in hot lava. There was nothing of consequence to do around here. He wheeled over to the one-room library and found that all the books excited him sexually, especially the dull ones. He certainly was in no shape to tangle with *Forever Amber*. No exercises at all till tomorrow, while the war heroes hogged the pool. How did he get on the nurse's quota? Geez, Casey, get your mind out of the gutter.

Funny, he could think "fuck," but he couldn't think "Christ." Into that nurse's pants.

He met some more people that evening, but not very decisively. He played checkers with an elderly Frenchman who skinned him alive, and he studied some more bridge. While puzzling through the bidding conventions, he thought—Uniforms are very sexy on women. Starch on top and wildness below. Thighs flying while the nursing cap stays primly put. How do women feel about paralyzed legs? Must be creepy for them.

Before turning in, he decided to make a sly tour. Might just run into something. Corridor 3, eh? If anybody would understand about bad legs, it was a nurse. Start there. Now look, God, sir, I'll only do it once, I promise. A sin, a sin, I know, but it's a church of sinners, look at all the saints who had a whack at it before they went straight. Write a confession out of this world when it's all done. Besides, I won't find her. It's just words in my head so far, no harm. Besides, look, it's also a test of courage. Confidence is essential in my position, it's kind of a special case. And she *likes* it, doesn't she? I mean I wouldn't seduce a virgin for the world.

Jesus, Mary, and Joseph—there *was* a party in corridor 3. Dirty laughter under the door, and bright dirty light. That must be the preliminary part. Brian tried quickly to remember what he'd decided about the moral question. Sin, courage. Polio made you a special case. That, my son, is a rationalization. Don't bother to try it on the Almighty as the boiling manure rises to your armpits. Hell isn't really like that. How do you know? Then he saw that thinking must now cease. His mind would filibuster till dawn if he let it. He must simply act. With a deep thrill of decision, he rolled his chair to the door and knocked.

The laughter snapped off. He probably needed a password. They seemed to be moving about in there, probably getting rid of the nurse.

"Who is it?"

"Casey."

"Who the hell is Casey? Anybody know a Casey?" Pause. "All right, come in, Casey."

When they saw him, Santini said, "Oh Christ, it's the Irish kid. Come in and join the party."

Five hairy GI's were sprawled around in their undershirts. No trace of nurse. They began hauling bottles and glasses from under the beds. "Boy, you had me scared there," said a redheaded guy about Brian's age. "Sam Rogers. Nix on the Ginger, O.K.?"

"You want a drink?" asked Santini.

"Yeah, I guess so." Might as well prove some kind of courage tonight. He didn't see how they could fit a gangbang in here anyway. It probably didn't work like that. She probably provided individual room service. He could see her silvering in by moonlight, purring softly—enough of that, Casey, for pity's sweet sake. The big thing now is not to choke on this drink here.

They'd filled the tumbler with Scotch and ice, and it burned like lighter fluid, but he was ready for it. He shivered the minimum and went "aagh," as if expressing admiration, and glanced around to see whom he'd fooled. Nobody was paying any attention.

"Listen, for the last time, does this chick Brenda put out or doesn't she?"

"Let's take it one by one. Murphy swears she does. Jackson isn't talking, but sources close to Jackson say he is paying top dollar for condoms."

"Oh man," said Rogers, clasping a hand to his groin. "I'd like to get my hands on that muff. For just twenty-four hours. Then you could cut it off."

"They'd probably have to."

"Ah, you guys are going stir-crazy. It's what the doctors call the will to believe. Nobody puts out for apes like you."

"O.K., you bastards. I'll find out for myself," said Rogers.

"When?" "Tomorrow." "How?" "I'll tell her I have this numb feeling in my dong that could lead to atrophy if not massaged immediately."

"She'd just send you to Dr. Pipgras. For a measurement."

Brian didn't feel drunk, but he sensed an animal menace, a stirring in wet jungles. These guys were trained killers. He saw their sweat shining in the moonlight as they stalked the wily nurse. Slipping wire round the sentry's neck, aargh! and then one by one into the tent, on hands and knees.

"Hey, kid, you just get here?"

"Huh? Yeah. Yesterday."

"Did they say when they're going to operate?" said Santini.

"Operate? What do you mean by that?" His voice sounded prep school. Would *fucking* operate be better? Easy to swear in your head.

"Yeah. That's what they sent you here for, isn't it?"

"Nobody said anything about operating."

Santini looked around. "Isn't it a shame? The way they don't tell guys."

"I personally think it's better if you don't know," said Rogers.

"You do? Boy, not me. The first time I got that dawn call, I shit my pants."

"Yeah, that's rough too. I don't know. What'd they tell you they were shaving you for, Joe?"

"A routine hygiene precaution. They say that hair collects fungi or some such bullshit. Don't you believe it, ol' buddy." Santini looked at Brian and shook his head. "When they come to shave you, it's the knife and nothing but the knife."

"I totally disagree with you, Santini," a fellow named Gene Something said. "Christ, you sweat all night when they shave you. Frankly, I'd rather not know."

"Just the footsteps in the hall and the knock on the door?"

"That's right." Gene nodded. "Anyway, maybe the kid's got an area where they don't have to shave. Like the foot."

"They shave the foot."

"Well, the kid looks kind of light on hair. How's the foot, son?"

"They wouldn't operate without permission," said Brian.

His head was buzzing suddenly, like a refrigerator. "I didn't give them permission."

"How old are you?"

"Seventeen."

"They don't need your permission. I expect your old man signed the clearance."

"He wouldn't do that."

"Yeah? Listen—you wouldn't be here if he didn't. What do you think this place is all about?"

"Cure."

"*Cure?* Salt Rock? There must be some mistake. The last time they cured somebody around here, Jesus Christ said he frankly couldn't believe it." Santini looked as if he was going to cry. "All right, maybe you'll be the lucky one. But you sure as hell won't get out of here without an operation. Man, that Dr. Pipgras is an operating fool. You notice, he's always measuring legs? Doesn't know what the fuck he's doing it for half the time. Especially when he's had a few belts. Christ, he sees three legs then. And if he finds one of them a centimeter out, you've had it. Zock, slash. Do you know, there was one girl in here who had thirteen operations correcting the first one? Her foot looked like a fucking medicine ball."

"Hey kid, you want to throw up someplace?"

"I'm all right."

"Had you pissing green there, didn't we?"

"Didn't believe you," Brian managed to mumble.

"No? That's good. You sure looked funny. You want another drink?"

Brian shook his head. Opening his mouth would be fatal. They laughed without malice. He shouldn't have burst into their room. This was what he got for it. He hung on a few minutes, for pride's sake, while they rambled aimlessly about Brenda's pussy, and then he left, and vomited up his humiliation in his own basin and cleaned up as best he could.

The Infante, the eunuch beyond price, sat on his fluffy cushions. The women petted him and dowsed him with perfume. The little prince is not himself today. He fell in with some rough soldiers, and they made him cry.

Brian flayed himself, in a drunken doze. He used to be a tough kid, by neighborhood standards. Nobody ever pulled anything like this on him before. God, he was soft. People had been too nice to him for too long. He'd forgotten the jungle watchfulness of male society, the playful pounce at the throat. Well, shit, he'd be ready next time. Santini's voice, somewhere in the dark: "You all right, kid?" Fuck off. Santini turned on the light and began combing his hair for bed, over the basin. "Christ, you really made a mess here." Brian dug his head down and burrowed into his doze.

The next day, Sunday, was hot—surprise. The veterans were hanging around the game room in clusters of stupefied silence. It was like a Civil War engraving. The garrison couldn't hold out much longer without water. "What's the matter with everybody?" Brian asked a guy.

"There was a bust last night on corridor 2."

"What happened?"

"Some nurse was caught with three guys."

"Yeah?" A sweet, vicious thrill, no denying it.

"Yeah. They're on the mat right now. Poor bastards."

"What about the nurse?"

"I don't know. Canned, I guess. Must have been a sweet kid, huh? A goddamn angel. Couldn't bear to watch people suffer." The guy scratched his nose. "I wish I'd known about it."

"I knew," said Brian.

"Yeah? You did, huh? You know, I sometimes think I spend too much time in the library."

The period of mourning extended about halfway through breakfast. Guys who had, guys who hadn't were all equally bereaved. "Things like that never last in this lousy mothering world," said someone at Brian's table. "Shit, you know she was due on 4 this very night? God-*damn*it." He howled like a puma. They began laughing after that and parodying their own heat, and by the end of the meal there was a hairy gaiety in the air. Brian glimpsed the little nurse slipping shyly past the dining room in her street clothes—impossible to believe she was responsible for these wild stirrings. " 'Bye, doll," murmured someone. "It's been real." The older civilians ate on solidly while the boys whooped.

He went to church after that, a small white chapel for Catholics, thinly attended this morning. A dozen very serious-looking fellows, conspicuously clean-living, not ones to be caught up in the Brenda devilment, you could bet. Brian felt unworthy. It was all terribly cheap and dirty. The girl was ruined, three soldiers were probably about to be court-martialed, and all the guys could think of to do was roll their eyes and gibber. Thank God or his guardian angel he had wheeled down the wrong corridor last night. Jesus, how could he face his parents? He almost dropped his missal at the thought. He could just see them at their window. His mother struck dumb with grief, making strangled animal sounds, his father frosty with contempt. "I told you, my dear. The boy is no good. It was a mistake adopting him from the gypsies in the first place." His mother proceeding to cry non-stop for the next fifty years. He wondered if any Catholics had taken advantage of Brenda, and how they felt this morning. Santini came in late and knelt at the back. He winked at Brian and held his head sympathetically.

Church was as white and clean as a nursery, and the priest was fat and kind as Aunt Jemima. Better than the lust-oozing soldiers or his own puke-drenched mouth. My God, how could he expect a miraculous cure after the way he'd behaved last night. Getting drunk was not so terrible, although it certainly felt that way. He didn't think it had become a habit yet. But those impure thoughts, ay yi yi. "You knew perfectly well that corridor 3 was an occasion of sin, didn't you, my son?" "Courage, confidence, church of sinners" . . . he remembered with sickly accuracy his little list of excuses. "Yes, well, you see, my son, those are the things the devil whispers to each of us to get us to sin. He's a very clever salesman, you know. He's got a different line for each customer."

"Yes, Father. So have you, Father."

I was disobedient four times and I told three lies. His confessions hadn't really changed since he was seven. Even if he confessed murder and rape, it would sound like three lies and one act of thoughtlessness. Brian began to wonder if he wasn't a little more childish in the religious area than other areas? And mightn't that be one of the things that had softened him? He felt too lousy to think it through. If he wanted a miracle, he'd better stick to the book. And clean up his language while he was about it. Sloppy thoughts, sloppy life. In such a small chapel every communion was noted. So he wheeled up reluctantly. He decided he qualified technically, but, landing on his furry tongue, the host tasted of prussic acid. Santini grinned from the back.

He determined to avoid the ribaldry that afternoon. Read a book or something. He tried writing home, but couldn't think of anything that had happened except the gangbang on corridor 2. *Forever Amber* was still by his bedside, but he saw the danger of books like that. Like for instance, they glamorize a girl who puts out and don't tell you how dirty it actually is. They leave out the filthy things men say about her, the cruel shit-eating grins. He thought of the guys howling over their breakfast as the girl who had been so nice to them crept away unnoticed. Christ, it was a vicious world.

He sat alone in his room with the flies buzzing and Santini's artwork torturing him with the same old lies. It starts out as a joke, and before you know it, you're crawling down corridors looking for pussy. He honestly didn't know if he could cope with it. He had a hopeless erection, primed with heat, disgust, a yearning to be good. If he eased it with his hands he would be damned for sure; a good resolution should hold up for one afternoon.

The priest in his head had one last shot. He pointed to the soldiers who had been found out this morning: shrunken, embarrassed, all the starch gone out of them, in the chilly judgment room. Not so impressive now, are they, my son? O'Monahan was a virtuoso on the wages of sin. Those same men who pranced around the halls clutching their groins and baying for pussy, look at them today. Well, maybe the priest was right at that, maybe that stuff *was* the real weakness, by God. A guy with his pants around his knees, squirming under a cop's flashlight . . . It was part of his own softness that he had masturbated to such slovenly excuses. He would do so no more. Christianity was hard, not soft.

The spasm of willpower cooled and strengthened him. The erection collapsed like an empty sock. He wheeled back out to the game room, feeling a gorgeous disdain for the soldiers playing their pointless bridge and chewing the slow afternoon fat. They were as pointless as the people on the railway platform, the drifters. Talking the silly gossip of their time and place in history, feeding, sleeping, dying, and leaving no trace. He, Brian, would vault past them, with willpower and vision. A cure was just the first step.

Sunday afternoon was visitors' time, and they began to trickle in—anxious men in rimless glasses, stout ladies in faded prints. Outside of the ones with an obvious mission, they were just sightseers: old people who liked to be around sickness, *young* people's sickness; retired real-estate men who could have gone to the seaside but preferred to be here, among the wheelchairs.

The patients went on with their business. The morning's poontang brouhaha was already a memory. Maybe it was just a gag; watch for that, Casey. You've been fooled before. A lot of life's terrors were just gags. The visitors walked slowly past the bridge tables, peering at the man who had to have his cards played for him, or the one who picked them up in his teeth (another gag, but they didn't know it), sighing softly and moving on. At the last table, up by the dining room, a big strapping patient, healthier than they were, rose as if to shake hands with them, and said, "Yowsah, yowsah, yowsah. Step right up and see the crip-puls. See them walk, see them talk, see them crawl on their bel-ly like a reptile."

There was a harsh howl of laughter, walling in the visitors. The boys' pussy had been taken away, but they still had this. The old people flinched and stood helpless under the whip. Sick people were entitled to their fun.

Brian found himself taking it up, without even thinking. "Yeah—see them groan, see them moan," he shouted. "Spot a twisted limb and win a prize." Hard, brutal kidding, the kind they did so well here. "We don't call 'em freaks, and we don't call them geeks, we just call them handicapped citizens with wonderful spirits. Don't feed them, just pray for them."

The visitors seemed to crowd together. Being laughed

at by cripples is probably no fun for an old man. Well, let them learn. We're tougher and better than they are. "Don't you want a relic? How's about a nice paralyzed toe, our Sunday special?" Brian had become a cheerleader, ushering the guests out. Several patients looked at him, and the guy who had started it said, "You're O.K., kid. Don't overdo it now."

Brian liked the place fine.

8

He got letters the next week from his parents and from both his aunts. It seemed that Blessed Herbert Weatherby was still fighting for his life—which, Brigid pointed out, made it a perfect time for a miracle. A miracle might very well clinch the case for his existence, after which canonization would be clear sailing. Dr. Steinmetz continued his troubled wanderings and had fetched up in Canada, where he was exploring the properties of elk sperm. The perfect sperm, he believed. Meanwhile, as Steinmetz waited for the elks to deliver, Portia recommended the enclosed article on carrot juice.

Brian took the enclosed article and tore it in four. The old girls were really pathetic in writing. Brigid labored on lined paper with the hand of a child. Portia's typing was blotched with inked insertions, words crossed out, and arrows running up and down the sides. He half expected to find a couple of arrows pointing at each other at the bottom. If he'd seen their writing sooner, it would have spared him some excitement. Anyway, what could you expect from a limey saint?

He did not, mind you, rule out miracles completely. They had been proved in Rome, by very stringent tests. He was still bucking for Lourdes. The big leagues of this business. But he was not going to weaken himself with low-grade bullshit. The soft pliability of the water in the pool still gave him thc impression that he might make it on his own. He surged his legs in and out against the feathery water—O.K., it was still the hip, but they were *moving*. A little more concentration and he might be able to force the message down past his hips and into the legs themselves. He twisted his forehead into knots and growled like a bear. Almost! He had read somewhere that people who conquered polio built up more confidence than they knew what to do with. So be it.

In due time, they made the new braces for him, light and streamlined as promised. But he was only allowed to wear them about fifteen minutes a day, in drills as strict as ballet classes. Anything more would lead to bad habits. In just this one respect, the place was bizarrely professional.

Meantime, the sight of people in wheelchairs began to seem normal. A wheelchair world. Even the GI's used them if they had the slightest excuse. Sick was good. Or so it seemed until V-E Day. Santini and another guy hopped wheelchairs that day and staged a race down the center of the recreation room to celebrate. Brian promptly appointed himself public-address system, with a rolled-up magazine for a megaphone. "Five laps, and no getting out of the chair to push it on the turns," he called. Cigarette betting was heavy, and even the old-timers were roaring.

Santini ran a dirty race from the start, banging chairs and forcing his opponent into the crowd. "They're in the stretch. Santini is cutting him off. Pow! Jackson belts him in the rear. And pushes him forward ten feet. Jackson tries to come up on the outside. Pow! Santini almost takes his ankle off. Jackson is getting out of his chair now. He's hitting Santini with his cap. The place is bedlam, ladies and gentlemen. Santini is trying to bite Jackson's hand. Jackson is mounted again. They're heading for the wire. Santini is zagging all over the course. Jackson is laughing so hard he can't roll, and Santini crosses the line to win the first V-E Day Classic. Jackson is still out on the track protesting . . . In fact, the stewards tell me that both men have been disqualified. Santini knocked over a bridge table and Jackson didn't pass the saliva test. No payoff."

Brian had never felt closer to the war than he did that day. Sick was no longer quite so good. The cripples would soon rise from their chairs and saunter off. And he wondered what kind of fear made a man willing to fake paralysis in the first place. Or exaggerate it anyway. From scraps he had picked up at table, one GI talking at a time, he pictured war as a solitary affair: a lone man coughing blood into the snow, lost behind enemy lines, praying for the Red Cross wagon to drive up like a Good Humor truck and bundle him into the warm safety of sickness. War was a great time for cripples. No one could ask a cripple to fight.

After the Japs were beaten, the GI's would pull out, leaving the lifers, the professionals. God, he didn't want to be left with those.

Meanwhile, he kept up those little bursts of resolution, but bridge kept taking his mind off his cure. He had proved to be a pretty fair player with a great memory and an almost visual sense of other people's patterns. Such and such would play a round game, somebody else was rhomboid. Made no sense, but it worked against average to good players (it was no good against the crazies). He won second prize in a house tournament and would have finished first except for a triangle who suddenly turned into a trapezoid, doubled and redoubled.

It was still a stupid waste of time, and he felt guilty about it. For hours he would forget his mission completely, would even be annoyed to have to break for exercise, and then, while Miss Prendergast cranked, would proceed to replay hands instead of attending to his tibia. Miss Prendergast was an assembly-line physiotherapist who jerked limbs to some private quota, so if he didn't try, nobody tried. At night, he thought about willpower, but what was the good of thinking about willpower at night? His eyes closed on a vision of aces and kings.

Santini decided to chance the Japanese war and announced himself recovered. He rolled up his Petty girls and threw them in the trash can. "My wife is kind of stuffy," he explained. "Did you really have polio?" asked Brian. "You can't fake it, can you?" Santini said, "Sure I had it. Everyone here had it. Maybe I just got better a little too fast." Brian wanted to say, "Don't go. Keep on pretending." If everyone pretended to have polio, it would be a better world. Besides, he didn't want to see his crazy friend replaced by some sick guy. He didn't want the healthy guys to leave him.

Santini's replacement was a gnome named Winters, a sickie for fair, with a barrel chest and legs like a bird. Brian could hardly bear to look at him, as he perched on his pillow Indian-style, fussily unpacking. As soon as enough stuff was laid out, Winters would flip his bird legs over the side, pounce onto his chair, and go skittering over to the dresser.

"Hey," said Brian, full of fun, "you know about the operations here?"

"Know about them? I ought to. I've had nine of them. You want to see my foot?"

"Not specially. Oh, all right." The guy had whipped off his sock. It wasn't as bad as Brian expected, not the swollen sea-green nightmare he pictured. But polio was still pretty damn disgusting.

"You've been here before?" he asked.

"Every year since I was three."

"How old are you now?"

"Nineteen." Now that was really shocking. Brian almost

said, "You're a liar," but saw how this might hurt. The man was an aging forty from head to foot.

"How's the talent this year?" said Winters. He began brushing his sleek black hair with military brushes. "Any good twat?"

"Geez, not much." This guy too? Brian could only think of three girls who were young enough to rate as twat and of these, two were grotesque. Number three was kind of pretty, but of course, she had polio, and Brian could never make time with a girl with polio. He was a leg man, and he couldn't face it.

"Well, we'll have to make do with what's around," said Winters, smoothing his mustache. It was obscene. This dwarf was duding himself up like a lover. Flashing his teeth and sluicing himself in after-shave. "I'll go out and do some scouting," he said. "A good-looking guy like you should have a girl."

Nothing came of it, that first evening. Winters returned empty-handed and sat on his pillow and talked sex, more than even the GI's did. He talked about girls he had had here in the past, and about a luscious waitress he was screwing right now up in Toronto. Brian tried not to visualize it—the first excruciating pass, the girl recoiling but trying not to hurt the little fellow's feelings, and the occasional freak conquest, with the little guy hopping about neatly on the bed, smiling, for all the world like Clark Gable, at his prize.

Brian had nothing to offer in return. Winters's activities would have silenced Errol Flynn. Besides, he didn't care to discuss his sex life in the same terms as this guy's. He shut his eyes and hoped Winters would fall asleep. But when he opened them a crack, he saw that Winters was still on his pillow, writing postcards.

The next few nights were the same. Winters would go on about luscious pieces of ass and great tits until Brian dropped off. Where had he learned to talk like that? A cripple for life, always between operations, he must have deduced that this was how normal people talked. Yet he didn't have it quite right. "Man, what poontang." Phrases that were meant to be funny came out as solemn as medical terms. He didn't know how to be dirty. Brian was glad he himself remembered the real world and still knew the difference between ass and *gluteus maximus*.

Then, just as Brian had become certain it was all just talk, Winters struck pay dirt. Not for himself, but for Brian. He said he had met a girl who was crazy for Brian's body.

"Who, who?"

"Anna May Tompkins."

"Anna May *Tompkins?*" She was one of the grotesques.

"Yeah, the nice little blonde."

Brian stared at the little Clark Gable grin. So this was what he meant by ass. Real *gluteus maximus* stitched and stuffed like a goose by a hundred unsuccessful operations. Anna May Tompkins looked like Mr. Punch, bobbing over her wheels, but to Winters she was a princess.

God, get me out of this beggars' opera. The thought of that little creature lusting for him, thinking he was attainable, gave him the green sweats. Yeah—this was what crept into your room at night if you had real polio. Not some strapping nurse but Mr. Punch, hopping in beside you like a frog, crooning obscene nursery rhymes. This was his league now, and he would be lucky to play as well as Winters in it. He looked at his own legs, thin as a concentration-camp victim's, and at his weak left hand, which would be a passenger in any future lovemaking, and thought, What the hell else do you expect? What else are you good for?

Winters, happy with his dwarf's world picture and his gnomish matchmaking said, "You're really a good-looking kid, you know that? Anna May said you look like a Greek god. Yeah. A Greek god. You know, you can have her in here any time you like."

For the next few days, Brian stayed mostly in his room. He couldn't stand to watch Anna May, who flirted like a courtesan under Winters's urging, and he was absolutely through with bridge. This whole place was a trick to get you used to polio, that was the magic formula and that was your cure. You left here a contented cripple.

He tried flexing the muscles on his own, and saw how futile that really was. It was all a lazy dream—I'll do it next month, or the month after, when I really try. All right, he was trying now. He stared up at the malignant calendar. Better by Christmas, better by spring. It was now midsummer, and not one damned thing had changed. Those stupid legs were dead. The babe on the calendar, Santini's last bequest, simpered at him. "Don't touch me, you deformed son of a bitch."

His father's next letter was not too well timed. "Dear Brian, your recent letters sound exceptionally mature and accepting. You seem to have learned wonderfully how to live with your affliction. Of course, your mother and I still pray confidently for your complete recovery. But if the Good Lord should decide otherwise . . ." Don't give me the Good Lord, please. Not you . . . "still have a wonderful life, all the stronger for the experience, sent for a purpose. Many people on two good legs . . . I think now at last I can write to you like this. You probably faced it before we did."

He fired back, "I definitely want to try Lourdes, in the fall at the latest. And in the meantime, I'd like to explore everything, I don't care how crazy it is. Even Dr. Steinmetz if necessary. Anything *at all.* I have not resigned myself to this one little bit." There is nothing mature about giving up.

Now to the embarrassing part. "Look, Dad, I know how hard I had to try to get you to send me here, so I feel funny saying it was a mistake. But it really is. They don't do *anything* here. The place is a complete fraud and the public should know about it." Yeah, I admit I had a good time. Another of their tricks.

That night, Winters told him not to be so choosy, he wished Anna May liked *him* so much. Yes, he admitted he'd made a pass at her himself, "but her heart belongs to you, daddy-o" (said as solemnly as a clergyman). Brian asked him to shut the hell up, and went to bed. His throat shook with rage over his damn disease and the people who wouldn't help him with it. Meanwhile, Winters wheeled around killing roaches, with hands as fast as any prize-fighter's.

9

His parents threw a party for his return.

The apartment was hung with a WELCOME HOME banner and there was a white cake with his name on it. Hennessy was along, sweating in his blue shirt, and Phil Marconi had his curly hair slicked down. Why were they all dressed up? It was like a funeral parlor, a lying-in. The guests all told him, with false-teeth smiles, that he was looking fine, looking wonderful. ("How do I look, Marconi?" he whispered. "The same," said Phil.)

"You're walking better, much much better, you're really coming along." If he turned green and crawled on his stomach, they would say he was walking better. It was meaningless. He missed the derision of Salt Rock. Here he was the only one of his kind.

When his Aunt Brigid told him he was walking better,

he said, "No, I'm not." This was the junk he'd listened to last year. He used to be flattered by it. "How'm I walking, Marconi?" He hoped that Phil would say, "You call that stuff walking?" but he just said, "Fine."

Toward the end of the wake, Hennessy edged over and said in a low voice, "What are the symptoms of polio, Brian?"

"Who wants to know?"

"I think I may have it."

"You're kidding." Brian's heart leaped an inch.

"I feel kind of weak."

"Yeah? Go on."

"My knee hurts."

"That's bad. What else?"

"I guess that's all. What do you think?"

Oh brother, if the boys down at Salt could get hold of this guy now, they'd have him pissing in his shoes. Let me at this virgin. So Brian thought, First I'll ask him if he sweats a lot. Fatso was rolling in sweat right now. Then I'll ask him if he's short of breath; he always has been, but he may not have thought about it before. Brian grinned an evil grin and shook his head slowly. Slowly does it, with bad news. Maybe a heart murmur—anyone can imagine one of those.

Then he looked again at the poor suffering bastard and thought, I can't do it. Fatso would fall down in a seizure. You couldn't play these games with soft, healthy people. "It's all right, Fatso. Everyone feels like that in the summer. Don't give it a thought."

"You're sure about that?" It was pathetic.

"Absolutely. Your knee would be the last thing to know." He started to describe how the symptoms worked, but caught himself in time. He wasn't going to be a polio bore. It was fun giving Fatso his reprieve, anyway, and Brian felt O.K. for the rest of the party.

He had sensed since his arrival that something was wrong between his parents. They were diplomatic with each other, but there was a sense of interrupted quarrel about them. They would go at it again, the moment his back was turned.

"Is anything wrong?" he asked, over supper.

"Wrong?"

"Yes, I think we should be honest with each other. I grew up a lot down there, you know."

They nodded. Growing up did not mean that you spoke freely, of course.

"There's nothing wrong, that I know of," said Kevin. "It's been a tough summer at the office, I'll say that much. There's going to be a building boom that's out of this world."

"Nothing wrong," echoed Beatrice.

"Well, that's good. So how about Lourdes?"

Kevin spread his hands. "How about it?"

"I want to go. Right away."

"There's a war on."

"Yeah, so I hear. I mean as soon as it's over." His mother

pursed her lips at the slight rudeness, but pursed lips broke no bones. His father overlooked it and said, "The Japanese may hold out for a long time. Hopping from island to island."

"Yeah, they may, they may."

"And travel restrictions will probably continue into the indefinite future."

"Yeah, well, of course I understand that. I just want to know if I can go the moment it's possible."

"That's so iffy, Brian, I don't see any point in discussing it."

"I'd just like an answer, yes or no."

"Give him an answer, dear."

"I told him, we'll see. He's going to have to go to school in a couple of months. We'd have to fit it in with that. *I don't know.*" He hit the table suddenly, as if it were a prison door.

"There's no need to shout," said Beatrice.

"All right, I won't, I'm sorry. I just want you to know, these decisions are complicated. You don't have to make as many decisions as I do."

"We *are* a cheerful group tonight," said Beatrice.

"No, no, this is good," said Brian. "I want to have everything out in the open. We've always been too polite around here. Tell me, Father, what is your real opinion about this Lourdes thing? Is it too expensive?"

"I could raise the money, I guess."

"And couldn't you get me a special travel permit or something? From one of your important friends?"

"Maybe."

"Good. Is it that you don't really believe in it, then?"

"I said it was an iffy question."

"I think you should know," said Beatrice with sudden breathless primness, "that your father has stopped going to church."

"Is that so?"

"Come on, Beatrice! You know that has nothing to do with it."

"I think it might have, Father. Why did you stop going?"

"Churchgoing is a personal thing. I don't have to explain it to anyone."

"I think you owe your son an explanation. Belief in God has a direct bearing on his cure. I think he has a right to know if a member of his family has lost his faith."

Her face was stiff, like an old lady's. Brian didn't want his side to be tainted with any more craziness. "It doesn't matter, Mother," he said. "I respect his right to stop believing. It's better than hypocrisy. I just want to know whether you think going to Lourdes is a personal thing too? Do your private feelings about the Church affect that?"

"I told you it was the travel restrictions," said Kevin. He looked at his son beseechingly. "I have to make very difficult decisions. I'll get you there if I can."

"Good. That's settled. Now how about Dr. Steinmetz?" He had never won an argument with his father in his life, and he didn't want to stop.

"Dr. *Stein*metz? That charlatan you were telling us

about? Brian—even *you* were making fun of him, remember?"

"Yes, I remember. But since then I've tried the respectable people, the regular doctors, and look what I've got for it." He thought of wheeling back from the table and pointing dramatically at his legs, but decided that was bush. It was too easy to switch on their sentimentality. "I've tried the famous specialists and I've tried their famous sickie-farm and their good sense. Now I'm ready to try a fool."

"And where is this Dr. Steinmetz?"

"I think he's in Canada."

"*Canada?* You want me to send you to *Canada?* And Lourdes as well?"

"Why not?"

Kevin looked at Beatrice: surely she would see the folly of this. "Look, I'm trying to be a decent man—O.K., there's nothing special about that, I know. I'm sorry I mentioned it. But didn't you say that this man experiments with *elk* sperm? Brian—apart from anything else, it's bad for you to start believing in people like that."

Beatrice said, "I don't see anything wrong with elk sperm."

"Right," said Brian quickly, before he could laugh. "I know it sounds silly to you. But most medical things sound silly, don't they? Look at penicillin. Made out of cow pies, isn't it?"

"Well, that's true." Kevin grinned and Brian almost grinned back.

"And isn't it really because the stuff he works with

sounds silly that people laugh at him? I mean it's not something silly about *him,* I bet he's no crazier than, well, Beethoven." They both giggled, as if this were the kind of wild discussion they used to have in the old days with nothing at stake. His father kept smiling at him to make him laugh.

"Yes, all right, I'll grant you the elk sperm," said Kevin. "I'll grant you whale blubber, if you like. But didn't you say something about leeches, too?"

Brian answered fast, to kill the humor, "Yes—and didn't they use leeches for thousands of years? Do you think people were crazy for all that time? Or do you think the leeches may just possibly have done them some good?"

Kevin couldn't scrape together another joke. "I just don't believe it. I never thought I'd sit in my own house and hear my own family recommending elk sperm and leeches. I must be going out of my mind."

"That's what the doctors say. And look at what *they* did for me."

"I think he should be allowed to try it," said Beatrice. "What have we got to lose?"

Kevin looked glassy-eyed. Wouldn't someone for godsake laugh? "Maybe we can find something in the city," he said.

They wrote to Dr. Steinmetz and he wrote back, a quite professional-looking letter, packed in brochures, describing various Steinmetz products—a vibrator, some kind of pump, a special Steinmetz honey contrived in Pennsylvania. He said he just happened to have a disciple in New York, a Dr. Schroeder on the Lower East Side.

So Brian and his mother went off to look for Schroeder. They found that the fruits of being out of favor with the medical establishment showed in his neighborhood. Flies drifted like buzzards over upturned garbage cans: sodden listless flies that you could catch with a sick left hand. Schroeder's building looked deserted. The downstairs apartments were gutted and the windows blown out. The second floor said MODERN DANCE STUDIO in rusty letters. The mailboxes in the hall had no nameplates, except for a piano tuner in 3A and Dr. Schroeder in 5B. Brian had asked his mother to come along, because his father's silent skepticism would have been a burden. Even a thing like this required faith.

He heaved his way stiffly up the narrow stairwell, gathering dust on his good right hand. It was terribly hot, and a deep breath would choke you to death in seconds. Still, Brian trusted it now more than the smart-ass salons on Park Avenue, with the bound copies of *Fortune*. Real miracles happened in dirt and darkness. He pictured Dr. Schroeder as a brilliant drunk with trembling hands, the kind who turned up as ship's doctor in the movies. ("Only three men alive know how to perform that operation—and you say you're going to try it in a tornado?")

He wasn't quite that, but a red-faced German with faded red hair and a white coat a size too small for him. Brian was glad his father wasn't here with his damn irony.

An enormous nurse took down Brian's particulars, while the doctor watched with bulging blue eyes. Doctors were supposed to leave during this part; it seemed unprofessional not to. Brian gazed around. Most doctors had so many diplomas on the wall, you wondered where they found the time; but not Schroeder. He just had the one, on yellowing paper, with his name spelled wrong. Was Ulm a university? or one of his qualifications?

"Now let's have a look at the boy," said Schroeder.

"You want me to take off my pants?"

"*Ja*, in a moment. But first I want to see something." And without further warning, he made a heavy lunge at Brian and drove two fingers into his throat.

"Ouch!" It felt like nothing on earth—a seam of sour lead on each side.

"You see?" said Schroeder triumphantly.

"See what?"

"It hurts, *ja?*"

"*Ja*. I mean, yes."

"You speak a little German, no?" The doctor gave a jolly chuckle, and the enormous nurse shook like jelly. "Dot's very good. Now, let me explain what caused you to say ouch. It was nothing less than the poison in your jugular."

"What poison?"

"The poison that causes the polio. Once your jugular begins to stop hurting like that, again you will be well."

"I don't get the connection. I mean, what has my neck got to do with my legs?"

"Look—I make the connection for you." He lunged at

Mrs. Casey this time and jabbed her neck. She was startled and her hat fell off. "You *see?*" He stood triumphantly over her as she bent for the hat. "That didn't hurt really? I mean, except for the normal pressure of the fingers?"

"No, it didn't," said Beatrice. Brian stared at her—hey, this was something, a genuine sign. Ulm or no Ulm, no other doctor had proved his bona fides so decisively. His mother smiled back, catching Brian's excitement.

"O.K., O.K.—how do we get it out?"

"Ah, that's where my little friends come in, my little leeches."

"Really? That's the only way?"

"Maybe, maybe not. It is one way, and it works." He was the soul of reasonableness. "They're very clean, you know, and they seem to know instinctively just the right amount of blood to take. Here, let me show you the little fellows."

He took Brian into a cubicle behind a curtain. It contained in cramped alignment a table and a bed and a bowl full of fat black beetles. My God—it was the Salt Rock nightmare come true. The roaches crawling along his neck and eating him alive.

"They fall off as soon as they're full," Schroeder explained. "They're like tiny little doctors, they know just what's good for you." He seemed awfully fond of them. The blue eyes sparkled with love.

I don't know if I can face it, thought Brian. Yet perhaps this was what the praying prepared you for: you had to go through your personal hell for a cure. Religion and science mating in squalor. Pain, dirt, and darkness, that's where miracles came from, not from spanking-clean offices and doctors with pink hands. Almost gagging in the heat, he said, "I'll do it. Let's go. Put 'em on me."

"Ah, no," the doctor chuckled his jolly-innkeeper chuckle, "not so fast. We have to prepare them. Diet and so on. We have to make them just the right amount hungry. The nurse will make you an appointment for next week."

They pushed back through the curtain. It was like a priest's hovel in Graham Greene, as opposed to an antiseptic Protestant church. "Miss Hoffman, give this young man an appointment for next week."

"Aren't you going to look at my legs?"

"Oh, *ja, ja*. Let's have a look at them."

Brian went back into the cubicle and took off his pants and braces. He made a point of staring down the leeches, to master them. He even put his nose to the glass. They looked like pure evil, dozing in their bowl, drunk on human blood. But they were angels deep down, sent to cure him.

From the way Dr. Schroeder peered at the legs, it was obvious that he didn't know what to make of them. He gave a slight push to the right one, and then pushed it quickly back for fear it would roll off the table.

"That's very bad," he said.

Brian nodded.

Dr. Schroeder looked closely at the left foot and pushed it up. "Can you feel that?" he said.

"Of course."

"Well, you better get dressed now." The doctor went out

quickly as if he couldn't stand any more. The silly so-and-so didn't know beans about polio. But he had the key to it, in that bowl.

Through the curtain, Brian heard the nurse say, "That will be twenty dollars, please."

A pause. "You want it *now?*"

"Yes, we want it now, please." Brian pushed through. Miss Hoffman stood at the desk impassively, and the doctor watched, obscenely. Mrs. Casey fumbled out her checkbook, and the nurse said, "The doctor prefers cash. It's better for his bookkeeping." Beatrice had eighteen dollars and enough for cab fare. They said they'd take the eighteen and collect the rest next week.

Brian knew there was something wrong with all this. He also knew his neck hurt and his mother's didn't. And that was the sturdiest hope so far. It didn't matter if they were crooks—heck, they probably had to be in their position. A sinful priest could say a good mass; in fact, the eucharist shone all the brighter for it. The big thing now was those black angels oozing drunkenly around their bowl.

Even Kevin seemed pleased—although Brian was on twenty-four-hour guard against being humored. Beatrice didn't mention the money. She made it sound as if they'd gone to a regular doctor. "That's very interesting," said Kevin. "So polio is just a pain in the neck, eh?" His way of not saying anything.

Brian was afraid to test his father's own neck, but realized, as suddenly, that he must. Maybe it was just men's necks that contained sour lead: then another dream would be busted, and he didn't know where to turn for his next one.

"Let me show you what he did." Brian wheeled slowly round the table. It felt strange laying hands on his father's throat. White, soft, unevenly shaved. Fumbling along the vein, he came to the spot right under the jaw. He'd never touched his father's neck before, or his chest for that matter. O.K., here goes. He pressed and looked close into his father's sweating face. Could he trust the old man to tell him the truth? Kevin's eyes were watery and bewildered. I'll know a lie right away, from that source.

"Is that it?" asked Kevin.

"That's it."

"I didn't feel a thing."

O.K., O.K.

Memory was uncertain about the next bit. It was certainly raining. His clothes were wet and heavy and hard to scrape off, even with the nurse hauling like a stevedore. They put him in a crisp white gown, tied at the back. Then he was walking up the stairs again—memory balking. He was scared out of his mind. Not just of the leeches, but of getting cured. He was scared of the moment when the strength would come snapping back. His memory stopped halfway; better to climb stairs forever than face that moment.

Beatrice smiled like a madonna. She loved him, up there on his little cross. To get well one has to die. One of the few things he knew for sure. At the first sign of life, he would scream and tear his hair and rip off his genitals, for expiation. He would go helplessly insane, and the cure would be pointless. Schroeder moved around him quietly, muttering in German. Devil's curses. Brian couldn't see under the lee of his own chin, but suddenly he felt one of the leeches landing on him with iron pincers, and then another, and then by tipping his head slightly, he could see two whole black columns. They were motionless as death, except for the feel of their jaws. His mother sat, smiling hope. The doctor rubbed his hands and watched.

Brian had no idea how long it lasted. Rain fell on the grimy skylight, sometimes heavy, sometimes not. Dr. Schroeder went out to clean his bowl. Brian ignored the dull pain of being eaten and just concentrated on his legs. Would they come back gradually or did it all depend on some one gob of poison? Sucked into a black jaw like a crumb off a carpet? The gradual theory was slightly the less frightening; but inch by inch, he had to give up on it. He stirred his legs gently from time to time, and Dr. Schroeder's eyes would gleam, and the doctor and his mother would yearn at each other wetly—yes, yes, little Willie will walk—and Brian would think, It's the hip, you idiots. Doesn't anyone understand polio around here? Schroeder's tenderness made his big lips drip.

Those were the slack moments, when the sweat turned cold and rusty in his crotch and his concentration snagged. When he felt that happening, he would turn up the willpower again to a scorching purple pressure—I will do it, I *know* this works. My mother's neck, my father's neck—he imagined blood vessels bursting in his forehead like light bulbs and his heart failing as the gauge on his willpower rose and the steam shot through his skull. Oh God, do it! Just do it! With Thy, Your, infinite power—so easy for You. Come *on,* then!

And then the first leech rolled off, in a blood-soaked stupor, and the next, and he knew it was all over. Christ! What a farce. It's not in the damn neck at all, everyone knows that. I knew it myself. Deliriously he tried to stand up, and another leech skittered to the floor. "Let's get out of here, Mother," he said hoarsely.

"It may take a little time," said Schroeder. "Call me again in about a week."

"What for?" said Brian.

"We may need another treatment."

"In a pig's eye, we may. You fat fraud. You're not putting those fucking things on *me* again."

"Brian!"

"Come on, Mother. Don't give him any money."

It was a silly thing to say, but Schroeder chose to take it seriously. He stepped into the entrance of the cubicle and blocked it, and Miss Hoffman loomed up menacingly behind him, as if she'd been listening for just this moment. "You better pay up," he said in a gruff fury. Brian was dizzy: Germans couldn't take a joke, he remembered. They were going to keep him here for experiments. It was a Nazi thing. Dirty white room reeling, hitting rock, sinking. His mother meekly unsnapping her purse, handing over bills.

The hand out, signaling, "More, more." God knows how much she gave him. And still Schroeder raged. "Young punks, guttersnipes," he said. He was crazy. With his huge red crazy face, he could easily kill them all. Tacky place to die. Brian tried to move in some unspecified way, and blackness came up like velvet from the back of his neck and smothered him gently.

He remembered going home in terms of a vague rattling in vehicles, a hearse drawn through the sewers, M. le Blanc the headless coachman, and then his father shouting him awake from the next room. God what happiness in that voice. What could it possibly be saying? "Damn charlatans. I promise we won't try anything like that again, Doctor. We must have been nuts." And Dr. Devlin, the family doctor, famous for diagnosing everything as flu, said, "I should hope not. I only hope the boy doesn't develop chronic anemia. His blood count is pretty low right now."

Brian realized that they had pricked his finger while he slept and taken out the last drop. That's why he was dead.

His mother said, "I still think it was worth trying."

A silence which he took to be embarrassment, then sounds of the doctor leaving. After which, the house was still. He's glad, thought Brian, with the kind of clinical detachment one needed for this. My father is glad it didn't work.

Kevin Casey took his vacation at home that year. He told Beatrice that he couldn't afford to take them anywhere;

he also told her that anyone who called her daughters Beatrice and Portia was a goddamn snob. He did not bother to lower his voice, although Beatrice still kept her answers down.

Aunt Portia made the mistake of showing up one afternoon, to see how Brian was doing. Kevin intercepted her in the living room. It was just more voices to Brian, who was dead, to all intents and purposes, in the next room, waiting to be taken away. The old Brian that you know and love, utterly dead, poor devil. He pictured his father sitting crumpled up under the fan with a bottle in front of him, like a desperate Englishman in the tropics, while a fluttery mission lady tried to sell him subscriptions.

In fact, Kevin did say, "Have you brought your magazines?"

Portia's answer was inaudible. The only person Brian really heard now was his father. "You haven't, eh? How the hell am I going to keep up with the daring adventures of Dr. Steinmetz? The last I remember, he was trapped in a cave with his chimpanzees, trying to collect specimens from them. Did he ever escape from the maddened beasts?"

Mumble.

"Yeah, the only thing that guy Steinmetz lacked was imagination. You really should read about this fellow Dr. Blatherskite who collects hippopotamus droppings in his hat—that sounds a bit more like it, no? Combined with the green mold in his ears, it produces the miracle elixir of the Indies. The health secret of the Aztecs, lost for centuries."

Brian smiled. He's talking to me, he thought. Making his case. The case for cynicism. Pretty good, too.

"You know, you seriously puzzle me, Portia. I'll never forget the way you used to give it to your pious sister Beatrice, for staying in the Catholic Church. Don't you know that this crap you peddle now is twice as wild as anything Beatrice ever bought? Hell, you might as well have stayed in the Church yourself and saved yourself from becoming completely ridiculous." The front door slammed. It made no difference.

"Yeah, to practice elk spermism and be a skeptic too—that's a bit greedy, don't you think? It seems to me the moment you left the Church, you began shopping around for any crutch that would hold you. Funny little twisty ones like Dr. Steinmetz. Rubber ones that bend when you walk. The Council of Trent designed better ones, believe me . . ." The bar was empty now in the long afternoon. He'd chased them all away, all the outsiders who wanted a piece of the polio. The Englishman crumpled still further, now that no one was watching.

"Oh Christ, though, I don't blame you for being scared. It's a scary business. Anything that helps—if it gets you to sleep on time, and if it keeps you from waking up crying—buy it, I say. I have my own little tricks. Oh yes, I do."

His voice sank, and Brian shut his eyes again. He liked it when his old man was being funny. He's a bit like me then—well, no accident, I guess. You can't disown a man who gave you your point of view. But this soft boozy stuff didn't say anything to him at all. He opened his eyes a crack as Kevin said, louder, "But don't cheapen the boy. Don't bring your miserable spinster fears around here. He's strong, strong in the spirit."

Ah, balls. Nobody's strong when God swings the old wrecking ball.

Brian wasn't mad at his aunts. They couldn't have done any more than they had. He wasn't really mad at anybody, just very tired. His parents had probably given him all the love they knew how. Not very intelligently to be sure, but it wouldn't have made any difference. Thank you all, anyway. Now, please go away.

He supposed they must be worrying about his apathy. That was probably why his father shouted so much. To all appearances, Brian must seem to be sleeping around the clock. He wasn't really. He dozed and daydreamed as he had when he first got polio, a kind of second coming of it. Then in the eye of the fever, his mind would become classically abstract—all ideas, no pictures. He could face anything in that condition: he could face being blind and chained to a rock, to take one example that came to mind. The trick was to slip from that utter whiteness into soft black fantasy. No hanging around the twilight.

Centuries passed in this way, and sometimes he imagined he was his own father sitting out there with a sick boy in the next room: shouting, "I'm not a bad man, I didn't do it to you." Of course you didn't: it was just some little old bug doing God's will. Nothing personal. I forgive me. His father stopped shouting at last. Brian heard his parents talking, quite sweetly now. He felt like Robinson

Crusoe waking from his storm, finding paradise. His father had returned to his religion, it seemed. Very nice. The very best crutches. Brian didn't want to think about anything in particular, so he kept his mind as vague as possible about this. When he returned to life, he would decide what he believed. But, luminous thought, *he would never put it to the test.* He would not under any circumstances go to Lourdes.

No hurry to wake up. He still had years to serve in the Roman legions, after finishing his course with Socrates. He smiled peacefully when his parents came in, to reassure them. Honestly, you didn't do badly. *Nobody* can handle this thing. I've taken up a lot of your time. Thank you all very much.

"I think it's mainly exhaustion. Salt Rock must have been a strain, and then this last thing."

"I blame myself for that."

"You really shouldn't. I went along with it. We had to try it."

There, you see, everyone's forgiven. His parents were resting now like himself. They had always been a good couple, and were so again. The polio year had been a crazy time for everyone. Becoming an extremely old man was an excellent solution for his father.

"And I still hope for a miracle," said his mother.

"So do I. I really do."

Right. But we won't put it to the test, will we? Promise me that. Also—you're both O.K., really. His father sitting out there, like St. Joseph, keeping his sheepdog vigil; his mother, dripping love like liquid gold. Good, good people. *Exceptional* people, in fact. He smiled to say, Please don't worry, I just want to sleep a few eons longer. Marcus Aurelius needs some advice. Flighty old bastard. Brian knew that when he woke up, he would be a cripple for sure.

All the wisdom blew away in a moment, he felt it go, leaving only the words, like empty peanut shells. The conversation was still in progress out there, it had never stopped, but Bernie Levine had come in. That was strange. Bernie sounded excited. Which was very very strange. Bernie had been sent to wake him.

"Now, would you mind repeating that, please, Bernie? For my wife." Why for his wife? Where his wife before? Brian wanted to know what everybody had been doing.

"Mumbles is in the hospital. I was over at his parents' place. They're all shook up about it."

"And they're sure he's got it?"

"Absolutely. Arms, chest, the works. He may not even live."

"My God!" said Beatrice. "That's terrible!"

"I'm scared," whimpered Bernie. "I was with him all summer practically. Just like I was with Brian last summer."

"Maybe your luck will hold," said Kevin, with the cool voice of the polio veteran. *My* voice.

"What's the matter with Brian?" asked Bernie. "Is he

O.K.?" Somebody better be O.K., or Bernie go nuts around here.

"I think so. He's had a temperature for three days. And you know, we actually thought he might have caught polio again, he had all the same symptoms. But it turns out you can't catch polio twice."

"Huh."

"He seems to be getting better now," said Beatrice. "His temperature's down—" a pointless lie, nobody had taken his temperature— "Dr. Devlin is a bit at sea with unusual sicknesses."

"He's a bit at sea with the common cold," said Kevin, quite his old self. "But tell us more about Fatso."

Fatso! So that was it! Brian woke all the way now, tingling with joy. Fatso had polio! It was like the first spring flower.

"Father O'Monahan was over there, talking to the Hennessys," said Bernie. "I guess he was trying to console them."

"Ah yes," said Kevin. "Yes, he does that."

"Brian'll be sorry to hear about it," said Beatrice.

Sorry? She couldn't believe that, could she? Now that he had a companion? Now that he might get Bernie too, and how many more? The all-polio world, which was second-best to a cure. It took him a moment to imagine any sense in which he could possibly be sorry for this. Then slowly he groped his way back to normal thinking: it must be tough on Hennessy's folks, for instance.

He swore he could hear elation in his father's voice.

Thank you for seeing it my way, Father. Beatrice sounded genuinely concerned, she was a finer character than they were. Finer, yet colder. The true feeling now was to rejoice just a little bit: not to sympathize whorishly with any damn fool who walked in the door, bleating about someone's troubles.

Bernie left, a haunted man, on the run from house to house—ha, ha! It'll get you, Bernie. God has X-ray vision and can see through any fig leaf.

Kevin came in and said, "Hey, you're awake. Hey, he's awake."

Beatrice came in, too, and clapped her hands like a girl. Who would have thought a year ago that they'd settle for this, to celebrate over. "Did you hear us talking about Fatso?"

Brian nodded, weaker than he thought.

"It's terrible, isn't it?" said Beatrice.

"Yes, it's terrible." And the three old hypocrites made a long face over it. A while after that, Kevin put on some records, including his collection of Irish jigs, and he and Beatrice did a couple of steps, the way they used to do them at the Irish Reeling Society before Brian had ever been thought of.

II

10 "Pick 'em up, Casey." His friend Baxter pranced a few yards ahead, clearing the snow like King Wenceslas. "They must be hangin' mighty low today, Big Casey."

"Fuck you," muttered Brian, stumbling along behind as fast as he could, snagging his legs against the drifts.

"What's that you say, Casey? Didn't quite catch you."

"I said, doan whip me, massah." They were just far enough apart for bystanders to overhear them, and Brian wasn't free to speak his mind.

The snow presented certain technical difficulties: layers of hard and soft resisting one leg and yielding smoothly to the other, coaxing him into a splitting skid. Meanwhile, Baxter was singing "Walking in our winter wonderland."

Brian couldn't move fast enough to silence his friend without enlarging the risk about ten percent on each step. Just too much. Passersby frowned at Baxter and his cripple-baiting, but Baxter was hard to penetrate. "In the meadow we can build a snowman," he crooned.

"Doan whip me, doan beat me." Brian surged forward, to get past a staring middle-aged couple: a salaciously tender lady and her utterly fair-play husband. Too fast. His crutch hit an ice sheet and shot out in front of him. He grabbed the other one and furled himself gallantly round it, like a marine at Iwo Jima, and slowly the crutch and he flopped sideways into the snow.

"Are you all right?" The lady was upon him. Oh God, in a moment she'd try hauling him up by the armpits, and her husband would start hauling *her* by the armpits, and they'd all wind up in the snow. By dusk, the sidewalk would be littered with bodies.

"It's all right, ma'am," said Baxter. "Some days, they just hang a little heavy, and down he goes. He likes to play, you understand."

Brian knew them by heart. He was a Columbia teacher. She belonged to interfaith organizations. They wanted to help everybody and they didn't want to interfere with anybody. So they rushed up to you and then they just stood there.

"Why do you *want* to embarrass me?" Baxter asked Brian. "Have you ever tried to analyze it?"

Yeah. The couple wanted to protest brutality, but suppose they were witnessing some kind of folk custom here?

They were pathetic. "Look, please go away, O.K.?" Brian told them, "I think your marriage can be saved, but it'll need work. Besides, I'm tied up right now."

There's no helping some people, is there, Percy? They didn't get angry, but seemed to enter new zones of indecisiveness. Perhaps I haven't converted you to the Nazi Party, but I've given you something to think about, eh madam? Brian went hobbling off with Baxter, leaving them standing there.

Polio in New York. An old lady grabbing you round the chest from behind, trying to help you across the street. The zest of hitting her in the ankle. The cry of "watchit" just after he'd fallen; the chorus of "take it easy's" as he lay spraddled.

Baxter was O.K., when you considered the alternatives. Even in a snowstorm. His teasing was tiresome, but better than nothing. The rest of their friends in the freshman class had walked on ahead for various reasons. It physically hurt some people to walk slowly. And, out here by himself in the slippery wastes, he would have been at the mercy of roving bands of do-gooders. "You remind me of a friend I used to have, guy named Marconi," said Brian. "It's all part of a pattern of rotten luck that has dogged me."

"Yeah? What happened to him?"

"He went to M.I.T. I must admit, old Phil surprised me with that. He wants to be an engineer. He never said anything about engineering before, but now it's all he talks about."

"Yeah? How come he's like me then? What sterling qualities of his are you keeping from me?"

"Phil likes to crap all over everything. He's a real cynic. Or at least he used to be. Now he's very polite about anything you say. No more jokes. I don't know what happened to him." High-school cynics must peak too soon. Marconi had sunk into himself for the last year of high school, as if life were just too unbearably sad. He stayed home all day and wouldn't answer the phone. Then he emerged with this thing on engineering.

"Funny how people change," Brian said. "This Marconi was a real bastard, I thought I could count on him to be a bastard forever."

"Sounds as if he grew up."

"Yeah, something beastly like that. Then we had this other friend—am I boring you?—named Fatso Hennessy, who got polio the year after I did, only worse. They got him in an iron lung in Colorado and there he sits. Well, it may be a coincidence, but Marconi went into his decline just about then. He never even liked Fatso before that, but now he writes him once a week, and last summer he went all the way out there to visit him."

"What secrets lurk in the hearts of men?"

"Damn right. Marconi took *my* polio in his stride, you'll notice. But when his enemy got it, he was overcome with guilt."

"Obviously wanted to kill the bugger. Feels responsible.

Simple transfer of his own self-hatred onto surrogate sibling, tweet tweet. Hence, no more need to be cynical, eh, my dear Sigmund?"

"You're a pisser, my dear Baxter. Upon my word." They'd picked up this English thing from the Jack Paar radio show, and Brian found it suited him uncommonly well.

Marconi was one part of a past that had died just like that. Brian saw none of his old friends now. That last year, clomping around Conception, was like a party that should have ended sooner. He had studied like a maniac the summer after Salt Rock to keep it from being two years, and by the blowsy standards of Conception he was more than ready to graduate. The first day back, he wobbled into class and was given a standing ovation. He didn't know what damn fool started it—some of the guys seemed embarrassed at joining in at first, which made him feel just marvelous, and then nobody knew when to quit. He decided that that dewy-eyed little creep Flynn might be behind it. One of nature's ass-kissers. Talk to him later. Break his legs and give him something to cry about. Griffin looked at Mulholland—I'll stop if you'll stop. They'd never liked Brian that much anyway. Don't clap for me, you bastards. Flynn kept it up several seconds. The rest had subsided. And Father Quinn had a special glint in his eye, as if maybe *he'd* given the order.

Subsequently, Brian was asked in due succession to run for class president and valedictorian and to edit the yearbook and all the meaningless shit a cripple can apparently claim by right. He began to wonder if every victory in life was going to be stained by pity, or was that a special Conception problem? He was the only guy in school who'd caught last year's blight, which made him some kind of a totem or scapegoat, the one chosen to suffer for the school's sins. He was even voted most popular, even though he went home early every day and had no social life at all. He wasn't popular, just respected. It was a bitter, lonely year that he was never to talk about much.

He swore then and there that he would never take advantage of his polio. Even scholastic achievement, that consolation prize for dwarfs and the half-blind, was not for him; though he couldn't help winning the state Latin prize.

O.K., Lazarus—you're on your own this year.

A new life, starting from scratch, with people who had never known him in the old days and who were free to hate him on his merits. Marconi, mourning over Fatso's iron coffin, could watch over the past for both of them. Brian had slipped out of the coffin and was alive. Well anyway, not to be too melodramatic about it—he couldn't very well make a fuss over Fatso, could he? It was like two ladies coming to a party in the same dress.

"To get back to serious matters," said Baxter, "what about the party Saturday?"

"I still haven't got a date. Joanie Finch was, it seemed, otherwise occupied."

"Yeah, she usually is. Kind of the way France was occupied. How about Nancy Selfridge?"

"Are you kidding?" Nancy was the most beautiful freshman at Barnard, homecoming-queen material and rumored to be something of a genius on the side.

"Why not? She likes you. I mean, she kept smiling at you, that time at the West End."

"She was drunk."

"To be sure. Still, in vino much good nooky, remember that. The guy with her had to drag her away, and she was *still* smiling at you, by God."

"Yeah, well that was nice of her." Brian couldn't explain, it broke the code, that a smile at me is different from a smile at you. He knew a motherly simper when he saw one; yet he must pretend now to discuss it in a sexual light. As if to give the only answer he knew, he slipped again in the snow and lay there: you see? This is our little problem right here.

"Goddamnit, Casey, haven't you embarrassed me enough for one day?" Baxter jerked him to his feet and lined him up over his crutches. "Now I just happen to have Nancy's phone number on me. Just one of my services. Why don't you give her a tinkle on the blower, old bean?" This British thing had all the makings of being a real drag.

"I'll think about it. She should be able to fit me in some time next April."

"She can fit you in any time, big Casey." Goddamn therapy. Now you see, Baxter here is trying to make me feel like one of the boys. It's nice to have a friend who'll do that, but he must be made to understand it isn't necessary. I have my own methods. Someday I will win a beautiful woman by brute achievement. There are women like that, who'll sleep with a hunchback if he's in *Who's Who*. And, of course, as women get older they are less fussy. But right now, I have no business going after a homecoming queen. I will be turned down, with the sickliest of regrets, and I will have that much less confidence for next time.

He sat, now, with his hand on the phone: not sure how he had got here. Anyway, this is as near as I should get. She did smile at me, and there was probably a tiny bit of sex in it, and that's fine. Now let's concentrate on becoming rich and famous. The women will beat a path to my door. Spoiled empty women with great bodies.

He was crouched on the edge of his bed. Very convenient, being able to live at home. Also, very constricting. (If I can't dance, I'm damned if I'll do dishes, was his motto.) Where would he bring his women, as the years went by? Oh Mother, how you surprised us. I was just showing Miss Selfridge my ulterior tibia . . . All this is getting us nowhere. He had to try that phone number, didn't he? *Brian who? At the West End, you say? Yes, of course. I have black hair, a thin Irish face. Surely you'd remember a man like that? . . . With Ted Baxter, eh? How is old Ted? Ted's in wonderful shape, thank you. Absolutely prime . . . I'd love to get together some time. This Saturday? I'm afraid not. Next Saturday, I'm afraid not.* He'd lose more confidence if he didn't make the phone call. She couldn't insult him as much as he insulted himself.

Anyhow, at least it would sound better in her voice. He braced himself and spun the dial.

"Nancy?"

"Who is this?" That wasn't such a hot voice.

"It's Brian Casey. I met you at the West End. I have a bad leg."

"Who do you want?" The voice was actually quite hideous.

"You mean you're not Nancy Selfridge?"

"Just a minute. I'll see if she's here."

Grunt. He tried to force himself to see the funny side. But why did he have to mention the bad leg? Did he think it would be good for at least one date? Goddamnit, Casey, don't do that again.

"Hello?"

"Hello, Nancy?"

"Yes?"

"This is Brian Casey. I met you at the West End."

"Yes, Brian."

"Er, are you doing anything Saturday night?"

"Well, sort of."

"That's too bad."

"What were you, I mean, what?" she fluttered.

"I was going to ask you to a party at the Sigma Gamma house."

"Well—I might be able to fit that in. What time?"

"I don't know. Late I guess." Holy mother of peace, he'd got her. "I'll call you back, if I can get past that dragon who answers your phone."

"All right. I'm pretty sure I can make it. And, Brian, thanks for asking."

Hot spit. Double hot spit. Nancy Selfridge. Jesus, the guys at the frat house would be creaming themselves. While the telephone fever was on him, he dialed Baxter and a couple of other guys over at Butler and asked them round for a little beer and poker. Nancy Selfridge–mm-mmm. He kissed his fingers and waved them at the crowd.

The guys from Butler were more than impressed, they were in shock. "Nancy Selfridge? The blonde? How do *you* rate, Casey?"

"God's gift to women," said Baxter. "She was warm for Casey's form the moment she clapped eyes on the little fellow."

"Please don't use that word 'clap,' it makes me nervous."

"Nancy Selfridge, huh?" Fellow named Harris. Iowa or someplace. "Oh well, what do I care. She's just a broad." Suddenly clutches his throat and screams. "Nancy *Selfridge*! Did you say Nancy Selfridge? Mother of God–Nancy Selfridge?"

"O.K., you want to play cards?" asked Brian. It was too much. What was he going to do with this extraordinary woman? He hadn't been on a real date since he got polio and couldn't even remember what you talked about.

"I don't think I'm in any shape to play poker," said Wendell, Massachusetts. "I think I'll lie down for a little while. Nappy poos."

"I hate to harp on this," said Harris, "but doesn't she go with Lundy on the football team?"

"She used to until Casey came along," said Baxter.

"Geez, you stole a girl from Lundy? What a man."

"Just tell me this," said Wendell, from the sofa. "Do you think she puts out?"

"Christ, what a way to talk about a goddess," said Baxter. "Wendell, you'll be working the West End for the rest of your days. Do you mean does she occasionally favor some lucky mortal with her celestial attentions?" Thoughtful pause. "Perhaps, perhaps."

"I asked you guys here to play poker, not to cream yourselves over my date."

"Oh, I misunderstood," said Baxter. "You really want to play poker, huh?"

They played for nickels and dimes, but Brian went at it as grimly as he would have for a fortune. "Geez, Casey, we don't raise that much around here." "Why not?" he said. Harris shrugged. "We just don't."

Brian shrugged back. What fun was it if you pussyfooted with this game, if you didn't get right up to the edge of panic? He was about to say, It's my house and we'll play my rules, when he saw that Harris was really looking itchy. In a minute they would be walking out on him.

"O.K., O.K.—what's the limit? Fifty cents?" Fucking sewing circle.

"We don't have a special limit. You know, you just don't push a guy."

Brian almost threw down his cards. What the hell is the point of the game if you just don't push a guy? But he didn't want them to leave. So for a few hands he tried playing their soft, second-rate way.

"You're too good for me, Casey," Harris said anyway. "I never played with a shark before."

"Yeah, where'd you learn this game? I mean *which* Hong Kong whorehouse?"

"I'm just getting good hands."

Poker was the excuse that kept them here, yet he could see they didn't really like it. Brian was wretched, not going for the jugular. He would rather just talk, in that case. But he would play on their terms.

"That's enough for me," Harris insisted.

"You want me to lend you some money?"

"No, thanks. I got to work anyway."

"Me too, I got a test tomorrow."

"Come on. One more hand." He dealt quickly, though it wasn't his turn. They looked at their cards listlessly. They might not like poker, but losing flustered and depressed them, like anyone else. Brian looked at what he had dealt himself—goddamnit, he'd come up with a full house.

All right, he wouldn't play it. He'd turn it in without a word.

"Casey?"

"A dime, I guess."

He couldn't do it, just couldn't. Try altering *your* poker game, go on. It's like altering your face or your attitude to money. Baxter raised him foolishly—please, Ted, don't say it so casually. That means you've got nothing, right? Harris's cards fanned wearily across the table. "Balls," he said. All right, you can still do the same, Casey. Fold quietly and treat your friend Baxter to a moment of happiness. Wendell was already on his way out.

"I guess I'd better see you, Ted." I'm sorry, I can't let you think you got away with it, can I? You can keep the money of course. In a minute they were all gone, and Brian was left with his pile of coins and IOU's, and two half-empty quart bottles of Ballantine.

11

To keep Saturday night at bay, Brian logged some time over at the library. He would never have expected it, he wasn't really the type, but books had become a great narcotic for him—Dickens, my God, what a writer, Balzac, Arnold Bennett: anyone who conveyed that the world was big and complicated as hell. The assigned work of a Columbia freshman was so simple and dull that it gave him ungovernable erotic fantasies; so he dipped outside his field. He hit on Bertrand Russell's *History of Western Philosophy,* and it was like meeting a dirty old man outside school: peddling the heroin of Atheism, as Father O'Monahan might say, through the needle of Doubt.

"Can you prove that you exist?" he asked his mother, as she made his bed that Friday morning.

"Of course I can. You can see me, can't you?"

"Yes, Mother. Of course. That's right."

Try it on Father. He may see the problem a little more clearly.

"Do you know that you can't really prove *God's* existence?" he said, over supper.

"Yes you can," said Beatrice. "Can't you, dear?" Kevin gave her a look. Who me? "That's right," he said. "St. Thomas does it at least five ways. There's first cause, and there's the argument from design, and I forget the other three. Was it *a priori*? Something like that."

"All right," said Brian. "Take first cause. David Hume really destroyed that one. He said that the concept 'cause and effect' is just a series of observations. It's just—"

"Did you learn that at Columbia?" said Beatrice, who had argued against a secular college in the first place.

"That's just clever-clever," said Kevin, prodding at his mackerel: the proof from fish, that's the one he'd forgotten. "Maybe I can't prove cause and effect, but every damn fool knows that it's there."

"Do they just teach you to doubt everything over there?" said Beatrice.

"Good grief, they don't even teach you that much," said Brian. "I got this from Bertrand Russell's book."

"Isn't he the man with three wives?" said Kevin.

"I don't know. It's not the most important thing about him."

"Well, it's good to know where your ideas are coming from. You see, Brian, Lord Russell is an aristocrat who doesn't take anything seriously. I believe he even raised his own children in the nude at one time. Can you imagine him with his pipe and all, and not a stitch on?"

"Aren't we getting away from the point?"

"Not really. Do I have to tell you why that kind of man would love to prove that God doesn't exist? You and I are not really equipped to deal with these ideas philosophically, but it's enough for Lord Russell's purposes that some doubt is cast on them. It's like hearing a rumor about a famous person. You're never quite sure afterward . . ."

Beatrice looked at her husband with relish. You see? He can handle anything you pick up at that Columbia of yours. Brian didn't push it—he'd forgotten how bog-Irish his parents were in this respect. They read *The New Yorker* and went to the theater; but when it came to the Church, they were a couple of toothless peasants. Well, he certainly didn't want to wind up going to Holy Cross or someplace to have his faith restored. If the religion issue led to that, to hell with it.

He tried to snuff it out gently, leaving no trace. "I certainly didn't mean that Russell disproves God—if you can't prove God, you can't disprove him either. It's a matter of faith, isn't it?" *Scripsi scriptum credo creditum fortiter ludere possum:* translated, let's have the conversation in Latin so we won't shock Mother.

"The Church insists it's also a matter of Reason," his father said doggedly. Since his own brief lapse of faith, he had become your basic devout Catholic, duty-bound to instruct anyone who didn't set the dogs on him first.

"Yeah, well, it could be. I mean, like I was saying this morning, you can't prove that *you* exist either, but it's not unreasonable to believe that you do."

"It sounds like a silly game," said Beatrice. Now that no loss of faith seemed to be involved, she quickly lost interest.

"It's good to come in contact with the best secular thought, if you're properly trained for it, as I think Brian is. It can even strengthen your faith." Kevin was still selling Columbia, which he *really* believed in. "Half my class at Georgetown left the Church."

The conversation was *aesthetically* painful. His parents' religion embarrassed him, like bad singing. Religion took talent. "I've got a date Saturday night," he said abruptly.

Is she a Catholic girl? His mother didn't ask that, of course, though his grandmother would have. Each generation slipped a little more into the bog of indifference.

"That's nice. Do we know her?"

"No." It's not Mary Murphy, who wheeled me around the high-school prom, if that's what you mean. It's a real girl this time.

He wanted to know if they were surprised, if they thought he was up to it. No, on second thought, he definitely didn't want to know. His parents' view of him would be misleading, and unlike anyone else's. His mother still acted as if he couldn't use the telephone: she called the dentist for him and the brace man. She would picture his date as fundamentally a problem in nurse's training. His father—ah, who knew what his father thought?

"So I'll be home late."

"How are you going to get back?"

"Ted Baxter'll take care of me." Better to lean on a friend than a parent: a step toward maturity.

"Are you sure you'll be all right? I mean Ted Baxter doesn't get drunk, does he?"

"Brian can take care of himself," said Kevin. "That is as long as *he* doesn't get drunk."

That was flattering. Now let's not talk about it any more. No more sex, no more religion. You'll never grow up if you keep discussing important things with your parents.

That night, he stayed awake war-planning tomorrow night with Nancy Selfridge. Did non-Catholic girls like that expect you to sleep with them on their first date? To judge from his friends' conversation, some of them did. How to tell which ones? And how much allowance must be made for routine bullshit on part of friends? Probably less in college than in high school. His new friends seemed more honest in other respects. Sex different? We'll see. Next question: assuming the best—where would they go to do it? Not here for sure. He had heard about seductions at the frat house, but couldn't imagine where they occurred. Check it out with Baxter. Maybe he knows a hotel.

God, Casey, you're a cold, scheming son of a bitch. He couldn't even remember what Nancy looked like, and here he was booking her into cheap hotels, frugeling her on the Si Gam roof and—all right now, let's not go into details or we'll be up all night. Mustn't leave game in locker room. I'm not really cold—quite the opposite. Have to keep it impersonal or I won't be able to handle it at all. Religious considerations? I'll be the judge of that. I don't think I owe God any favors, after what he did to me. That's self-pity, Casey—maybe polio was a blessing in disguise. Yeah, some disguise. No, I mean it—you're twice as smart as you would have been without it. Look at all the reading you got done. You could almost pass for an intellectual in certain obtuse circles. Also, this may be useful, *people don't envy you.* O.K., we'll call that a tie. But please, don't send round fat eunuchs like O'Monahan to tell me what's what. It is well known that the Irish are scared of sex and make some big virtue out of their fear. An Italian priest would say, Into the sack-a you go, big boy. And ask her if she's got a friend. Would he? That sounds glib. Did you learn it at Columbia? Anyway, as to confession, uh*uh,* I'm not telling my sex life to some prissy old lady in a cassock . . . glib, but I do know more about God than O'Monahan does. I've been touched by His hand. And I know one thing He doesn't do—He doesn't cure polio. Look, we already discussed that. His mysterious ways and all that—you bet they're mysterious. My father really agrees with me about God. Who knows what your father thinks? Not even your father. Some steel door closed in the middle of his mind. Behind the door, green greasy alligators, like everyone else. Will I give a good account of myself with Nancy? WILL I GIVE A GOOD ACCOUNT OF MYSELF? Not yet, you fool. Down boy. Oh my.

Three hours' sleep was not enough, but it would have to do. Just spend a normal day, now. You're not seventeen any more. You're, my God, almost, well, it's an improvement, nineteen. Old enough to drink and fight for your country. Let's have a little suave around here.

By afternoon, he was sexually exhausted. It had leaked away like gas. Another shave, another tub. He sought refuge in grooming: hosing down the old armpits, what? Or how about a dab of after-shave in the groin? it can't hurt . . . Ouch, it certainly can. What more can I do to enhance my loveliness? He sat on the toilet seat, bathed in steam, and thought, oh my God, another problem—how do I get a you know? Ask Baxter for one? It could be the social gaffe of the year. "Hey guys!"—Baxter was no man to keep these things to himself. "Casey wants a *tweet!* He thinks he's going to make out with Selfridge on his first date." How about one of the guys at Butler? Same objection. Goddamn, he wished he knew what was expected of him.

The only alternative was to get on over to the drugstore, slipping up-ice on 116th Street, and just ask for one. You think going to confession is difficult, you should try this. "That'll be, er, three Trojans please." And five Hail Marys. He swore he would not let the religious thing get to him again, but then he thought of the slimy rubber things strewn like leaves under the hedges in the park, ten Our Fathers' worth in each of them, the wages of sin.

That's just an aesthetic matter, not materially affecting the *gravitas peccati* one way or the other. (They put the dirty parts of the moral theology book in Latin, the greatest spur to learning ever devised.) Now, then. Question for our experts: is Trojan a brand name, or is it generic? "I'll take three of your house brand, please. Whatever you personally recommend there . . ." Would the druggist sympathize with his flounderings? Did druggists have a code like priests and doctors? Levine worked in a drugstore one summer, and he was pretty funny about the customers who wound up ordering toothpaste or Bromo out of very embarrassment. So it seemed there was no code.

He could imagine some kid like Levine regaling his friends: "Yeah, this guy came in, all cripped up—and he didn't even know you have to have a marriage certificate. Yeah, and not only that, but he didn't know you have to be individually measured for them!" To hell with the Trojans, they were sinful anyway.

Maybe one more shave would help. He had been in the bathroom over two hours, and twice he had heard polite footsteps outside. His parents never bothered him in here, but they would have to use the place sometime. He decided to skip the shave and take his chances on that rugged look.

Instead he took a nap, and immediately imagined Nancy Selfridge braying at him: "You mean you haven't got one?" "I just happen to be a Catholic." "Well why the hell didn't you tell me?" The screaming woman in the bushes. "Send me one of your friends, at once."

All right, he'd get one. Three? Was he up to three? Or did you use them more than once? He was beginning to feel like an old rubber himself, foul and crawling, discarded by man and God. His precious seed flowing into the city sewer, where it belonged. What a joke to think he could do this lightly, with his training.

Grimly he set out for the store and barked his order for three male contraceptives, and was handed them without incident.

He could barely croak out a "hello" when he finally saw her. She kept him waiting in the dim lobby of the girls' dormitory, and he spent the time reminding himself that sex would not occur for the first five minutes at least.

To his relief, she seemed to expect to do all the preliminary talking. "I hope this kind of dress is all right. You didn't tell me what kind of party it was." The dress looked O.K. to him. He didn't know what kind of party it was; a track suit would probably do splendidly for the Si Gam.

"Black is usually all right anywhere," she said. "But I'll die if I'm the only one in a cocktail dress."

She was supposed to be smart, she looked smart. Maybe she'd stop crapping around in a minute.

"How are we getting there?" she asked.

"Friend has a car." It was only a few blocks, but he didn't wish to impress his date with one of his twenty-foot slides onto the trolley tracks. So he had badgered Baxter into getting out his heap.

It wasn't a bad car, actually—the thing about Baxter was that he was rich, bless him—but it gave one something to talk about. "Hold on to the door, Nancy—it has a nasty way of flying off. Messy business. I'll work the siren. The rest of you dogs, get out and push. With any luck, we'll make it." This stuff would keep them occupied while he wriggled into his seat.

"Hey Baxter, I can get you fifty big ones for this. I have connections at the city dump. No? You Armenians are a proud little people . . ." Nobody was laughing, not even Baxter. To begin with, this was not Marconi's uncle's Chevy, but a brand new Oldsmobile 88. Also, possibly, Baxter did not laugh after dark. Brian suddenly felt high-school: on his last date, two years ago, insulting the car was just the thing.

Nancy started up again, asking whether he came from the city, and whether Baxter came from the city, and Baxter's girl Perry, who came from the main line, whatever that was. Nancy averred as how she loved the city herself, especially the crisp clear days and the tingle in the air. Shut up, you dumb broad. How could you become sexually aroused by such bullshit? She sounded like a housewife from New Jersey. The gorgeous body was just something she was passing through.

"I grew up in New York," said Brian, "to the crisp clear sounds of, 'Outta my way kid, straighten them papers, put that back or I'll kill you.' You know, from those picturesque little guys who run our quaint cigar stores, and those colorful taxi drivers of ours. By the way, have you noticed that all cigar-store owners are exactly the same height?"

No response. This was a guttersnipe approach to a glamorous evening, was it not. Baxter said that they would ruin the skyline if they put up a U.N. building here. Out of sheer nervousness, Brian said he thought the skyline was overrated.

They arrived at the Sigma Gamma house and Baxter let Nancy and Brian out and drove off with Perry to find a parking place. Baxter looked stern as a judge in the dashboard light. Better shape up, Casey. Brian wasn't strictly a member, but a regular guest of Baxter's. Nobody else knew quite what to do with him. Boy, I certainly messed up in the car, he thought, as he hoicked up the stairs. You know what it is? I'm not a gentleman. That's what it is, Master Pip, right enough.

He guessed they had located the heart of the party. At least, this was the room where they had shown the stag movies last week and he had almost fainted. But was this all? just couples necking to old Artie Shaw records? Somebody edged silently along on the sofa, leaving a space for Nancy and him. Should he apologize to Nancy? I mean, she must have expected a real party, not just notes for a party.

"What are you drinking?" asked Baxter, who had followed them up.

"Just Coke for me," said Nancy.

"Tsk, tsk. Perhaps our wild Irish friend will change your mind about that." He winked at Brian. "How about you, tiger?"

"I guess I'll have a rye and ginger ale."

"You're kidding."

"I am?"

"Yes, you are. Believe me."

Maybe if I was standing up, I could hit him with my good hand, or kind of fall on top of him. But he'll be long gone by the time I'm up.

"All right, get me the correct thing, Mr. Taste. And make it snappy."

What gets into these Baxter-type guys after dark? In the daytime, he's a bum like everybody else. But at night, *voilà,* pussycat. Brian found himself watching closely: would he bring him a frozen daiquiri or a pink lady? Or maybe a mango chutney frappe?

Baxter brought him a Scotch and water, and went over to an adjacent armchair and started right in to neck with Perry. Well, Jesus, there was nothing special about that. Anyone can be a gentleman, if that's all it takes.

Nancy looked up at him with sultry eyes. How'd she manage that? The housewife saucers had narrowed miraculously. She had left her Sunday-go-to-meeting manners in the car.

"You're a strange boy," she said; so help him, that's what she said.

"Ah, you'd noticed," he shot back.

"You're laughing at me. I can tell."

Although the couples each acted as if they were alone under the stars, they must have been aware of each other, because they seemed to move in unison. Signals ran along the sofa cushions—Brian felt like the first day of dancing school. Should he start to neck now? He'd forgotten the little he knew.

Last week, this same crowd had whistled and popped its cheeks over "The Randy Desk Clerk." "My ma gave me a nickel to buy a popsicle, but all I want is chewing gum, chew-chew-chew chewing gum," was how they greeted the act of fellatio. The air still carried traces of it: the cheap hotel room, actors made of grey genital, yipping students. The real business of sex, not this garden-party crap.

"I'm not laughing at you, I'm laughing *with* you, honey," he said. A certain amount of talking seemed necessary, any old crap would do. At what point in the inanities they should begin to neck he'd better leave to her, he guessed.

"Do you laugh at a lot of people?" she murmured.

"Just the funny ones," he murmured back.

"Please. Be serious. *Bri*an."

"I'm trying. It's not easy."

Not easy for her, either. She straightened up and reached for a cigarette. Her face hardened to flint as she squinted over the flame: hey, that's good, hold it. Brassy, tough platinum blonde, in an expensive bar. Not that mewling little girl in the car, squealing over crisp autumn days, and not True Romance rushing Joe College at the frat house, but the real lowdown thing.

"I'm serious now," he said, and pulled her closer with his good arm. "Now," he repeated, and pressed hard on her mouth, not kissing, just pressing, until their teeth clanged. Her arms tensed, as if to push him off, but then she seemed to resign herself to it: it was part of the deal, the dating contract, putting up with the occasional gorilla.

Don't do me any favors, he thought. He pulled back

slightly himself, embarrassed at the amateur lunge, and came back more smoothly. She stroked his hair in return, content now with this slumberous compromise, and very sweet it was for a while, her mouth working gently against his, and her body softer than dreams.

But did one go on like this all night? His back hurt, and he tried another angle, and another. It was like carving a roast. "How far'd you get Saturday night?" He knew the Monday talk. "You get the tit? Outside tit or inside? Just the bra, huh?" He decided he'd better push on.

She let his hand linger on her breast for just a moment, his trophy for Monday. ("You didn't have to pin her, I trust." "Are you kidding? The price of my pin is complete surrender.") Not bad for a first date with a campus queen, but suddenly not good enough. Brian played to win. He put the hand back quite sharply and held on—not, he realized, enjoying it all that tremendously. It was too much like clinging to a rock.

Outside tit? O.K. Not bad, Casey. Wouldn't let you go any further, eh? He understood that you were a damn pantywaist if you stopped before they ordered you to. So he plunged his hand into the black V-neck and groped through lace until he'd got the nipple itself. Eureka, guys. Plant the flag.

She was looking up at him, unresisting. "Did you just want that?" she asked.

He held it lifelessly, pointlessly. The bra rasped against his hand so he couldn't circulate it. Meanwhile, the others necked on obliviously, still as statues, knowing better than to do that sort of thing in here. He'd made a damn fool of himself. Nancy's eyes were big again, with sexless pity. Little boy didn't know what he was doing. She had let him have the breast, like a child.

He disentangled his hand, and for a second he could have hit her with it. "I'm sorry," she said. "It's all right," he said. "I like you an awful lot," she said. "I'll bet you do," he said. They couldn't start necking again. She was an expert in these things, too damn expert. He was on to her stinking game. Since thirteen she had known how not to hurt a guy's feelings, how to keep his respect, the exact inch of terrain to surrender each time out. She even knew how she wanted to be talked about on Mondays. That whore look was no accident.

"Come on, I'll get you a taxi," he said. Too embarrassed to look at her, obscurely angry: yet some dirty little part of him still wanted to impress her. "It didn't work out too well. I tried to work too fast." One of his rare mistakes, gracefully acknowledged. "You're too attractive for your own good."

She didn't say anything. They went down the stairs and got her coat. She looked sad and more human than before, with none of her fixed faces—though perhaps that, too, was fixed. "The human look can be obtained by—" They couldn't find a cab, of course, and so he walked her slowly back—it was a scene they both wanted to get out of, but they had to walk slowly. He concentrated maniacally on not falling: that would be the living kiss-off end. At her front door, she kissed him quickly on the cheek and ran in.

To hell with her. End of that. Of course, he wouldn't tell anyone about the tit; couldn't really imagine why people did. He walked a few steps, and flung the three condoms far away into the snow.

12

He spent Sunday morning in church, to clear his mind. The droning incantations of the crowd at Corpus Christi (where they dialogued the mass in English) and the inscrutable dance of the priest might fashion him a mood. Despair was out of the question, he'd come too far for that. How about becoming a recluse like Marconi? Phil had one invaluable secret: he knew that the examined life was a pile of shit. It was just too all-round embarrassing: you didn't have to be crippled to feel it. Marconi was a special case, though. Amazing spiritual gifts. A rancid saint. Would probably be a priest if it didn't require *some* faith. Phil had barely enough of that for engineering.

It would be nice to escape the world of bodies somehow, of clumsiness and sympathy. To become a superbrain in a glass bowl, feared by earthpeople. *Hated* by earthpeople. Or Christ up there, cursed and despised of men. Bleeding to death, and still man enough to be despised every inch of the way. To be so strong and make such a statement that, if you were dead in a ditch with your legs and arms beside you, people would spit on you. That was manhood for the handicapped.

Brian ate his crippled friend at communion with shuddering relish and stayed all morning to watch the repeated sacrifice. By the ten o'clock mass, he could almost imagine the priest's face, twisted in a smirk, as he slammed his switchblade into the Host. This is the God for me: a God who would rather be horsewhipped, bad-mouthed, and killed every day than pitied. He even hired these priests, his own blessed goon squad, to sacrifice him around the clock. Of course, the old ladies tried to pity him. Easy for them—they hadn't been there. They knew not what they did.

The hypnosis was working: the pounding disharmonies of those flat Columbia-area voices, like waves that couldn't get together, would have him levitating and jabbering Latin in no time. Christ, of course, wouldn't be seen dead in this place: He's dead drunk out in the snow right now. Spitting rainbows of blood. If you want me, that's where you'll find me, madam. In fact, that's the *only* place you'll find me. You don't fancy me, eh, with the tubes sticking up my nose and that hole in my throat? Pity. Because no man goeth to the Father, except through me. That's it, brother. Right through that hole in my throat.

No, I'm not sorry for myself, not a bit. Look at how I talked to Pontius Pilate just now. And the women of Jerusalem. "Weep not for me, but for yourselves and your children." I don't want your pity, ladies. Go home and tremble for yourselves. I get along very nicely. I am broken, you see. Nothing more can happen to me. Baxter, over there in the crowd—now that's a different case. How would you like to be broken, my good man? We'll see when the time comes. And why it's Selfridge, the town whore, I've always liked whores. Oh, not that way, believe me; not the way you think. I know too much. Procreation is a nasty business. I sometimes wish I'd never invented it. But when a customer ignores them afterward, that's different. Now that's real feeling. Like mine. Yes, a whore laughed at, or pelted with rocks, that's God in there, that's me. But don't weep for her, you fat fools, weep for yourselves.

It was the last mass, one-ten, and Brian had arrived beyond words at a still scene in a meadow where Christ sat calmly buffing his nails while his tormentors wailed and thrashed. Cut off your legs and follow me. We can't, Lord, we just can't. Imagine asking this guy for a cure: he'd send you something worse, with his blessings. Cautiously, now, let us return to this prosy old church, bumping down on the black-and-white landing strip. Whether these thoughts he'd been having were blasphemy, he really didn't know, or even if they had any connection with the Christian religion. They were *his* religion, he knew that for sure, and he had no trouble believing it. If he had anything to say about the love of Christ, it was a cold, silver object, not the hot, gold stuff. For once, he didn't get mad when the lady next to him tried to help him up. Poor crazy lady, trying to meet minimum requirements among the beatitudes. He even staggered against her, giving her charity a real workout. Now *that* was real Christianity for you.

By Monday his head was clear as a bell. "You'll notice the slight spring in my limp." He'd won. Baxter sought him out and grilled him about what he had done with Selfridge, taking her off so early. Where, what, how many times? Trousers up or down? "You just do it to talk about it, don't you?" said Brian. "Some truth in that," said Baxter. "But not the whole picture." Baxter, grinning, red-faced from his Sunday beaver hunting in Foxglove County, Mass., or his polo in the snow—I know better than that now, thought Brian. Trailing around with this guy like a mascot. Baxter's guest to life.

He wasn't going to be any recluse, he'd tried that at Conception and he wasn't the type, but he did decide to stop seeing that bunch. He couldn't lick them at their own game, so must simply think of something else. A million on the stock exchange by the time I'm a senior, was one idea. Pay for his women, cash on the barrelhead, no psychology, no crapping around. He bought a *World Telegram* and studied the market; bought another one; found the same sense of pattern he found in bridge. Ah ha.

Unfortunately, money was a dirty word at the Caseys'. Kevin used the word sometimes, Beatrice never. Playing the market would be like dipping your hands in shit. Brian made some mind bets for a couple of weeks and found he would have made a small profit already. A solitary vice, making circles on those squalid columns—IBM couldn't miss, that was his ticket. He suddenly saw the whole thing, electric typewriters, giant mechanical brains, and when the war with Russia came, business machines to drop on the enemy. He felt the fizz of a new temptation: he must get some liquid capital, or whatever they called it.

"How much do I need to get started?" he asked Baxter after a history class.

"Hey, where you been?" said Baxter. "You're letting Selfridge go to waste, you fool."

"Yeah, I'm sure. Eating her little metal heart out. Listen, I'm talking about money. Mazuma. The long green." He flicked an invisible ash. "Spondulicks, my good man." "Yeah? W. C. Fields spoke *higher* than that. Why you always get that wrong, Sam?" Baxter quivered. "You fool, you bloated idiot . . ."

"Lorre speaks faster than that. So, how much do I need to start investing?"

"I guess you could start with ten."

"Ten whats?"

"Ten thousand. That's for a *small* start."

"I see. Could you lend me a dollar till Friday?"

Still, the dream of gold bricks piled up in the closet was too good to shake. Old Ebenezer Casey, cackling in his nightgown, showing his prize to some enormous blonde. The big kid going all to pieces, crying and laughing and tugging at his nightgown. "What a man!" The brain in the glass bowl shook convulsively.

Meanwhile, his mother was going the other way, getting a thing on voluntary poverty. By sheer concentration, she managed to look a bit like a European refugee who was down to her last dress. "The war was a punishment," she said, over dinner. "What else can you expect if you're rotten with materialism?"

"Weren't we in the middle of a depression when the war started?" asked Brian.

"Well, that was another punishment. And we didn't learn much, did we? Look at us now, like pigs at the, er, zoo. All those cars and washing machines and labor-saving things while people are starving."

"Don't you think we deserve something after all that punishment?" asked Kevin. He was making some good money this year, and his wife's conversion came at an awkward time. Brian could tell that his old man liked money. Not talking about it probably made it worse.

"Punishment? We weren't punished half enough in this country, if you ask me. A little rationing, a little inconvenience. You can't truly say that you were *punished*, dear."

"Oh no, *I* wasn't punished. But some people were. I mean the ones who lost sons."

Awkward silence. Lost sons. Brian continued to think about the stock exchange. Look at it this way, God. The other guys have legs, I'll have money. That's fair, no? I was punished during the war, wasn't I? A little cash would equalize that, and I'd consider it settled. Wouldn't bother you again. O.K., I know how you detest arguments like that. I'll take it downstairs to the other guy."

"What are you grinning about?" asked his father.

"Nothing. I just thought of something."

He's happy, our boy is happy. Isn't it wonderful, our boy is happy? The beaming, merry-peasant faces of his parents brought on an ungovernable urge to tease. How about giving them the look of quiet pain instead? "It's nothing, Mother. Just . . . nothing." Hopping sedately to his room, as they rose awkwardly, napkins to groin like Greek statues; meanwhile, Brian busting a gut laughing.

To hell with it. Money. That's the thing.

The next morning, or the one after, he just happened to notice his mother's purse, on the radiator by the front window: a blue number, with the gold spangles chipped and missing, a couple of them still sparkling in the sunshine. He'd always wanted to see inside one of those things. It might give a clue to what women were up to. His rummaging hand dragged out a Kleenex with streaks of pale lipstick, a tortoise-shell comb, twenty-six dollars and thirteen cents. Very revealing. His hand settled on the bills. His parents still gave him a child's allowance, it was one of those things that hadn't grown, and he thought, "She owes it to me anyway." Then, "She doesn't want it herself." Then, after a lingering caress, "Well, those were interesting thoughts." He released the cash, and clicked the purse shut.

He decided to analyze the thoughts. One curious part was that right and wrong hadn't come into it at all. He could recall half-thoughts and coded bleeps like, twenty-six isn't worth the risk; five wouldn't be noticed, ten would; cripples would make great thieves. Hey, that last one was worth saving. He could see himself heaving along supermarket aisles, stuffing his pockets to bursting, and clanking out through the check-out counter. Or staring at natty floorwalkers until they looked away for very shame, and then quick, the Hope Diamond. Precious stones, sir. Turn their pity to good coin. Or how about terror? Lurching through the fog like Jack the Ripper. Ping, goes the little shop bell. "We're closed for the evening, sir. Sir? . . . ooh ooh, it's aargh"—Casey's twisted shadow falls across the shopgirl, his hands move with amazing dexterity.

No kidding, he could probably pick up a nice piece of change as a sneak thief. Undignified to be caught, of course; but undignified for them, too. They'd probably let him go. Or at least get another cripple to search him. His constitutional right. Anything to take advantage of their sentimentality. Even his parents, by God, would bend over backwards, not to suspect him. That's a nice ruby, dear. Now go to bed.

Just a morning's thoughts like any other. (Did everyone talk to themselves like this? If not, what did they do with their heads all day long?) Then one day the next week he found himself staring like a dream into an actual cash register that had been left open, and which twinkled with crisp new bills. The owner had gone out back, looking for an electric heater for Brian's room, and his mother was back there with him. A stack of verdant twenties, fresh lettuce. What's up, doc? There was no time to think about it, maybe five seconds, to judge from the voices and position of the feet. His mother usually wound down and succumbed to sales talk by about the third item. He found that his thoughts were all in order, and remarkably serene. Test of nerve, this first time. Just a game. Pursuing his analysis. He would, of course, never do it again. Carefully, he peeled off five twenties, no more: not hurrying was part of it. He moved away a few feet, and began scrutinizing lawn mowers. The register rang behind him, his mother had paid for the heater. He imagined the man frowning briefly, something vaguely askew in the lettuce patch, then shutting his machine firmly. There are some things people don't want to know. Brian turned with an innocent, bored blink. "All set, Mother?" The guy had a weak face, he wouldn't follow it up.

When he got home, he called a brokerage house and found out how to buy a share of IBM.

Things, according to the older, wiser Casey, tend to have a crooked recoil: you expect it on one shoulder and it hits the other. Part of it was that he felt like a jackass about the theft. Not guilty—sex had all the rights to that—but sheepish. A sheepish, if you can imagine, jackass. They had a rule about this kind of thing on his block. He and his middle-class friends used to pinch fruit off a stand on 125th Street, but you quit doing it by fifteen at the latest—if mentally retarded, you had till sixteen. After that, you left it to people who needed the fruit. (Canon law MXI: "*Fructem relinquite pauperibus.*") He felt now like cashing his share and mailing the money back anonymously. "Your obedient servant, Fitzroy, son of Raffles."

But being a jackass wasn't the worst of it. He could live with that. The worst of it, the rich taste he couldn't get rid of, was that he'd really enjoyed it—hearing the feet, the voices: finding in the stupefying dull sounds of a hardware store the pleasures of fear. And then, taking the money *slowly,* prolonging the fear like a wine-tasting. It was better to be seen committing the worst crime calmly than to be caught doing nothing nervously. A jerky move over by the lawn mowers and Mr. Felt would have looked into the cash register. No connection, but that's what he would have done. People fear suspicious behavior more than real activity. Hell, you could have the precious gem *mailed* to you, if you knew how to behave.

He was satisfied at first just to have the philosophical insight. He tried writing a story about it but found himself instantly bored—he wasn't a writer. He'd rather be written about. A writer was just a servant to the people who did things. Maybe if life hadn't cast him in a passive role, it would have been different: but a crippled writer was too much. What he really wanted, there was no escaping it, was to do it just once again, to see if his theory was right, and to relive that juicy moment in the hardware store. To be fully alive again for five seconds—Christ, he'd even pay for it.

Too bad it was out of the question. It brought back so

many things he had been forcing out of his mind—waiting to release the ball until you could hear the linemen's breath; sinking foul shots while the sweat swam into your eyes; going a little further with fear than the others. And then, as a reward, to find fear opening the senses, so that you felt the cracks in the earth, smelled it, knew its twenty-seven flavors; saw things from the side of the eye, caught highlights from the river, when they played down there; knew by the odor which man was guarding you. Stay with fear, and it will show you sights, boy, take you where no man has trod. And now he had found something nice in the fear line that he could do as well as *they* could, if not better, and it was considered shameful and neurotic. "They ought to make a sport out of larceny." "They already have—they've made them all out of larceny." Ah, wisdom. Who needs thee?

He gradually fought the temptation into an obsession. Just once more—and maybe try putting the thing back the next day? No, putting it back would make the whole thing ridiculous. Like returning the money people lost at poker. You've got to pretend the game is real, to extract the honey from it. Anyway, *I'm not going to do any of it.*

Casey's winter slumped and wheezed into early spring. Baxter gave up on him. Selfridge had found a poet with terrible teeth. Crazy. No friends for now, a *de facto* recluse. On odd afternoons, he took the bus downtown to play his new game—a game like the stock market, like life itself. He visited all the big stores and figured how he *would* rob them, if he had the criminal mind. He checked the fire exits and men's rooms—no, that was the wrong style for him. No use being furtive—better to exploit his high visibility. Fall down and let them put you on the elevator. Stuffed like a goose with goodies. Have heart attack over there by the desk—no, that's going too far. They'd immediately start feeling under coat for pulse. Find grandfather clock. "Can I help you, sir?" "No, I'm just waiting for my mother." Right now, he was trying to look occupied in Lord & Taylor's. He was checking to see if ladies' stores might be better than men's. True, you were more noticeable, but they didn't keep trying to sell you things. The house dicks were presumably training their eyes on the broads. A man working these stores would surely get a footnote in criminal history.

He practiced his unobtrusive stance, waiting audaciously by the information desk itself, with the slumped resignation of a male appendage. "Waiting for my girl friend." Better than mother, less sinister somehow. You poor guy, you'll have to pay for all this, won't you? Sympathy, a bonus. For a grown son, dragged here by the hair by Mom, they would probably feel contempt.

"I'm waiting for my wife." Really? Hooded gaze at that one. Well, it was worth a try. In two and a half hours, only three queries. "Still waiting?" Four. "My girl friend goes a little crazy in these places," he said, with a thin, unmemorable smile. "You know how women are."

The game was O.K. as far as it went, but it was finally just more wisdom. As he stood in Bendel's on Thursday of Holy Week, watching the salesladies swoop by, he felt like a store dummy. They seemed to notice him less, the longer he stayed. But perhaps they were registering him a little more every minute. He would never know, unfortunately.

He had long since figured that the thing to steal here was the soft fabrics—some of those spring dresses would fold up to nothing, he bet. One would simply hump over the counter, and finger them with that bored expression. "Will Mother never be done?" Time the staff in their rounds so you wouldn't have to look up suddenly. Pick out a dress and crumple it casually into one's bosom. His bulgy winter coat would hold a full wardrobe.

And what the hell would I do with a spring dress? Sell it to the Mafia. Give it to Nancy Selfridge. Throw it on the floor and make her bend for it. Not important. The thing is to see if a beautiful abstract plan can be brought to throbbing life, right? Elevator, maybe seventy-five feet away. Two girls chatting—the little blonde tends to gaze around while her Italian-looking friend is talking. Better wait till she starts talking herself. My own saleslady, the one who keeps asking if I'm all right, has disappeared. Women take, what, about three minutes in the can? Tugging off the girdle, grunting back into it—God knows what happens to the stockings, it's no business of mine.

In the quiet, dull shop with the whispering girls and the purring rug, he began to feel the same giddy thrill he had experienced in the dust and metal of the hardware store. The ominous smell of pots and pans had been O.K., but the feline menace of cloth and soft perfume was better, classier. There was more variety to this game than any of the famous ones, which were played in fixed settings. Mannequins gestured at him like enemy linemen. He had landscaped the place to a fare-thee-well, knew where all the living people were, and which of the inanimate objects had souls. To the mannequin with the two-way radio wristwatch, he said, "Would you tell my girl friend I got tired of waiting. She's wearing a checkered coat." He planned every step, all the way to the bus. The dress would be stashed under his belt by then so it wouldn't shake loose, and his features would convey blank animation. Fine American boy. Damn pity about his handicap.

You're not really going to do it? He wished he could hold this moment forever, the timed shopgirls, the eddy of customers (drawing away from him for sure: their collective mood was homeward), the boiling clarity of his mind. "Have you ever been alive, madam?" Lady gift-wrapping an Easter bunny. His side vision was simply fantastic. Both flanks were covered. A cluster of shoppers to the left formed a screen of blockers; a woman making a fuss to the right drew the flow of eyes that way. Not an interesting enough fuss to hold them for long, shrill but monotonous. Half a minute, call it. The elevator finger began moving sedately up from the basement and the crowd below stood moonstruck, staring at it. Opportunity in sufficient quantity can constitute temptation. But of course, he had already decided. His exaltation depended on his doing something now—he had no *right* to his exaltation if he didn't do something. The devil was a nut on small bills like this. He began to walk, sensuous to bursting, to the nearest counter. The carpet was spongy underfoot, like good turf, and all the joy he had ever known in sports ringed his head like frosted diamonds. The fabric was absolutely luscious, and profoundly sexy. Heaven would be lined with this stuff. He could fondle it forever. This red number would be nice on Selfridge. Or the green one for Mother. One, two—O.K., the green one—three. Slowly, voluptuously spinning out the joy to screaming point, he slipped the dress into his coat. He looked around blandly, not focusing, the way celebrities do. Now for the stately trudge to the elevator.

One jog step, two. Three. Four. "What are you doing, sonny?" Where the hell did *she* come from? A grey-haired lady with rimless glasses had a hand on his wrist strong enough to make his fingers fly open. "You'd better put it back," she said.

It would be undignified to argue with her. He pulled out the dress and handed it over. "Where do we go?" he asked.

"Home," she said, "as fast as you can."

"Aren't you going to arrest me?"

She looked him up and down. "No," she said.

Ludicrously, he wanted to hang around and talk to her. How did you get into this business? Did you spot me all along? Was it just hopeless? But she wasn't a talker. He hobbled to the elevator, making up answers for her. "Leave it to the professionals, sonny. You looked around too much —real pros don't do that. You're a marked man from Abercrombie's to Zeek's Appliances. Have you thought of psychiatric help?" He pushed into the elevator, and she was still beside him. A compliment, in a way. "Very plucky of you to try it in your condition. In view of your handicap, we won't say another word about it," he imagined her saying.

She saw him to the door, old enough to be his mother, and he slushed out into a sodden spring rain. More fucking wisdom, it was all he was allowed to have. They wouldn't even arrest him. He took the number 5 bus home, and nobody offered him a seat. And for the first time, until now, he felt like shouting, "Offer me a seat, you bastards. You've got everything else."

13

Brian's interest in politics up to now had consisted of nothing heavier than arguing with his father about labor unions and such. Kevin, your old-line Democrat, without much stomach for it, would defend the "union principle," but then admit they were all corrupt in practice. Brian: "What's the good of a principle if it *never* works out in practice?" Kevin: "You, a Catholic, can ask that?" His father had acquired the slyness of the hen-pecked, of the man who sneaks a drink in the closet. Upright Catholic that he was these days, he still liked his bit of mischief. Brian assumed Beatrice had squeezed some of the starch out of her husband but couldn't remember when. It was such a cliché to be a know-it-all about one's parents. Brian was sold, right now, on the mystery of the human heart, and he was sure that Mauriac and Péguy could flush some amazing secret out of his parents. Or if they couldn't, they couldn't. (Yeah, he felt good this year, couldn't explain why.)

Avoiding clichés also formed the basis of his whole political position, as it became advisable to have one. He was certainly not going to be any youthful radical—how banal can you get? Everyone knows that youthful radicals wind up as chairman of the board. The conservative position was more glamorous, and he was impressed by Tocqueville on revolution, but his ancestry nixed that. It might be chic for a Jew to be conservative, but it was hopeless for an Irish Catholic. At home, he liked to heckle his mother about Dorothy Day and the radical pacifists ("What's so spiritual about dirty fingernails?"), but at school he just took the line that everything was very complicated, and that nothing was as simple as his opponent thought.

"Don't you believe in anything?" asked his new friend Woody Kline.

"Not much."

"Don't you think that skepticism is kind of a youthful pose?"

So it was hard finding a position. The clichés were everywhere: nice, though, having Woody as a friend—a sharp nervous fellow in a lazy body, who told him he was very smart for a goy. "I can improve your I.Q. twenty points if you'll submit to this simple little operation." Woody and Murray and Seymour, a whole bunch of new friends, all tugging him gently to the left. They couldn't get him to support Henry Wallace, though. "On aesthetic grounds. Four years of that prose and the language is finished." "Elegant detachment is very Catholic," said Woody, who was on to his weakness for originality. "Radicalism for its own sake is very Jewish," said Brian and added, "When you're a successful dentist, *then* we'll talk."

He was continuously puzzled at the way he made friends. He pictured himself as this hard, lonely man—sidestepping the Byron cliché as best he could, only to land splat in the Bogart, O.K., O.K.—but somehow, he could always count on a few people liking him, even when he didn't want them to. One reason was that he was easy to fall in step with after class. For the same reason, people were always asking him directions. Also, he could be pretty funny, not great but adequate, so he attracted the wags. (Funny people *need* each other, he decided, and are ready to overlook gross incompatibilities.) And then maybe there *was* something mysterious about him, eh? a secret wound that fascinated people. O.K., Byron, move over. There's room for both of us.

His new friends were, as a class, physically inept. They weren't always running on ahead of him. In fact, left to themselves, they probably moved even slower than he did. Woody hardly moved at all, but lay on his bed playing Bartok records and planning the revolution.

"We're going to use you as a figurehead, with your permission. You have a lot of Idiot appeal, and God knows we need an Irish Catholic."

"Do I have to tell you what happens to revolutions,

Woody? First, they devour their young. Right? Then, when the romantic figures like me have been liquidated, some fat-faced little accountant moves in and runs the place like a military hospital. Meanwhile, all the biological checks and balances that keep the system healthy have been destroyed. Everyone knows that about revolutions."

"Catholic *shit*. Equilibrium, preferably with me on top. Don't you know that history is movement, for Christsake? Revolutions are happening all the time—good ones, dumb ones, blind ones. Do you think any professional revolutionary could have achieved the changes this country has been through since 1900? Christ, you must have read history in Latin, if you think history has equilibrium."

"I believe in organic change. Manipulated change is artificial."

"Christ, you bought the whole crock, didn't you? You think maybe labor unions are organic? Ask my old man who got his head busted in a garment workers' strike in 1935."

"You lie."

"Nevertheless. *Somebody* got his head busted. It doesn't matter who. Listen, Casey—it isn't a question of deciding whether you want a revolution—you've got one—but which kind you want."

"All right. I'll take one that's made in America. We know our own tastes better than Uncle Joe does."

"That's funny. You get your religion from abroad. Why not your politics?"

And so on. Brian felt that Woody really didn't want to resolve these questions right now, but wanted them to last forever, like summer picnics. "You don't *really* want a revolution, do you Kline? You might have to give up your apartment, for one thing." "I don't know. We'd only have to start another in five minutes to straighten out the first one." Seymour Rankin said, "*I* want one. What the fuck else are we talking about?" "No—Woody really doesn't. He's a professional revolutionary. That's different. A revolution puts him out of business."

Brian found he was beginning to do more talking than reading. He'd been by himself too long. There was a virile affection in this kind of talking, like old heavyweights embracing. Yah, they cuffed each other and snarled, but it was just a way of saying, "I love you." When he tried the same thing at home, though, his mother thought they were real blows, and a couple of times she left the table in tears.

"Dorothy Day is *not* a neurotic."

"All right, all right. If you say so. She isn't. But tell me—what exactly is the point of erecting a pigsty like that in the middle of a slum? I mean, that place of hers on Mott Street is crumbier than any tenement *I* ever saw."

"How many tenements have you seen?" asked sneaky Kevin.

"*That* is a dirty question. I can only say, it *must* be crumbier, because you can't *get* any crumbier. The rats are eating each other down there. And you know what? She won't ask those bums to clean it, because it would be an affront to their dignity."

"Well, it would," said Beatrice. "Those people have been dehumanized, don't you see? By the system. Anyway, a clean floor isn't that important."

"Boy, *you* think it is. You clean *ours* every day. And don't you think maybe that's why we have dignity and they don't? For godsake, Mother—do you think the poor are different from us? How condescending can you get? Don't you think they'd like to have clean houses too? But then you get these romantic slobs from the middle class coming down and saying, 'No no, dirt is *good*. Keep your nice dirt!' You know, if there's one thing that keeps the lousy system going, it's people like Dorothy Day." How'd he arrive at that point? Quick, Mandrake, think of something. I'm smarter than they are. "No, I mean it. The Rich Catholics just love her. 'The poor are *better* than you,' she tells them. 'Right you are,' say the Rich Catholics. 'We are but miserable sinners, the lowliest of men. We wish we had your strength, Miss Day. Now, there's a dollar and get lost.' So, they get to keep the real big money and feel humble into the bargain, and Miss Day gets to be called a saint, which is probably all she wants anyway, and—"

"You don't have to make a speech about it," said Kevin. It was true, there was no affection, no old heavyweights about it. He felt more like a shyster lawyer talking them out of their homestead.

"You twist everything," said Beatrice. "Just for the sake of argument. I know you don't mean it."

He didn't know if he did or not—he was just trying it out. To her this was cold and empty, like everything else they did at Columbia.

"Have you given any more thought to law school?" Kevin asked politely.

"Yeah, I haven't made up my mind yet. Listen—Mother, I know Dorothy Day is a great woman and I wouldn't have the guts to live that way myself. And if we're going to have this system, and maybe we should, then somebody has to look after the people who get broken by it. All I am saying is that if you want *real* change . . ."

It didn't help a bit. He had attacked Dorothy Day, hadn't he? The average mind, he understood, worked in dense murk. Lunging at shadows of comfort or distress. Her eyes filled with tears—now, even after his retraction. Well, maybe the average mind was right. He had attacked Miss Day, that was the reality of the thing. His mood changed: ideas shouldn't really be all in fun. They made people cry. All those guys sitting on their butts, playing Revolution: guys who had never worked a day in their lives, or witnessed a death. His mother was right to cry. His friends and he were the biggest cliché of all, smart-ass college kids. Dorothy Day was real, she had done something, but they could shoot her down for a gag. They could also confuse the Beatrice Caseys and weaken the faith of the murk dwellers, just for the sake of an argument—a cozy, just-us-boys argument. It was time now to give up this childishness and find a faith of his own. If he could. His father coughed sympathetically, as if he understood the problem perfectly.

"I don't know, Woody. I'd sign up for the revolution right now, if there really was one, and if I could really believe in it. But you can't believe in something just for the sake of believing in something, can you?"

"Can't you? That'll come as news to the great American public."

"No, I'm serious. It's not so easy for Catholics anyway. We've really worked all the combinations on faith, you know? Faith from memory, faith from tricksy argument, faith for the sake of the children. We're exhausted by the time we get to politics."

"I know," said Woody. "As a Jew I've been vouchsafed certain insights. And you and I *know,* as the heathens do not, that true believers can actually get by without that much faith."

"How can this be, Mr. Bones? You talk in riddles."

"Listen—take some old priest working the barrios in Brazil, or some Marxist brewing up a storm in Beirut, and ask him how much he believes. He'll blink at you for a minute, wondering why the hell you're wasting his time, and then he'll mumble some line a twelve-year-old wouldn't swallow. Fact is, they've completely forgotten. They're wrapped up in, you should pardon the expression, the existential situation."

"I'm sure you've been sent to me for a purpose, Kline. But what could it be? I mean, if these people have forgotten what they're doing, aren't they a menace?"

"Yeah, that's one catch. That's why we-who-know have to purge them now and then. But seriously, though, what you chose is a way of life, and you *know* whether that's right or not."

"Ah, you secular mystics. Just know, huh? In the blood would that be? Or in the brave cojones?"

"You've got to get over the Reformation *some* time, Casey. I'm not talking about private judgment, if that's what you're worried about. I'm talking about the various collective judgments that are reasonable at any one time. Ally yourself with the best of these and see what happens. If you're lucky, history will pat you on the head and hurry on to its next appointment." The Sunday picnic stretched before them. But Brian wanted to get somewhere this time.

"You know, Woody, I keep taking your arguments home to Mother, and then I make up ones for her to send back to you. We're not getting anywhere. Let's put it this way. I guess as a Catholic I find *any* worldly cause kind of idolatrous—I mean, in five minutes it has its own God and its priests and its junky dogmas, and you just have to start stoning it again. Tell me what's wrong with that."

"No—it's a perfect attitude for a revolutionary. Catholics make terrific revolutionaries, you know."

"But I keep telling you, I don't trust revolutions. They turn to shit after that first good night in the beer cellar. I can only buy *ad hoc* setups, where something good seems to be going on. Like, for instance—" Saints forgive me—"Dorothy Day and *The Catholic Worker*."

"Isn't she God down there? With bums for priests and pacificism for dogma?"

"Shit, Kline—you've got to rest those ruthless powers of analysis sometimes. Do you want to sit in the bathtub and play the trombone all day, or do you want to do something?"

"You've got it at last, Casey. Welcome to the Party."

The next part was disappointing. It seemed that Woody wasn't exactly a Communist—the Berlin–Moscow pact had embittered him at the age of nine, and he'd been shopping around restlessly ever since. It was kind of pointless to be a Trotskyist, what with the old man dead, and nothing seemed to be jelling right in the postwar world. Tito might be worth watching, allow that the murder of Mihailovich may have been dialectically necessary, but there was still something of the gangster opportunist about him—move his country a few miles further west and he'd be endorsing Wheaties. China might be interesting in a year or two.

"Look," said Brian, "if I'm going to do something, I want to *do* it—not just sit here twirling the globe like Lowell Thomas."

"The thing is probably to build revolutionary cells and hand them over to the best power bloc, when the time comes."

"That is just a bunch of words, and you know it. You're still playing, aren't you, Woody?"

"Maybe. Maybe I stop at this point. I'm just a recruiter with a cute smile."

Brian proceeded to ask him the names of groups that were doing things; he didn't know any. Where do we begin then? He couldn't say. The thing now was to lie down again and savor the latest step in one's own development.

"The trouble is," said Brian, over his second quart of beer, "I don't give that much of a shit about developments in Lower Slobovia. You can wait forever for help to arrive from some Communist International—like the Irish waiting for the French Army to pull into Wexford. O.K., maybe the Chinese will finally float a gunboat up the Hudson and lay siege to New Jersey. So what?" He belched a golden mouthful of Ballantine.

"Now who's playing? I'm talking about the future of Latin America—how to weaken the almighty Fruit Lobby, little things like that."

"And I'm talking about fixing up New York City. Tearing down some slums. Giving the colored man a break." He said the words awkwardly, forcing new passions into existence: he hadn't thought about the colored man in years.

"Ah, a meliorist. A little Band-Aid for Madame's cancer?"

Brian suddenly felt suffocated; he wanted to smash the china teacups and take a flaming torch to the guests. Woody's fat, indoor face was like a madam's, inviting him to stay in the whorehouse, the whoring word-house, forever and ever. "You talk too fucking much, you know that Kline? Twenty years from now, you'll still be lying on your back, keeping an eye on developments in Ecuador."

"It's a way of life," said Woody. "I thought you liked to talk."

"Yeah. But it's not a disease with me. What the fuck are *you* doing for Madame's cancer, by the way?" Woody stood, as if to prove he could. "It's no use, Casey. You're an incurable athlete. You think talking will weaken you. It will, too." Woody yawned. It sure as hell had weakened *him.* Still, he would become a teacher someday and sign things. He would send his students into battle. If they felt up to it. Brian had learned a lot from this bastard, but it wasn't enough. Still, it was nice being called an athlete again.

"You're a dangerous man, Casey," said Kline, after a long silence, and opening one eye.

"Ah yes, oh swami? How's that?"

"You want a prophecy? A priceless insight?" He pressed his temples with his fingers. "I see a man stalking Dublin in his trenchcoat. I see a post office . . ."

"Get stuffed. What do you really see?"

"I see a man of little faith and much energy, the most dangerous of your curious human species. A cynical man of action. You could wind up on either side of this thing, you know."

Brian thought, I'd better not believe this or it'll come true for sure. "What you see, Kline, is a storm trooper. You're always seeing storm troopers. Not that I blame you. After the recent unpleasantness."

"Thanks." That wasn't funny. Brian hurried past it.

"Also, you're so dingdong passive that anyone who paces the floor looks like a track star. I just said, Let's do something, and you head for the bomb shelter."

"Maybe, maybe. Anyway, I don't want you in *my* party. You're too rough. Turn in your card and all your bombs."

They had another quart of Ballantine and talked about movies.

14

Analyzing the campus like a bridge hand: the political activists were deuces and treys this year; the aces and kings were the political dropouts. The guys who knew the mythical Kerouac and typed their haikus on toilet paper. The political groups had to be kept going, like Protestant churches, by *somebody*. But the best people weren't doing it any more. The Wallace fiasco had knocked the stuffing out of them. Harry S. Nonentity would now proceed to nail down the Iron Curtain for good, and spangle the globe with good U.S. Steel.

"What do you say we just give up?" Brian said to Woody one day.

"And enjoy the imperial decadence, you mean? Not me. I have a commitment to my father's busted head."

"I myself have half a mind to cultivate my own garden for a spell," said Brian. "Under a spreading nuclear umbrella."

"I love it when you talk, Casey. All those words and everything."

Actually, part of Brian's brain *was* attracted by the imperial vision: Roman legions marching out through the gate of Janus. American soldiers with the Sun on their helmets, manning their checkpoints—just *as a picture,* he liked it better than the scruffy losers, the pale-faced clergy of the Left. You'd be inhuman not to.

"I guess there's some of the fascist pig in all of us," he said.

"Yeah? You find that?"

"A little bit, sure. Be honest about it, Kline. Don't you get just a small aesthetic boot out of a well-drilled army doing its stuff?"

"It makes me sick."

"O.K., O.K. It was just a passing fancy. So what do you propose we do now? Please don't say call a meeting. I couldn't stand another meeting."

"Fucking snobbery."

"Fucking condescension to you. You're just as bored by them as I am. You know perfectly well that the jerkoffs do all the talking at meetings, the little farts with the five-part questions. Mark my words: the Left will bore itself to death at meetings before the enemy even finds us."

"You're right about fascist pig. What do you want? A well-drilled army? Or one smart guy named Casey to take the place of meetings?"

"He doesn't have to be named Casey. Look, Kline. Are we that committed to inefficiency? Let's have a little Stalinization around here. You know what happens at meetings. After everyone has voiced his scruples and registered his outrage, we finally agree to draft a telegram. 'We, the undersigned, wish to deplore . . .' 'Denounce,' shouts Fred the Fart. 'All right, denounce. Denounce in the strongest . . .' 'Most unequivocal,' screams Jerry Jerkoff. 'That's two words, at night letter rates—' "

"O.K., skip the crap and get to the story point."

"All right. 'Denounce in the strongest terms the continuation of nuclear testing. Signed, the Turn Left Society of Columbia University.' The cable arrives at the White House. The blood drains from the Chief Executive's face. 'By God, fellows, this alters everything. I've just heard from the Turn Left Society.' "

"Very cruel and very easy," said Woody. "The boys in the German High Command would have roared over that one. The pathetic little people with their puny telegrams."

"Hey, you're really sore, aren't you, Woody?"

"Damn right I am. O.K., a telegram isn't much. I happen to think it helps. Maybe we can think of something better next time. But Jesus, what's the good of anything, if we give up the principle of discussion? What's the good of the Left if you sneer at the farts and jerkoffs?"

What good indeed? "I don't know, Woody. I really don't.

I believe all the same things you do. I think capitalism is a pile of shit. I think New York City is a crock of crap, and it's the best we have. So? I can't see a string of Henry Wallaces setting things right."

"That lousy campaign," said Woody. "How many generalizations can you draw from one lousy campaign?"

"Plenty," said Brian. He looked around. Cold winter light curtained the window. A depressing time to talk about anything. The aimless conversation had finally bumped against something bad. There was distress in Kline's face—you're not my brother after all. That, Brian swore, was all that happened that day. The well-drilled army had done it: yeah, face it Casey, you admired *that* one too, the one Woody's thinking about. Brian had always feared that when they got to the end of their argument, he would be on the wrong side. Woody looked at him and shrugged. Brian nodded. "O.K., then." "You want the rest of this beer?" "You have it." Time to move on.

Kerouac's disciples didn't appeal to him at all. Through the agency of a classmate he got himself invited to a couple of their parties, and it was almost as bad as going to meetings. There were always the one or two original guys, and hordes of imitations. The "hmm, good tea, man" crowd. Zen had its own Fred Farts and Jerry Jerkoffs. Intolerant bastard, Casey. O.K. then, I envy them. I am the real brain in the glass bowl. I cannot take the road and screw Mexican peasants on the hoods of hot rods. I envy those who can.

He didn't even chance smoking the tea, until he'd tried it in safer circumstances; and beer did not set you up right for this kind of party. Still, he made some friends. Brad Jackson, who took off his pants when he wanted people to go home. Gary de Falco, who shouted, "You all eat shit" whenever he felt he was being ignored or slighted. At the second party Brian got a chance to ask them both over to his place for a beer. If he could get the originals without the imitations he might find something he could use. They arrived the next afternoon with jugs of Muscat. His mother took one look and actually left the house.

"You wonder why I've asked you all here," said Brian.

Brad waved his hand. "Never gave it a thought."

"I wanted to ask you how you stand the company at those parties?"

"What company? I don't see any company at those parties."

"I see. Next question. Who did you vote for in the last election?"

"I think I can answer that for you," said de Falco. "I voted for Won Hung Lo, great white hope to topple Ming Dynasty."

"Fine American," said Jackson. "Great war record."

They gave Brian some marijuana, which made him giggle. They called him Philosopher Casey and asked him his plans for the Chinese New Year.

"No spesha plan. Liberate coolies. Try get closer to number 1 wife." Brian snuffled with laughter at his own multicolored opacity: his face, which he could see very well from inside, was red and rheumy as a dragon. Aarf, Kerchow. Fire ran up and down him like a maddened elevator. They played some Andre Kostelanetz records, the hottest item the Caseys owned, and Brian shook with glee, especially over the violins. The others paid no mind to him. After a while, de Falco said, "Kostelanetz eats shit. They all do, you know." And Jackson said, "They don't write music like Beethoven any more." "Listen," said Brian from his underwater home, "this isn't Beethoven, it's Jerome Kern." "I know," said Jackson. Brian shrieked.

"Gotta go now," said de Falco. "You've been a wonderful audience."

"Don't go," said Brian. "You just got here."

"Been here for two hours. Muscat's gone. Say hello to your mother." They were undulating toward the door already.

"Wait! You! The one with the striped ass!" shouted Brian. But they were gone. He shaded his eyes with his hand and dry-heaved with laughter. He was still agitating when his mother came in, sniffing, with a shopping bag. "What's the smell, Brian? What are you laughing about?" she asked. "Nothing. You–just–look–so–funny!" He fell sideways, and his gut landed on a spike of laughter and ground itself out. She helped him up, and he sat trembling slightly. She looked frightened but didn't say anything. After a while he calmed down, and nothing more was said about it.

Disgusting, sloppy, wasteful. Made a fool of self. Got to

keep a clear head. 'Sall I've got. Still idling irregularly. Missing a cylinder or two. He had a slight relapse that night, or a sunburst of memory. Muscat and marijuana, making their last rounds. Got to do something useful, mustn't fuck up like those guys. Have been given great gifts, my son, therefore great responsibilities. Mustn't squander them in the bath water. His head right now was a damp cellar with people bumping into each other and shouting "ouch" and "ah ha!" and he was happy to wake up to a clear blue day and find his mind bright as silver.

He decided he might as well give the Turn Left Society another whirl, just for something to do. The losers with the gravy stains might look better after his afternoon with the winners, the windblown lords of creation. Woody Kline raised an eyebrow when he saw Brian come in, and so help me turned his back. Geez, you know, the guy hates me. He's had time to think. Do I mind? No. Fuck him. Try to win him back? See if I can?

"Hi, Woody. Sieg Heil and all that."

"You shit."

Never win him back that way. Ah, well. Having enemy not all bad. At least somebody's thinking about you. Promise you'll never change, Woody. Promise you'll never grow indifferent.

They took their places on rickety auditorium chairs, and the meeting droned to life. It seemed there was a crisis of leadership. Chairman Zeke Snyder had defected to the Right with a snarl. "Must have been something he read," said Deputy Chairman Rankin. So they needed a new boy, and would somebody like to propose someone. Woody's name came up, but he said he wasn't the boss type. Fucking prig. He in turn proposed promoting Rankin, who smiled demurely as if sources close to Rankin felt that he would not refuse a draft. Brian was amusing himself making up a speech for Rankin—"Unfortunately my opponents have seen fit to take the low road. They have resorted to Goebbels's tactic of the Big Lie and the unsupported smear—" when he heard his own name mentioned. Someone must be kidding.

He looked back at Woody, who was glaring at him ferociously from the rear left corner. O.K., Woody, you asked for it. "Would Member Casey accept the nomination?"

"Sure. Why not?"

"What kind of answer is that?" bawled Woody. "You think this is a joke or something?"

"I'm sorry I offended Member Kline. I was shocked by the question. Let me try again. Yes, I would be honored by the nomination."

Woody was on his feet. "Maybe Member Casey would like to take another minute before deciding. It's my understanding that he doesn't approve of meetings or popular assemblies of any kind."

Your bid, Casey. Wait till they're all looking. Slowly does it. Like stealing diamonds. Now. "Member Kline must be referring to some facetious words I had with him in private. I didn't know you were taking them down, Woody. Obviously, gentlemen, I wouldn't be here if I didn't approve of meetings."

A little too smooth? Maybe. We'll see.

"You make it sound pretty sinister with that 'in private' stuff," said Woody. "I'm sorry I broke the seal of the confessional, Casey. Most conversations are held in private. I just thought you might like to be reminded of your own convictions."

"Thanks. Was there anything else?"

Woody took a lunging step forward and flung a hand through his black hair. Brian thought he was about to shout "Strike!" No idea Woody was capable of such passion. Don't underrate the little people, Herr Commandant. Woody was locked in some terrible moral struggle. To go on now, he must expose more of that private conversation, and it obviously went against his conscience. Big sissy. Brian smiled. Go ahead, I'll truss *you* up in that conversation and carry you out in it.

"I have reason to think this guy is not suitable," said Kline.

What reason, what reason?

"I don't believe he is in sympathy with the purposes of the club. I believe he is an ambitious guy who would like to run anything he could get his hands on, just for the sake of running something . . ."

"I don't know if psychiatric evidence is admissible," said Brian. "What about someone who is afraid to run *anything?*" The medical twist reminded Brian, as he seldom was these days, of his legs. They would be an ambiguous factor for an onlooker to weigh. Was this same embittered cripple compensating with crazy power drives? Or was he a wise man matured by pain? You be the judge. One thing that was clear was that his enemy was standing and he was seated. He looked up at Woody with a mild, peaceful expression. "I may be ambitious, Woody, but remember, I didn't ask for this nomination."

Woody sat down. He must have sensed the flow of sympathy, which was rushing down toward Brian. "Casey admires the German Army," he said desperately.

Anger now, or lose it all. Very slow burn. Long glare. Then—"Are you kidding, Woody? That's the meanest, craziest thing I ever heard. I don't know why you don't want me to have this job, I thought you were my friend; but I didn't think you'd go this far to stop *any*body."

"What exactly did Casey say to you?" asked Rankin grimly. There were only about twelve guys present, but there was a nice little smell of danger. Get him now, boy.

"I don't remember exactly," said Woody, "but I remember what he meant."

"*I* remember," said Brian. "I said I had an aesthetic admiration for precision drill. I didn't say anything about Germans. Obviously, if I admired the Nazi Army, I would not be attending the Turn Left Society. Unless Member Kline believes that I joined it in order to get myself nominated, so I could take it over and silence a vital voice on the Left."

Woody must see by now that his opposition had guaranteed Brian's victory by acclamation. "Christ, you're even worse than I thought," he said, directly to Brian, and stalked to the door. Hell, I've made a fool of him, thought Brian. Why did I do that? It wasn't necessary; and besides, he was half-right. More than half. "Look, Woody—if I get elected, I hope you'll stay." Woody hovered over his galoshes, paying no attention. Brian wanted to add, "Look, I can honor a contract. I'll run it the way you want me to," but of course, that would be admitting his guilt. "We *need* you, Woody." Woody stomped down on his galosh. You can't argue with a cripple, can you? Take the job, cripple.

Brian could do no more. Technically, Woody had insulted him. Magnanimity was O.K., but truckling was out. Too bad. It was messy and regrettable. One shouldn't have to shed blood.

He didn't get his acclamation. A couple of members trusted Woody and viewed Brian now with sour-eyed suspicion. Interesting. They would doubtless resign, after a talk with Kline, leaving Brian in charge of nine members, plus two absentees. What the shit did it matter? Tomorrow he would start recruiting, and make this club something *worth* fighting over. His veins ran carbonated cream as the votes were counted. Hot damn! "Five votes for Casey, one vote for Rankin." That wasn't something so very terrible he'd done to Kline. Woody had botched the German Army story hopelessly. The guy was unbalanced on the Nazi question. "Eight for Casey, nine for Casey." Hell, he turned on me first.

"Would you like to say a few words?"

Here was a game he could play with anybody. Woody had lost within the rules. Brian stood up slowly, locking his knee braces. His legs were part of his political equipment now, part of the game. Which made it all quite different. "I'd love to," he said.

15

Broaden the base. Get outside speakers. Offer free silver. He buzzed with plans. Stage a protest. A student strike against nuclear testing, on the steps of the Low Library. Prod the university's fat ass. He sat in his room, trying to calm himself with agendas. He knew that what he needed now was sex, in massive doses. Not cold mechanical masturbation: he could pump till dawn, without rooting out the excitement. He had to pass it on to someone else.

Go out and have a drink, anyway. Talk brilliantly at the West End Bar. To a small audience of semiparalyzed soaks. He went quietly down the hall. His parents still snored out of tune. You'd think that they'd have worked that out after twenty-five years. Shut the door quietly. Did he really want to go to the West End? It stank of compromise. So many second-rate evenings died there in squalor, he wanted another *victory* tonight.

He took the subway downtown at 116th Street instead. The car was mysteriously full for the time of night. Yellow faces bounced and shook in the dirty light. Let me make you a speech. *That's* why I've brought you all down here to my subway. Goddamn, he wanted to see that look again. The look of blind attention in the guys' faces. He would get that look from a woman someday or die in the attempt.

Only eleven people had heard him tonight. God knows what his first large crowd would do to him. Couldn't do much more, he supposed. You can only take in so many faces anyway. In fact, he remembered just two, Pete Simmons and Jerry Wineberg. Both guys rather surly in real life. A speaker receives devotion that nobody else is allowed to see. Like a doctor examining women patients. Cool off now with more plans. Cancel the protest at the library. Helling around Columbia is like setting fire to your own playground. Move it downtown. Pick a pressure point, where a dozen guys can snarl up the whole city. Reroute all these yellow faces that travel forever on the subway. Get arrested? Of course. But make great speech to the police. And another great speech in court. Also speech to warden, chaplain, and man who brings breakfast. The yellow faces nodded, glassy-eyed.

He got out at Fiftieth Street. He'd heard about a bar. Didn't know if he had enough money. Buy a drink and see.

A flossy, dead-looking place, as advertised. Man in white, polishing glasses, like surgical equipment. Two suicide blondes at the far end of the bar. Hard to explain, but whole scene extremely sexy. Better think of another plan. March on City Hall, maybe. Lead it in wheelchair. One of the girls came up. "Buy me a drink, dear?" He nodded. Her face was creased, but when you thought of how she got the creases, you saw that it was a fine, sexy face. An honorable face. Worthy of his debut. She sipped her drink and put a hand on his knee. Came up with a handful of brace. Had the politeness to leave it there.

"Where you from?" he asked.

"Iowa."

"Why did you leave?"

"Everybody leaves Iowa."

"Miss it?"

Shrug.

He wanted to know more about her, but could find no reasonable questions. Married? Hardly the thing. Like her work? Live near here? Live near here.

"Do you live near here?"

"I have a room at the Coronia. Sometimes I stay at my sister's in Jamaica. It's nice up there."

Fine girl. He put a hand on *her* knee and was surprised at the harshness of the nylon. Was this what German girls sold their bodies for? Incredible. Nylons and cigarettes. It was a ridiculous exchange.

"Have you been to Jamaica?" she asked.

He shook his head. "Do you come here every night?"

"Most nights." She looked uncomfortable. Interrogations probably had bad associations.

"You must like it," he said. "Would you like some more tea?"

She shuffled under his hand, as if to escape. But he patted her knee and smiled encouragement. "It's O.K., I don't mind what you drink. Tea is good for you."

She smiled back, uneasily. Poor woman. Don't worry, I'll do the talking. You just sit there. He asked her if she'd ever made a speech. No? He had. It was fantastic. You know, a bit like *your* work. The excited johns. At the end, who has had whom? I don't know. The speaker is the one who gets paid.

She looked as blank as she probably would have if a crazy customer was whipping her, but she picked up the reference to her work and seemed about to protest. She didn't really do this for a living, you know. But she let it pass. The whole thing must be so goofy and boring. She slid her hand further up his brace until it rested on his groin. Damnit, he was trapped in there. She extricated him. It was a kindness. She smiled slightly past him. Her breath came heavy on his face, and a smell that must be lipstick. It was all much warmer and heavier than he had expected.

"Can we go to your place?" he said.

"I can't leave here till the bar closes."

"Then?"

"I don't know."

"What do you mean you don't know?"

"I'm not supposed to."

What the hell kind of racket was this? She was into him for two tea and sodas. Was he just paying for her conversation? and her desolate company? God, talking to her was like sitting alone in a cheap hotel room. Off an air shaft.

"Can I have another drink?"

"Are you kidding?"

She pressed his groin again. Brian noticed the barman frowning. Maybe she was exceeding her duties already.

"Got to go to bathroom," said Brian. "We'll discuss it when I get back." But when he turned round a moment at the men's room door, the bartender was talking to her, and when he returned to his seat, she was back at the far end with her partner.

He sat down storming. God knows, he did not feel very good about what he was doing. But such as it was, he should be allowed to do it . . . he glared at her, but she wouldn't catch his eye; glared at her friend—how about you, honey? Have some nice tea with Brian? The bartender was watching him now, like a fat cobra. "What's the matter with you, Jack?" said Brian. The bartender looked away. "What kind of joint are you running, Jack? Would greasy little clip joint describe it?"

The man was polishing glasses again.

"Christ, why don't you pee in them? That's even cheaper than your finest oolong."

The man glanced at the window. "You'd better get out of here, kid."

"That's a great line. Did you make it up yourself?" Brian

shouted. Different speeches for different audiences. He would get a rise out of this animal somehow.

The man kept looking at the window. Probably some police friend passed the spot every now and then. Brian wouldn't have a chance. They could make up any story they liked. Unspeakable shakedowns would follow; mother sobbing quietly in police station, father smirking. We should never have adopted the little buzzard, my dear.

O.K., some honor was salvaged. "It's a privilege to be thrown out of your little shithouse. I'm only sorry for the people who have to stay." He headed sedately for the door. "You have my sympathy," he said to the girl. "Are you sure you don't want to come with me?"

Her eyes were blank, even of fear and embarrassment. She wouldn't look at him. The bartender watched him all the way to the door. What a lousy system. Girls living like that. "Did your mother ever think it would end like this?" he called to the bartender.

When he hit the sidewalk, he found the excitement was still with him, worse than ever. He still wanted that woman, dull heaviness, smell of lipstick, and all.

He stood indeterminately outside. Forty-five minutes to closing time, a long time to be standing innocently on a sidewalk. Two cops did pass him, with the same bilious stare as the barman. There was only one expression in this town, dull hate. New York was like a huge retarded family with a history of syphilis. God, he hated this town tonight, and its whole sick bloodstream, graft, shakedowns, mean yellow eyes. "What do you boys get out of life?" he wanted to ask the cops, but decided better not. They would pick him up on the way back anyway, and have him before a crooked little magistrate in no time, a greedy venomous hunchback who happened to be the mayor's brother.

He could just make out the burned-out sign of the Coronia Hotel, a block away. He'd passed it before, a dimly lit walk-up with the lobby on the third floor, and often wondered what kind of people went there. Now was the time to find out. O.K., Mauriac, O.K., Greene, he thought as he pushed open the grimy glass door a minute later and started up the stairs. Sin was supposed to be like this. The last time he'd been up stairs like this, he was looking for a miracle. This time, he was looking for something a little more reasonable.

You could hardly call it a lobby: just a space with a teller's window. A fat lady peered between the bars, another cheery New York face. "You want a room? It's one-fifty, cash in advance."

"No, I'm just waiting for someone."

"Who're you waiting for?"

"I don't know her name."

"Well, you can't wait here, buddy."

"Is that right?" He leaned against a peeling wall, facing her. There were no chairs, nothing, it was just a space. Was she going to call the cops, or throw him out herself? After giving him that just-watch-it-kid-that's-all glare, she went back to her paper work, whatever the hell that might be. Hey, you notice something, Casey? Nobody ever *does* anything around here. All is empty menace. He wanted to go over to the grille and shout, "You're all under arrest."

Twenty minutes to go. Awkward standing here, back, shoulders stiff, hands sore with sweat on the crutch cross-pieces. Acts of defiance take their toll. A skinny girl in a slit black skirt came up the stairs and gave him a long, slow look, presumably an invitation. If so, no thanks. He wanted Miss Iowa tonight. He wouldn't take an ounce less. Besides, she had touched him, it was like an engagement. The girl picked up her key, mumbled into the grille, shrugged. They both looked at him, and he smiled charmingly back. Nobody knows what to do with me. A white American cripple can go anywhere.

Another girl came up, heavy-assed, heavy of soul, with barely enough energy to look him over bleakly, before picking up her key and disappearing. This must be the after-theater rush.

Ten more minutes. "Your friend won't be coming now."

"I'll wait," he said. What you don't know, madam, is that I am the deputy mayor's son. The one who went all queer. Surely you remember? Everyone in this town was so sunk in corruption that they all feared each other: they didn't know how much power the others wielded. Maybe this wasn't such a bad system after all. He'd have been arrested ten times over in a civilized city.

His mind kept turning back to Columbia politics, to help the time drag past. The bars had been closed for half an hour now, and Miss Fu Manchu looked as if she was getting ready to close up shop. Thrilling wrestling match between the Irish champ and the fat lady. He couldn't give up now. He'd even take the skinny one, if necessary. Or grab the subway out to Jamaica and scour the streets.

The fat lady seemed to be lingering now for his sake. Embarrassment? Kindness? What secrets lurk in the hearts of men, eh, Graham? He was frozen to the wall, kept taut by the act of balancing, wondering what the hell he was doing here: hoping for two minutes of mortal sin with a plain girl on a dirty bed, that's what. Even a whiskey priest would give up and go home at this point. But I can't give up, you see. That's the thing.

She arrived at last, and when she saw him, she gave a real, full-bodied start. Beautiful. The man with the questions had followed her here. The vice squad was sending out its special platoon of gimps to trap her.

"Hi," he said.

She just stared.

"I waited for you."

She got her key and again the two ladies looked at him. Like two spinsters staring at a cat burglar.

"Which is your room?" he said. Miss Iowa looked at the teller. This was it. Throw-out time or victory. The fat lady shrugged helplessly, the big pussycat. The girl started toward the adjoining corridor where all the girls had gone, not beckoning him but walking slowly, as if to allow for his pace. He'd won, because they didn't know what else to do with him.

"I only have eight dollars," he said. "I can send you more."

She nodded. Any sum would have done, or none. It was strange. He had expected, he now knew, to be treated like a child, the ladies explaining why it was all impossible and finally bundling him into a cab. But somehow he had overpowered them. Oh, he was hot tonight. He could have overpowered anybody tonight.

The room was even fouler than he expected. Great morose stains on the sheets, and when he opened the little drawer by the bed, a teeming muddy contraceptive lingered from the last visitor. Go boy, wallow. It was his trysting place, his rendezvous with love. The shrine was scented with dust and day-old sweat. He reached for the girl's hips to haul up her skirt, but she walked away and whipped the skirt off herself, a simple wrap-around job held by a safety pin, to reveal a panoply of garters and stocking tops and sweet, mottled thighs.

He sat on the bed, the better to bury his head in the looming softness. But again she outfoxed him. She took off her pants with the same sexless economy and sat down beside him, unzipping his fly in a businesslike way, as if preparing him for a medical examination. In a moment she was playing with him, and he had to admit it was very nice, until he realized she was bringing him to a quick boil just to get it over with. He pushed her away.

"Hey, not so fast. I want to enjoy this."

"Ooh honey, I can't wait. I want it so badly." He'd never heard such a silly voice. He wanted to slap it out of her.

"Well you'll just *have* to wait," he said, and flung his face at her legs. She squirmed a moment and pushed at his hair with her hands. "Oh honey, I want it so badly. Put it in now."

"Shut up," he said, and kissed her thighs and her hair until she was still, and then finally, though the angle was awkward, kissed her pussy itself, very wet and slippery, a delight he'd wondered about so often, very strange, the smell a complete surprise, though he'd heard jokes, the whole thing not so much wonderful as infinitely surprising. She was trying to play with him again, and again he pushed her away. The vice squad must have its money's worth. A quiet, tactful struggle for supremacy—her eyes were apprehensive when he squinted round at them (God knows, there was no describing the position they had gotten into now), and her voice was stock-company seductive, but her methods were still crisp and professional.

One way and another, he did all the things he wanted to, glaring down every eruption of impatience (hate me but remember me), and when he was ready, he refused to let her get on top, though she thought it might be easier for him that way. Childish perhaps, but he had a premonition he could call the tunes better from up there.

Right he was (God, the mind was clear tonight). She began to buck and writhe immediately, with passion as trumped up as her stupid voice, urging him to come and flood her with delight. But he held firm, and the writhings mixed with his own stillness produced perfection, the lay of a lifetime. A million-dollar mistress could do no more —and this was just a two-bit whore trying to polish him off fast.

Sensing the hopelessness of it, she gave up and lay still,

and he commenced his own deep motions. "Are you nearly finished?" she asked, all the tenderness gone. If she'd been doing him a favor, it was long used up. Good. He shook his head on her cheek. Christ, I'm a bastard. Has anyone ever gotten more for eight bucks?

He wished now that the clarity of mind would go away. One did this to stop thinking, damnit, to encounter God or the devil in speechless wonder. Well, not tonight. Too greedy perhaps. As he ground on, it began to feel mechanical, and he thought, shit, Casey, you're a superficial character. And he thought, the poor girl has had enough, I mustn't outwear my welcome. For a moment, he thought he'd left it too late, but then it came thundering out as sweet as could be. And when Cinderella looked around, the room was hideous and yellow with filth and the girl was old and pathetic and her thighs were fat, listless splotches. "Have you had enough?" she said in an old lady's voice. "I don't know," he said. "I really don't." Then he added, "Thank you."

"Don't forget to wash yourself, and leave the money on the table."

He hadn't even taken off his pants. She hadn't seen him in his naked beauty. Tough nuts to her.

She watched him leave, relieved, angry, who knows? Out in the lobby the office was shut, but the fat lady was waiting by the wall. A speech for madam? No speech. Awfully tired. Please excuse. She watched him to the stairs. He said "Good night," but if she answered he didn't catch it.

Remorse? Oh sure. Pale catechism remorse, almost gone

by now. He controlled that argument himself. Forgive me, I have loved much. Also, dirt remorse, cheapness remorse. That terrible room had seemed like a lovers' bower to him for a time. And he had exploited the girl worse than any bartender. Much to think about on the way home.

Exultation? Oh yes. Fantastic.

16

The Turn Left Society got so big it finally burst in three. Woody Klinc, fighting with kamikaze persistence, set up a Turn Left Society to the Left of Left. Ex-Chairman Snyder tried to start a Revised Turn Left Society on the Right, a special End of Ideology wing, but that in turn split like a firework, and Brian's branch remained the main onc.

They did some page 8 things, like picketing Ibn-Saud at the Waldorf and Cardinal Spellman during the grave-diggers' strike, which Woody Kline called a politics of gesture. And they got in some Marxist lecturers who Woody said were out of date—doddering windbags and tabby cats. "Is it just my breath?" Brian cabled him from two blocks away. "That has a lot to do with it," Woody cabled back.

One saw quickly the limitations of a society like the Turn Left. It appealed, like religion, to only one kind of temperament—somewhere between the jock and the theatrical. The rest of the campus chewed its own corner of meadow. To appeal to them, you had to put on a show of a kind which involved changing your nature. Brian gave it a try, with his special orgy committee, which held a mass meeting to discuss the possibilities of spring orgies on Morningside Heights, the proceeds to go to Harlem redevelopment. "Christ, that's a cute idea," bellowed Woody, and Brian had to agree.

Politics purely as a game was an incurably minority sport. Nothing Brian could do seemed to attract the best minds on campus—well, even he was getting a bit bored with Ibn-Saud. Meanwhile, the new Zen masters cackled at the club's earnest efforts, and Woody said, "You're playing, Casey, it's all you can do." Be nice to impress old Woody. Crucifixion and resurrection might just do it.

By spring, Turn Left had become pretty much a social club. Brian rented a clubhouse out of subscriptions and all kinds of non-political people began dropping in with tennis rackets. "When are you having your first tea dance?" cabled Woody—telegrams being their new hostility gag. "You really like me, I mean, deep down, don't you?" Brian asked Kline the next time they met. "No," said Woody. "Deep down, it's worse."

Still, Woody was his political conscience. In a last effort to be serious, Brian called a special meeting to propose that the club set itself up as a real student government, sort of a shadow administration to haunt the real one. "The last refuge of feudalism," he told them, in that lovely musical voice. "A campus consists mostly of students—so naturally, they're on the bottom. They have no voice at all. The faculty is in the middle, so they're allowed a little squeaky voice, but no power. Then you have the magnates, the trustees, call them 'absentee landlords,' with no connection with education whatever, nothing but their fleecy pigskin wallets."

"To save you having to make a speech—I don't *want* to run a university," said one of the new members. "And I don't want to run a hotel either. Being a guest is better, believe me."

"How do you feel about prisons?" said Brian. It stopped the sniggers like hiccoughs. Quick dirty shots were sometimes best. "Anyway, I'm not talking about running the place, I'm just talking about minimal representation . . ."

"And the greater glory of Casey," shouted Woody.

Shut up, you fool. I'm doing this to impress you. "Look, Kline, why don't you play your old records at your own meetings? You can be sure of not being interrupted there."

"Numbers game," said Woody. "You're boasting about your big fat membership again."

"Yeah, what you call a numbers game, we call democracy. Listen, Kline, we happen to have a subject tonight and we'd like to talk about it, O.K.? The subject is student government."

"We already have a student government," whinnied somebody.

"You're referring to the Toothless Wonder, I believe. Look—I'm talking about power."

"Bet your ass you are," said Kline.

"Students *don't* have real power," said Zeke Snyder. "So why pretend they do? What kind of progressive-school charade you playing, Casey?"

Brian answered him, and the next, and the next. But soon they were arguing with each other, and the meeting spun out of control. The magic wasn't working worth a damn.

"Order, order," he shouted. A pause, and then another roar of argument. God, they were maddening. Some clown was talking about women in the dormitories. Somebody else wanted to know where he could park his car during gym class. That sense of a monster rally with the hundred-foot flag behind him and one spirit in front of him had evaporated into meaningless student babble.

"Order." No pause this time, no chance to use his weapons. Goddamnit to hell. "Shut *up*," he screamed.

"Temper, temper," said Woody.

"I adjourn the meeting," he said and walked stiffly off the platform, trying to contain his suppurating rage, trying not to look like a stage villain thwarted by John Doe. Nobody paid any attention. He headed as calmly as he could for the subway to see what he could find downtown.

He resigned from the Turn Left Society next day. It was true what they said about intellectuals—all sexless playboys, using their brains like water pistols. He was especially disgusted with himself for having taken their admiration seriously: admiration was just another fad around here. Vanity, my son. Anyway, looking at things more coolly. There were no real politics on campus, because nobody had real interests. It was like playing poker without money. He concentrated on his studies and on plans to get into law school. Then, a place in the cabinet. No messing around.

Being funny was already a little harder, drier than it used to be—a safety valve, consciously resorted to. As a junior, he understood why they called some jokes sophomoric: giggle jokes, sloppy as sophomore drinking. He hated Columbia now. People like Kline could beat you at Columbia, because they didn't play for money.

He still lived at home, damnit, and his mother picked up after him. It used to irritate him to be fussed over, but there wasn't much he could do about it. As long as he lived, old ladies would want to carry him up the stairs. It was over a year since he'd hit one with his elbow. Real maturity.

"You forgot to dust the desk," he told his mother. If she was going to tidy for him, she might as well do it right.

She was expert by now at dusting around him as he worked. Being slaved over was a mark of kings and cripples. It's how you look at it. "Watchit, Mother." She was trying to dust under his papers. "You're disturbing my chaos." She did as she was told. "And don't be so meek about it," he said. "You don't have to take that stuff from me." She smiled uncertainly. Long hours of kidding, hectoring, talking half to oneself, had altered their relationship somehow. Gradually, unnoticeably, he had gained verbal ascendancy. Maybe talking to someone who was down on her knees so much was what did it.

"What do you want me to be when I grow up?" he asked facetiously.

"Happy," she said, quicker than he expected.

"Is that all?"

"A good Catholic man. And happy."

"What do you think Father wants me to be?"

"I think he'd like you to do well at something."

"Is that all?"

His mother paused. She was almost dusting his hands by now. Look, we don't analyze each other, dear, except on very special occasions.

"I think he wants you to be a great man," she said vaguely.

"Why can't he be one himself?"

"I don't know. He is one in his way."

"No he's not. Come *on,* Mother. What happens to people? He's a talented guy. A witty guy. Yet he hasn't made a good joke in nine months. And you *know* he's just a hack architect now." He held up a hand to silence protest. "He doesn't *read* anything any more. All he ever says is, 'I think I'll turn in now, busy day tomorrow.' Is this something that just happens to men? Do they all crawl into a corner and die? Will *I* get to be like that?"

"I don't think so." She looked as if she wanted to get

out of here, to get away from this talk. "He works very hard."

"Yeah, but he doesn't get anywhere. You know when I think he gave up? Around the time I got polio. And he didn't want me to go to Salt Rock. It was like he'd lost his nerve."

It was very bad form at the Caseys, taking oneself too seriously. To suppose that he was the cause of his father's decline—supposing his father *had* declined—was insupportable presumption. Beatrice bridled, a touch of the old fire.

"Didn't *want* you to go to Salt Rock? Have you any idea what he went through to get you to Salt Rock?—he was already working eighteen hours a day to pay for specialists and physiotherapists and all. Yes, he'd be up all night with his drawings sometimes. Things were quite strained around here. He even drank a little to keep his strength up. Of course that doesn't work, you know, and don't you ever try it . . ."

Oh Jesus.

"I think he was so relieved when that was over that perhaps he hasn't been quite so ambitious since."

Oh double Jesus. Shut up. Don't tell me *now*. About your sacrifices, about my own callousness. Or about how the game was fixed and the victories meaningless. I honestly don't think I can stand it. His mother looked at him: she must see a furious face, the skin screaming. She said, "Is anything wrong?" Nothing. I just killed my father, that's all, the way I'm supposed to. You've brought him to me in your mouth, like a dead bird. Only, you're dead too. Yeah, Brian Casey has cut a swath on his way to the family throne. His mother edged away and resumed dusting, busier than ever.

PART TWO

The Perkins Papers

1

The street hadn't changed: the wall was still straight and the houses looked like a row of grandfather chairs. The apartment couldn't have changed much either. It still had a forties look to it, a greyness deeper than dust, Brian Casey's log cabin. They don't build them like they used to. The sofa was worn to a thread, but there was a mobile over by the upright piano that got us up to the fifties, I guess, and a leather chair you couldn't get out of without help. I could almost see Brian's wheelchair in the doorway, and the two parents looking at him with strained smiles.

I wasn't that interested in them right then, they were just another late-middle-aged couple, ice-cold clues. Kevin looked the more youthful and with-it of the two, with rich white hair and an unlined face. But his style was as dated as the apartment. I also sensed an old Irish politician in there somewhere, or maybe I was reading that in: anyway, a dishonest charm. He didn't drink any more, according to my sources, but he made you think about drinking. Beatrice Casey looked older than her husband, as if she took trouble right on the face instead of wherever he took it, but most noticeably she looked starved for someone to talk to. Well, I get that feeling about most women her age.

At that point, it was just a job.

I talked with them at length about Brian's conquest of polio. I was there officially to work on a campaign biography in which conquests of polio are very much the thing. When I hooked up again with Brian in Indiana, he was sarcastic about that, said that it was a fake and he didn't want to be known as destiny's cripple; he also said, "How do you conquer polio—you just *have* it." But I insisted on putting it in. We had to do something with it.

Besides that, there's a personal problem here. The only sickness I ever had myself was the measles, when I was seven, and so I have an unholy respect for pain and disease, and I find it impossible to believe that polio could have been quite the casual experience he describes. Anyway, I laid it on medium-thick in the campaign biography, and he laughed and said, "Your book made me cry. But believe me, Sam—" And he told me his stories of Salt Rock and the leeches with bitter high spirits, reminding me a little of one of those GI's of his at Salt Rock, trying to make his young listener sick.

I am, of course, the young listener, Sam Perkins from Newton, Mass., guessing what it was like to be growing up in 1945, or maybe trying not to; trying not to be distracted by old movies, fashions, phony nostalgia, cars. It can't have *felt* that different. People didn't go around thinking, This is 1945 and this year we're dancing the jitterbug and reading *A Tree Grows in Brooklyn,* or whatever the hell they were doing. They just did it. It isn't important to Casey anyway. He is definitely not a décor man.

The campaign biography came and went. It was reviewed along with eight others in the Big Paper, and the man said, Well, it's more honest than some. I allowed that Senator Casey lost his temper and swore a bit, took a drink and hated football. Honesty was a big thing in our campaign and that kind of ersatz revelation was the way we did it. (In fact, Casey loved football, but he thought it good for the public to confront a politician who didn't.)

After the puff-job was done, Casey said, Let's get together some day and do a real book about me. And in a way we did, as you shall see. Except that by now I sometimes feel, who needs *you,* Casey? I have the warp of his soul so well from listening to him in cars and airplanes and both of us half asleep in hotel rooms that I can tell the truth far better than he ever could. Call it presumption or ghost writer's revenge, but nobody knows a man the way his speechwriter does.

One other thing I should warn you about, and then I'll get out of the way. I once dropped out of a creative-writing course at Harvard. The teacher said, "You've got to make up your mind between Raymond Chandler and Edith Wharton; and whatever you decide, don't ever again try to tell a story from more than one point of view." I saw what he was getting at and I went straight into politics.

We were looking desperately for a candidate that year as usual. It was my first crack at the vote, and I didn't realize that one was always looking desperately for a candidate. This was the first election ever held as far as we were concerned, and if we didn't find our man, probably the last one. Grim.

Solemnly my friends and I stalked the state capitols, interviewing any charlatan or windbag willing to give time to a bunch of politically illiterate undergraduates. I formed a loathing then and there for minor politicians, who seemed as superficial as actors and nowhere near as entertaining, and who were at their absolute worst with children. No black man ever saw more condescension on the hoof than we did that winter. Nor do I ever wish to hear again a sermon on patience and how there are no easy solutions.

At the same time, I formed a grudging admiration for the stars, the ones who could charm the socks off you in the length of time it takes to shake out of the next urinal. These may turn up on any side of any issue, and in my slightly older opinion are a bloody menace and should be banned from public life.

Washington was a bit better. I'll take senators over governors any day—wider interests, I guess, and less encrusted in grey-faced hangers-on. At first, we were certain we would find our man here. The four most promising of them were thrillingly blunt with us, firing off opinions that would surely have shocked their constituents out of their tennis shoes. Washington was so unreal, and they were so buffered with immunity, they could say anything they liked.

Until that is, we got to the Issue. That was something on which even a minor senator might be quoted on the front page. A look of calculated vagueness camo over our boys, then the patience sermon and allusions to top-level briefings. If we knew what they knew. This took out two of them, two of the best. Since they had a real shot at the Presidency, they wouldn't take the one chance that would make it possible. At this writing, they're both still waiting, a little farther back in the pack than before.

This left us with Senators Jenkins and Casey. Jenkins had manifest dentures and no power base. He alone could speak out on the Issue and be guaranteed no hearing at all. A soft-on-Communism charge hung limply on him, and nobody could be bothered to remove it. Needless to say, he seemed ready to run at a moment's notice.

Casey had the opposite trouble. He was, at first glance, too slick, too good to be true. He had New York-power base to burn. He'd made some money of his own somewhere. And he'd come out on the Issue at just the right time—not too early with the cranks, or too late with the schemers. He was a star all right, young, presumably dynamic (who ever heard of a young listless politician?), handsome, with a look of stoic endurance that he'd obviously earned—notice the slight way he shuffles his legs, must be very painful for him. In researching Casey's past, I talked to a couple of old polio hands, and they said that that was one thing they couldn't stand about Casey: the way he reminded you. It was a violation of the code and made him a bad man. But then they didn't know politics. Also, they were terrific polio snobs. Nobody knew but them.

"Excuse me for not rising," said the senator.

"Hm, all right, of course." We grunted with alarm.

He asked what he could do for us, and we said, Run for President on the Issue. We were down to our last senator, and our finesse was shot to hell. The bastards had worn us out.

"Well, I'd need a little louder demand than that, wouldn't you say?"

"Sure, sure. But would you be interested?"

We named our groups, and they sounded pretty silly in a senator's office, but he nodded and said, "It's a start. I think student politics is going to have a good year. Anyone like a cigarette?" He flashed a silver case. "Only tobacco, I'm afraid. Amherst, Harvard, Radcliffe, and Tufts, eh? That's a pretty good concentration. Could you deliver New England for me?"

I guess we tittered. We had learned our political manners and recognized that heavy joshing style, the language of the heart for politicians. Casey almost made it attractive, though not quite. He had the voice—a touch of the

New York streets, mixed with your favorite professor's intonations: impossible by now to tell which was laid on which. And of course, he was more intelligent than the others.

"It's a tempting suggestion. But you people would have to promise you wouldn't just play at it. You'd have to go out and find yourself a coalition and bring it back in here, kicking and screaming in a sack. And I never met a coalition that wasn't revolting. Union jackals and black con men and students—wait till you see the students you'd get. Not little ladies and gentlemen like yourselves."

"Yeah, well."

"And fund-raising—Christ, I wouldn't ask any decently raised child to plug into *that* sewer."

"Aren't you busy?" I asked. "I mean, I hate to take up your time."

"No, that's all right. I like to talk." He smiled at me. Down boy! "Leave when you get tired. There aren't many people here in Hellfire Swamp who really like politics. Gossip, now that's something else."

We were charmed, flattered, sold for life. He canceled two appointments, and made funny cracks about the dignitaries involved. Then a not-so-funny one. "Senator Smithers keeps a camera in his asshole to catch the perverts." Wrong joke for this group. Sold, unsold. As if he wanted to sell us all over again. You liked me as a nice guy, now try me as a rat. Let's get down to essences here. Trying to keep cool as the hot charm poured over my head. Something disturbing about his lunging playfulness, the big-dog virility some politicians have. Why is he doing this for us? First impressions hopelessly mixed. Shadow on long Irish face. He's lonely. He's playing with us. My sick liberal humility. Maybe he really likes us. I don't know anybody who knows how to meet celebrities properly, even minor ones. Let's face it, what I mainly cared about that day was what he thought of me.

"I'm sorry. I'm in a silly mood. I had lunch with the President." He was looking at me again. My face had told him something. Uncanny. "Would you *like* to be President?" I asked. "I honestly don't know," he said.

We left, dazzled by this routine display of political sex, our first, his nth. We could *have* him. All we had to do was perform one trivial little task, like carrying all the grains of rice in the kingdom up Pike's Peak. "Mr. Perkins," he said to me.

"Yes?"

"Look me up if you want a job."

It wasn't magic, of course, but a very old trick. I wasn't the brightest of the bunch, but henceforth I thought I was. Also, that we were mystically tuned in to each other, whether I liked him or not. Our group did not get Casey to run—we couldn't have elected a mayor of Worcester—but his availability became known eventually, and a coalition just as hairy as the one he predicted began to form, and the country had a candidate on the Peace Issue, as it presented itself that year.

Politicians' memories, my foot. He held my hand a minute, and my elbow too, as if to say, I wouldn't be doing all this if I didn't remember you, would I? "Perkins," I said. "Yes, Perkins, that's right." "Job," I said. He could smile and think simultaneously like no one I ever saw. "Where are your friends?" He'd got it. "I don't know. I lost them someplace." "Excellent. You have the makings of a politician already."

He released my hand, which sank back to my side, more dead than alive. He later told me that he got that grip from pushing a wheelchair. But I figured it was from trying to prove there was nothing wrong with his hand. That's the kind of difference of interpretation you'll find right along.

"The only thing that bothers me is that you may be too much of a politician. I see you've cut your hair. That's a bad sign in a young man."

"I'm sorry."

"There are two possible theories about you, Perkins. Maybe more. Either you're an opportunist, who dropped the rags and feathers of your generation the moment you were offered a respectable job. Or else, you never belonged in those rags at all, but wore them to escape attention. Maybe you'd *really* like to be Humphrey Bogart. Could you be a bit of a fraud, Perkins?"

I hoped to Christ I knew what he was getting at. Job interviews were like walking on fiery eggshells. "I'll bet I know why you asked that, Senator. You're testing my wit and resource, right?"

The smile. "Maybe that's it. Would you get one of those bottles and make yourself a drink?" I went over to his sideboard and slopped out something: Scotch, I imagine. I didn't want to flunk drink pouring. "Yes, something like that. Actually, I picked you because you seemed less like a politician than anyone I had ever seen. A good minor poet, maybe. Minor, because it's middle class to be major, isn't it? Perkinses don't need that kind of thing."

"My branch does." What kind of snarling, bog-Irish crack was that? More testing? I observed that he didn't take a drink himself. Irish desk sergeants seldom do. Ah well! I was looking for a candidate, not a buddy.

"The politics I can provide myself. I don't need that from my assistants. A courtesan doesn't need whores-in-waiting. Christ, half the people in this town should be taking lessons how *not* to sound like politicians. Which is where you come in, Perkins."

"I think you just like saying 'Perkins,'" I said. This was the biggest gamble of all. Did he like to be kidded? The transcript doesn't mention that my mouth dried slightly as he stared at me: so it sounds like a pretty slick exchange.

"You think that's it." He changed faces again. "O.K., Sam." O.K. what? "Have you ever written a speech?"

"Nope. Not a real one."

"Would you like to try?"

"Sure. In fact, I already did." I pulled out a tattered copy of an Issue speech I had spent the last week on. He flipped through it. "Who am I supposed to be talking to?" "I don't know. Anybody." "That's impossible. Every speech has an audience built in." He tossed it aside. "It's too political. Anyway, I can do my own peace speeches. That's easy.

What I want is a speech explaining my oil depletion votes. To the Vassar chapter of the A.D.A."

"How *do* you explain them?"

"The less you know about that the better. I don't want to cloud your mind with information. How would you *like* them explained?"

"Look, Senator, I cut my hair. But I draw the line somewhere."

"I'll say this for your crowd, Sam—you dish out jokes better than you take them. All right, I'll tell you what I'd like you to do about oil depletion and other embarrassments. I'd like you to study those votes and see if you can spot the trade-offs yourself. Check the votes of the oil senators on Medicaid, welfare, and other Eastern luxury items. But don't do it like a politician, don't cackle over your findings. Allow your mind to drift above the trading aspect and into clear skies. Be funny, be lyrical, be whatever you damn please. The kind of thing you and your friends want to hear is what I want to say."

I left the drink untasted on his desk and went off to look for his files. I was prepared for it to be boring, but not as boring as it was. I almost quit that first afternoon. Listen carefully, you people out there. Politics is dull. They hire people like me to paint a face on it with lipstick and all and then write poems about it. O.K., away we go. A bill for the old folk here, a bill for the *rich* old folk there. An oil vote for a pro-union vote—and the unions made to sound like choirs of angels. I can still imagine Casey's voice and smile. "Which of us was the cynic that year, Perkins?"

2 I must say, looking back, Casey chose me well. He was absolutely right about my fraudulence—I was about as hip as Dean Acheson. I wore the clothes and I sprawled in doorways, but I felt like an idiot. I had been raised not to call attention to myself, and dressing like a pig was the way we did it. He was even right about Bogart. I had read every private-eye story ever written and had even tried to write one myself in grammar school.

Politically, I was perfectly suited for Casey's house prig: the kind of high-minded young puritan who was flooding into politics that year and clamoring for a voice. My feelings were passionate but not deep. I would be fascinated by my first compromise. Casey explained all this to me later, in some car or other; it's what he thought he saw sitting in his office that day, and Casey was never wrong about things like that. He also told me, though he didn't have to by then, that he liked to hire high-minded people because they would do dirtier work for nothing than low-minded people would do for hire. True. If the candidate so much as intimated to me that a principle was involved, it was like unleashing a rattlesnake. A low-minded person would at least have watched his own skin and thought about tomorrow. I stopped at nothing.

I didn't see him again for a few days, being down in the vaults cleaning up his past. I tried to imagine the charges against him; then I'd put on my false mustache and run round to the other side of the desk to answer them. It was a cinch to find those trade-offs he mentioned, and not so much harder to make it sound as if he'd gotten the best of each one. All right, he had voted for a wretched Supreme Court nominee, but the nominee was defeated anyway, as Casey must have known he would be, so the vote was a pure trading counter and for it Casey got everything but a warm water port for New York State. And so on, from triumph to triumph. Joan of Arc should have had such a record.

Boredom turned to glib fascination once you had the key—this was real politics, boy, not that stuff they taught at Harvard—and I ran up a gorgeous brochure, full of lines like WHICH of these men is the real patriot? I panted into Casey's office like a St. Bernard and laid it at his feet. He had two friends in there that I didn't recognize, man and woman, "Hi, there," didn't really notice them, how'd you like it, huh, huh?

"Let me know the next time you plan to drop in, Sam," said Casey, who looked as if he'd been interrupted in mid-hump. "I know your generation is supposed to be casual, but mine isn't. Not on your fucking tintype." He swore like someone who'd been raised not to, so it made you jump.

His two friends looked at me with large expressionless eyes. I was obviously a joke of a kind they didn't especially care for. They looked like movie people or publishers or something.

"What have you brought me?"

"It's a fact sheet."

"A fact sheet, eh? I thought I told you to avoid those things at all costs. O.K., let's see it."

I handed it over, feeling as if my collar were sticking up in back. He read fast, with a diagonal swing of the head, and began right away to laugh.

"What's so funny?"

"Nothing. It's beautiful. It's the most shameless campaign document I ever read." He shook his head. "You idealists." He laughed some more and said, "Listen to this, Maggie: 'The root trouble with our system is that some candidates are simply too good for it.' That's me, darling."

"May I have it back, and I'll be on my way."

"Wait a minute, Sam. I'm sorry. Don't ever walk in without warning. While I'm showing off to my friends. O.K.? Now why don't you wait outside till I get rid of them." He winked at them and they smiled. Corner of Sunset and

Madison. I walked out into the slanting rain or the pitiless sunshine or whatever the fuck was going on that day and all the way back to my hotel room.

He didn't call till the next day, which gave me time to brood. He's a bastard, I thought, but maybe the country needs a bastard right now. "Elections in this country have degenerated into popularity contests." I ran it through my mental typewriter. "Senator Casey has never feared hurting feelings in the cause of truth." I could already hear him laughing over that one. The snide son of a bitch.

Well, I didn't have to like the mother. If it took that kind of character to oppose the war, I must find a way to make that kind of character attractive. (E.g.: another marvelous Casey story—the time he told a newsman to go fuck himself. Change that to pompous newsman. Change it to pompous, *powerful* newsman. Delete the "fuck.") And goddamnit, he was honest, whatever he said.

"Honest? Not especially," he said, when we got together that afternoon. "Honesty is just a form of rhetoric. It isn't what politics is basically about."

He was all charm again today, with nobody else present—academic charm, at that. "You might as well see my worst side, if we're going to be married. Have a drink or something, and we'll discuss the thing you wrote." I didn't move. Politicians are always saying, "Have a drink." It's just one of the things they say.

"O.K., let's start with the basics, because the next thing you write has to be usable. We don't have time for on-the-job training, and I haven't got money for an editor. The first obvious fact is that if I was that good, you'd have to hide it. People would resent hell out of me. Secondly, I'm not that good. To tell the best lies you must study the truth more closely. I am not the greatest American since Dolly Madison, or even Willie Sutton. If you look at those trade-off votes, you will perceive that in every case my opponent could claim the same statesmanship as I. In Texas he could say, 'I voted for you all.' In New York he could say, 'I was never blinded by sectional interests.' Same for me. I may need Texas myself someday."

"Are you telling me there's no difference at all?"

He touched my hand and I thought, Please don't squeeze, the finger you busted last time hasn't mended yet. Even a chairbound politician will find some way to get his paws on you. "Medical students are expected to throw up at their first operations," he said. "Politics is much worse, believe me. No, of course there's a difference. But maybe not as great as you like to think."

Not great enough to worry about, either. And touching me doesn't help, buster. There was, of course, still the war. But I was afraid he was going to tell me he was trading that off for the next World's Fair.

He never took his eyes off me, and after a while I wanted to slam my face shut and say, Stop reading. "Maybe I'm more of an idealist than I let on," he said. "We must never let the public know, if so. And while we're on the subject of honesty—I don't know where you kids learn to write like that. If I want political clichés, there are lots of old men in town who need the work. Be true to your own style at least, Sam. That's where honesty really *is* important."

Bullshit, buddy, I thought. Honest prose is the biggest con of all. Look at the English. I had one question for him, as soon as he stopped crapping around, and my services hinged on that. "What do you say we write a real fact sheet," he was going on, charmingly, "describing all my deals and precisely how they were made? Yes, throw in the car and the call girls, what the hell. You can even make up a mistress, but be sure the facts check out. I don't want to be caught in a lie about a serious thing like that."

"Look," I interrupted, "would you just tell me one thing on the Bible of your choice. Can I trust you about the war?"

He nodded. "Yes, that's the one thing." Deal.

He invited me for a weekend to his country place in Maryland. Next week, we would start work in earnest, for the New Hampshire primary. For now, we would play. Checking my diary again, I find that my thoughts about him were fresher and simpler than they appear here. He was a little too flashy for a small room. Or let's say, he could be until he knew you disliked it. I think he hired me partly to remind him how the Ivy League sensibility worked—necessary after grunting around the clubhouses too much. For a time, I marveled that a man with a mind so much like my own could have got so far in politics. Ha! He had a closetful of minds, I just had the one.

If you are the least bit observant, you will have noticed by now that I am not. If I had to describe his office, I would say it was average. Neat-looking. A desk, a couple of chairs. Now let's get on with the dialogue. You would never know from my account of it whether Casey liked paintings or music or French cooking. Luckily, I chose the perfect subject, because Casey never showed the least interest in any of them. His house contained some hunting prints and what might have been ancestral portraits, if the Caseys had been here since 1700, but Fran Casey told me the pictures came with the house. The record collection was standard O.K. stuff—Beethoven's Fifth and Sixth, Bach's B Minor Mass—but Casey talked right through whatever was playing, his only comment being, "Isn't that kind of loud, dear?" As to food, I don't think he had noticed a mouthful from the day he was born. He ate like an electric shovel, unless he felt like talking, in which case he didn't eat at all. The food at his place was awful, and several times that weekend, I got the feeling I had stumbled into a Trappist monastery by mistake. Though I must say, his wife took good care of him, within the monastic Rule.

Since he looked like our best bet for candidate of culture, I asked him who his favorite composer was, and he snapped back, Beethoven. No further comment, no early-period/late-period spinach. Hmm, painter. The Flemish were pretty good. Rembrandt. I asked if he liked any Americans, and he said, Do I have to? And I said I thought so, but I'd take a poll on Monday. And we were off on the subject of cultural nationalism, while the Pastoral went its rounds unheeded.

The funny thing was that he seemed like a cultured

man in public—probably our best bet would be a "Home on the Range" facetiousness about this. I guess he could have managed a verbal interest in culture, everything got plowed into words with Casey. I pictured his real ancestors crouched in a peat bog, with nothing to do but talk. And occasionally push each other over. O.K.—how many Irish painters can *you* name?

Despite his narrow interests, he never ran out of things to say, and I didn't get too bored. Casey was a good host. Having emptied life of art, culture, everything, he filled it up again his own way, as he must have done for himself during those months of convalescence. I pictured him sitting up in bed in a bright, empty hospital room—reinventing the world in his head, leaving out (sick man's license) anything that bored him. I took him up on several of those drinks he kept offering, and sneaked a listen at his Beethoven and had an O.K. time.

Fran Casey was a real surprise. If there was one thing I had been sure about with Casey, it was that his wife would be a political asset. Chic, dignified, or some adjective I'd never even thought of—the perfect political woman, brought to you by Brian Casey. But she wasn't. Frances Casey was a political disaster. She looked like an upstairs maid and talked like one, too, when she talked at all. Outside of taking excellent care of the senator, she seemed to have no characteristics at all. I could only suppose that Casey had put a hand on her knee when he was seventeen and been forced to marry her on the spot. The price of being a Catholic. I scoured the place for a wedding picture, the kind that bad novelists find so revealing, but discovered none.

"Do you indulge in church?" Casey asked me on Sunday morning.

I jerked my head, no. My parents had separated when I was twelve (my father's high-mindedness was the unofficial ground), and my mother had sent me to a Catholic school for a couple of years; and religion had given me the shakes ever since.

"I guess speechwriters don't have to. Candidates still do," he said. "Even Catholics. And even in the South. It may be a wicked religion, but at least it's better than your atheistic pornography."

I asked him whether the country wasn't ready for a bad Catholic yet, and he said, We'll soon see. And I asked him if he'd go to church if he didn't have to, and he said, None of your damn business. Religion is a sacred thing and we don't talk about it, thank God. I offered to go with him, but he said he didn't want me converting, it would unbalance his team. He got into his car and his wife chauffeured him off to church.

Fran had been to a dawn mass herself, so she came back early and set to work on the senator's lunch. I decided to corner her in the kitchen. Up to now, she had been smothered in Casey's conversation and I hadn't heard a word from her. She looked, flushed pink by kitchen steam, as if she might just conceivably have been pretty once, in the dullest way possible; but she had been soaked too long in Casey's character. There was something sodden about her arms and the way she moved her feet.

"How do you feel about the senator's candidacy?" asked Sam Perkins, boy reporter.

"He's very excited about it," she said. Soddenly.

And how do you plan to decorate the White House? Like a dungeon, I know.

"Where are the children right now?"

"Kevin, that's the oldest, is at Loyola," she said quickly, like an old prayer. "Patricia is at Mount St. Mary's," and so on, down the roll of Irish names, six in all, each away at some place with a saint's name. It sounded like a put-on to me. The few Catholics I still knew had names like Brunswick and Stacy, and went to Harvard and Radcliffe. I wondered if Casey had always planned to go into politics, starting right in with his kids' names, laying the common touch on them at birth. Or was he really a Pat and Mike Irishman all the way? (Or was I, perhaps, a howling bigot?)

"Religion is sacred, we don't talk about it." Clever son of a bitch. I know he believed in God, but on whose terms I never did find out. Otherwise, being Irish seemed to be just a tool of the trade: high-style Oscar Wilde for one bloc, and a kid at Loyola for another. Behind it, an empty house and a wife who wouldn't talk.

"I hope this doesn't seem out of line, Mrs. Casey, but your husband's a very complicated man."

"What do you mean?" she asked without turning. What was she cooking, anyway? So far I had seen nothing but potatoes—another hideous put-on. Remind him to get in some blintzes. He's already got the potato vote in his pocket. "Well, maybe he isn't," I babbled ingratiatingly.

"I mean, with politicians, you figure everything is done for effect, but maybe it isn't at all. We think they're cynics, but maybe all the cynicism is in our interpretation." Oh, good grief. Well, what do you say to that, Mrs. Casey? Was she as confused by the question as I was?

"I know it's none of my business," I plunged on desperately, "but if I am going to be working with the senator, I really should get to know him. I don't mean anything nasty or, you know, secret."

She turned round, blinking and red as a roast now from her work. I don't know what I expected next—some raging revelation: "He's a beast, I tell you," or some understandable variant of "get lost"—but I certainly didn't expect what I got. As primly as a little girl reciting her catechism to the bishop, she said, "My husband is a very great man."

She had to go fetch Casey from his prayers after that, and when he got back, he seemed charged by the experience, and suggested we get right down to work. He said that sermons were a great time for thinking about politics, but he must have been thinking right through communion too, because we talked the rest of the day, and it was like hanging on to the coattails of Mercury, and I fell into bed that night too exhausted to write it up in my throbbing diary.

3

"If you ever got to like me," Casey said, almost to himself, "you wouldn't be so useful to me." This was just a warm-up toss. I was to find that something about car and plane travel brought on a rush of suspect illuminations. He always seemed playful in the back of a car. Also in a swimming pool, or any place where nobody else had legs either. Christ, he was hysterical in swimming pools.

"You'll be relieved to know I do not demand loyalty," he said. "Peerless efficiency will do."

We were driving back to Washington to clean up his desk, and were mauling around a fund-raising speech for the evening, breaking our toil with Casey's own special word game, which he called Sophistry. My reading of the above fortune cookie was (1) I enjoy playing Machiavelli. (2) I can make friends any time I want to. If you don't like me, it's because I choose it so. (3) and (4) and (5). I was working on these when the bell rang and he gave me another. "Friendship is a basically unfair relationship," he said. "Now where was I?"

I wanted to talk politics, not this stuff, and I hoped it would blow over soon. "What do you mean, about friendship?" I said, yawning mentally.

"Epigrams shouldn't have to be explained, just topped. Ten points off your score and back to undersecretary. All right, just this once, since you're new here. To put it Thomistically, friendship disturbs the balance of nature. In practice, it always means, 'I'll take something from him and give it to you, so you'll be my friend,' and at its worst, which is most of the time, it means, '*You'll* take something from him, won't you, honey, and give it to me, because I'm *your* friend.' It's an offense against *justitia* and *ipsud quod rem*."

Was he serious? St. Thomas, *justitia,* a world without friends? "How does it feel to be trapped in a speeding car with a medieval fanatic?" he said.

Casey's idea of fund-raising was quite a ways from mine. In fact, I didn't see how he could worm a penny from anyone his way. It threatened to be one of the dullest speeches ever delivered. No jokes, no fervor. "It's all right. I'll read it with a throb in my voice and a twinkle in my eye," he said. "Just make sure the figures on steel are right. I may be using last year's."

"You mean you did them from memory?"

"That's right." Son of a bitch. This owl is God.

"One thing to remember, Sam. These are very important people. Jews on the way up, Wasps holding, Clyde Jasper, the dignified Negro. I wouldn't insult them with a lively speech." He smiled, wallowing in his plush throne. "They just want to know if they can trust this man with their children's teeth."

Out of the car, he was like a fish beached. For public appearances, he used a dignified wheelchair, but on private missions he heaved along on two canes, dragging his hips behind him. He seemed annoyed when I accidentally walked on ahead of him, but when I dropped back, he said, "Go on, go on." I never did work out how fast he wanted, or whether I was making up the whole problem myself—the kind of goofy impasse that has to be kept in mind throughout this account.

Behind his desk, he was yet a third man, restless, looking for things to do. We'd had our jollies out in the car, now I was just a pair of legs, like everyone else he hired. He even put on stage glasses to emphasize the distance between us. His secretary, Jane Donohue, came in—a beautiful chick, though it turned out she was from a good convent—and he said, "How the fuck are we going to win New Hampshire on one appearance a day, Jane?" Was he trying to shock her? Jane didn't raise her head. "Is the whole state supposed to come and see me in my fucking suite?" he continued. "For Christsake, tell Jack to get me some exposure up there. I'm not the blessed infant of

Prague." Search me. "Sam, go off and write some speeches. I have to round up a staff today."

"Any special kind of speeches? Or just the regular assortment?"

"I haven't got time for jokes. Find out what's eating the farmers and tell it to stop. Jane, tell Jack to interview the volunteers, and tell him to throw out the ones with scrofula and obvious brain disease." Time for his jokes, but not for mine, you'll notice. "We still haven't got a campaign manager for New Hampshire. There must be some pompous asshole looking for work up there. Get Jack on it."

Jack Spritzer didn't have a title. Even when the campaign had developed a Byzantine hierarchy, with no fewer than five official campaign managers, Spritzer was just Jack. He had his own special relationship with Casey, and he looked with impartial loathing on everyone else in the operation, including me. A little redheaded fellow, ex-seminarian, something that had grown out of the back of Casey's brain and incubated in his hat on some black day.

I spent the afternoon among the crops, staring blankly at alfalfa yields or whatever the shit they grow up there—the merciful censor has blanked it out for me—and that evening we flew up to New York and Casey gave his speech. He had fixed it so he didn't have to eat the dinner, but rolled in with the coffee, to a round of hollow, calculating applause, from the better class of capitalist pig.

"Excuse me for not rising," he said. I winced, but the line drew a sympathetic burble, as it always would. He told some jokes that weren't in the speech. And then he gave a *speech* that wasn't in the speech, the kind of witty, charming speech I'd been pleading to write myself. I believe he used the steel figures. Otherwise, the whole morning had been a waste of time.

I raged in my doorway, where I stood parked like a waiter. Even a boring speech becomes a point of pride after a while, and I yearned to hear any line of my own, however feeble. In lieu of that, I began to phrase my immediate resignation. What the hell did this egomaniac need with a speechwriter anyway? I was too mad to notice at first how the fat cats were taking their cream. But the purrs began to reach me, wheezetittering chuckles and a strange sigh of business confidence that translates, "Good man, good solid man." And when it was over, they exploded with a passion of approval that would have sent Hitler to bed happy. "My God, he's one of us. He's against the war, but he's one of us." Casey sat there, head forward, staring at the future, like Churchill. The virility that was too much for a small office, the St. Bernard breathing on your face, was just right for large dining rooms and sports arenas. I found myself clapping too, and grinning and nodding at some banker, who was looking around for agreement. Every vote seemed important at that stage of my innocence.

A swarm of black dinner jackets closed on the head table. They wanted, like teeny-boppers, to touch him and get his blessing. Flint-faced tycoons, grinning from ear to ear, jostled down the defiles between tables. But they were mass-arrested by Jack Spritzer's voice.

"Attention please, everybody. The senator is very tired. He'd like to meet you all and thank you personally for coming. But he has to save his strength for the challenges ahead. So—on to New Hampshire!"

It didn't sound very inspiring, coming from Spritzer. A cheerleader shouldn't have adenoids. A grumble of disappointment was followed by a dispirited clap as the senator wheeled out the back exit. My banker looked round like a frustrated baby—"I didn't get to touch him, waaah!" I thought, You heartless bastard, can't you see he's a cripple? And then I thought, Oh Christ, Casey's made a mistake. They don't want weakness in the Presidency. If they do pick a cripple, it'll be out of superstition—they think he's stronger than other people, inner strength and all that. They're all mad about strength. It's all the bastards have got.

I made a note to tell Casey this, after my resignation, a parting gift to pay for the weekend. Other politicians could show fatigue, Casey never. He would have to kill himself to prove his strength.

But when I found him, he wasn't tired at all. In fact, he seemed to be planning some kind of a party with Spritzer.

"What happened to my speech?" I croaked.

Casey looked around imperiously. As if to say, What speech? You mean *my* speech, don't you? You don't have speeches.

"Look, Senator, this is pointless."

He relaxed his Churchill face. "I'm sorry, Sam. It was

my mistake. This wasn't the crowd I expected. One look, and I knew those people had no dignity at all. Have a drink and forget it. I overrate the rich, it's an Irish weakness." Not enough? "I promise I'll give that speech to *someone*."

So I let the resignation ride for now, and gave him my advice about being strong, to which he listened thoughtfully.

"You're probably right," he said. "I hadn't thought of it. Funny, it's the kind of thing I usually *do* think of. Maybe you've taken over part of my brain already. I guess I should have told them I'm flying to Los Angeles for a giant rally, shouldn't I?"

I felt flattered to be part of his brain and all and pleased that Casey hadn't taken *immediate* credit for the idea. One of the local Reform Democrat ladies, who had helped round up the moneybags for tonight, looked in at that point and said, "Couldn't you *please* go out and talk to them, Senator? We're not raising half the money we'd hoped."

I'd forgotten about that end of it. I looked expectantly at Casey, and couldn't believe what I saw. He was pinching his Adam's apple and flapping his jaws soundlessly. "His voice is gone," said Spritzer quickly.

"Oh my God," said the lady, and backed out. *We haven't even reached New Hampshire, and the candidate's voice is gone.*

Casey laughed like a kid as soon as the door had shut, and Spritzer made a mirthless, burping sound. This was the team we were going to win with? "I'm sorry, I just can't take those people, Sam," said Casey. "I can't talk to them for five minutes without insulting them."

"Where do you expect to get your money then?"

"From people who want a good President." He had a trick of going serious on me, absolutely unfairly. "I thought you and your crowd were looking for an honest unhypocritical candidate. Well, you got one, you cynical little bastards. So please don't ask me to crawl to the rich on my very first night. O.K.?" I really had nothing on the spur of the moment to say, and he paused long enough to make this clear, like a matador patting the bull on the horns. "Good night, Sam. I want to talk to Jack for a minute."

Whatever party they were planning did not include humble speechwriter. I wandered off to the servants' quarters—actually, across town at our hotel—wondering how he could be so good and I could be so bad.

4

I guess I should say a word for myself at this point. My original intention was just to be a device, like the teacher said, a disembodied point-of-view, but I can see that assumptions will be made about the gaps I leave, and that if I don't explain myself a little, you will make somebody else up to play my part—a vacuous, slow-witted chump who is always being bested by the senator.

In fact, I was to win several of our arguments, or at least think I had. I was much more radical than he was, in theory; but I found that, as I bumped full-skull against the real world, I despaired more than he did of getting things done. You can't possibly propose this or that, I'd say, they'll lynch you out there. And he'd say, Why not? God knows, I had flung myself against moving automobiles in the past, and there wasn't anything I wouldn't picket. I had been in the Youth Movement indecently long and people were beginning to talk. But I was a timid speechwriter. Casey told me my encounters with the cops had impressed me more than I realized, that letting yourself get arrested again and again *weakens* your confidence vis-à-vis authority. And I said, Bullshit. Your willingness to say daring things only proves how trivial you think words are. Perhaps, he said. On the other hand . . . God, he loved to talk when the jag was on him. Through the long night, after six speeches and a thousand handshakes, he'd still be at it, eyes shut in the back of the car, like a maestro practicing his scales after a concert. Competitive, coquettish, or just a lonely winding-down in which he hardly seemed aware of his listeners—usually only Jack Spritzer by then, gloomily pulling on his freckled nose (he hadn't the guts to pick it outright). Then Casey'd say, "Oh Christ, words! You're absolutely right," and fall asleep just like that.

To get back to myself for one more delightful second—I was politicalized to the back teeth in those days. But with this one wrinkle: since my father had already fought for every hopeless cause going (and, in fact, was still at it), the only way I could kill him properly was actually to win something. So I tried to be as pragmatic as hell, and I looked at Casey the way a chef looks at a cow: all I could see were the lines around the steaks and chops. His marriage was a bit we'd have to throw away. There was probably some way of serving up the children. Private lives don't matter much, when a famine can take out ten million of them at a stroke, and Casey's was just something to hide or exploit. This, in some ways, made me the ideal dum-dum observer or Dr. Watson figure.

Our primary strategy was fairly typical for that year, when candidates were chosing primaries like smorgas bord and where it was possible for the leaders to miss each other completely if mutually agreeable. We opened in New Hampshire, of course, for the early newspaper coverage, and to show our Eastern-seaboard muscle. Skip Florida ("It's a disgrace to win in Florida," Casey). Make two killings in the Midwest, preferably in a state that the other candidates had overlooked and another from Group B, just to keep things simmering. Our money, the way Casey was behaving, would not stretch to more than two all-out campaigns, but we could count on some mass suicides in the others. Then plunge it all on crazy old California.

We drove around New York State the next day, which seemed like a funny way to get to New Hampshire. "This is where my real strength lies. Weakness here is the fatal split in the pants." He checked in with various upstate pros, on what principle of selection I didn't yet understand. He didn't seem very friendly with them, and I wondered what good the trip was doing. "It's a very feudal region up here," he explained. "They like an arrogant snot." Pause. "Anyway, they've got one." One little guy, who truckled disgustingly and hung on the window of our car wheezing Sen-sen, was told for his pains to buy a new suit. A bunch of guys in Utica crowded around shaking hands, and I swear the senator wiped his own with a handkerchief while they were still standing there. Ah well —integrity, I thought. It's what we wanted. I didn't need another speech about that.

Still, "How the hell did you manage to win up here?" I asked him.

"Raw ability."

"You didn't get any help from those guys, did you?"

"You're damn right, I did. Those are my loyalest supporters. You should see the others."

Time for another round of Sophistry? "They have children, just the right age by now. They have wives. That's where the support comes from. Women and children are very puritanical—they respect rudeness, it's so nice and plain."

"I thought you said they were feudal."

"Well, there you are," he said, smiling and smacking my knee. "The truth is never simple."

Was it fair to say that he just despised the local-politician type? "In some ways," he said (jubilant at spending *a whole day* in a car). "There's certainly no other business that would employ most of them. If you talk to them too long, the failure rubs off on you, sure as leprosy. Still—they play my favorite sport, so they can't be all bad." Yet he could be charming to them, too, when he felt like it. God knows why, he was nice to a fat fool in Suffern, swapping dirty jokes and pounding him like a football coach. "What happened to your integrity?" I asked about that.

"Needs a rest," he said. "Moderation in all things. Or

as Augustine puts it, '*Moderatia in omnibus, a fortiori in mini-bus.*' Or don't they teach Latin at Harvard?"

A hilarious day—but was this a campaign? The only cloud in my personal sky was that he would not tolerate pot within fifty feet of him—something we would have to conceal from the youth of America. We drove back to the city quietly. When he didn't talk, he really didn't talk. Wouldn't even answer questions, like a spoiled kid. In the hotel lobby, leaning on his crutches, he broke his monastic silence. "We accomplished a lot today, Sam, believe it or not. But God, it's depressing. All those little turds want is job security. They don't care how rude you are, if you offer them that. *Real* integrity could afford to be polite."

He meant it about being depressed, and I didn't see him again for several hours. New York wasn't a bad place for this to happen, but he had told me to hang around the hotel, so I found myself lobby-sitting like an old ballplayer, staring at girls and potted palms, whichever grabbed me most at the moment. I was all dressed up in a suit, the quickest cultural surrender of all time. I thought of falling in love with Jane Donohue because she was there, and then remembered a convent girl who had literally crushed my hand between her knees—just a little girl, too—and I decided to let it go. My precious hands were in enough jeopardy from the senator's handshakes. Maybe one of the campaign volunteers would come to my sexual aid eventually: muse to the senator's speechwriter, it beat working the mimeograph machine.

From time to time, Spritzer would cruise the lobby, pick

up a personage at the door, and escort him back to the elevator. I decided there was something needlessly furtive about the senator's doings. When he wanted to talk business with his upstate pros, he would shut the glass partition in the car, and I'd see him mouthing his deals. Afterward he'd make a cleansing crack to dismiss the man from his system, but he wouldn't tell me what they'd talked about. He told Spritzer, of course. At this point, some old family hatred, passed down from Cotton Perkins himself, and kept alive by my two spooky years with the Benedictines, stirred in my sleepy gorge. Spritzer was probably an unfrocked priest who performed black rites with Casey upstairs, in a hair shirt and a derby hat and silk vestments with Hibernian A.C. on the back. I was sick of the two of them, and wished I'd spent the day with a real politician, learning something useful.

By eleven o'clock, I could stand no more. I was about to go out and catch a dirty movie or something when I saw someone I recognized from the papers, Tim Houlighan, the Democratic state chairman, waddling across the lobby with Spritzer for tugboat. Politicians probably have the faces they deserve; but in that case, what terrible thing could Houlighan have done? I stood up. What the hell, Casey would only throw me out, it would pass the time. I followed them up and knocked. Spritzer opened the door a chink. "Hi, Jack." "What do you want?" "I want to come in. Haven't you ever been lonely in a big city?" Spritzer didn't know what to do with me, and he couldn't just stand there, so I pushed him and the door gently back and walked in.

If Casey was annoyed, he didn't show it this time in front of the grownups. "Hello, Sam. Come on in. I'd like you to meet," etc., etc. Maybe Casey wanted to get rid of Houlighan anyway. He looked like a lout.

"I'll certainly think about what you said, Tim." First names could sound stiffer than titles when Casey used them.

"I'm not through yet," said the chairman.

"You're not?"

"No." He held to his chair like a bag of cement. "I have to remind you that what you want now is a lot different from what you wanted then. A U.S. senator is a freak as far as state politics is concerned. He's got no patronage, and he's got no power. He's just a fucking ornament. You won it, because it wasn't worth our while opposing you and upsetting the things that really counted."

"Is that all it was? I love to learn these things."

"You bet it was. We didn't want to split the ticket, and a lot of good boys can always ride in behind a peace candidate."

"What about the state convention?"

Houlighan spread his hands. "Same thing. It was a three-way fight, which could have torn us apart. We couldn't have won a thing with the other two lunks anyway."

"That's what I thought." Casey paused, the old matador trick. "You know, you people fascinate me, the way you can explain anything by the old rules the moment after it's happened. Too bad you can never explain anything before it happens. The truth is, you don't know what hit you at that convention, and it seems you don't *want* to know. You're like an old World War I general, and a losing one at that. Hell, that stuff didn't even work against Dewey or Javits."

Hey, do we really want to offend this guy? Some horrible instinct of compromise, much deeper than my trendy radicalism, was showing its ugly face more each minute. But taking things personally was a luxury Houlighan didn't allow himself. "Dewey and Javits played those rules too, only better than we did. So does every successful politician who ever lived. The new politics is a myth. It's just another act for a pro to master, if he has the time."

Casey smiled. "That's pretty good, Tim. You'd noticed that, huh? Have another drink and tell me more about it." He looked at me with a baiting expression, while Houlighan bent to his pouring, and whispered, "Sam, *you* knew the new politics was an act, didn't you? You're a bright boy. The youth constituency has to be picked up by someone. And they're so damn ignorant, you can do it without dropping a stitch with the regulars. Right, Tim?"

"I wouldn't know about that." Houlighan saw no reason to waste time on me at all—the only real difference between an old pol and a new one. "All I know is that you may become senator while the boys are asleep, but you'll never become President that way. You have to plug into the system, right now, and at all points."

"Does that mean I have to smoke those lousy cigars?"

Houlighan grunted. Joking was strictly for show, not for private use. "You have a lousy rapport with the boys. Word gets around if you can't deliver your own state."

"I'll deliver it."

"That's not enough. You have to *look* as if you can deliver it. Don't let that victory go to your head, Brian. A lot of U.S. senators don't know balls about politics. They'll never know how they got to Washington."

"O.K., Tim. What do the guys want? As if I didn't know."

"I've got a list for you, back at the office. Why don't you come round about nine?"

"I was planning to be on my way north by then."

"I suggest you come round."

"I suggest you mail it."

Another grunt. Another trivial display of integrity. "I'll tell you something you won't find on the list, Brian. Those boys are only human. They have pride. It isn't strictly necessary to treat them like dirt." He glanced at me. "Listen, kid, so you can remind the boss from time to time. You probably despise those guys yourself, because they remind you of your old man, right? And you think they're all on the take."

I thought of my father, Jonathan Perkins, in the A.D.A. and the A.C.L.U. and way into antivivisection. Always on the take, my my. "Well, they're not. They're in politics first of all because they love it, something you kids haven't proved yet, by the way. And a nice visit with the senator makes their year for them. It justifies them, makes them feel like somebody. Who knows, you may not even have to *give* them so much, Brian, if you're nice to them."

"They sound pathetic," I muttered, but Houlighan believed kids were to be lectured at, not heard.

"So just remember that, O.K.? I don't want you to compromise your famous cool style, and neither do they. Christ, it's votes for us all. That part of the new politics I accept. But, you know, Brian, a little smile from you is like an embrace from a normal guy."

"That's swell, Tim. I'll remember that. A little smile from Dracula goes a long way, eh? Listen, we never talked about New York City."

"You tell *me* about New York City. You know what you got and what you need." As it turned out, they both talked about it, at exhaustive length, but I'll spare you the tiny details. What impressed me most about what followed was that through the whole conversation, neither of them mentioned New Hampshire, or anything outside the state, and absolutely no item of substance arose. So this was politics, eh? I began to appreciate that glass partition in the car. Could it be that I really didn't like politics after all?

"O.K., now what about Brooklyn?" Yeah, what about that, huh? Fascinating little borough. Casey was very serious now, showing off his great memory and discussing neighborhoods as if he was moving pins on a map in his head. I assumed this would snow a dope like Houlighan, but the chairman was much smarter than I expected, within this particular fish bowl. He did some thumbnail sketches a novelist would envy of various clubhouse leaders, not just flat trade talk, but the feuds and drunken insults and who needed money to send the kids through college, and which widower was beginning to play the field. I couldn't tell what was important and what wasn't. Politics was basically gossip, and the old people would wear us out with it. In the next few weeks I was to meet, besides working hacks like Houlighan, countless ladies who followed politics like soap opera, and men who clung to it like baseball, crowding into meetings for company, and licking stamps for a sense of purpose, now that the kids were grown. How could anyone under thirty with a few months to spare in the summer compete with these withered addicts?

"O.K., Tim. Send me your list and we'll take it from there." They parted cordially, grabbing elbows and such, and wishing luck. There was no way of knowing whether they liked each other or not. Spritzer took the chairman downstairs, leaving me with the Master.

"You know," Casey said dreamily, "I'm going to take that guy's pants."

"You are, huh?"

"Yes. I did it before and I've got the knack."

"With your new-politics act?"

He smiled. "Don't take that too hard, Sam. The kids' instincts are good, and we'll honor that if we can. But they are also much too dumb to govern, you know that. It's better this way."

"What about educating them?" I mumbled gruffly.

"Sure, we'll try that. But politics is a pretty dull subject, you know. I thought you were going to fall asleep a couple of times just now. And we were pretty interesting, as these things go. And you know, by the time you've got the education, you'll be another shriveled old fart anyway, and your education will be out of date. Good night, Sam, and sweet dreams."

Shleep, thash all I want. Jush li'l shleep. Drunk with fatigue, I hauled my knees onto the bed and lay there like a starfish. Politicking is great exercise, as mind-dulling as my old sport, track, and just as I passed out, I thought, We'll show them the kids can take boredom, and dish it out too. I didn't care too much for what he said about the new politics, but by Christ, he was better than Houlighan anyway, and right now, pettifogged and gerrymandered and bleary with sheer process, and with my hard-won identity damn near washed away like a dirt road in a flood, I wasn't too sure what the phrase "new politics" meant anyway.

The phone rang instantly. "Sam, you sleep too damn much. Come up here, I want to talk."

Up yours, Senator. In a very sincere way. But he'd rung off already. Casey's insomnia was malicious, I decided then and there. He would have nothing to say to me. I passed an early-morning whore in the corridor, on her way home from work, with tired, burned-out eyes, and I thought, You and me both.

You and me and *Spritzer*. The little shit was already up and about, exuding evil like morning dew. He came out of Casey's door and followed the girl to the elevator, and got in with her as if she were a big wheel in Bronx politics. And I thought, Is there nobody he won't see across a lobby? There couldn't be anyone as evil as Spritzer, it must be my mistake. Actually, I had nothing against him except his face, and the air he gave off of "He's *my* senator, I tell you, not yours."

"Morning, Sam. How are you on devaluing the dollar one more time?" Casey sat framed against the window, a portrait of the statesman in red-silk pajamas.

"I'm absolutely against it, chief." I yawned. "Aren't I?"

"No, no. Think again."

"I'm for it?"

"In certain grave circumstances, yes, you are. The dollar is nowhere mentioned in the Old Testament. It is not sacred. It is for man's use. O.K.—now, go thou and write it up."

I was still terribly sleepy. "Write what? I don't get it."

He turned peevish on me. "I expect a certain amount of intelligence from my staff. I assume you know some basic economics. Otherwise you wouldn't have asked me to run for President, would you?" Was he angry now or what? And if so, why? "I mean, you wouldn't go all the way to Washington to tell professional politicians how to do their jobs if you didn't know what the fuck you were talking about, would you?"

"If that's all you wanted to say, I'm going back to bed."

"All right. Only be out by noon, or they'll charge you an extra day."

The above is a much better game than Sophistry. I believe it was invented by the Chinese in the tenth century B.C. and brought West by large black rats. It is called Diplomacy. Observe—if I walk out, I've taken it all too seriously. If I stay, I've capitulated. Casey could make up these scenes all day like chess puzzles.

"I know about economics, I just don't know about *your* economics."

"O.K. At least you're awake now." He began, still grumpy, to explain his position, and I listened with the lower half of my left ear. Actually, I didn't give a damn about the dollar, which I thought of as a crazy capitalist toy that wouldn't sit up straight and which wet itself in your lap. I looked around at the unmade bed. The senator must have had a terrible night, what there was of it. The sheets were churned and mangled and ripped in several places. His legs must have come to life and kicked the hell out of them. I also saw what looked like a stain right on the mattress. Christ, how'd he get a nosebleed way down there?

Spritzer came back in and stood by the door. Casey was still rolling on about the dollar—liquidity and floatability and the exquisite sensibility of currency. "Almost like a woman, as the French minister would no doubt put it." Spritzer looked as if to say, "I'll hear your confession now, but we can't do anything about that mattress."

I have a pretty disgusting mind if you encourage it. I fantasied now that Spritzer had seen the painted nun home through the snow and was back in time for the abbot's sermon.

If Casey had really had a girl in his room, he was a better man than I was. Four hours a night is not enough for a sex life, or even a sleep life. It looked as if even so accomplished a lover as myself might have to suspend operations for the duration. I thought about Jane Donohue fleetingly, as a fighter sniffs ozone, just to keep going. Could a relationship founded on tits alone long endure? Don't know, no opinion, never heard of him. Next, quick quick like an old movie, Casey in his wheelchair on windy corners, shaking hands with puzzled New Englanders; on his crutches in the snow by a factory gate—a man pushing by, thinking it's a handout. Another saying, "Were you in the war?" "Sure I was. Purple Heart at Okinawa." Winks at me. "God bless you for that, anyway." Casey in empty halls, because the advance man made a mistake. Casey at frowsy banquets. "What we want to know is, what do you plan to do for the morticians of America?" Some crazy convention in Manchester—the advance man thought it was worth a look. "I don't plan to do *anything* for the morticians of America. Unless I decide to investigate them." Well, there go the morticians. Casey manifestly pissed off, deciding to instruct. "Every man is at his smallest and meanest in a group like this. Look at lawyers, look at doctors—look at politicians if you like. I'm reaching for something bigger in you . . ."

"You a Catholic?"

"Yes, ma'am."

"You are, huh?" The lady had nothing to further that. She was drunk as a bat and had forgotten the question.

"I am and I'm proud of it. But I'm reaching for something bigger than Catholic, too."

"Bigger than *Catholic?* What's bigger than Catholic?"

shouted a man. Oh Christ, they were all stoned. All the morticians were drunk out of their skins.

"A purple, ball-pointed Methodist elephant. Good evening, ladies and gentlemen."

Casey was mad as hell in the car. "We're wasting too much damn time," he said. "I thought you said you knew this state, Harris."

"These are pretty good turnouts for New Hampshire," said the advance man (or, in this case, boy).

"The hell they are. I know this state better than you do. Here—give me that list." He grabbed the list and went through it, slashing with his pen. "There. Now fill in the gaps with real meat. And if you can't do it, get some elderly shut-in to help you. Christ, just because you're a volunteer doesn't mean . . ."

"It means I can quit, at least," said Harris, just like that. "Stop the car, will you, Pete?"

Casey watched him go in silence. Then he shrugged. "Touchy little creatures, aren't they? You'd never see a pro do that. Christ, these kids."

The next meeting we went to was a little better, except that an old lady tied him up for ten minutes with a question about my father's old subject, animal vivisection. He was elaborately courteous this time, maybe in memory of the lost advance man. "Could you try to phrase that in the form of a question, please?" "All right. Last year in our nation's laboratories, countless thousands . . . and these figures only go up to last August, mind you." This time he was too polite, and he lost the others. The weak anxious eyes turned inward again, to whatever usually occupied them. On the way out, an old man with a hearing aid came up and asked Casey where he stood on the war. Our antiwar candidate sighed and patted the man's arm.

"Bad timing. Christ, I'm rusty," he said, in the car. "I should have said, 'I shall give animal vivisection my highest priority. Next question.' How's that—too sarcastic? God, I'm sleepy. Don't wake me for any audience of less than five."

It was impossible to believe we were getting anywhere. We hired a couple of new advance men, but they were just kids (well, almost as young as myself), and they kept lining up meetings with little reform groups that they thought needed the encouragement. They also had no sense of geography, so we were always shooting randomly up and down the state, to address groups that looked too young to vote.

"I thought you hated kids," I said, after one fiasco.

"I wish I could afford to," he said. He looked out the car window at the snow, and when he looked back, Mr. Hyde was gone. "Actually these kids are pretty good. I can't reach the adults in this state, but they can. I don't understand adults at all."

We couldn't afford polls, but sneaking a look at the other fellow's (we had a spy in Governor Chesney's outfit), we saw that we seemed to be completely stuck. The antiwar vote was frozen solid up here, and so was everything else. Chesney's escalation-with-honor policy (our name for it, not his) held at around thirty percent. Representative Sprigg and his peace-from-inside-out theory was good for another twenty-five—Sprigg maintained that protest prolonged wars, if it didn't actually cause them, and that a domestic cooling off would quickly spread to the battleground. (Note: his guru, the historian Jethro Fine, had so far produced five volumes proving that wars were the pure expression of domestic friction, and Fine was the pop highbrow of the year.) Our worst enemy, Senator Fielding, only commanded about fifteen percent himself, but was a powerful negative threat, because his campaign was aimed straight at us. "This country cannot afford to lose a second war" was his slogan—shabby, because we hadn't strictly speaking lost our first one yet, according to our own official history. His secret weapon was the Vatican concordat with Peking, and the papal encyclical *De Reconsideratione*. If you've ever tried to write a speech explaining an encyclical, you'll understand the size of the monkey wrench that Fielding threw at us.

"I suppose Fielding and Casey are really the best of friends," I said to Jane Donohue, in one of our rare, breathless tête-à-têtes. "Old polo partners, etc. Isn't that how politics really works?"

"No, they're real enemies." She had a nice mouth when she talked. I felt like an explorer beginning to find Eskimos sexy.

"Why? Anything personal?"

"I think so. Envy maybe." Jane thought that everyone envied Casey. She was a one-woman groupie, as possessive as Spritzer, and if I wanted to get her in the sack, I would have to imitate the boss down to his limp. (Sounds cruel, but old nurses get like that.)

Whatever was eating Fielding, it was a damn nuisance. Casey had to deliver a speech in an out-of-state Protestant seminary declaring his complete independence from Rome and practically reading himself out of the Catholic Church. A slick job which he wrote himself, full of references to Cardinal Newman and Bishop Pike, but what a waste of time.

"We need a new constituency," said Casey, as we drove back.

"How about ministers?" I said. "You knocked them dead tonight." Casey certainly did know how to talk to clergymen, with the little urbane jokes and the gentle humanity. I was impressed, and so were they, beating their shiny pink palms till the sweat ran. And the devil take it if their napkins fell on the floor.

"Ministers, market gardeners, multifarious milliners, that's my crowd," said Casey. "The trouble is, all the hard stuff is nailed down by now. Labor, business, the teeming black populace of New Hampshire—all the people who know what they want. All that's left are the vague men of good will. The compassionate set."

We decided he ought to project more concern. What kind? Vague concern, of course. I wanted him to say something specific about socialized steel, a hot number right then, but he said, "Let's save that for California. Late at night, to a group of students, after the papers have closed." I was mildly surprised at his caution—sounded almost like me for once. Spritzer chose the moment to glare at me venomously. "He's my candidate, all mine!" I wouldn't have thought any more about the steel question, it was like a hundred others, talking politics is like raking dead leaves, if Spritzer hadn't glared so hard. As it was, I looked up the senator's voting record the moment the car stopped and found that if Senator Fielding were to call us a cat's-paw of the steel barons, we were on a sticky wicket without a paddle. Oh shit.

At what precise moment a campaign starts moving is hard to say. Maybe the movement is just in one's mind. I'm told that some campaigners can swear they're moving, and end up with fifty votes. Anyway, it's a nice trip while it lasts. One moment, we were a messy little family, Donohue with her special relationship with Casey and Spritzer with his—and I no doubt with mine, which I was too close to see. The next, we were in the middle of Mardi Gras, with people swarming through the headquarters, kids who'd hitchhiked from Tacoma, old pros loping through like bassets smelling something they liked. "I was here first," you wanted to tell them. But you'd never get back your little personal campaign now. An odd result was that Donohue had dinner with me, and we talked about ourselves for a change. Or at least I did, and she gave signs of listening. The sack could not be far away.

Casey seemed unruffled. Whether he was a humble man, or a man so proud he didn't have to show it, I honestly couldn't tell. He often made me feel that the two were the same. "Political good fortune is part mystical," he said.

"Only a fool would take credit for it." I certainly couldn't trace where ours was coming from. Was it Senator Waldo's endorsement, or the article in *Time,* or some throwaway line of Casey's own that hit the public right? I gave myself modest credit for my special Casey stories mailed to our more childish columnists—Casey refusing to eat pizza in the Italian neighborhoods ("You wouldn't respect me") and flinching from babies (there were no babies, I had to invent them) and denouncing apple pie—which must have sealed up the cynical twelve-year-old vote. But there's probably no one moment. The kids from the West had started out weeks ago, when the campaign was dead. So maybe the *Zeitgeist* ran along a curve in time. "Just keep sacrificing those goats," said Casey. "Make sure the Jujube is happy."

The Jujube was delirious. You could feel it in the streets, a week before the primary, even when you walked far away from headquarters; or maybe I just carried it on my clothes. We had the crowds now, huge by New Hampshire standards, and the group face had changed. The New England suspicion had cleared like a cloud. Casey hadn't changed a hair, but he suddenly had charisma and seemed like a great man. Maybe it was the vague concern that did it—though Christ knows it *was* vague. We seemed to say less and less each day, and get more and more thunderous applause for it—until I began to think we *had* said something and I'd missed it. (My own progress note: guilty about this drop in content, but knew deep down we hadn't changed, and besides I wanted to win.

People talk about how reality corrupts politicians, but it happens twice as fast to their staffs.)

Up to now, Chesney, Fielding, and Sprigg had refused any kind of debate, for the very good reason that Casey would skin them alive. Suddenly they had no choice. Sprigg still held out, on the theory that debates were innately divisive—even if the contenders agreed about something, they had to pretend they didn't, the last thing our troubled nation needed. Just as well. Sprigg was one of the slowest-witted men I ever met, and it would have been murder. With Casey the murderer.

I guess the debate seemed spontaneous, but God knows we prepared for it: not just rehearsing our flexibly firm positions on everything down to the great sliced-bread controversy, but how to make Fielding angry and Chesney stuffy. "I sometimes think you really want to be President," says I to Casey. "Not necessarily," says he to me. "I just want to win this particular debate."

I was interested to meet Fielding, and maybe ask him on the sly if he wasn't kidding about the Peking concordat. He was on the face of it the perfect type of the lovable scoundrel, and I had a theory that he was a secret humorist. I looked up his voting record and found that there was no kind of skulduggery he could safely accuse Casey of. He'd sold out to *everybody*. He had even, for a brief time, converted to Catholicism, possibly to get a judgeship. I wondered if we could use that somehow. "Is this the young idealist who walked in my office a few months ago?" said Casey, still shoveling *that* old crap at me.

"Well, why not? He started it."

"You must know by now, being over twelve, that in this game you are defined as much by the mud you throw as the mud you receive." He winked. "Get somebody else to do it."

"Are you serious?"

"No, I'm not, for once," he said. "Fielding isn't running for President. There's no point wasting good mud on him. In this state, we're racing the clock, not the field."

"What do you mean?"

"Tell him, Jack. I'm busy."

If I had to get my answer from Spritzer, I'd as soon not know. I finally figured what the old mystagogue meant was that none of the others was running for President—it was three mechanical rabbits and one greyhound. If Casey didn't win big here and in his other two states, he was through. The smile would freeze on our fat cats, and the kids would hitchhike off to the woods and raise berries. (Like, we tried, man.) The big boys would keep out of the primaries as long as they decently could, all the way to Detroit, the convention site that year, throwing Fieldings in front of our wagon as long as they could. Casey liked an air of mystery around his thoughts, but the veriest boob could have worked out this one.

The debate you'll remember, so I won't go into it. Casey wanted to sneak a little national time ("for the Party") and the others reluctantly agreed. So we all trooped into the CBS building in New York like a herd of gypsies and squatted down in one of the control rooms and whooped it up in our infectious way. We had a giggle when Chesney brought up the South African question out of a clear sky —a very big issue in New Hampshire. I sweated out the steel problem, but I don't think an outsider would have spotted anything. Casey suggested a referendum on it, knowing damn well this country doesn't have referendums. It's a perfect way to consign a subject to oblivion—call in the People. Fielding's best material was so far below the belt you couldn't see it. Casey raised the religious issue himself as we had decided. "Certain murky allegations, slithering like rats in a dark alley." So much for that. I take credit for discovering that the World Council of Churches had sent a representative to the Vatican–Peking talks who recommended closer ties for Protestants, too. Fielding, the old heathen, simply writhed.

The next day, the critics noted Chesney's weak good nature (he seemed so delighted to be on national television at all that Casey couldn't get him to be stuffy about anything, only foolishly affable: he just kept grinning and saying, "I don't think we're very far apart on principle") and Fielding's black, inexplicable rage. There *was* an explanation for that, and I knew what it was. I had seen Fielding in the studio before the show and he was already glowering for practice. I introduced myself as planned, and he said, "So you work for that son of a bitch, do you?" He wasn't a secret humorist at all. "Just because he's a Catholic doesn't mean he isn't a good person," I said, goading him further for the show.

"Catholic? What the fuck has that got to do with anything? That bastard will sell you out regardless of race, creed, or ability to pay."

Casey wheeled over to see what was happening. He looked sleek and sharp, with a slight gangster shininess under the lights. "Are you trying to lure my kids away, George? I know how you envy my appeal to youth."

"Yeah, I know about your appeal to youth, you prick."

"The grannies are dying and leaving you, George. Too old to pull the lever."

"They'll never say that about you."

"Also, you envy my youthful appearance and athletic build, isn't that right?"

I had never thought about Casey in terms of physical violence, but suddenly the air was thick with it. Unfortunately, Fielding couldn't hit him now, and he couldn't hit him next year, and this would eventually drive him crazy. Casey's face seemed to croon to him—go on, hit me. I won't mind. Fielding turned away in disgust. And I thought, Never mind, boss, you'll get someone to hit you someday, if you keep it up long enough. Casey's hands slackened on the chair and I suddenly realized that he had been planning what to do with Fielding's first punch—pull the arm out of the socket, slip a half nelson onto his opponent and drag them both to the floor. Casey would be a menace to society if he couldn't get someone to wrestle him real soon.

"I think he's ready now," said Casey, smiling; and so was Casey himself, as smooth and calm as you saw him on CBS.

I was still curious about Fielding, so I decided to slip off the reservation and talk to someone in the enemy camp, across the corridor. Fielding's entourage was a lot older than ours, old newsmen, old ad men, and just plain unadulterated old men. But they were quite friendly and detached, having started out way before the age of ideology, and they talked like rich sportsmen, training turtles to race each other. "Don't you know?" said Fielding's manager. "Casey stole his girl."

"Jesus H.," I said. "Catholic father of the year, eh? You mean to tell me that the fate of the nation rides on the love life of two middle-aged men?"

"It's happened before. Besides, this was no ordinary girl. This was George's wife."

"No shit."

"Yeah, they used to be very good friends. Business friends, you could say. George didn't even know what was going on—what the hell can a guy in a wheelchair do to you? Then Ellen got the divorce, and good Catholic Casey said, 'Gee, that's too bad, kid. I really wish I could help you.' That's a sweet guy, your boss."

"And I suppose Ellen slashed her wrists into the sleeping pills."

"Not quite. She drinks a bit more these days. But then, who doesn't? She was only a kid, George was very proud of her, but what the hell, I don't think he'd have minded so much losing out to another kid. Why am I telling you this by the way?"

"Beats me."

"Well, for attribution: there is nothing personal about

this campaign. George Fielding works hard and he plays hard, and his victory over alcohol is one of the great stories of our time."

"Right on," I said.

My only reaction right then was attaboy, Senator. The debate was about to start, and even the turgid network waiting rooms crackled with excitement. The knowledge that our boy had cuckolded one of the enemy gave me reassurance. The moral issues could wait till we'd got out of the arena and the lions had gone home. I saw Chesney wandering about like a man in a dream, so I smiled and waved, and he stepped up and shook my hand, with speechless fervor, though we'd never met. He was ready, too.

The debate was in the bag right then. Casey seemed to dance by himself, in the shadows in the moonlight, using the other two as occasional props, like Astaire dancing with a flower pot. I was only afraid he might seem too flashy. But the dials in Casey's head tell him when to lay off that and play the statesman. A mismatch all the way, and I got a vicious thrill out of it, knowing what I knew. Afterward, Fielding and Chesney shuffled their papers importantly—Casey didn't have any, of course—and smiled briefly at each other like adults, who know how to keep things in proportion. But outside, Fielding was like a beat-up old man. The rage had burned out his engine, and he almost needed help to the street door. His manager appeared to be steering him by the armpit.

"So long, George. It's been fun," said Casey.

Fielding took a step sideways, straining away from his

manager, and I thought, This is it. They'll fight for sure, there's nothing else left. "So long, cripple," he said, and hobbled out. Casey grinned in pure diabolic triumph.

That should have been the end of the day, but campaign days have no shape. I couldn't sleep, what with replaying the debate and trying to cut little speeches out of it. So I went down to the bar in our hotel, where I saw a couple of red faces I knew, two parboiled newsmen, who nodded and went on talking. I assumed they were talking about Casey, because I assumed everybody was talking about Casey—such is the vicarious paranoia of campaigning. And I was all set to tell them they'd got their facts wrong, when I realized they were talking about Fielding instead.

"He certainly hates Casey, doesn't he?" I horned in, trying to direct the conversation to something I understood, Casey.

"Yeah, I guess so."

"You *guess* so? Why the hell else is he running? He hasn't a snowball's chance of winning. And he doesn't seem to believe in anything special."

"And it sure cuts into his drinking," said Rust Gates, the older of the two. "Jesus Christ never gave up more for his country than George's two quarts a day."

"So why's he doing it, if he doesn't hate Casey?"

"Well you see," said Gates, "Fielding's a bit of a dirty old man, in some ways. He had a little trouble with the Revenuers a few years back."

"Yeah, I remember." One of the dirtiest spots on his

utterly filthy record, as a matter of fact—undeclared campaign contributions stretching from here to Bermuda. Possibility of censure by the other crooks. God knows, I wish someone would think up a fresh kind of political scandal, a new line in muck.

"Well, the most amazing thing happened a couple of months ago. He got a complete clearance from Justice. Wasn't that grand?"

"Yeah. What does it mean?"

"It means he can keep the money and bathe in finest bourbon the rest of his days. Yet here he is, out stumping the country for the sake of all of us. Makes a man proud." A boring drunk, but all I had.

"Explain, oh master."

"Well, who the fuck do you think runs the Justice Department? Santy Claus? You think they *give* away clearances? Dwight Morris saw a chance to cut off a peace candidate at the knees. So he let Fielding out of his cage."

"You can't prove that," said his friend, speaking for the first time.

"Unfortunately not. Not in a court of law. That's the only place a wife can't testify against her husband."

"You got it from the old lady, eh?"

"Yeah. Phone up Ellen Fielding any time after midday and you'll hear the whole story. But you can't use the damn thing." He burped sadly. "Of course, everyone knows how he hates Casey, too. His staff are practically handing out brochures about it. It's the cleanest motive for running they can think of. Everyone prefers a crime of passion to the regular kind."

This was too bloody much for me. "You mean the rivalry's a fake?"

"You're full of shit," said the friend, "if you think that."

"O.K., I didn't go that far. I just said that his staff has to remind him every day how much he hates Casey, so he'll remember to snarl. Fielding's too drunk for a crime of passion. How the hell do you think he lost his wife in the first place?"

"You're still full of shit," said his friend. "Don't you believe him, son. At a certain time of night, he thinks he's a cynical newspaperman."

"Fuck you, Cassidy. What are you drinking, kid?"

Nothing, it turned out. It was three in the morning and I had to be up by seven. So I told them good night and headed for my room. Thinking, If you hang around the press long enough, you'll believe anything.

Now that was certainly the end of the day, right? I had learned enough *Realpolitik,* or fakepolitik, to last a year. Time now to go to bed and digest it all. But the phone was ringing even before I got in the room.

"Where the hell is Spritzer?" Casey's voice sounded German war movie.

"How the hell do I know where the hell is Spritzer? He lives his own life, thank God."

"Goddamnit, I've got to have Spritzer." Then, in a note of wheedle, "He's not in his room. Are you sure you haven't seen him?"

"That's right." Nobody could want Spritzer that much.

"Well—in that case, would you mind coming up yourself? Right away." He paused. "And bring some money." What money? I didn't have any money unless he needed thirty-two cents in a hurry. But he'd already rung off.

You go too far, Senator Bighead. I almost rang back to make a noise into the phone. But his voice had sounded peculiar, as if he was forcing the arrogance. I decided to take a look at him.

"Come in," he shouted, before I'd finished knocking. But I didn't have a key and he couldn't get to the door. "Come in, come in." He began to shout as if his bed were on fire. Then, in a lower voice, "Let him in, or I'll crawl over and do it myself."

Silence. My God, he'll do it. I don't want to see it—I could just picture Casey looking up at me from the doorknob. What the hell scene was I in for now? Had Fielding come to kill him or what? I found myself banging on the door like an idiot, there in the middle of the night in the middle of the Hilton.

The door opened slowly. I flinched, but it wasn't Casey. It was a blonde with her blouse ripped, paperback style. The odd thing was, she was holding one of Casey's braces in her hand. She obviously didn't want to let me in, but she didn't know what else to do with me. She was a victim of one of Casey's situations. He was sitting up in bed to the left of our picture, with his legs folded under him and his face going three ways at once.

"Fielding must have sent her," he said quickly. "It's a

frame. I let her in, I thought she was room service. And she began tearing off her clothes."

"How come your braces were off?" I don't know why I asked. It was as if we were checking his story for weaknesses.

"I wheeled over," he said carefully. "Then I got back into bed. That was a mistake, I admit."

"Crap," said the girl. "I don't know any Fielding. I just want my money."

"We'll have to pay her something," said Casey. "We can't afford a scandal at this stage of the campaign. Have you got a fifty, Sam?"

"For what you wanted, it's a hundred. If I did that stuff."

"So, you didn't do it. Give her fifty, Sam. And, baby, tell your friend Fielding that he'd better think of a better trick for next time. Nobody's going to believe I raped a big healthy girl like you. Not in my condition."

She didn't say anything. If he wanted his frame-up story, he was welcome to it, as a professional courtesy. It was just another john's fantasy to her. Son of a bitch thinks he's running for President. She held out her hand to me, still gripping the brace as a hostage.

That would have been that—except that I didn't have the fifty. "Couldn't you write a check?" I croaked.

"Not in my own name. Can't you see, that's just what Fielding wants? In Spritzer's name maybe, or yours."

"I don't take checks," said the blonde, her usual helpful self.

So there we were, me with my door handle and the blonde with her brace, and Casey fighting for control. Rosie or whatever her name was could not break the tie. Her mind had frozen. Did she take American Express? I wondered. Casey was trying to regain his TV form, and I was confident he would any moment. He stared at her imperiously, trying to break her proud stupidity; but she was strong. Meanwhile, I was working out ridiculous little deals that were too silly even to mention.

Don't ask me how long, an hour, thirty seconds, something like that: Casey's glare suddenly broke against her face, and astonishingly, his own face seemed to crumple completely. In a voice I'd never imagined, creamy with self-pity, he said, "Can't you see I'm helpless? I'm tired. We'll get you the money in the morning. I swear to God." He was close to crying.

The kindhearted prostitute stared back with utter contempt. She might be in a cheap line of work, but she'd never crawl like that to anyone. "Here—" she threw the brace at him and it clunked on the floor. "Keep your fucking money." She pushed my hand off the door handle and went out, without leaving a name or address.

Casey sat for a long time, in a species of trance. He didn't ask me to leave, and I didn't want to. I know it sounds crazy, but I honestly thought he might try to kill himself. I've never seen a face readier for it. "It weakens you in some ways," he said to himself. A regular hour must have gone by this time, and I saw light under the window blind. Maybe he was safe now.

I began to open the door, and he said, "You didn't believe a fucking word, did you? About Fielding and the frame-up?"

"It doesn't matter."

"You can quit when you like. Jack'll give you your money."

"I didn't say I wanted to quit."

"I didn't ask you." He wouldn't look at me even now. "I can't have someone working for me who's sorry for me."

I remember after that walking down the corridor, staring at the carpet with sanded eyes; and rocking gently in front of the elevator; and thinking, as *he* might have been thinking, Maybe he shouldn't be President after all.

5 By morning, I was trying to take a lighter view again. The fact was, I wanted to stay in the campaign now. I wasn't sorry for him in the least. Even without the whore to show me the right attitude, I would have been disappointed in him, though. If he couldn't handlc that, how thc hell was he going to handle the Russians? I know it sounds goofy, but I was so used to seeing him as a candidate that I couldn't judge the scene in any other way. I guess I also disapproved of a man paying for his women. I didn't care how many senators' wives he racked up. But whores were something else. How could he hope to cope with the balance of payments? On the plus side, I had to admire his stam-

ina. Jesus, after the days he put in, to even *want* to do it—the electorate would be proud of such a toro. Remind me to start a rumor. Not really so funny. That look of ultimate weakness canceled out everything good I could think about.

I had slept late because nobody bothered to call me. When I went down to the desk, I found that Casey and Spritzer had checked out and gone back to New Hampshire, leaving an envelope for me with a trifle of money in it. What was I supposed to do—just give up and go home? Or offer my services to another politician? Maybe my scout group and I could scrape together another peace candidate, out of leftover mud.

Unfortunately, Casey was still the only game in town. I walked around New York for a couple of hours, imagining myself highlighted against the buildings by great camera work. Loping toward some girl who was loping right back. It was a bright, clear day, warm for the time of year, and it felt pretty good to be out of politics. I got as far as Central Park and lay on the hard winter ground, as we kids do, and rolled my man-of-distinction overcoat into a ball and stuck it under my head. And, naturally, I thought about Casey.

Goddamnit, even an utterly colorless candidate is hard to get out of your system. Campaigning welds you together at the hip. Casey, I found myself thinking, read that whole scene differently from me last night. He thinks people are still sorry for him. It's a mistake he makes about people. Maybe they were sorry for him when he was a brave kid.

But nobody feels sorry for a middle-aged man, whatever his troubles. I thought of ringing him and telling him he would always be a shit by me. It might help.

Then, still thinking away, I came to my old friend, the Catholic Church. I remembered the kids at school discussing whether they really burned you for masturbation, or was it scare talk? Maybe Casey was ashamed to be found in a sexual situation of any kind. I hadn't thought about that. I assumed he had to be fed girls to keep up his strength, and he only worried about his failure to cope with the whore *politically*. But he might not see it like that. Maybe he had to end the scene at any cost, even pride, for religious reasons. I didn't know whether this made things better or worse. At least it meant he would only crack in certain private contexts.

I still had to decide what to do with myself. I'd left my bag at the Hilton, but I couldn't afford another night there at my own expense. I'd cashed Casey's modest check, which just about paid for carfare back to Boston. As the afternoon wore out and I watched the people drifting aimlessly around the park, I decided I'd been out of politics too long. And I thought to myself, How many Presidents of the United States would know how to get a crazy whore out of their room at five in the morning anyway? It has nothing to do with executive ability. (And besides, he wouldn't have a glassy-eyed speechwriter at his side in Moscow, but someone like Henry Kissinger.) Oh, what the hell—I'd start hitching back to New Hampshire while there was some light left. It didn't do any harm to look in.

The next day they voted, and I wasn't going to miss my climax, after working so hard to get the girl.

It was a tough hitch and I didn't think I was going to make it in time for the primary. Slept in Hartford Monday night, if anyone wants to know. The next day I got lucky and caught a right-wing trucker who took me the last long leg. "What are you doing up here?" he asked. "Visiting my parents." "Good. Casey's brats are all over. But you look like a nice clean-cut kid." So do you, buddy, so do you. I had to endure some crap about so-called educated (who, me?) and who pays their bills for them, but I had a last lick coming. When we reached Concord, he said, "Where do you want to get off?" and I said, "Just take me to Senator Casey's headquarters, he's like a father to me." He stopped the truck then and there, and I had to walk half a mile in the dark and the everlasting snow, but it was worth it. The bastard had got me back into politics.

I hardly recognized Casey's place that evening for all the banners, bunting, and froufrou. The workers were at full pitch of their devotions, churning round and round in the glare, and it took a bit of getting used to, with my frostbite and my streaming galoshes. Nobody's eyes seemed to focus right, and I've never been bumped into so many times without apology. I saw Jane Donohue, and she came up and kissed me passionately on the lips, tongue and all. "Where have you been?" she panted. "I stayed in New York. Fixing things," I said coolly.

It seemed voter turnout was terrif. Jane still used words

like that, a real old-line Catholic. It seems she had been on the phone all day, and so had everyone else, lighting a fire under the farmers. Every vote in the a, b, and c categories (that's down to the "what? who?" crowd) had been tapped. We could not fail.

The senator hadn't arrived yet. In fact, no one had seen him all day. He was believed to be resting. So of course I conjured up an immediate nightmare of Casey brooding over his humiliation in New York and deciding to withdraw. By my reading of him, this was just possible.

The returns began to come in, and they would have done credit to old General Thieu's organization work. But this only moved my nightmare into a new phase. That proud, lonely man would never withdraw if he lost or only won small. But a smashing victory would tempt him like sin. The kids were out of their collective mind by now, screaming and grabbing and hugging anything that moved. Jane was practically raping me with excitement, and I thought, Yes, yes, one could do it right now, as a purely political act. But this was just the kind of scene that Casey would love as a setting for his irony: an old-time political rally, acted out by children, yeah. Now, tell them it's all off, to go home and be kind to their mothers.

I guess I have a lot to learn about proud, lonely men. At the height of the peak of the orgy, he rolled in with a big silly grin on his face, parting the crowd like Moses. He didn't look like much to me, because I knew about this hairline crack down the middle, but he must have looked like God to the others. It was easier to scream along with them than to stand in pompous silence—after all, it was our victory as much as his. "We're number one," or some such inanity. "Yea, Casey."

The political football was turning into a real horse race. Yah hoo, sis boom ba. Besides, if I didn't shout, I'd lose what looked like my first big chance with Jane. I turned to her for a squeeze and I saw she was kissing somebody else. Ah, these convent girls. I spun her around, and with wild empty eyes she applied the same kiss to me, without even starting a new one. What we were all kissing was Casey, of course, using each other, in his phrase, as the bread and wine.

He tried to make a speech, but it was impossible in that noise. And I'll swear he looked disappointed for a moment. But the hopeless crazy grin came back. Earth has no happiness like unto a winning politician. He wheeled out again, to whatever kind of evening he'd planned—God, what could satisfy him tonight? (I later found out he spent it taping interviews with the press.) Jane and I grabbed a bottle of campaign booze and went off speechless to her hotel room, and she made love like an electric angel. It was worse than taking advantage of a drunk. And I thought, If she calls me Senator, I'll really have to leave; and then thought what a shit I'll be if I hang around here to the end.

The next day, I called on Casey. He was still grinning, only his number-three, or watch-out grin. "I thought we'd lost you," he said. "I hear that kids have no stamina." Translation: "I'll get even with you, you bastard, if it takes all summer." Sam Spade Perkins's features showed no expression.

"Well, we've got to start work on Wisconsin and Indiana," he said, every inch the gruff leader. But there was no way he could impress me right now. Could he stand having me around in that case? He contemplated his next move, a possible cat's-paw sacrifice. "I know what," he said. "Why don't you skip the next two primaries and do a campaign biography? I can use the same speeches out there—I doubt they've reached Indiana, or ever will."

"What kind of campaign biography?"

"Flattering. Ruthlessly honest. You know." He smiled—you know what an old sinner I really am, don't you? He'd found a use for me after all. Spritzer glowered. *I'm his confessor, not you.* "No, seriously," said Casey. "I know you can't do much within the limits of the form, but do what you can. Try to be a little more honest than most, O.K.? A few laughs, a few tears. Get my father to help you. In fact, get him to write it. He'd love to. And then pick us up before California."

I assumed he'd hire another speechwriter in my absence, or even two, but I didn't mind. He wouldn't use their speeches, either. And I was happy to step back from this madness and get my own bearings. Did I really want to support a candidate with a crack down the middle? Or did every candidate have one? Finally, could Casey be trusted in the clutch? Looking up his old clutches might help.

So I returned to New York to hunt up his old man and

his first law associates and even his pal Phil Marconi who, according to Casey, "knew something." Marconi was still in the engineering game, successful by the look of his carpet, a big, ragged, melancholy man, with a crucifix behind his desk. He remembered that polio autumn moment by moment, and reproduced it for me in more detail than I wanted, and so graphically that I could feel the shadows closing on Our Gang. It almost seemed that life stopped for Phil that summer. At least, he showed no visible interest in the present. Did Casey back out of fights as a kid? Goodness no. He fought forty minutes to a draw with the meanest black kid you ever saw—a kid who had the rest of us terrorized. So, that was a relief. I asked Marconi what he thought of Casey as a possible President, and he looked at me warily, and said, "He's quite a guy."

If he knew something, he was too kind or tired to tell it. I was ready to go, but Marconi had one more thing to say about the old days: "We had another friend, Joseph Hennessy, who was scared out of his mind of getting polio. I used to razz the poor guy about it. Then you know what? Next year, Joseph did get it, and a few years later he died in an iron lung. A very regrettable thing."

He stood up. He wore a vest, and he had a slight stoop and premature silver hair. He evidently was not the man to ask about the miniskirt or cigars for women. He lived in that world only by an oversight. I might get a flicker if I asked him about the latest Bing Crosby road picture or how the Brooklyn Bums were going to do next year. I shook his hand, and he said, "Remember me to Brian."

I turned at the door, expecting to see a kid in knickers and a cardboard helmet. But he was already back at work designing bridges for the now-people.

Kevin Casey must have stopped his watch the same day as Marconi. He was the curator of the next period, the first winter and spring, and he took me through it in a bluff chamber-of-commerce way, stressing the laughs they'd had, thanks to Brian's soaring spirit. I didn't really want all the names of the doctors and stuff, but I got them anyway. He told me that people had tried to sugar-coat polio for Brian, but Brian had insisted on being told the facts about it. Beatrice Casey stared out the window at the dirty old river—was it clean when Brian was a boy? I wondered. Time had fixed their seating arrangement like an architectural blueprint. Kevin had the sofa to himself these days, Beatrice preferred a hard chair by the window, and I was stuck in the leather bucket, with my legs sticking over the edge like old laundry.

"What do you remember of that period, Mrs. Casey?"

She looked at Kevin. She remembered pretty well, I guessed, but what good would it do? "Brian was very brave," she said. "Kevin remembers better than I do."

That was their combined version of it. But both were eager to talk to me separately, and tell me how hard those years had been on the other. Nice people, I guess.

Kevin went out, leaving his wife first ups. She gave the impression of being on a spiritual retreat of indefinite duration. But if she had finally gotten to the truth of the matter, the only good she thought she could do about it was pray for people, and be kind. She told me word for word how she had felt when Brian took sick. "I think we did every possible thing wrong. But it doesn't matter. The Good Lord knows better than to leave these things up to us, doesn't he? I think Brian turned out pretty well after all, don't you?"

"Fine," I mumbled.

"The only thing I regret," she said, in a lower, more confidential voice, "is what it did to my husband. I'm afraid Brian was the whole universe to me for a year or two, and I ignored Kevin. Nobody should be the whole universe, should they? It isn't fair to anybody. Kevin is just as important in the Divine plan as Brian. I think the biggest mistake we both made," said this surprising woman, "was taking it all too seriously."

Brian had told me I wouldn't get anything much from his parents, that they never talked about anything personal. But that must have been just in the family. To a stranger, she was anxiously personal. She even gave me to understand that she had stopped sleeping with her husband for a while, because he had left the Church. "Catholics were strange in those days. Thank God for John XXIII, at least in my case. It was a terrible thing to do to Kevin, a terrible blow to his confidence. Thank God—" she looked at me closely: this was official—"he's all right again now."

I knew this was getting me nowhere as far as the campaign biography, or my own doubts, went. But I couldn't think of any direct way to get what I wanted—"Madam, would you trust your son with the doomsday button?"—so I hoped she would stumble on it herself.

"Do you think maybe Kevin ignored *you* for the sake of Brian?" I asked, just to keep her talking.

"I wouldn't know about that," she said. I make my confession, he makes his. I shouldn't have spoken. It had woken her up. She said, "I shouldn't be telling you all this. You won't be using it in your book, will you?"

The stupid thing was I didn't give a damn whether Kevin ignored her, I was just being sociable. There was probably a lot in those two I didn't get, because I wasn't interested in them personally, with millions dying in India and all that. Kevin Casey took his turn next, with his guard up as high as it would go. He repeated his wrinkle-free, wart-resistant version of Brian's childhood, almost too good for even a campaign biography. He kept glancing at me to see how much I was buying. Something about him suggested that he would edge his chair up any moment and tell me the *real* story. But he never did, not advertently. He told me again what a fine woman his wife was. Yeah, yeah. "Didn't you draw apart a little over Brian's illness?" I asked, hoping to crack him on something, anything. "What makes you say that?" he asked quickly. "Nothing. I just thought something like that might happen."

He sat back and puffed his chest slightly, suggesting that a new and larger untruth was being cooked up in there. "Things like that bring people together. I would say it definitely strengthened our marriage."

He looked away, perhaps to smile. He was an intelligent

man who'd learned that intelligence gets you nowhere. When he looked back, it was to say, "I thought Brian handled himself well in the debate, didn't you? How many delegates do you think he can count on now?"

Ah politics! I'd forgotten about you for a moment. There is no fun like instructing an amateur, and I wasted the rest of the session showing how much I'd learned. The scavenger in me surfaced only once, when Kevin Casey offered me a drink, and I almost said, "I'll have one if you'll have one." If I could nudge him off the wagon just once, I'd find my crock of gold or whatever.

He had learned all the words about politics, and it seemed like a lively discussion at the time. But looking back, I realized they were the kind of bright disconnected questions a good hostess might ask who'd heard your field was such and such. What about labor? How now Dade County? I wouldn't say he was faking an interest in the campaign. But he was so busy doing his duty, being the perfect candidate's father, that he had no time to work up a set of feelings of his own. Above all, he didn't want to *embarrass* Brian. These were awfully nice people.

I heaved out of my bucket and said I'd call again. I felt as if I were leaving a sick room which was being kept in readiness, with fresh flowers. Brian never came home, they said, but he saw them in Washington sometimes. Offhand they seemed like another part of the cow I couldn't use. I didn't realize till later how Kevin might have decoyed me past their hiding place. After all, Brian's irony had to come from some place, didn't it?

After that, I found an old teacher who said that Brian was brilliant and a member of the Turn Left Club who said he was memorable and Professor Woody Kline, who said he was a no-good, low-life son of a bitch. Casey had insisted I see Kline. "Look, he didn't ask for the candidacy," I said to this boyish-looking little guy, who was sitting in a castle made of books, his study. By this time I was a pretty fair devil's advocate, or speechwriter. "You'll find Casey never asks for candidacies," said Kline. "He just finds out where they're going and arranges to meet them." "Isn't that true of all politicians?" I asked. "Otherwise, we'd never get any Presidents at all." I was pretty pleased with that one. Kline was supposed to be some hot political scientist, and here I'd pinned him to the mat with laughable ease.

Kline pulled out his pipe, obviously to gain time, the poor bastard. "No, it's only true of professional idealists like Casey. Practical politicians have to squat down near their interests and hope something comes along. Sometimes they wait all their lives." Casey's memo had said, "You might as well hear the worst, and his name is Kline," but so far he hadn't talked about Casey at all, only some abstract idea of Casey. He had reduced Brian to a character in a professor's equation—a dream inside a dream. You've got to understand, I'd been in the pit, man, and smelled the sweat, so this guy seemed a little unreal. If Kline knew how many interests Casey was squatting on in real life, he'd have something to be shocked about. "Mind you," he rambled, pointing his pipe at the class, "it's not always bad that idealists can travel light and meet trains, if there's nobody else there. Let's just say I don't like Casey's face."

That was more like it, I guess. What was Casey like in those days? "An opportunist, a scrambler, a Catholic Sammy Glick." Ever see him scared? "Jesus, what was there to be scared of at Columbia?" I still couldn't come up with the right question. So I said, "If you could only see what a slobby campaign Casey runs, you would never call him an opportunist again." "Yeah, slobby like a fox. I'll bet he just happens to work longer hours than anyone you ever met." "How'd you know that?" "He always did."

Heart, cold. Bile, rising. Tell me, were there any political irregularities? He told me about their falling-out over the German Army, and Casey's machinations with the Turn Left Club. I began to suspect that Kline would have found the rise of George Washington distasteful. But what was that about the German Army? "He admired it, that's all," said Kline. "He admired holy hell out of it in fact." "How do you know?" "I could tell by the look on his face when we talked about it one day. He was like a stained-glass window."

"Hmm," I said, if you can actually say such a word. "I guess you must find him slightly incredible as a peace candidate, huh?" "Bet your sweet ass, I do," said the professor and winked at his own devilment. "In the crunch, Casey is a power man. It may be the cripple thing, I wouldn't know. He also worships his own intelligence too much. He may be against this war, because it isn't a very bright one, but wait till he comes to a really intelligent war. Mmboy. Look at it this way, Mr. Perkins—what else has Casey got to believe in, besides his own strength and intelligence? He was brought up to believe with all his heart in an all-loving God, and this God proceeds calmly to knock the legs out from under him. So much for faith. After that, it was him against the universe."

It was believable, like most professors' stuff, if you're in the mood. The only trouble was, it made Casey sound too attractive. "That's just theory," I said. "Theory about cripples, theory about Catholics. I never met a cripple with a power complex in my life." I'd never met any cripples at all, but was sure this would hold up. Next he'd be talking about Negroes being good athletes.

"That's true. Man cannot think without general ideas, yet there *are* no general ideas." Kline by now was lying on his back with his eyes closed, boring himself to sleep. Geez, I was glad to be out of school. "Of course, it's a personal thing, when you come down to it," he said. "That doesn't mean it isn't real. Political science is simply an adjudicating among prejudices."

Enough of this small talk. "Do you really hate the guy that much? Or is it just a habit?"

"Oh yes. I hate him all right. Casey fooled me once into thinking he was O.K., and you can't forgive a man for that, can you? Besides—he stole all my secrets. You probably thought he got them from St. Thomas, huh? Forget it. He's a turncoat Kline-ean." He smiled sadly, trying to make a joke of it. "But who knows, maybe Casey is what politics is really all about and I'm teaching a lot of crap. I'll be working against him, anyway. If he's right, my whole life is a waste of time."

Ah, you airy-fairy professors, what do you know? I was so full of being in the pit and smelling the sweat that I never got Kline's wavelength until I got it later from Casey. One funny thing is, I got a feeling he really admired Casey, the brother who'd taken to big crime. People who know only one politician tend to take him too seriously. I stood by the door a moment, hoping to settle this. "If it was between him and Senator Fielding, what then?" "I'd take Fielding any day," he said, without opening his eyes.

That settled it. A nut, a palpable nut.

Who else did I fail to get anything out of on that first trip and what else did I fail to learn? I did learn that Casey had fought that plucky fight with polio. That he refused for some years to go to sports events. Conquered that O.K. and now went all the time. That he had done brilliantly at law school, but had goofed off in practice. He was busy reforming one of the local Reform clubs, and caused annoyance at his firm by using the secretaries on political business. The only cases on which he'd exerted himself specially were ones involving important clients (hiss) and voluntary civil-rights cases ('ray!). He'd defended a nasty price-fixing operation (boo) and spent a summer in Mississippi (right on). He'd made a lot of money: enough for a President, almost enough for a junior partner.

It was beyond me to assess a lawyer's honor. My sainted

father once told me that a lawyer is like a doctor who's always being asked to save Hitler's life; and my father's refusal kept us pretty damn poor, too. In politics, Casey's record was fine—but then, so was every New York liberal's. There was no test, no way of telling what he'd do with a national constituency at his back.

Ruthless rise? All rises are ruthless. In Reform circles, the ploy seemed to be to outflank your opponent's idealism. Casey had done O.K. He'd played chicken on the peace issue with a decent fellow called Winespun until Winespun had gone over the edge, calling for unilateral disarmament. At which point, Casey stood at the brink and shouted "irresponsible" down into the ravine. Presto, congressman. Then the thrilling scamper around left end again for the senatorial nomination, a beautiful thing to see. He was the anti-boss candidate, yet he had all the bosses he needed (all of whom became, of course, anti-boss bosses, by association). God knows what he told them. His little pipe attracted rats and children both. He had the kids, the blacks, the new politics—yet lots of rich white supporters too, and his crack core of dirty old pros. Well, no use worrying about where he got them, he wouldn't be here at all if he hadn't.

And in the Senate campaign there was his curious appeal to old ladies, muddle-headed hard-hats, and suburbanites looking for the perfect insurance policy: stargazers of all persuasions; avalanche. "Casey appeals across class and across generations," I found myself mouthing. I was learning slickly for my slick book. What did I want for myself?

I didn't like his strengths and I didn't trust his weaknesses. Or, as we say in Sophistry: would this man crack late at night if his braces were taken away by the Chinese ambassador? Or would he arrange a world in which the unexpected was already taken care of? And which was worse?

Before returning to the trail, I looked in on my old man, who was already heading up a lawyers-for-Casey committee and who thinks the senator is a great American. It bodes ill for our chances. The only encouraging thing I learned was from an old guy who worked in Casey's congressional office before anyone had heard of him. "Hustle? Oh you bet," said the old sage. "Take credit for other people's ideas? Naturally. He wasn't running for Pope, you know. But I'll tell you one thing, the actual work—you know, the nasty stuff that goes on between elections?—he actually did some of it. That's pretty rare among name-brand politicians." Was the country ready for a working President? I don't mean working for re-election, but really working? Maybe if he did it quietly . . . Another guy said Casey quit working the day he made senator. That was more like it. But it was all self-instigated gossip. There is no truth about politicians, only versions. Your mother would lie to you about her pet candidate.

I picked up our own little hero in Indiana and was surprised to find him still only life-size and almost smothered in a huge organization. Wisconsin had been a slight disappointment—no fewer than five candidates claiming moral victory, including us of course. I kept only half an eye on the campaign, partly because of my precious doubts and partly because I had to rattle off the biography in time for immediate publication, hard going even for brainless shit. There was no avoiding it, since he'd payrolled the research, but I felt as if I was carrying out Casey's trash for him, and that he'd given me the project to test my humility after that fiasco with the whore. And, of course, if we stumbled any place along the way, the book would be a lame duck or something. Casey at this point was rumored to be having an affair with an actress who was following us around, and I hoped this would keep him out of mischief for a while.

Indiana was also inconclusive. All the big boys ducked it, and we were left grappling with a dim favorite son named Harrison, an undignified exercise. We had to wipe him out to get anywhere, but he had all kinds of mysterious out-of-state money, and Casey ran a sulky campaign: he thought we shouldn't have entered in the first place, and he got even with his staff by giving his dullest speeches—some of them mine. After one bomb in Indianapolis, I almost asked him never to use my stuff again. Other people's words bored him, and I could have read it better myself. But I still believed in peace, I guess, so decided to hang in a little longer.

California was another story. This state brings out the ham in politicians, and Casey was made for it. Besides, he had a field to run against here ("I couldn't sprint against that cart horse in Indiana. I would have looked cheap"). Here he had one of his friends from the Senate to go against. Russell "Billy" Wilkins, the Southern moderate, who had just switched to peace, and was trying to see if there was enough of it for both of them. My interest pricked up at this—another peace candidate gave me a choice, too. There were plenty of others, enough to get stuck in the door we hoped. But Wilkins was the main new ingredient.

"I welcome my friend Senator Wilkins to the cause, however late." Casey rehearsed about twenty variations of this phrase on the plane. "My victory—I mean our success—in New Hampshire seems to have clarified Senator Wilkins's thinking miraculously." He was looking forward to the land of the goofy orange groves and even sang us an Irish song, "The West Awake," in a light tenor voice.

We ran into Wilkins in the Beverly Plaza in Los Angeles, and I was encouraged to find him one of the most charming men I'd met so far.

"How are you, you old son of a bitch?" he said to Casey.

"I was fine until you announced. When the hell did you discover peace, Billy?"

"In the snows of New Hampshire."

"We'll nail you on that late conversion."

"We'll nail you on that hasty decision. I waited until I had all the facts, my friend. I do not assume that my country is always in the wrong."

They laughed, and it crossed my mind that this guy might be too nice and boyish for politics. Could he handle the Russians? Did he have a crack down the middle?

"We shouldn't be seen here fraternizing like this," he said. "We're supposed to hate each other's guts, aren't we?"

"No, no," said Casey. "It's different with peace candidates. We have to outnice each other. I always have time to visit with my old pal Billy."

"In normal times I would agree. But I just can't seem to get that old-buddy feelin' with the nation like it is and all."

"O.K., try it that way. But you'll find my way is best. And if you want any other tips on how to be a peace candidate, feel free."

"I'll do that. Nice talking to ya," he said to me. "Give my regards to Frances," to Casey, "and try to stay in drafts, do you hear?"

I was afraid that Casey wouldn't have the heart to run against him. But when I mentioned this to the master, he laughed and said, "Well, right now, I don't have to. We're running as an entry. We'll just count the combined peace votes this time. Don't worry, Billy hasn't the legs to make it to Detroit."

We were in his room, and he was in his favorite perch, by the window. Los Angeles stared sleazily back, a riot of laundromats. "Christ, what a city. How can anything be so vulgar? Yeah, I love it."

Spritzer looked in and Casey looked annoyed and Spritzer looked hurt. This was their new routine. "Was there something you wanted, Jack?" Casey was obviously bored with his flunky. Was he planning to change flunkies in midstream?

"I'm tired of politics," he said to me after Spritzer had huffed out. "And Jack doesn't know anything else. I know it's a lousy time to bring it up. No, I'm not tired of it, I'm scared of it. I'm scared that someday I won't be able to stop smiling and nodding. You know, you have to pretend to be an extrovert at first, and then suddenly you don't have to pretend any more, and finally you can't get back inside. California could be the place where that happens to me." Oh, a talking jag. Come back, Spritzer. He was reminding his Ivy Leaguer what a sensitive man he was deep down. "You know that bit in your manuscript where you say, 'The senator likes to go off by himself and think and get reacquainted with himself'—what a load of garbage. I haven't done that in years. Or what about, 'He always has his beloved history books along with him.' I haven't cracked a history book in years. Those books are just weighing down the luggage."

He already had me ashamed of that damn manuscript, and I'd done only one draft. He'd forced me to praise him, to get even with me for knowing his weakness, and now he was sneering at my praise.

"It isn't too late to destroy it," I said.

"What was that? No, it's O.K. As garbage goes, it's very high quality. I don't know." He flexed his hands, as if to find if there was any strength in them. "This is a shitty occupation. I should be thinking about the great issues of the day, but I'm too revved up to think. The great issues are decided by a group of mechanical morons who can't stop smiling and nodding. You go along with that, Perkins?"

"Absolutely, boss."

"Ah to hell with you. Let's get drunk and forget politics. You know what? I'd like to see my kids. Do you think we could fly some of them out?" A representative sample, no doubt. He'd said this before and nothing had come of it. "I love my kids, do you know that? Especially Whozit, the little one. Christ, I'm a lousy parent. I can't even tell you their ages. When I think of how my parents loved me and how it fucked me up—no, that isn't fair."

He suddenly wanted to talk about the past, his new hobby. Maybe it was the only kind of reflective thinking he could do under pressure. I got out a bottle at his instruction and poured us both a belt. He was doing this to tune himself for the game tomorrow—groveling, snarling at his own unworthiness, laughing at himself. "Did I tell you about the time I went into mourning when they discovered the Salk vaccine? I cried like a baby." I couldn't tell if it meant anything or was just an exercise. There's a lot I don't know about this man.

"What do you think about the German Army?" I said. He laughed. "So you met Woody? Yeah, of course you did. You know what I think? I think Woody was the one who admired the German Army. You know, like Puritans and sex?" He looked over: buy that? No? "All right, no secrets from the speechwriter. Sure, I admired the German Army, Woody was absolutely right. You'd have had to be out of your skull not to in those days. Marching with their legs up like chorus girls." He laughed again. "Woody despises cripples, you know. Woody is so hostile he doesn't dare leave his room."

God, that playfulness—bounding around wildly now

that he trusted me. "Marconi? Death by Catholicism and threw away the key. The Church knows a lot of ways to beat you if you're not smart and tough enough. You won't find out anything from those guys. You have to come to me!" He coughed with laughter and then shrieked, "And I for*get!*"

Drunk as a lord. For collectors of trivia, let it be known that Casey has a very weak head and generally despises alcohol, like anything he can't lick. In this case, he probably wanted something to help him sleep. He hadn't slept more than four hours a night since this thing began. I had to pick him up now like a male nurse and dump him on his bed. I'm skinny for this kind of work, but his legs weighed like a child's, seeming to make an unfair, uniquely Casey-like claim on me, and I had no trouble at all. After that I went looking for Spritzer—I was damned if I was going to take off his braces for him. I'd never be able to work for anyone else if I did that.

6

I couldn't have gone to work for Wilkins right then, even if I'd wanted to. Not only would it have been a brutal trick on Casey, but peace candidates just don't do that to each other, it would have hurt both of them. My chance would come after California, if Wilkins made a respectable showing. This may sound cold-blooded, but remember, the country still hadn't chosen a President, and I knew less every day whether Casey was stable enough to handle it. To make things worse, he would hardly talk politics with me at all any more. Every time I tried to discuss issues with him, he dismissed them with wisecracks ("there's enough politics in the home without dragging it into public life"). He didn't even seem much interested in the war, although it was heating up again to the point where a peace candidate could be in trouble. Senator Wilkins was emphasizing what's right with our society, and I suppose I should have been glad that Casey didn't do anything as silly as that: but I also got the feeling he was just too lazy to think up a new speech. Casey had chosen this freaky moment to decide I should write a serious book about him; or at least to play a game of, "Suppose you were writing a book about me." "I'm a much more fascinating character than I realized," he said. "Reading about myself every day in the papers has whetted my curiosity. What is this Casey all about? What does he want? I expect even you are interested to know by now."

Only politically, sir. But Casey no longer valued me politically, if he ever had. He had three new speechwriters now, and although I still went through the motions, I had graduated irreversibly to crony. He began to tell me what his father really thought on such and such an occasion, as if I gave a shit what his father thought. "I wasn't so sure about my mother," he said. I told him reluctantly what she'd said about him, not having the character to withhold information, and he nodded and said, "Ah, that explains a lot."

"O.K., now what about this war we're supposed to be fighting?"

"Which war was that?" You can see why I thought of jumping to Wilkins. I hadn't signed on for this.

"Talk politics, damnit," I said.

"You're just not the political type, Sam. I always knew

it. We'll make a human out of you yet. Anyway, politics is overrated."

"You picked a fine time to decide that."

"I agree," he said. "It's something every President should know."

I didn't want to live in the past with him and his family and Phil Marconi. Those people were dead and he'd die, too, from thinking about them. But he seemed to need a quiet place in the past where the heat of the campaign couldn't reach him, and the worst of it was that he seemed real when he talked about that, while his public side seemed phonier each day. I frankly believe that campaigning is bad for people and should be disallowed by law.

Casey's current image featured lazy strength—after all those months of campaigning, what a tiger. One afternoon we got mobbed in a supermarket parking lot in Los Angeles, and I thought, Jesus, he'll panic, he's helpless—at least, I know I panicked. But he sat there throughout, calm as a quarterback, while the crowd mauled at his chair and almost heaved it over. He actually picked up a crazy-looking kid and held him out as a shield. "Steady, boy," he said. Our secret-service man was jumping up and down in a frenzy, and I was shouting, Get back and You're all mad, and other useful slogans. Any idiot could have tipped him over and left the crowd to tromp him to death in seconds. The perfect assassination. But Casey just grinned at me and said, "You see?"

"Come on, there's a way out through the store," said Spritzer. But damned if Casey didn't want to stay. If he made it to President, he'd be dead in a week. We wheeled him out anyway, and I got a thick lip running interference, and Casey kept shaking hands all the way, dragging people along on his chariot.

"Politics is a contact sport. You've got to let them feel you. It proves your existence." He was excited as hell back there among the boxes in the A & P storeroom. "You've got to feel *them,* too. Catch their grace on your hands." He wanted to go out there again, but we calmed him down, and within minutes the crowd had disintegrated, leaving its soul to Casey.

The crazier he got in private, the harder he campaigned in public, reading the gospel in Mexican-American churches, walking through Watts on his crutches, giving the peace sign, everything but wearing an Indian bonnet and doing a rain dance. It was pretty sickening, and I told him he was going to lose his intellectual constituency, and he said, "No, no—you don't understand. I am being simple for the simple people. It takes a big man to do that." He smiled. "Mind you, the simple people must wonder what the fuck I'm doing, going to church at my age, but it goes over great with my intellectual constituency."

The polls fluctuated wildly, as they will in California, depending on the tides and the phases of the moon. Wilkins wasted valuable time being nice. But then he or someone must have noticed that while Casey was also nice, his supporters were sons of bitches. We, or they, did some terrible things with Wilkins's voting record, which was almost identical with Casey's, except for the inevitable Southern specialties. To begin with, we printed it, a dastardly thing to do to any senator's voting record. And, of course, we printed it in screaming red type for the bad parts, invisible ink for the rest. I asked Casey what had happened to that clean campaign we were running, and he said, "Ask the boys. Wilkins is tougher than we thought, I guess."

Anyway, as I say, Wilkins or Wilkins's people noticed and got right sore and began trying to rip Casey personally. "Fop, dilettante, political playboy." To answer, Casey had only to wheel his chair stoically across camera. "Easterner, ivory tower, egghead." Get out the chair again. Focus on calloused hands. Did Casey mind being used in this way? Not on your life. "Early in the game I decided I couldn't hide it. It was on Jones Beach or some place, and the little kids were staring and the grownups were peeping and, you know, looking away quickly, and I thought, O.K., you want a show? I'll give you a dandy. The hunchback of Notre Dame in Technicolor. And I've been doing it ever since."

Wilkins was always the gentleman in private, and when they met shortly before the debate, he managed to say, "How's the ol' fop doin'? Christ, this is a ridiculous business, ain't it?" But I had a feeling their friendship was just about over. Politicians often use live ammunition, whatever it looks like out there. "We're going to get you people," muttered one of Wilkins's goons. "We'll think of something."

It sounded like a witch's curse, but I didn't see any way even a witch could get at Casey. Maybe his private life? No. Everyone likes a sexy politician. Possibly to be on the safe side, Casey split with his movie actress—at least she left his room in tears one night and took her name off our ads. I hoped he'd take up with a nice quiet ex-nun or something, who wouldn't interfere too much with his work.

Not a vestige of high-mindedness left, you'll notice—in me or anybody else. The loftiest of our young people were cruising around town, planting mustaches on Wilkins's posters. Casey was all for it—kids are supposed to have fun, he said. I was at least seriously looking forward to the debate, because I still had hopes for Wilkins, although my team spirit tugged me apart. Both candidates had resisted confrontation as long as possible, on the grounds that peace candidates do not fight, but those crazy polls, which showed them alternating on top of and underneath a landslide, had driven them to it. "If my opponent establishes a clear superiority in the debate, I shall yield," said Casey. "Peace is more important than personality." To which Wilkins shot back, "Do you want the country run by a flashy debater, or by a man of experience and proven judgment?" They both knew the morning line.

General question: did Casey mind losing a friend like Wilkins? No and yes. Losing a friend meant you were getting somewhere, it was real. It also meant you were a little lonelier, with only a few million people left to count on.

Our team had by now grown so big that I didn't even know all the names. And I sensed a snarling envy in the lower depths at my own closeness to the leader. Spritzer spent most of the time at campaign headquarters, bossing the young volunteers mercilessly and asserting his own seniority: I, too, could be close to the leader if I had the time. The politicking that went on in that place, down to the smallest flea on the dirtiest hippie, would fill several grubby volumes—in fact, already has, so I'm spared the task. Even listing all the campaign managers and advisers that came and went would bore you to stone: and we'd stocked up on girls to appease Women's Lib, which didn't seem to bother sexist-pig Casey too much. Presumably he rode herd on the whole mob, with a network of personal relationships worthy of the Vatican. And he still got mad when I burst in on private conferences, bless him.

Spritzer looked at me with deepest loathing whenever I stumbled into headquarters, and I felt a blinding pain in my left buttock as the voodoo needle sank in. So I was surprised one day when he sidled up and said, "We're all that's left of the original team. Do you think we could be friends?" "I doubt it," I said, before I had time to think. There was no way to take it back or soften it or fuck around with it any way, shape, or form. He stood there, pulling at his damn nose, which should have been ten feet long by now. Then he nodded and said, "You're just like *him,*" and went back to his desk.

Things had also cooled between myself and Jane Donohue. Maybe her confessor had gotten wind of our night of nights in New Hampshire, which by the way was not duplicated in Indiana (polls too low). Or maybe she felt she'd betrayed Casey. Anyway, she refused even the most demure invitations, on the grounds that she was tired and busy and washing her hair—that is, until election night, when the same damn thing happened as before: the excitement burst out of her in every direction, and she moaned my name and held my throbbing maleness and rained hot kisses on my upturned face and all that great stuff—but before we get to that, I should say a little something about the debate and the hairy ending of that California primary.

"What job do *you* want in the Fifth Reich?" said Casey. "Commissar of Culture good enough for you?"

"There ain't going to be no Fifth Reich if we don't haul ass," said I. It was the afternoon of the debate, and Casey had decided on a marathon paddle in the pool. His bird legs straggled and shimmered in the green water, and he was busting with life.

"What the country needs is more local fiestas, a Manhattan county fair, compulsory five-day drunks, no excuses. In honor of what, though? What do we have instead of saints? Maybe we could start canonizing our own. Like the queen's honor list in England, every year we dub a whole lot of new saints. Wouldn't that turn the country around, huh? All those rich shits tripping over each other to be on the President's holy list."

"Look, Senator, I know you need your rest and I hate to be a bore, but what are you planning to do tonight to keep this debate from being a waltz? What the hell are you going to disagree with Wilkins about?"

Do you know what the son of a bitch did then? He splashed me. "Don't take it so seriously, Sam. Life is only a dance."

"And the kids who followed you out here," I said, blinking on the chlorine. "Are they taking it too seriously, too?"

"Most likely," he said, squinting at me. "Don't worry, though. They're having a ball."

I got out of the pool, as pissed off as a man can be. The campaign was making him completely childish. I didn't feel like playing the solemn young fool to his Father William, so I left him cackling to himself, and got dressed and drove down to headquarters, where everyone's thoughts were riding on the performance of this scheming opportunist. A couple of reporters cornered me and asked how Casey was preparing for the debate. I wanted to say, "Playing in his tub," but I was now "sources close to Senator Casey," if not "the senator's office" itself, so I babbled lies about relaxed and confident and tanned and fit. Why one does it, I don't know—the spirit of the campaign speaks through you. A month ago, I would have said that Casey was just crapping around making bad jokes, but since then charges of fop had been leveled, so my seismograph said "dignity." I told the press he was home brushing up on his facts. Casey didn't deserve it, but his staff did. They were all tensed up for the walk down Main Street, and I only hoped Casey wouldn't crack completely and start babbling about the Manhattan County Fair.

He was still chuckling when I saw him in the studio.

"They tell you that politics isn't a charm contest. Don't you believe them. I'm going to have to reach deep into my bag to outcharm Senator Magnolia tonight, sho sho."

I began to wonder if he wasn't deep into the bag already, but his breath smelled O.K., and the eyes were clear blue. (For some reason, they were grey when he was bored or out of sorts. Fascinating, eh?) I mumbled something about fop and playboy, and he said, "No, no. Out here, fop power is good. You can't stop a fop from reaching the top—have a million buttons made up immediately."

Cruel bastard. I was his butt now, the court fat man, his sadism reliever. That was the price of his intimacy. Of course, he was going to hang tough in the debate—wasn't he? Well, he had a national platform now—was that really all he had ever wanted? There was no chink in his playfulness, I honest-to-God couldn't tell what he was going to do.

Wilkins went off first with as dull a statement as I ever heard. He had followed Casey's lead in not stressing differences, so there was nothing to do now but suggest what a fine, experienced fellow he was. The nation owed Senator Casey a debt for throwing down the gauntlet of peace (yea, *sic*), but now it was time for a man who would bring the party together in Detroit, a man with wide friendships within the party at every level, a man snooze . . . I could hear the nation's sets going off with an atomic click. Wilkins, as I hope I've indicated, was a funny fellow in real life, a Yalie, and a very sharp bond lawyer. But he was so busy now emphasizing the perils of government by Eastern smarties that he had dumbed down to idiocy. As one of your finest types of Eastern smartie myself, I foresaw difficulties working with this guy. Was it possible he might not even *want* me? Good grief.

I doodled away at a gauntlet of peace, set in a field of tits, my specialty. Wilkins was dead. The voters he was aiming at died last year in a body. If Casey came on funny, they were both dead. What do you want to be when you grow up, Sam Perkins? I drew an *enormous* tit, enveloping the rest. *That's* what I want to be.

I figured Casey's best bet could be to sag toward the middle on the dullness issue. If he was just a little livelier and funnier than Wilkins, he could still be a pompous ass and collect all the charisma marbles as well.

Wilkins sat down, his very backside looking earnest and statesmanlike, and the camera switched to Casey. By God, his brow was furrowed. What madness was he up to now?

"My friends [no fellow Americans for Casey], you might suppose from Senator Wilkins's pleasant and largely meaningless opening remarks that there are no issues worth discussing in this country of ours any more. Every four years we stage these little pageants. A little shadow-boxing, a grimace here and there, the old dance of the politicians. I'm not sure we even make it as entertainment any more. Anyhow, you would never guess that while we waltz before you, to the strains of a nineteenth-century clubhouse, that millions of black Americans . . ." Oh Jesus, that was it. He'd saved it till now. "Our cities are powder kegs, our countryside a desert . . . peace for what? Peace for whom? Senator Wilkins's own voting record raises grave questions about this . . . he claims to have friends in every section of the party. That's really too bad. I suppose that means friends with Governor Faunce and Congressman Winters and every white racist that ever spat on the Bill of Rights. I can't think of a shabbier claim."

Peace candidates don't do this, eh? I'd been trying to get a strong civil-rights statement out of Casey for months, and he had said, "No, it'll divide the peace constituency. And if we don't get peace, "they ain't gonna *be* no civil rights, boy." But now he was launched into the most moving account of black suffering I've ever heard from anyone of any color. I resisted him, knew that I was watching the dirtiest fraud of all time, but it was, as you will recall, a hell of a speech, and if there were no tears in Casey's eyes, it was only because he was too strong and manly to cry.

Wilkins's people must at least have considered this possibility, and prepared some arguments. But there is no argument against eloquence. Wilkins seemed deeply unbelieving, but he managed to croak out some stuff about his deep concern for black people, and he dug up some piece of token legislation he'd sponsored concerning equally clean washrooms. And he said, "You won't get peace unless the whole country wants peace, and the whole country includes the South, my friend." Casey interrupted (against the rules, but what are rules when a man is overcome by passion?), "Then I don't want peace. If it means crawling to racists, begging for votes, I don't accept the terms."

Woody Kline was right. But what did it matter? "Fortunately," Casey said in his next turn, "I take a better view of the South than you do, Senator. The times they are a-changing down there, and maybe someday even the politicians will notice it. In fact, I sometimes believe that the only thing holding the South back is the men it chooses to represent it. And furthermore . . ."

He went on about party reform and from that to something else, until there was no way for Wilkins to get back to the Negro question. When Billy did bring it up in his summation, it was in the form of a maddened bleat. The audience remembered that he'd lost that one already, they'd heard it while their attention was still working and had digested it as fact. While Wilkins tried to zip his fly after the horse had escaped, a friendly cameraman played on Casey, and that mobile face, drawn, sardonic, grave, conveyed four hundred years of black oppression better than any old field hand with rickets could have.

After that, the usual jostling, the sense of lights being turned up, no need to wait for the ref's decision. I went out in the corridor to sniff for repercussions. Casey was wheeling out of the studio, serene, a thin film of sweat on his forehead after a light workout. Wilkins came up swiftly behind, expressionless, and bent over and said, "Why'd you do it, Brian?"

"I had to do something. You were getting too good."

Wilkins shook his head, as if to say, My ma told me it would be a dirty game, but Jesus Christ. You're too rough for me, boy.

"They'd have cut you to pieces in New York next month, Billy, and we wouldn't get *anyone* through to Detroit. It's better you die here."

"They gonna cut you in the South now, boy," he said in his mockiest accent. "You didn't have to do that. You'd have probably beat me anyway."

He walked away, giving me a polite nod—there goes my other peace candidate. Shit. Wilkins was hunched over until he got to the door, then straightened up with the first scent of night air. He walked out of the building a free man. Brian watched him go, himself trapped in his chair and in his head. I wanted to leave with Wilkins myself, but there was no place to go. "I wonder if he's right," murmured Casey.

The small meaningless groups broke up, and I was left with the senator for a moment. He was frowning, and the fun was out of it. Had he panicked? Anyone can be brave in a parking lot. But had he played a card he didn't need? I found I was thinking his thoughts myself. So nervous about winning this trick that he'd blown the finesse. He worked it through and then looked at me to see if I had, too. "Did it ever occur to you that I might be sincere?" he said.

I shook my head. "Not for a minute."

"No? Pity. I just might be. You don't know very much, do you?"

"And what about the peace constituency?"

"Fuck the peace constituency," he said, and rolled down the corridor and out to his car.

Time for one more poll, and let's hope this was the right

one. It showed us creaming Wilkins, and just about edging the rest. If the right combination of people dropped out, we still lost (that is, assuming you can guess which way a California voter will bounce); if only Wilkins dropped out and threw us his support, we won. We waited for Wilkins to concede, we knew he'd lost the stomach for it. He was just not such *merde* as candidates are made on. After a couple of days, we sent him a friendly note, suggesting a meeting, but we got no answer. Casey was gloomy and abstracted. "I hit him too hard," he said. "Why do I always do that?" Then he said, "Well, where was I? Salt Rock, where our brave boys sat out the war?" Before I could get in a word, he was into his account of the South, which was an understandably rancorous one. The debate and Wilkins's refusal to concede made Salt Rock sound like Devil's Island.

We were sitting in Casey's room the day before the election, and I was listening to this stuff absolutely numbly—my moral judgment or whatever you call it couldn't cope with Casey any more and had just gone to sleep—when in burst, and I really mean burst, one of Wilkins's young workers, a Southern peacenik named Hobbs. "You know what's happening over there?" he shouted. "Wilkins is talking about throwing his support to Blount."

Casey's face said, just for me, Don't burst and don't shout; don't come into a room like a B-movie character. But his voice just said, "What the hell?" Blount the moderate hawk was five points below Casey in the last poll. Wilkins's support could put him over.

"He says he doesn't think you'd make a good President, however right your policies are."

"He thinks that Blount would?"

"Not specially. Just better than you."

"Christ, these Southerners. Peace comes and goes, but race goes on forever."

"He says it has nothing to do with race. He says he agrees with you about that anyway, and if he came from New York, he'd be the first to say so."

"Yeah, well that's the point," said Casey. "Where he comes from *is* the issue, not him."

"I absolutely agree with you," said Hobbs. "I thought you were wonderful in the debate, Senator. You really said what was in your heart."

This was pretty sickening. The little chap had already fallen under Casey's spell, the quickest hypnotic subject on record, and would sell out his own region or anything else. "If he goes through with it, can I work for you?" Panting like a lapdog he was.

Casey drew himself up tall in his chair. "You bet you can, and bring your friends. We can take Blount. I'll be glad to have Wilkins out of there on any terms, it'll clear the air." He looked at Hobbs with his campaign face. "We'll strike a blow for the real South, right, Mr. Hobbs? In fact, we'll take Wilkins's own state from him in November and teach him a little politics. I'd be honored to have you, and any Southerners I can get, working for me."

Hobbs left, still panting. And Casey said, "Son of a bitch." Pause. "That mealy-mouthed, magnolia-scented fuckface. I'll kill him." Pause. "Did I tell you about the leeches yet?" One last pause. "Some other time, I guess. I'd better tell Spritzer to get some boys over to Wilkins's place and start peach-picking. You and my talented staff of speechwriters, start kicking around the following thoughts for tonight's humble statement. I stand alone as I stood in New Hampshire. The politics of deals versus the politics of principle. Now at last we know where Senator Wilkins stands—in Dixieland, ass-high in cotton. No, change that to, Wherever the South wind blows him." In five minutes, at the speed of an auctioneer, he had snapped off enough phrases to sort into three speeches and had talked to Spritzer on the phone and told him his door was wide open to Wilkins's brats. His Irish was good and up, he'd gotten somebody one-on-one at last, and he began wheeling around the room like a one-man band, throwing out more ideas than any staff in the world could use.

I went to the next room, where the speechwriters lurked, the monkey cage, as we called it. I left the door open a fraction, to hear if any Wilkins people came over. Within half an hour, the parade was on. Since we all knew whose speech Casey was going to use—his own—we crowded against the door like the seven dwarfs. What we heard was the sound of strong men drowning in Northern charm. Here we were, the firm of Messer, Fishbein, Masi, and Perkins, four graduates of Casey's charm school ourselves, four royal favorites, listening to the pitch that had won us in the first place. We began to grin. Hank Messer turned on me with Casey's extra double-dip sincere look and laid a warm hand on my wrist and began to mouth along with Casey in the next room. Phil Masi looked at him meltingly. "Oh gosh, Senator, I'd follow you *any*where." "Like oh, wow," breathed Howie Fishbein.

We began giggling, and pretty soon Casey wheeled over to ask what the hell was going on in here. "The last guy thought it was a children's birthday party, but I said it's always the politics of fun at our place." He was between visitors for a moment so I took the chance to tell him we'd been admiring his technique and just couldn't contain ourselves. And he frowned a moment, not sure how to take it, and then he said, "You mean, I need your he'p, young man, I really do?" He put his hand on Messer's the way Messer had put his on mine, and gave him the Look. "The real South, boy, the real ding-dang antebellum *Souf*. Oh—you say you come from New Jersey?" He winked and everyone laughed, and he said, "Tone it down, boys, O.K.? We're doing great."

There was no point going on with our joke, now that Casey had made it for us, so we shut the door and got down to our unavailing speechwriting. I picked up the phone to pass the time and heard Casey's voice on the other extension putting through a call to Wilkins. Naturally, with my morals in their current state, I kept listening and this is what I heard in the apple barrel: "You're making an ass of yourself, Billy. You'll look like a man of no principle at all, and besides I've got all your people." "Congratulations," said Wilkins dryly. Casey tried again. "Look, Bill, try to understand, you don't have anything to hand over to Blount. So you might as well not try." "You give me my people back if I stay in? That's mighty white of you, Brian, if you'll pardon the racist expression." "Of course you can have them, Billy, they're still yours. It's just that they won't work for Blount. And listen, when this is over, let's have a drink." There was a moment of silence, no breathing at either end, then Wilkins, slowly, luxuriantly, in souped-up Southern: "The way I see it is this, Brian—if you've got all my people, you're sitting pretty. It's damn nice of you to call and try to keep me in the race, and I appreciate it. Truly. But with your people and my people, you really don't need little old me." "All right, cut the crap," said Casey, with a false laugh. "I don't think you really come from the South at all." No response to little joke. Casey: "Obviously, I don't have *all* your people, Bill, or I wouldn't be calling. I have enough of them to make you look bad, but not necessarily enough to win." "Don't worry about me looking bad, Brian. I'll look fine where I want to look fine, and I don't give an f about the rest." Pause. Wilkins's breathing well. Casey off thinking somewhere. Finally, "Look, Billy, you think I'm a shit, right?" "Something like that." "And you don't think Blount is a shit, right?" "Blount's just a regular old hound dog, like the rest of us. I know his smell. You smell funny." "Oh Christ, Southern wisdom." "Hoped you'd like it, Foxy." "So what happened to peace?" "Nothing much. Just say I lost it in the sands of California. Just say that, if Casey wants it, there's probably something wrong with it." "Just go out quietly, will you, Bill? I don't need a ringing endorsement, just a murmur of approval." "You know who I'm sometimes sorry for, Casey? Those kids you're debauching." I stiffened. Save your pity, coonskin. "Kids have no knowledge of character, and only a rat would take advantage of that. I don't trust anyone with a big youth constituency." "Just fucking go out quietly, and say something nice about peace. You don't have to mention me by name. Geezus, Billy, we used to be friends, didn't we? I'll campaign for you next time." That voice again, that panicky voice. "Sorry, Brian." Click, long pause, click.

I ran round to see what kind of shape he was in. He looked O.K. "I trust you heard that, you debauched kid, you. Wilkins's right about that, anyway. I'll bet you never listened in on other people's conversations before you met me, did you?" He wheeled back to his desk. "O.K., we'll just have to win without him. How's the speech coming?"

"Did you really think you could talk him out of it?"

"I guess not. But it was worth a try."

I went to the monkey cage and picked up the drafts. He read them quickly and said, "They're not nasty enough."

"Well, we thought, you know, manly regret was the thing."

"No, I want to nail the bastard this time. He's dropping out because of the race issue, remember that. Now he's showing his true colors. What the hell can he say, that he doesn't like my face? Try for cold anger, will you? It happens to be what I feel for once."

I went back and tried to summon up some cold anger. Thought of calling room service to order some. Debauching kids, eh? No judgment, huh? Let me at the pussycat. But all I could hear was Casey's pleading for his endorsement and for the rest of his people, a whine that got worse in my head till it sounded like a dying cat. Casey on the wall, helpless. Meanwhile, the real Casey was wheeling around noisily, and the next time I went in to check, he said, "You know what I need, don't you?"

I knew, but I was damned if I was going to get it for him.

"No, you don't know. You're too innocent. Forget it." He went on wheeling and I went back to my speech, thinking, so help me God, if he needs a woman, *somebody* should get him one. We couldn't have him going on the air in this condition.

We dumped the drafts on him and went out for a bite, and we heard Wilkins's abdication speech on the coffee-shop radio. The suspense played hell with my ham sandwich. Wilkins had decided, it seemed, after studying the polls, that his presence could now only serve to divide the party and confuse the meaning of the result. He was grateful the party had so many fine candidates that he wasn't needed. He wanted to thank his fine staff—their effort had not been wasted, no effort was wasted. As for himself, he was way behind on his fishing, and wanted to learn his children's names again. That sounded like the real reason. He'd simply lost his stomach for it.

"And in conclusion—" I licked some mustard off my

finger, and just left the finger in there– "I am advising those who have worked for me, and who believe in the things I believe in to–" Christ, I bit myself– "vote their own consciences."

Pandemonium, in my head at least. Wilkins, you're a goddamn prince. Messer clapped my back, completing the confusion in my mouth. "Hey man, he did it. Or he didn't do it. I forget which." I weaved my way to a phone.

"Did you hear it, Senator? Have you time to change the speech?"

"Yes, I heard it."

"Wasn't it great?"

Casey answered slowly, as to a child. "You'll never make a politician, Sam. Sometimes I envy you. It's just possible he may have killed us. Come on up and let's see what we can do."

Well, I'd have figured it out eventually. I only need a little help. The big news was that Wilkins was *not* throwing his support to the peace candidate. He didn't even mention peace. If he'd gone further and backed the hawk, he would have left himself open to Casey's counterattack. Any idiot could see that.

Casey greeted me with this: "You know, I've just about had it, Sam." He had a drink in his hand, but wasn't drinking it. He'd offered himself a drink, and now he was stuck with it.

"I didn't know he was that nasty," I said.

"You don't get to be a Southern senator unless you have a killer streak. It's not that nasty, really. I should be able to handle it. It's just that when you've been playing chess for seven months and are on your eight thousandth move, you can get tired without warning." He sat quiet for a moment, as if planning his resignation, then said, "O.K., what are the options?" A nerve twitched under his eye.

He decided he could think better lying down, but that was a mistake. Exhaustion hit him like surf. He lay there gasping, and I went and brought him a cold sponge and doused him down with it, and I even found myself chafing his wrists like a fight manager. I guess his mind still worked, but his body was gone. He'd scheduled a press conference just before eight, to make the eleven o'clock news in the East, and he said, "Jesus, where am I going to get the strength for that?"

I suggested calling it off, but he shook his head. Any sign of weakness would complete the day's rout. So he just lay on his back, breathing deep and thinking strong thoughts. At ten of eight he motioned me, and I picked him up like a Raggedy Andy doll and propped him in his chair. "Jesus," he said. "Oh Jesus," and I understood he might actually mean this for a prayer. "You know, Sam," he murmured, "I'm really a nice guy. Let that be our secret." Raving, poor bugger.

We wheeled him to the elevator, slumped down like a Halloween dummy, and I thought, We're delivering a corpse to the White House. Dead on arrival. The elevator had to make several stops on the way down, and Casey made a reflexive effort to straighten and smile slightly. Then he seemed to remember that you don't need every voter in the country and slid down again.

We got him to the ballroom, where the vultures were

gathered. I saw Spritzer over by the microphones and I drew a finger across my throat. That means something else in TV, I guess, but Jack seemed to understand and stepped smartly to the microphone and said, "The senator will just make a brief statement tonight. No questions, please." Good old Jack, never lets you down.

Casey kept his head down as we wheeled him through the reporters, and I wished I or someone could lend him just five minutes of strength. The goddamn sleepy-strength image had drained him. My great advice. The one candidate who must never be tired. He got to the microphone, and I thought, Oh, it'll just be a routine Casey miracle. His face would be smooth and calm, the old bugger had just been spoofing. Hadn't he? He looked up at last, and his face was death—he suddenly needed that blood the leeches had taken. His mouth moved and his forehead sweated and nothing happened.

"Excuse me," at last, the deep voice, scavenging desperately for power. "Senator Wilkins's announcement, on top of a slight viral infection (not bad), leaves me somewhat at a loss for words. Not my usual problem, as you know. I should like to begin by saluting my old friend's gesture—Billy, if I may break the rules and call him that, has put party above self and principle above party. He knew that we both stood for the same things, but—" his face went blank, at least to the trained eye, a real blackout— "but you can't cut a nomination in two and give it to two people like a communion wafer." He frowned. He hadn't meant to say that. "What you can do, of course, and perhaps it's a little early to talk about that, but then again, why not? is talk about another office closely allied to the Presidency. I believe that Senator Wilkins would make an admirable choice for that particular office. And wouldn't it be a wonderful change to offer the voters two men they want instead of one they want and one they can't stand?"

What the hell was he doing? Yeah, yeah, new politics and honesty. But even old unpolitical Perkins could see that Wilkins's supporters weren't worth a Vice-Presidency. I would like to be telling him that now, in my tired, superior voice. "Casey, you don't know shit about politics." All our V.-P. bull sessions had concerned men of the Great Right Center. Blount, Waldo, someone who could deliver the deadheads.

Casey seemed to regroup around this new idea: he was pleased with himself, he was dancing and jabbing again. "I have been thinking of this ever since Senator Wilkins announced, but for many reasons, I thought we'd better have our contest first, fair and square, without the smell of a deal about it. That's the tradition in our party, and it's a good one. And it was, may I say, a heckuva contest. Billy hits hard." He touched his jaw ruefully, and the little dogs laughed. "My, does he hit hard. But he also hits fair. I believe I gained from this contest, and I believe the public gained, too. I won't say we were Lincoln–Douglas, but we did our best. So, Billy, if you're listening out there, no hard feelings and come on over. I need you, boy."

Short statement, indeed; there was no stopping the bastard now. "I understand that what I've done tonight is considered 'bad politics' in some circles. I hope so, anyway. I suspect you are as fed up as I am with the kind of good politics that harnesses two men with nothing in common, in order to attract a majority with nothing in common, and provide an administration that suits nobody." Casey next fielded an invisible grounder to his right: ah hah, you think I'm a silly liberal idealist who doesn't know his ass from a sand dune, eh? "The funny thing is that 'good politics' in quotes isn't even good politics any more. Half the people who would have voted for me will vote for my opponent if I sell out on the Vice-Presidency; and half the people who would have voted for my opponent will vote for me because *he* sold out on the Vice-Presidency." Casey! You know the Real Majority can't follow dependent clauses. "It is, then, my belief that my position *is* the majority position in this country, and by God, I want a fair chance to prove it."

He was revved up enough to answer questions all night, but to my surprise he wheeled out quickly. I saw why in a moment. "Hey Senator, how come Wilkins didn't throw you his support?" bellowed an inconvenient reporter. Casey waited till he was near the door, then said, "He told them to follow their consciences, didn't he?" A laugh, or more a grunt of approval. Casey caught it at the crest. Then rolled out with, "Most of his young workers have come over already," in a lower voice, suitable to a half-truth. "Hey Senator, what's going to be the platform on race if you and Wilkins are the ticket?" But Casey was gone.

I decided to let Spritzer take his temperature tonight.

As the repercussion man, I moseyed about, unobtrusive as hell, for a few more minutes. "I thought he seemed a little tired," said a reporter. "Geez, who wouldn't be?" "He looked better than Wilkins, and Billy's only been going a few weeks." They were all heading for telephones or cabs, and I couldn't very well stop one and ask him if he thought Casey had blown it. I left the room with one bunch, and then came back and left the room with another bunch, but nobody would answer my question, since I didn't ask it. Finally, there was no one left to go out with but Rust Gates the cynic, who had a weekly deadline and was shuffling slowly toward the bar to think things over.

I pulled alongside and said, "Well?"

"Well what?"

"What do you think?"

"Fifty cents takes my opinion away, at your favorite newsstand." He kept walking, but I knew he liked to talk, so I tailed him into the bar and sat on the next stool with what I took to be a disarming grin.

He held out through one drink and then said, "New politics, my ass. Wilkins gives him just the people he was talking about, the ones who have nothing in common with him. South, West, and middle everything. Willie is their kind of boy, a genuine Norman Rockwell. Tell me, when did the two boys cook this one up?"

Cook? This raw deal looked cooked to someone? Or was this just the product of Gates's warped intelligence? He had the worst record for prophecy on the beat. Still, he was right about Truman in '48, wasn't he?

"You don't have to tell me," he said. "It smells of deal

a mile away, but only to the trained nose. With the unwashed, he gets it both ways—a reputation for rejecting deals, and a beautiful little deal. That's some fancy politician you're working for, sonny."

I wanted to leave and tell Casey about this, but Gates now insisted I stay and have another drink, and I guess I owed him that. "You know, I didn't like your boy at first. Wrong kind of Irishman, you know? The kind who'd really like to be an English gentleman. That empties a man out, a silly ambition like that. But, goddamnit, anyone who knows his craft like Casey is O.K. with me."

I expected the captain to be sitting coolly aloft, dictating memos. But when I phoned his room, Reverend Mother Spritzer said he was out like a light and slapped down the phone in a pet. I wondered if Casey was up to two whores tonight. No, not even Casey.

I already knew Casey's opinion of Gates. To wit, "Rust loves all the clubhouse shit and he'll sit up all night with some drunken hack from the Bronx lapping up his inside garbage. He thinks that's what politics is all about, the poor romantic bastard." Still, it was the only opinion I had to go on, so it loomed large.

But now suppose Wilkins decided to jerk the rug? Was there time for that? Yeah, before the polls opened. Was there any way of getting in touch with him? I phoned Wilkins's hotel, not sure what I had in mind, just whimpering at someone I guess, and was told Billy had already pulled out. I spoke to Hobbs the Fink, and he said Wilkins had gone home right after his own announcement. I asked if Wilkins was likely to come back at Casey in the morning, and he said he doubted it. Billy had seemed just sick of the whole business. I didn't rate Hobbs highly as a judge of the human heart, but I held the slender thread and swung from it until a phantom Jane came shimmering through the jungle trees and the mango swamp to rescue me from these aggravations.

7 Wilkins did make a statement, saying he understood the offer to be a campaign pleasantry, and that under no circumstances would he consider the Vice-Presidency. He was making no recommendations to his supporters, who were grownups (a few of them anyway) with minds of their own. Out of state, out of mind. The item appeared in the afternoon papers, and I doubt it affected a single voter.

Casey went into his election-day swoon. Down at headquarters, we got up a game of football, using a roll of toilet paper as our ball. It streamed down over the pass receivers, who went bucketing blindly into desks, knocking off as much paper as they could. We played like bloody savages, even contriving somehow to break a window. I keep asking myself what I felt that day and other days—you must have felt something, you dummy—but I didn't feel a thing. On four hours' sleep, it's a happy animal life. Sleeplessness is an indulgence: never trust a politician who boasts about it. All right—write that thought down, you lazy bastard. It's an authentic Casey, worth at least five cents. Somebody crunched me into a desk as I reached for a piece of paper, and then grabbed my head and pushed my nose onto the typewriter keys and said, "Write us a speech, Plato."

A couple of afternoon papers said that maybe Casey was *too* clever; and I thought, No, he's just tired. He always acts clever when he's tired.

Anyway, Casey was a mythical beast. The only reality today was the gang at headquarters, whooping for a winner. After we'd used up all the toilet paper, festooning the joint so it looked like the inside of a hangover, we drank a jug of wine and listened to rumors by radio or on foot or just rumors made up in the office. Word was that the vote was light—how could that be? Was all this drama for nothing? Could all those people have something better to do than think about us?

Spritzer put his arm around me. "How's it going, Sam?" I was too startled to resist, but went limp in his arms and did the dead man's float. Jane, as previously reported, was working slowly into an erotic trance. Turnout better upstate—good, good. Always fine sensible people upstate. Mexicans, no action. Orange County, quiet so far. O.K. with us. Maybe the rednecks were overconfident with

Wilkins out. Then, the big news, a late-afternoon swell in the Negro districts. That had to be good, didn't it? Or did it? Blount had been making mild interracial noises since the debate, figuring he'd found a vacuum (politicians are a scream), but the best he could do was "Negroes-need-lawn-order-more-than-anyone," or "Let's save the coons from each other, guys."

What did Casey do with himself on election days, anyway? Horrible to contemplate. Spritzer said the instructions were to leave him alone, so I left him alone. It wasn't his day, it was ours. He was just an excuse.

We were good and plastered by the time the returns came in, and we howled and groaned every time the board changed. I necked with Jane and Spritzer necked with the two of us and Hobbs, the Wilkins man, tried to put his arms around the whole mess. We were peaking too soon, there was nothing much on the board. Casey went ahead 75 to 9, then he was behind 201 to 102, from those crazy little districts that vote early and try to act smart.

Now we needed Casey himself to keep us going, but the rumor mill had gone haywire from overwork. "I hear he's left town. Yeah, gone home to New York." "He's having a breakdown in his hotel room." "He's hiding out in a monastery." We got scared at every crazy one of them, and Spritzer decided to break instructions and call the hotel. The girl at the switch thought that the senator had gone out. Where, where? Dunno. Somebody thought airport. Jesus. Had he checked out? Dunno, connect you with desk. The pile of us were all over Spritzer by now, trying to get our ears into the phone. What the son of a bitch say? They switched us to hotel dry cleaning by mistake, and dry cleaning got sore at all these nuts breathing into his phone and hung up. Hank Messer shouted, "That's the last time you get to clean *my* pants, John Chinaman." We dialed again and couldn't reach the hotel at all. And when we finally did get through, the girl said, "We are not entitled to give that information." We all shouted at her at once like loons. "To whom am I addressing?" she said, and we all wailed different things, F.B.I., dial-a-prayer, all kinds of shit, and then began to laugh and scuffle. Spritzer left us there braying into the phone, and went off to find a cab.

The early swings and the wine had conditioned us not to take the board seriously, so when we went back and saw that Casey was now a thousand behind, we shrugged—more smart asses out there in voterland. Ho hum. We picked up a few points, then took a truly sickening dip: 5,000 down. Up a little, down, holding. There were thousands of votes to go. Watts, for instance. Oh—you say Watts is already in? Well, upstate then. Dear old upstate. The farmers and all that. Backbone of the nation. Upstate is going badly so far? Oh Jesus.

The possibility dawned slow as dawn over Nome, Alaska, that we might just possibly be going to lose. I had considered it, of course, as one considers old age and death, but I had never really believed it. I had no set of feelings for it, no way to handle it. My first thought was, Will Jane sleep with me even if he loses? The faces around me were stricken, orphaned. The drunks had sobered up and were close to tears. Jane was squeezing her handkerchief and biting her lip, somehow closing herself round her sorrow. It's not the end of the world, I thought, and then thought, No, the end of the world would probably be more fun.

Come on, Casey boy, Casey babes. Drive, man. Time was running out on us now. We didn't take any more dips, but we didn't rise either, but settled at 5,000 back and went to sleep there, and the numbers began to drain out. Casey rolled in quietly at some point and we didn't even notice him. He shushed the few who did, and watched the board calmly. Then Jane saw him and began to cheer tearfully, and everyone took it up, and suddenly Casey was the greatest man who ever lived, we loved him, it was tragic what the boneheaded electorate did to men like him, wave on wave of cheers, expressing a hundred rare feelings, the most nuanced, complicated cheer ever put together.

He wheeled to the board, and I suddenly saw that his wife was behind him and two boys that I recognized as his sons. Sons of a gun—so that was it: not streams of whores beating on him and other politicians' wives and his own campaign bunnies, wearing down his cleverness, cooling him to normal, but this. The all-American family. Incredible.

He held up a silencing hand, which was cheerfully ignored. Fran Casey, I noticed, looked quite chic, as if experts had been working on her. The boys were handsome and healthy-looking, though one was grumpy and the other was nervous. Normal enough, I guess. Fran Casey smiled nicely, not too broad, just pleasant, as if she'd had a pretty nice day, seeing the shops and all.

The cheer wore out at last, it had said all it had to say, and the gang buzzed for Casey to answer it. He still looked beat as he had last night, but his number-one voice was back. He introduced his wife and kids, and said we'd be seeing more of them between here and Detroit. Cheer. Detroit, eh? "Right now, things look pretty bad, and I wanted to speak to you before they look worse. We still have an outside chance of winning. But I want you to hear what I'd say if we lost. I would say—" and he hitched at his knee— "that I've been down before, and I've gotten up before. Life has not always been so wonderfully easy for me. Years ago, the Almighty saw fit to give me a handicap, as if to say, 'We'll see what Casey's made of,' and I accepted the challenge. I learned to get up off my ass, if you'll pardon the expression, and fight. I learned to walk, with the help of my wonderful mother and father, whom I can never thank enough and who will be joining us shortly." What the fuck? "And I learned some humility down there, too. I learned that you can't walk by yourself, however big a man you are. You need the help of others, as I need your help now." The audience cheered for itself modestly. "So let's imitate the Almighty for once and see what this campaign is made of; let's test it and see if it can get off its back and fight. I know what I'm made of and I'm pretty sure I know what *you're* made of, and I'll tell you this—if the Almighty can't keep me down, I'm goddamned if Governor Humbert—K.—Blount can." Ecstasies. Among suddenly popping bulbs and some kind of spotlight that had just been wheeled in, his parents advanced solemnly to greet him, his father, the big white-haired phony, and his mother with her secret expression. I hadn't seen them all together before, and as his mother stepped up to peck her son, I thought, She's disappointed in him. She expected something better. But that was ridiculous.

Spritzer came pushing past me in a businesslike way, and I realized he was steering a cameraman into position. They were setting up for the concession, or the non-concession, and getting in some homey stuff as well. It was just routine politics, all the other candidates had probably sent for their parents by now, if they could get them out of the bars, but it made me sick with Casey.

"Isn't he wonderful," murmured Jane, and squeezed my hand as if Casey had just declared a victory.

"It didn't change the board any," I snarled, and she pulled away for a horrible moment.

But amazingly it did change the board. If anyone still doubts Casey's divine powers, I can only report that his sudden surge began within five minutes of the end of his pep talk. I don't know, maybe he'd figured it that way, maybe he'd analyzed the districts that remained and had shouted himself to the best of both worlds again—an indomitable-in-defeat speech and a victory as well. It is also possible that I was overrating his cleverness.

Nobody's lonelier than a cynic, ask Casey, Sr. When the numbers began to tilt our way, the crowd went crazy for good. They had been through the Valley of Death with their leader and were loaded for bear. Nothing on God's earth could stop us now. Jane kissed me full-mouthed, cynic or no, and I capitulated on the spot. Call me a rat, but I'd been planning all day.

She insisted we stay for the victory speech, but my mind was already under the covers and I didn't take in much. At one point I found people clapping at me, and I realized I had been singled out—"Sam Perkins, my loyal, gifted, and may I say highly critical speechwriter. Whenever I find myself slipping into the morass of clichés, old Sam hauls me out." Not tonight, I couldn't.

It lasted forever, and I was afraid that Jane might be over the hill. But never underestimate a good case of religious hysteria. When Casey wheeled past us, she fell on him with a huge kiss—it's you I really want—and the old whoremonger kissed her lightly back, inflaming her for hours to come. He shook my hand and grinned that knowing grin, *aren't I a devil?* He knew I knew the score but assumed my forgiveness. When I didn't respond, his smile thinned out. *Don't be a sap. I did what I had to.* After that, his parents shook my hand blankly and the whole caravan wheeled out, with Spritzer pushing the chair to leave Casey's hands free, leaving me with my spoils.

I guess I should say a word about Jane here. I didn't really like her. There was something incurably school-marmy about her, at least outside of the sack. Her conversation bored me, the way opera bores me: that is to say, I would literally not hear whole paragraphs at a time. For instance, I still don't know why she moved to Illinois when she was three or what happened to her father in the war. I'm not sure what it was about her, it was just conversation like anyone else's. In fact, she was above average intelligence. Maybe it was the flat Midwestern voice or maybe it was the resolute sunniness they teach them, that somehow comes out so bright and cold. But I think it was mainly this Catholic thing of mine. The ones on the campaign seemed to belong to a private club—and that was where they really talked. With the rest of us they were just polite. Or so I felt.

Except, except. That night in Los Angeles she talked, wild, blasphemous, sometimes incoherent talk. I wasn't even sure she was talking to me half the time, and I didn't care. Just to turn all this on was enough. And her body beat time to her words, writhing and banging and clinging. Sex object, you say? Yeah, that was me, all right. She called out Casey's name and I thought, Well, I'd rather provide the body than the name. In fact, I was proud to stand in for the senator. But then she said, "I'm sorry, I didn't mean that. Don't get angry with me." Whoever you are.

She was so unlike herself that I felt I should talk to her differently; but I didn't know how, and anyway, she didn't seem to be listening. So long as it was all a dream, it didn't count. Between sessions, she was terribly restless, putting her legs over mine, kissing my chest, putting my hands on her breasts, anything to get me going again. I was too busy to think, but was whirled up in her sense of damnation. I can still feel her wet hair against my face and her desperate fingers, which seemed to insist we get it all done in one night, so it would be one sin and not two. Myself, wishing it could be spread over, say, six months or so.

I can't explain it, but the fact that I didn't like her made it better in some ways. To get this little holygirl, this little halfnun ladyjane goodybird crying for what I had to give —there was a sweetness in that, no getting around it. She seemed annoyed when I was slow recovering from, I think, the third round. We were falling behind on our sin-production schedule. Daylight ended it for good, one didn't do these things by day. She got out of bed and showered and dressed and left almost in silence. At the door she pressed my hand and looked at me, as if to say sadly, "You should be ashamed of yourself." I swore she couldn't go back to her elder-sister style with me after that. But she could and she did. And I thought, O.K., I'll settle for those nights; she can do what she likes with the days.

8

Casey flew home the next day with his wife and sons, and we didn't see him all week. He took Spritzer along, not for company, I was told, but to answer the phone. It was difficult to pretend he was in vibrant touch with his campaign, because we never got to speak to him at all, and neither, I later learned, did Spritzer, who had to make up Casey's instructions himself. Jack also gallantly concocted bulletins about how the senator was hitting the history books and doing a lot of heavy thinking. But Jack told me later that Casey was just locked in his room most of the time, and nobody knew what he was doing. Fran brought him his meals in there, and his sons visited him as if it were a sick room. Weirdly enough, fits of laughter were noted during these visits. As if Casey really loved his children after all.

When he returned to our little treadmill, the campaign seemed to taste different. Fran Casey traveled with him now, displacing us court jesters, and she began to emerge as a public figure in her own right. Her basic personality was so vague that it seemed possible to turn her into anything one liked—a saucy Irish girl with a serious side, or vice versa. We even discovered that she wrote verses, love poems evidently directed toward Jesus. Wild.

We saw more of his parents, too—his old man proving to be quite a snappy speaker in short bursts, ideal for communion breakfasts. Politics might save this man yet. We couldn't get a word out of his mother, but she had a great sad smile. Various sons and daughters came and went, all reasonably presentable and breathtakingly forgettable. I don't like families much, it turns out. As the only child of an only child I resent all those relatives a Catholic can summon up at will: trustworthy mediocrities taking work from us clever scoundrels.

Jane said, If you were Irish, who else *could* you trust besides your relatives? It was back to chilly banter again, so I set to work with my ice pick. I told her that I refused to confine myself to election nights indefinitely, and she laughed and said, "I'm not sure I like you on other nights. You seem kind of stuck on yourself." To Catholic girls, everyone is stuck on themselves except little St. Francis of the Elves.

So I attempted prodigies of self-abasement, and told her at intervals how insecure I really was, and how my cockiness was just a defense for a basically sweet person, and she laughed again and said, "All right, I believe you.

But I still don't like you. Not enough. Not enough for that." "How much do you have to like someone for *that?* As long as you like *that?*"

I'll never learn. She had some special dispensation for election nights. But there just weren't enough of those. The New York primary is a proxy kind of thing, I doubt if her confessor would accept that as an excuse. And the same went for Mickey Mouse primaries all over.

"Haven't you heard of *aggiornamento?*" I ranted. But it was hopeless. I would sneak over to her desk afternoons and murmur, "I hear Michigan's in the bag," but it didn't arouse her at all. She said, "After the campaign, we'll see. My head's all over the place right now." Would that it were, I thought. "Supposing I told you I had a terminal disease?" "I wouldn't come near you." Hopeless.

Still, midsummer was O.K. Casey seemed to have recovered from California, or was skillfully patched up, and was campaigning as well as ever. He was a riot on talk shows and had perfected his determined stare for the big rallies. It was all show biz, "and why not?" he said to a summer-school audience at Chicago U. "The ancients used to put their leaders through irrelevant tests, just to see how they were at irrelevant tests. (Or if the ancients didn't, they should have.) Politics is nothing but a series of irrelevant tests." He had a rule that you should talk earthy to intellectuals and literary to the slobs. And it is to his credit that he never kept this rule.

"You disapprove of me, don't you, Sam? Well, fuck you," he said one day, apropos of nothing.

That's how it was in June. I told him I didn't think a new politician should wave his family about like an old one, and he told me to go to hell. "There aren't that many votes in the Harvard Yard, Master Perkins. A lot of Americans still come from families, you little bastard."

Cold and mean, as ever, as we zeroed in on Detroit. I was committed completely to the campaign and not to him, and if he had eaten a live baby on television, it wouldn't have stopped me now. We had to win. Why? Never mind. We had to win.

The campaign bio came out, the fastest publication in history, typed on rice paper by maddened midgets. I counted ninety-three typos. In July he said, "We're falling behind on the in-depther, the story that couldn't be told. Where was I?" And I thought, Why don't you get yourself an analyst? And then I thought, It's probably against his religion.

I owed it to the campaign staff to listen. One boring thing was, he was always at terrific pains to make himself sound normal. His childhood was a yawn—nobody ever had such a normal childhood. "I know you're supposed to hate at least *one* of your parents, but I could never swing it." It was only when he got to the polio period that this broke down. "Yes, I—must—admit, yes, I was kind of selfish around then. But why didn't they tell me they were making those sacrifices? Ah—I don't know. I suppose I would just have said, 'Some big deal. You should see *my* sacrifice.' Kids are impossible, excepting yourself of course."

I felt I liked him in this period and no other. His legal career was another yawn. He said only one interesting thing about that. He said, "You know, if I'd stayed in that profession, I'd have probably forgotten I ever had polio. Polio is no very big deal, believe me. It does not, contrary to appearances, scar you for life. In fact, come to think of it, I did forget about it for years and years. But in politics, you use everything."

I took it all because I wanted him in shape for Detroit. Christ, I'd have done anything to get him in shape for Detroit. Perhaps he knew that and was taking greedy advantage. Until he made even himself sick and said, "God, I'm tired of myself. Tired of thinking about myself. When this goddamn business ends, I swear I'll never think about myself again."

"Why wait?"

"You can't help it, Sam, they *make* you think about yourself. This is the most egocentric exercise ever devised."

Was he going over the past to check his fitness for office? Was that why he was going over every last detail? He looked at me with a liverish eye, and I could suddenly picture his father slumped over his bottle, talking to himself. "There are no clues in the past," said the old mind reader. "None. You're always either too kind to yourself or too hard on yourself. Let's forget the whole damn business. Could you tell Fran I want to see her?"

And yet, he would be back at it the next day. Was he good enough? Or was he like his father? He read himself into Kevin's thoughts and prowled there like a caged tiger.

"My success is all my father lives for. He doesn't like me much, how could he? but this makes up for it. And of course, he's only alive in the most technical sense of the word." Then shook his head. "How do I know I'm not just as dead as he is? Just because I don't act dead. Look it up in Descartes or somebody."

This was not getting him in shape for Detroit, so I said, "Don't worry about it so much. You don't have to be that great to be President."

"President?" he said, looking up vaguely from his distant thoughts. "What President?"

Delegate counting was our sport now, and we played it night and day. Spritzer, who to my embarrassment proved to be a political wizard, traipsed all over the country picking up strays. Casey didn't want to see them that much. He said, "I'll play the hand I've got. Give the other guys a sporting chance." Still, the delegates poured remorsely in, with Spritzer's whip licking their tails, and Casey, loathing himself for it, charming them on. It suddenly looked as if victory could not be avoided. Wilkins came out against us, but no one could remember who Wilkins was by now. The offer of the Vice-Presidency was forgotten, or remembered as a fiendish ploy. We were free to bargain with a fascist if we needed one. Our natural enemies, the old party warlords, came around to bend the knee everywhere we went. Tim Houlighan flew out to Fort Wayne to ask for Casey's help just to get on the New York delegation. His pants had been stolen, as promised, and almost the only New York regulars who survived were the ones

Casey had seen upstate that first day. And imagine, I didn't even know he was thinking about that stuff. "You've taught me a lesson in politics," said Tim. "You're an Irishman, after all." That mess in California had done it. Nobody wanted to fight any more. Casey had reeled out of that state hemorrhaging badly and hearing the birdies, but at least he was on his feet. The others had had to be carried out. Great little system we've got here.

It looked as if the convention might be a waltz. He wouldn't need too much strength for that. I hoped he would relax now, but when we checked into our hotel in Detroit—desolate war-torn Detroit—his fur was up and I didn't know what to expect. "How does it feel now that you can see the white whale?" I said jovially.

"Christ, I can't see it yet. Two more months of campaigning is all I can see." We were looking down at Cadillac Square, where the Presidential run would begin. His face was so tight it gleamed. "Would it be pretentious to ask if this cup could be removed from my hands?" he said. "I'm serious."

"Don't you want it?" This was unthinkable. We'd have to lock him in his room if he started talking like this.

"Yeah. I guess I want it. I'd be pretty damn foolish not to. The thing is, it seems immoral."

"What does that mean?"

"It means, there are things you can hustle and things that you can't. I never really thought it would get this far."

"Well, it did. Christ, Brian, Senator, sir, you can't seriously think of dropping out now?"

"Can't I, you little snot rag? I'll think what I damn well

feel like." I had to put up with this, of course. I had to humor this monster until the votes were counted. "You know, I've been praying a lot lately. I believe that stuff, you know. And it doesn't come out good. The Jujube is sending back bad tea leaves."

Oh God. Religion. At this point. "Yeah. I still pray to God for help," he said. "I haven't the guts not to. I spit out the words like vinegar. What the fuck did God ever do for me? Still, I came to depend on him during that time. It got to be a hobby I could turn to. The more shit he shoveled at me, the harder I prayed."

Is that a fact, sir? I couldn't think of anything to say remotely connected with that. But he seemed to expect something.

"You're just nervous," I said, "and this stuff comes into your head. The important thing is a whole lot of people believing in you and depending on you out there."

"The *important* thing? You're telling me the important thing? What kind of shit is this?" He was malevolent again, as if he were praying. "You think people believing in me is important? What idolatrous garbage is this? You think God is less important than that bunch of pimply ass-kissers believing in me?"

"Well, yes. I mean there's nothing you can do about God, is there, and you can do something about us."

"There's plenty you can do about God. You can obey His will. There's not much of a fuck you can do about anything else."

For a moment I wavered. Maybe he was going crazy, and we should let him pull out quietly. But then I thought,

Crazy or not, he's our candidate. "I'm sorry you feel like that. But you know you've got to stay in."

"Listen," he said, and the hatred poured pure and black and serene. "Listen, you little paper-thin, secular windup toy. You've never had a thought more than an inch deep in your whole lousy Wasp life, have you? And now you're sitting there with that half-inch smirk thinking, How can we con this nut into the White House? You'd betray your mother and spit on the Host to get me in now. Yeah, even if you knew I was certifiably insane. You little turd, I thought *I* was immoral. If you don't get mad now, if you try to be nice with me and jolly me along, I shall despise you as long as you live."

Was he *trying* to get me mad? It was such wild stuff. I'd thought up to now he was just doing it to clear his mind. "I'm used to you," I said. "I know you too well to get mad."

"Yeah? Listen, kid—supposing I told you that I used my polio, that I resurrected it for political advantage, to turn people's pity into votes? Supposing I told you that?"

"I'd say you'd been wasting your time. You didn't need to. You could always make it on your own. In fact, your polio means just as little to other people as you say it means to you."

"I see." He nodded. "That's very interesting. Maybe I don't believe it, but it's interesting. Now, supposing I told you that I didn't give a shit about the peace issue, that I was just using that, too? What would you do then?"

"I guess I'd have to walk out."

"O.K., why don't you do that?"

This was too damn much. I've seen some heavy bullying, but this was too damn much. If he was that mean and cruel—I didn't see what distinguished him from our incumbent President.

"Are you just trying to get rid of me?" I said, squinting at him.

He grinned. "I'm sorry, Sam. Why do I always do that? Trying to get even with my two-legged friends, I guess. Are you becoming a little more human, Sam, a little less Harvard?"

"Fuck Harvard, you lace-curtain mick."

"Attaboy, Sam. Don't take it lying down. Yeah, you're getting there. Would you like a job sometime? How about a drink?" He laughed and laughed. "I'm going to take a nap. I feel a lot better." He rolled alongside his bed and flipped himself onto it, a neat, delicate process. He shut his eyes. "On to Detroit," he said, although we were already in Detroit.

9

He was *my* candidate, I'd found him, I didn't care if he *was* unstable, I tell you. I sat in the hotel bar, drinking like an old pro. And I was able in no time to convince myself that his rages were completely controlled, the Jesuits had taught him that, in fac' he was *saner* than . . . no, don't overdo it now. Still, to be scared of the Presidency was proof of sanity, wasn't it? Bet your ass. Casey saw, as any rational man must, that the job was not built to human scale. In fact, his humility would make him wunnerful Presh'dent, someday.

If I needed any further arguments to bolster the case I was committed to anyway, I had only to look at the other politicians in Detroit that week. Compared with those leftover meatballs, Casey was a mass of throbbing humanity. They were all over town, painting their noses red in any building that served liquid, and I got a perverse pleasure seeing these wretched of the earth sporting Casey buttons and Casey hats. They couldn't have looked funnier in "Voltaire" buttons.

It was all business that week. Casey went from caucus to caucus, telling the good old boys not to worry, their jobs were safe. "I know that local professionals are the meat and sinew of politics. What the hell, I'm an Irishman. I *like* politics." Irishman indeed. It wasn't like Casey to call himself names like that. But if it worked, I was for it. Six months ago, I'd have wanted him to remain his cool self to the end. Hell, six months ago he would have. But when you see that little gold chalice, you break into a run. "Let this cup pass from my hands—hell no. Drink, drink."

"This is pleasing you, eh snot?" he whispered to me after one of these nights of shame. "This craven sellout is to your taste? Remember, I'm just doing it for you and your friends; you know, the ones who believe in me so much." Anything you say, sir, just promise me you won't go insane.

As usual he didn't sell out quite as much as I wanted him to. He always gave an equal and opposite pitch to the reformers. Having assured the old boys that their jobs were safe, he attacked the whole business of jobs, to wit: "Some people can't see beyond their own jobs. That's why American politics are so damn tacky. The politics of jobs never dreamed a dream or paid its dues on a vision." Nobody seemed to mind, or even notice. And to me: "Tell me when your little stomach gets sick. I'm doing it for you."

He was doing it to amuse himself, in my opinion. Anyway, since I didn't get quite the thrills scourging my conscience that he did, I decided to let him go to hell on his own. I went singles to some delegate parties and found myself reassuring earnest moon-faced ladies from the cornbelt that Casey was a prince and that nothing was closer to his heart than agriculture. You'll be glad to hear that the old Eastern smartie got his comeuppance more than once. "Do you know what's going *on* in Cumquat County?" "Wha?" "Yeah, right here in Cumquat. Ever since Sheriff Wintergreen died." Why the hell was I telling these people about politics? I didn't even know the names of their state capitals.

Well, you know about conventions. No matter how dull they try to make themselves, to show how America has truly come of age, they still have all the silly excitement of kids' birthday parties. If you've happened to miss one, the next closest thing would be wandering around a county fair with a straw hat and a jug of moonshine. I tried slyly to seduce Jane into sharing this mood—wasn't it almost like an election night, huh?—but she was quite chilly and reserved, no doubt suffering a seasonal complaint, which was a damn shame, for both of us. Ah well—on with the mad night life of Detroit.

"Alabama casts its . . ." To hell with that. This isn't a

political account; as Casey says, I'm not cut out for it. God knows what I am cut out for. My final break with Casey was not the result of a return of political honor, far from it. I doubt if I'll ever be bothered by that again, or even by an interest in politics. It was a silly personal matter and I'll get to it in a moment. But first, a couple of unforgettable vignettes. Reeling to the convention hall, arms linked, Casey's famous battery of speechwriters. Ejection from the floor, for not having the proper credentials, or any credentials at all. Near arrest for trying to steal a pass from a sleeping delegate from Montana. It was like a cattle market out there, except they'd removed the price tags from the delegates. "Jesus, it's better on television," said Hank Messer, so we barged around the ramps like four jolly members of the class of '04, looking for a set. We wound up in some kind of press tent, and I said I was a stringer for Time–Life, and the man said, "That's funny, I'm the managing editor." Oh well, they all say that. "Have a drink anyway. Your secret is safe with me, Mr. Perkins," he said. So I thought, O.K., smart-ass, just for that I'll have one. Next scene, Casey's famous speech on the party platform. He was as usual breaking all the laws of man and beast, turning up on the floor so soon, but he made even this sound like just what the country needs. "This is not a constitutional monarchy. The candidates had darn well *better* talk about the platform . . . Anyway, the following are the things I believe, and if events should so ordain in the next few days, these are the things I shall practice, *whether they're in the platform or not.*" Pandemonium.

"Every President in this century has come as a blinding surprise to the electorate and often to the party as well. With me, should you so choose, you will know exactly what you're getting. And I would like to take the opportunity to tell any delegates who may be bound to me that so far as it is legally possible, I am releasing them now. I ask no man to vote against his conscience. I want, if I should be so fortunate, a mandate so clear that it can be followed for four years, without anyone ever saying, 'Wait a minute, we didn't mean *that*. That was just politics.' Well, for the last few days, I've been playing politics myself, and enjoying it—what the heck, I'm a Democrat [you'll notice he cleaned up that Irish crack], but I'm not playing politics now. This is what I want." He held his speech aloft. "I want it in the platform—and I want it *out* of the platform—because I believe with all my soul, it's what's best for America."

There followed the most radical speech he had ever given, the one I'd begged him to give months ago, an incomes policy with fangs down to here, a health plan that wasn't actually drafted by witch doctors—well, you remember it as well as I do. I looked at Messer and he shrugged, "Not me, boss." It was Casey's own speech, presumably even typed by himself to surprise even us. And I thought, seeing him from the outside for a change, God, this man is impressive. He made me fleetingly proud, yeah little me, to be an American. No one in our history ever had more courage than Casey was showing right this minute. He had made sure on the personal level that I would not be impressed by him—a hero-worshipper was no use to him—but this was the real man all right.

Then Sam the Slow looked around at the journalists' fishy faces, and remembered the real reason he had been hired, namely because he was such a well-meaning jerk. There was no way of getting this far-out platform through. And now he was defying the convention and saying he was sticking to it whether it got through or not. What kind of crazy Irish courage was this? He was cutting his throat beautifully, as befit him, on national television, but he'd be just as dead afterward. After which, he would be one more of our famous liberal saints, a man who was just too good for us. And I could hear him saying, "Wasn't this what you wanted too, Sam? Weren't you and your friends looking for an impossible saint, like your father before you?" Hell, no. We weren't looking for this at all. We had to do something about it immediately. I could picture Blount's people getting cautiously off the floor, and God knows who else's people. And meanwhile, this elegant death wish of Casey's had left us without a peace candidate at all. He had led the kids into a defile, he had even killed Wilkins, the other guide, and left us there to die. Christ, proud to be an American.

Messer and I rushed out of the tent, as if we had somewhere to go. Maybe we could wire Wilkins or something. Or maybe we could write another speech for Casey, saying he was only fooling. Or—maybe—we—could . . .

Casey had left the floor at the wrong end, and when we got there, he had left the building. And when we got to the hotel, the skittish fellow had left his "keep-out" instructions. So we raced around in circles, and we got Wilkins on the phone and enjoyed his rich Southern laugh to the full, and we played jayvee politics with every delegate we could find (they were noncommittal to a man). "He didn't mean it, you can trust him," I raved. They were very nice to us considering. Naturally, you can always trust a man who doesn't mean what he says. It's how the horse race bounces.

Up in my room now, puffing a much-needed joint, looking for patterns in the fog. Why had he fought so hard against Wilkins and Fielding and the rest, if he didn't want to win? You know why. Because he wanted to get this far, within spitting distance of the championship. So he could spit at it. It all fell into place, gentlemen, all my prejudices about Irish Catholics and about noble losers like my old man, and all the other snot in my system, when word came through by phone ("word" is just released, like gas, in convention cities; nobody knows where it comes from) that a lot of his delegates were holding. Some of them had to, because of binding primaries. Some because their wives and children threatened to leave them if they didn't. And others had gotten wind that it was a brave speech, of course, and were all for bravery, so long as it's in good taste.

I went down to the lobby to suck up more word. My guru Rust Gates materialized at my side at some point (you only have to rub a bottle) and confirmed what I'd heard. "He proved out of town he was a politician, therefore a crook, therefore someone they could trust." Gates was happy as a child with an electric train. "They know that platforms are meaningless, from which it follows that courage about platforms is meaningless. Casey will be no more bound by his speech than he will be by the platform itself. He'll be bound by the commitments he's been making privately, like everyone else." He clapped my back. "What a performer!"

A roller coaster is no place to try thinking. But could Gates's Mad Hatter view of reality possibly be correct? I honestly didn't know. It was possible that Casey had tried to lose and found that he couldn't. Or it was possible that he was enjoying a last hand of poker at the summit, with the odds exquisitely assessed. You tell me. My main feeling was that I'd made a consummate ass of myself with the delegates, and I hoped Casey never heard about it.

The platform vote came the next day. Casey's last-minute proposals were rephrased and vagued-down and inserted in the form of subclauses, which made it all the usual self-contradictory hash. I don't even know who did it: his fancy-pants speechwriters only worked tea parties and supper dances these days. President Casey would certainly be able to live with this platform, since nobody would remember a word of it. Spritzer told the press that Casey was not dissatisfied. "You can't expect a great party like ours to agree about everything. Agreement is not possible this side of the grave. After that, you must ask the Republicans." Spritzer read the words woodenly, so they sounded cheap and mechanical: still, they would probably read O.K. in the papers next day. "It is much better than we expected a while ago. Our crusade has already borne fruit." The thing about platforms in general is that it's impossible to concentrate on them even when they're right in front of you; so if Casey wanted to call this one a personal triumph, only the strongest intelligences could question him.

Repercussions were that the convention was going swimmingly, despite my personal deaths. We'd won all kinds of seating fights and procedure fights as the enemy lay down obligingly in front of our wheels. Casey's grass-roots machine was now said to be a miracle of organization; yeah, the very same rabble I've been describing—well, I guess we did have some great people out there, the ones that I'd never even met. Andy Provo from Massachusetts, Peggy Klipstein from Ohio, no one will ever know who deserves credit for what, so we give it to the leader to be on the safe side. Word from the streets was that Casey was being hailed as one of our truly great men.

I wanted to see him myself and share in any smugness that was going. I found a lot of people at the hotel who wanted to touch the leader and breathe his healing cigar smoke. But the orders were still, nobody gets to see Casey. Well now, what the hell—who was important around here and who wasn't? The others at the desk looked at me, young workers, campaign bunnies, favored writers. Pride demanded that I go on up.

Spritzer waylaid me, of course. "I wouldn't go in there if I were you."

"Who the fuck says so?"

"Don't worry. He isn't seeing me either. I even had to make up those quotes."

"That figures," I said. "What's the matter with him this time? Why the hell isn't he seeing his own people? Doesn't he owe us something?"

"I don't know," said Spritzer. "I really don't."

"I'm going in," I said. Why does one have these moods? Casey's secretiveness had embarrassed me enough. He had no secrets from me, goddamnit. I'd had the run of his soul for months, and he wasn't going to pull rank on me now. I wasn't going to go back to being the new boy, scuffling my feet in the corridor. Stuff like that.

I pushed Spritzer to one side, a little touch of violence that really primed me. I had a duplicate key, the only one besides Spritzer's, and I used it like a lord. "Casey?"

It was a decorous scene. Casey sat by the window in his wheelchair and Jane Donohue massaged the back of his neck. She looked like a queen and I wanted her, right now, in front of him.

"So this is it?" I said, like the Count of Monte Cristo, or somebody, as I immediately realized, making me all the madder.

"*What* is it?" said Casey.

"You two." Jane glanced at me, a little apologetically, and went on with her rubbing. She didn't mind being used, she'd been raised that way, but she might as well be used by the best. Casey looked me up and down imperturbably, that strange look of sizing me up physically, of counting my legs and arms, of deciding that I didn't belong in the ring with him.

"I don't mind if you think the worst, Sam. At my age, and in my condition, I'm flattered."

"None of your goddamn games." I boiled over all the way. "It's your goddamned condition that *gets* them."

"Oh, so you do think so, don't you?" Casey smiled. "Yeah, polio's important. You can win it or lose it, but it's important. Anyway," he said briskly, "I'm glad you finally found something you care about, Sam. Congratulations. Many people never do. The campaign has not been a total waste." Thanks, Father Flanagan, I needed that. I backed away, awkward with rage and humiliation. I swear I thought for a moment of picking him up and flinging him on the floor. He knew it and grinned. Try it, kid.

"Do you have enough for your book yet?" he said. "Or aren't you the man for it?" I slammed the door. Spritzer leered at me compassionately. He'd been there before. I would have thrown up on his shoe if my timing had been better.

Final snapshots, literally. Casey accepting the nomination with yet another great speech. I didn't hear it or read it, being long since out of town. I got it later from the press files, along with the pictures of Casey with his arm around Fran, his colleen, fresh as a shamrock, and the pictures with his parents, lit like waxworks by the flashbulbs, the family morgue. Father pleased as Punch; mother still looking as if she'd have preferred a priest. Strange.

10

Your guess is as good as mine as to why he lost the election that year. If you've read the usual *post-partum* sludge, you know that Casey's medium-narrow defeat was at once a triumph of charm and a failure of nerve, an exercise in voter education and a serious misreading of the nation's mood. All that crap. I leave it, with my fragrant blessings, to people who see life that way. Who believe that the nation has a mood and that they know where to find it.

For myself, I'd be content to know if Brian really lost his voice in Wyoming and why Spritzer left the staff for a week in late October. You can't see those little pinwheels from outside. Did Brian succumb to the campaign bends again, or did the sturdy presence of Fran Casey (not to mention Jane's neck rubs) steady the old boy? Did his death wish kick up again, and some scene in the night catch him at a bad time? Or did he actually do his best? Don't ask the court jester. Brian stuck to his principles throughout, which Rust Gates, in a disillusioned piece, said proved he wasn't serious (see Gates, "Rather Be Left than President"). Then again, the incumbent manipulated the issues as only an incumbent can manipulate. The conditional cease-fire two nights before the debate must have knocked the shit out of Casey. Some people said he's just making a record for next time, and some people (mostly Woody Kline in *Dissent*—see "He Didn't Sell Out—That Was His Sellout.") said he was trying to prove that leftism couldn't win under any circumstances, and—well I won't bore you with all the things people said. I apologize for the way politics keeps creeping in. My concern is with the private Casey, if I can find him and keep his eyes from wandering.

"He was too good for them," said my father, playing on my old prejudices. Father is a real Christian, a ring-tailed loser, who could sour you on any candidate. He worked his ass off for Casey on the local level and got a pleasant note from Brian for his pains: was he any relation to the young man who used to write his speeches? And if so, how was I keeping? My father even had the nerve to tell me I didn't understand Casey. Said I was a liberal perfectionist. Wow. And also I got a card from Jane, suggesting we get together now that her head was clearer. Talk about rubbing it in.

Having failed conclusively at novel writing, I decided to try my hand at the New Journalism. Casey seemed like a great subject for a non-fiction novel, mainly because he was all I had. He was still very much a live issue. On the one hand he was already a plump virgin-martyr for the liberals: a second defeat would put him in the top ten. On the other hand, he liked to win. Which side would prevail? Referring to my notes: "Victory is vulgar, Sam. Great men don't have to win. Victory is essentially for losers." This is just the boss funning with his houseboy. Turn the page. "You're an incurable little snot, Perkins. You'll never understand anything." That indicates we're approaching Detroit and he's biting at his dog leash. "Always remember there is more to life than politics. Then again, there is less to life than politics too."

So I took my notes and added my own super neo-journalistic, non-fiction fiction techniques. You know, those great little touches like "he cleared his throat." What puzzles me, on rereading the whole schemozzle, is that I find I come out of it looking like a bum. And don't think I didn't try to make myself look good, even to the point of putting myself down charmingly in places. Maybe my sterling qualities don't show up in print—like a mirage that can't be photographed. Or maybe I'm still seeing myself Casey's way, imagining him leering over this and winking at his smart-ass friends.

What's even worse, Brian Casey looks better than he should on paper—and don't think I didn't try to make him look bad. His *vices* are the things that don't photograph.

A good politician knows how to make a good record even on the john. I thought that an inside book was the one way I could beat him, but I'm not sure I don't get hurt worse than he does. There is, for instance, a tone in my voice that I can't stand and I can't shake. "Put myself down charmingly." Jesus Christ, what a phrase. Needless to say, Casey put me on to this tone.

Well, O.K., I've still got the manuscript, I can change it, touch it up. But words are so damn hard to control. There's no way I can make you like me now, with that fucking tone. For instance, that scene between him and me and Lady Jane. How can I convey what it was like losing to this guy? Not just Jane, who I guess I never really had, but anything. I hated that sense of I've beaten you and don't you forget it. I knew just how Senator Fielding must have felt when Casey stole his girl. Brian couldn't simply beat you, he had to ride through you in triumph. Also, there was a sense of I've taught you a lesson, haven't I? And worst of all, there was the knowledge that he *had* taught me a lesson: forced it down my throat like castor oil. "There is more to life than politics. Then again, there is less to life than politics." I thought I was past the age when a grownup could put me down like that. Yet in our last game of Diplomacy, with me holding all the pieces, I'd wound up stomping out of the room shaking with baby rage. I still stammer when I think about it.

The Campaign Casey is all I know for sure. Since I started this two years ago (how time drags when you're having fun), I've talked to everyone I could find who might add to it—law partners, old political rivals, and assorted Casey-watchers—and the truth is not in them. People just aren't rational about politicians. I got a swollen breastbone from the finger-jabbers, the guys who say, "You remember the Rizzoli contract, kid? The time that Flanagan was indicted? Well, Casey's campaign manager signed the affidavits." Proving that Brian never drew an honest breath. And I lost a lapel to the little clinging people who told of unknown acts of kindness that St. Francis would have given his cassock to have thought of. You know *why* he saved the thruway, don't you? To give access to the old people's home in Snaggletooth Bay. It could have been any politician under God's grey sun. I decided to stick with what I knew.

Out of God knows what quiet desperation, I decided to have a last wistful crack at Fran Casey, who at least had been there through the whole thing. She was the blindest witness Casey could have chosen, but she might have heard something.

I can't say she was particularly pleased to see me. She had lost her campaign bloom and returned to sullen privacy. Brian was off someplace lecturing, his new vice, and she was home, keeping things dusted. I almost gave up on the spot, but decided to sweat out a cup of tea with her and run through some of my incisive interviewing methods. We had our tea in the garden, though it was a dull day.

"Tell me, Mrs. Casey," I said, swirling my tea bag to put her at ease, "how do you feel now that it's all over?"

"How do you mean?"

"You know, feel," I explained.

"It's been over a long time now."

"Yes, I know. I mean, how *did* you feel? When—it was all over."

"I guess I felt relieved."

"You did?"

"Yes. Brian's much happier, much more himself when he's not running for things."

"That's interesting," I mumbled incisively. She gave me a sharp little look. Who was I anyway? Was I a friend? I smiled ingratiatingly. Oh, this was ridiculous.

"Yes," she said. "Campaigning gets him, you know, excited."

Another look. Was I really O.K.? The secret of interviewing is to find someone who wants to talk. There's practically no way you can botch it after that. "You knew him pretty well, didn't you?" she said, and I nodded. "I mean, I'm not telling you anything you don't know, am I? He's not himself when he's campaigning. All those women and things."

I gaped.

"Oh, I don't mind about that. I know I'm not much of a prize myself. Brian was very lonely when I met him. He told me once he was just shy with girls. Besides, he needed someone to look after him the way his mother did. He's like a child, you know. But it gets him so upset. He feels terribly guilty about it. He's deeply religious." They learn that voice from reciting the sorrowful mysteries of the Rosary, I believe.

"Why did he have you along after California then? If he was all excited or whatever you say?"

"I don't know. Maybe he needed me again and thought a wife would help. Or maybe he needed votes. I don't mind, either way."

"Wouldn't he have calmed down in the White House?"

She put her arm to her brow as if to ward off glare. "It's just politics. He was so much happier before he went into that. He had a choice, you know."

"He did?"

"Oh yes, he almost became a law teacher at one time. Then he needed more money for the children and he went into law himself, and then he spoke so well they asked him to run for things. But teaching's what he really wants, you know, reading and thinking and living a quiet, ordered life." She sounded like a parody of our old campaign brochure.

"Has he told you this?"

"Oh, often. He knows that politics is bad for him. At the end of the campaign he asked my forgiveness for everything he'd done to women, and to men, too. *My* forgiveness."

The old fraud. Was there no end to his goddamn games?

"I don't understand these things," she said. "I only know what I see. He *changes*. It's like an occasion of sin, if you know what I mean. He *knows* he shouldn't be in politics."

She actually began to sob. This poor deluded lady had bought the whole worthless crock from Casey.

"What about his children?" I asked vaguely.

"Yes, he's even a better father when he's not in politics.

He really wanted to be a good father. He said that being able to have children at all was a wonderful surprise for him. He said . . ." Too much. I sat staring at my tea bag, while she pulled herself together. Then she burst out again, "When he's campaigning, he doesn't even *recognize* them. I think it's a terrible profession."

"How is he now?"

"Now?" She looked up smeary-eyed. "He's much better now. Reading and thinking and praying again, too, if you can understand that. And seeing more of the children, too. You probably don't know what this means to him." It sounded awful.

"So you don't think he'll run again next time?"

"Dear God, I hope not."

After a moment she added, "I don't think he will. It frightened him last time, getting so close. He's really like a child, you know."

Could any of this possibly be true? Was this the real Casey—a saint juggling politics in front of the Virgin?

"His mother spoiled him terribly, he admits it himself," she concluded. "He needs someone like me." I refused a second cup of tea and decided on the spot to put in a call to Spritzer, who was still running Casey's office in Washington.

Looking through the living-room window at Fran Casey mopping up the tea things, I listened to Spritzer's rasp, friendly as could be now that he had his senator to himself again. "I wouldn't quite put it like that. What Brian actually said on election night was: 'Imagine eight years in the White House with that woman!' Well, you know what a kidder he is."

The worst of this story, and I write it with relish, is that Brian said that line to entertain Spritzer. I don't believe he meant it. There was some part of him in this house, Mrs. Casey could not have made it all up. But he hid it like a saint guarding the Eucharist. Fran shook hands solemnly as she saw me out. *Do not understand me too easily, young man.* Jesus, you too.

His kidding is, of course, the problem. At the moment he remains in the Senate, thinking and praying or whatever he does, and with a Presidential election coming next year, various young activists are out looking for a peace candidate. Casey has indicated availability. Jesus Christ.

Just to remind you of who we're talking about and to clear your mind of Mrs. Casey, let me give you a last blast of the authentic Casey sound: "A bastard who knows he's a bastard is the worst bastard of all. Still, he has some kind of inner life, and that's supposed to be pretty good, isn't it? Ah, what do *you* know, you little dash dash dash? . . . Black rage, eh? Tell me frankly, sir—would you rather be black or have polio? and who am I supposed to rage at? Don't tell me about your suffering, sir. I detest monopolies. Ah, forget it, Sam. They may have suffered, I sure as hell haven't . . . try it like this. So much injustice in past cannot hope cure now stop Suggest hands full cleaning up block stop. Okay, festoon it with gut rhetoric, and we got ourselves a broad base . . . The Jews? The national I.Q. would sink to 63 if they went away. However, they must expect to suffer for being so smart. Nobody likes people to be that smart. Meanwhile, Israel should have a phantom jet in every garage . . . You know something [yawn] Sam? The Master only calls lepers to the head table, so just admit you are one, and get up there boy. Fake the sores if you have to, no one's counting. Just *wanting* to have them is a sign of [yawn] I forget. Theology is very complicated. Anyway, Sam, just remember—a Casey can always beat a Perkins at that game. You'd make a lousy leper. Nothing personal, O.K.? Who wants to eat with a bunch of sick people anyway? I often wonder what the Master sees in them . . . Sinking fast. Take a letter here in vital heartland of New Jersey wheat capital of little man not one scintilla of one iota in allegations of my opponent who has unfortunately taken low road . . . you know something, Sam? God has been very good to me. Yes, he has, the old bastard [snore]."

They say it's going to be different next year. More kids and women and blacks than ever are going to take part in the electoral process, i.e., vote, partly inspired by Casey's run for the roses last time. I sincerely hope they will have the maturity to reject this man, who despises kids, exploits women, and—well, I don't know how he is with blacks because I never saw him with one (I guess he admires their gall, though, and he says they make great audiences). But I'm afraid he's just their cup of tea. Every one of those groups is masochistic in its own way, or so it seems to your little-league philosopher. Look at what I took from him—and didn't he know I would? So Casey will wheel his throne among them—seeing healthy people on their knees is all he asks of life, the rest is spinach—and they'll sing Hosanna and "Hail to the Chief" and other Christian hymns. A crippled king for a crippled world, they crucified him once but here he comes again. A nice act, but I have a hunch that Casey's father ain't in heaven.

At this late date in the manuscript, I thought I'd check some of my theories with an old political crony of Casey's. I knew he'd sneer at the politics, out of very pride. But I thought he'd at least be dazzled by the psychological insights. No dice. "He never talked like that to me or any of the guys," he said. "That religious stuff."

"Yeah, but he said those things."

"Well, he was just being literary." He withered me, the way they all did. Literary was make-believe, a case of milady's vapors. "Yeah, but he said them," I insisted.

He looked at me a moment with those boiled-potato eyes they issue to inner-city pols and said, "You know the one mistake I thought Casey was making was hiring young jerks like you. But I was wrong, and he was right, as usual. He's got every kid in the country on his side this time—and you know how he got them? From practicing on *you* every day." He laughed. "Jesus Christ, supergimp. That's a good one."

I couldn't believe it.

"Where did a clown like you get a smart idea like that?" I snarled.

"He *told* me. You were sitting in the front seat of the car one day and I said, 'That's some staff you got,' and he said, 'That's not a staff, that's my violin.' Christ what a politician. He could make DiMaggio think he was really a ballplayer at heart."

Big fat victim—it was you he was practicing on, not me. I got it right the first time. Literary is real, not that crap you deal in. Yeah, he saw you standing on a railroad platform years ago, on his way to Salt Rock, getting smaller and smaller and going nowhere. And he saw you next to his bed, rubbing your fat hands and telling him God was on his side, and picking him out of the snow and saying, Take it easy, son. And he said, Someday I'm going to get that mother. I know because he told me. I wrote the book, you see. He's my character.

The fat pol just laughed and laughed. Casey would probably have laughed too. Because I was on that railroad platform myself, dwindling to nothing, as Casey shot off into the night looking, once and for all and to hell with all of you, for that miracle cure they'd promised him. Not a cure for polio or anything trivial like that, just a cure for not being God.